Revenge
of the
Ten Pound Poms

Lynn Peters

Also by Lynn Peters

Novels
Immaculate Misconceptions
Premature Infatuation
Reading Between the Lies

Collected poems
Why Dorothy Wordsworth is not
as famous as her brother

ISBN:979-8-630307422

To Lucy and Jonathan.

And John, of course.

In the 1950s thousands of British families rushed to swap miserable post war Britain for a life of warmth and opportunity in Australia.

This is the story of one of them.

> My bonnie lies over the ocean
> My bonnie lies over the sea
> My bonnie lies over the ocean
> Oh bring back my bonnie to me
>
> Traditional folk song

ONE

'My bonnie lies over the ocean…'

Chapter 1

February 1999

Rose

He came to see me today. You could have knocked me down with a double decker bus, if one hadn't done it already. He said, 'Mum, are you all right?' I said, 'I'm seventy nine, in intensive care with a tube in every orifice, what do you think?' Well you've got to laugh, haven't you?

Do you know, he didn't look a day older. Not like me, even my crows' feet have got crows' feet. He was settling down for a nice chat when my sister piped up, 'I think her mouth is moving. Is she trying to say something?'

What did she have to butt in for? She sent him off to get a nurse and when I woke up again he'd gone. But he'll be back. They said he wouldn't come but I knew he would.

Chapter 2

Rose

I was having a quiet doze, there's just an hour after lunch when they've sent the visitors out and you can get a bit of rest without them whittling on, then I opened my eyes, and she was staring right down into my face. Gave me such a fright.

'Rosie,' she said, 'are you awake?' I thought, well I am now, breathing all that garlic in my face. I could see right up her nose.

'I'm Lesley,' she said. 'The O.T. That's occupational therapist. Have you seen one before?' She had a blouse on with a waistcoat over, and a long wraparound skirt, very arty crafty. Bare legs. We never had bare legs, not pasty white anyway, and not from choice. In the war some girls used to paint a line up the back but you could see it wasn't a proper seam. This woman wouldn't have to bother, she had blue veins doing the job for her.

'Occupational therapist?' I said. 'I'm too old for an occupation, I'm on pension.' I was just kidding. Occupational therapist, indeed. I might be old but I'm not stupid.

She laughed. Mouthful of grey fillings and a gold bridge at the back. 'No, no one's trying to send you back to work. I bet you've worked hard all your life, you're entitled to a bit of a rest.'

She was looking at my hands. I used to have beautiful nails. When I first went to work, I used to put polish on them, dark red. I never wore make up, didn't need it really, and the men didn't seem to miss it, I always had plenty of attention at the engraving factory. I went in and out in all the right places and in those navy dungarees with my red shirt and my dark hair... It was a smashing job, I can't think why I ever left it. At the time we all thought we worked hard, but we didn't know the half of it. They always say hard work never hurt anyone, and the ones who say it generally never did any.

The girl who brings the tea round has got good hands, but her nails, they're those long stick-on ones. Purple with little pictures painted on them. I said you want to be careful when you're picking your nose, you could end up doing your own brain surgery.

'Are you listening, Rosie?' asks the O.T., like she's known me all her life. When I was young you didn't have all this first name malarkey. 'I just want to ask you a few questions. Is that all right?' She had her voice raised, enunciating very slow and clear like she was talking to a foreigner. But I'm not a foreigner, not any more. I live here now, where I was born. I haven't even got an accent, by the time I'd unpacked my luggage it was like I'd never been gone.

'Just a few questions. Is that all right?' she says.

'I can't hear you,' I say, playing along. 'You'll have to speak up.' So she says it again, even louder and slower which makes Mary in the bed opposite laugh, only then I'm sorry I've drawn attention because she comes out with the questions we've heard them ask the Time Travellers – that's what we call the ones who arrive not knowing where they are or what day it is.

'Do you know what the date is, Rosie?' she says. As if it makes any difference when you're my age. I know that Monday is pension day, and which days Corrie is on, and that Friday is when Joanie calls in on her way to the charity shop, and that's enough for me. But as it happens there's a TV listings paper open on the bedside table, I like to know what's on even if I'm not watching it, so I tell her the date and she looks very happy with that. Then she says who is the prime minister and I get that right too, and I tell her that I also know we're coming up to the millennium, which you'd have to be half daft not to, it's on the news every minute - half the world is going to be partying like there's no tomorrow, and the other half is heading for the hills because they think there isn't going to be a tomorrow! I say all that, thinking we'll have a laugh but she nods and looks serious and asks me am I'm worrying about it? No sense of humour, that one. So then we do mental arithmetic which is add two to five, then take six from eight. Me, who did the accounts for the farm for thirty years! But she's impressed now, I've gone up in her estimation. She shows me a picture of a cup and a house and a car, and I have to name them. I pretend to struggle, just to make a game of it, but I see her looking concerned so I answer up quick. Don't want her sending me off to a funny farm just because she's got no sense of humour. Then I have to demonstrate that I can get from the bed to the chair unaided, and I'm getting irritated now, because it was only a fall I had, anyone could trip off a bus platform. Even her with that long skirt if she's not careful.

So then I'm in the chair and she says can I remember the objects she held up for me before. But she didn't hold up any objects. A cube, she says. Red. And a green ball. I look down at her bag and they're there on the top. But she's made a mistake, she didn't do that test with me. I look across at Mary but she suddenly gets interested in her magazine and pretends she wasn't listening.

It's the young Japanese one changing my dressings today, Susie or Suki she's called. She's much gentler than the sister, a big Irish woman with a sadistic streak. You know when she's planning to make you suffer because she says, 'This won't hurt,' then she rips the plaster off like she's stripping wallpaper. But Suki lifts the edge of the dressing gentle as gentle, and the sad look on her face as she whispers, 'I'm so sorry,' you'd think it was her own leg she's that careful. Apparently I've got some ulcers or something from where I tripped up. They'd be fine if they'd just leave them alone and let the air get to them but you know what medical people are like, always think they know best.

Suki says, 'Will your daughter be coming?'

I say, I hope not. Mattie's another one who'd be fussing around thinking she knows best. I spoke to her on the phone, I said, what's the point of you coming all this way, spending all that money? Buy yourself some clothes, you could do with them. I remember how she looked when I picked her and her waste of space husband up after one of his business trips. What a sight she looked – scruffy old jeans and a tee shirt that had never seen an iron. And he was even worse. Mattie said they only dressed that way for travelling, and I said that's even worse – think of all the people across the world who have seen you turned out like Worzel Gummidge.

'And do you have other children?' says Suki.'

I tell her about Bobby and Richie, and my grandson Warren, and my granddaughter Tamsin who has a baby already. She isn't married but no one bothers about that any more. My other granddaughter, Sandy, is a career woman, and I don't think she's bothering at all.

'And your daughter, Mattie,' she asks, 'has she got children?' That's the only problem with Suki, she's always asking questions. Say one thing for the Sister, she doesn't go in for a lot of chit chat.

'No, my daughter hasn't got any children.'

'It must be lovely, having grandchildren,' she says.

I say it is. But it's not like there's any skill in it. You have children, they have children. They have some more children. It's stopping having them that's the problem. When I worked at the factory, the engraving was something to be proud of. Me, earning more than every man there, having them threaten to go out on strike because I worked too fast and it made them look bad. But proud of having had kids? You might as well be proud of being able to walk.

Though come to mention it, walking's something I would be proud of. You should see me shuffling down the ward on this zimmer frame – clop doink, clop doink.

'Are your grandchildren coming to see you?' asks Suki. She pauses with the dressing in her hand, gazing at me with her pale clear skin and eyes like slivered almonds. The new dressing is so white it could have been washed in

Persil. 'Or do they live far?' she asks.

I tell her they live far, very far, even further than where she comes from, though it turns out she's only from Basingstoke.

Later on, Enid comes waddling in from Surgical which is higher up the social scale than Care for the Elderly. They have little televisions with headphones attached to your bed and you can make a phone call and everything. Enid is in for her piles and they must have left a wad of dressings in judging from the way she walks. Still, at least when she sits down she won't need a cushion.

'They'll be planning a home visit,' she says when she hears about the O.T. Enid always knows everything.

'I'm not going on a visit,' I say, 'when I go home I'm staying home. Anyway what's a home visit?'

Turns out, they take you home, see if you can walk up your own stairs and make a cup of tea. And if you can they still bring you back, even though there's a bed shortage and a staff shortage and an ambulance shortage. I say it sounds like there's also a common sense shortage.

'It's protocol,' she says. 'If they don't bring you back it messes up the paperwork. That's important these days.'

I'm about to argue with her but just because she thinks she knows everything it doesn't mean she can't be right sometimes.

'I'm walking a lot better now, aren't I?' says Enid. I tell her it's not bad considering she's got a jumbo pack of incontinence pants stuffed in her knickers. Enid laughs and rolls her eyes to the ceiling. She's like me. Old enough to know that if you don't look for the funny side you're going to be pretty miserable. Unlike Mrs Morris in the next bed. She wouldn't see the funny side if it poked her in the eye. From the look on her face you'd think it was the end of the world – though judging by all the doctors who come hovering round her, maybe it is.

'If you get the chance of a home visit, you ought to go,' Enid says, heaving herself up. 'It's an outing if nothing else. What have you got to lose?'

She shuffles back and I lay there remembering. Len, elbows on the table, sleeves rolled up, eager look on his face. He was a good looking man, with those narrow eyes that I thought were like Clark Gable's. And so young. Was I ever that young?

All this looking on the bright side is exhausting. I lay back on the pillows and pretend I'm asleep. Immediately I'm back there, back home with Len, back in the time when we were still happy even if we didn't know it. 'Len,' I'm saying, let's do it. What have we got to lose?'

Mattie

We got home and Nanny said if I put her old apron on, I could help with the potatoes, so she gave me one to peel but the skin wouldn't come off, and I was still on my first one when she'd finished the whole bowl.

Bobby was playing with the pegs on the oilcloth. Nanny called it oilcloth. Mummy called it lino. Then Auntie Joanie came home and we did drawing on the backs of menus. Nanny used to bring them home from work, piles of them. They were like little books, with a picture of a beautiful lady glued on the front, and inside there was a separate sheet that said what the food was. There was a tassel and a ribbon holding it all together. The ribbon would be gold or red, or sometimes in royal blue.

I used to take the tassels off to make belts for my doll or to tie up my hair. You could draw on the back of the menus, or round the edges of the writing on the inside.

One afternoon Grandad came home and gave us sixpence each. I thought Nanny would be pleased but she was very cross. She said, 'You've got money for them, but when it's the housekeeping it's blood out of a stone.' He grinned at us and winked so Nanny couldn't see.

Grandad was the one for playing games, Nanny was always too busy. Sometimes he'd play Ludo with us, and he'd knock the dice off the table, and when I picked it up I'd see he had moved his counter forward. I'd say, 'Grandad!' and he'd give his wheezy laugh that made his shoulders shake. Nanny would say, 'Are you cheating those children again?' Sometimes he'd nudge me and wink and we'd get Bobby to pick up the dice from the floor and Grandad would move my counter on as well. Grandad taught me how to ride a bike. He walked along holding the handlebars so I didn't come off but I still couldn't balance so he said he'd put stabilisers on it.

After tea, Daddy would come for us, or sometimes Mummy if she was on early shift at the engraving factory. Mummy used to say I was the apple of Daddy's eye but he'd laugh and say, 'No she isn't. She's the apple of my pie!' Daddy could juggle and do magic tricks which we all liked, especially Auntie Joanie, but if he took too long Mummy would come banging on Nanny's door wanting to know why we weren't home already. He played piano too, he could play anything you wanted. When he played honky tonk Auntie Joanie used to dance with me. Or sometimes Daddy would play and she would sing. I'd shout, 'Auntie Joanie, sing the rabbit song!' That's what I thought it was called when I was little, but we still called it that and everyone would laugh when I said it. Auntie Joanie would sing the verse and I'd do the chorus all by myself.

> 'My bunny lies over the ocean
> My bunny lies over the sea.
> My bunny lies over the ocean.
> Oh bring back my bunny to me.'

It was my favourite song and even though I knew the word was 'bonnie', still a bunny is what I thought of. If I had a pet I wouldn't let anyone send it away

Rose

Enid from Surgical brought a picture of her sister in Australia for me to look at. Her son brought it in for her. A woman with a dodgy perm squinting into the sun. She's standing outside a brick bungalow on a wide lawn that's parched brown. Could be anyone, could be anywhere. But Enid's got a hunch we might have met up. Which is barmy. Even if you were actually looking for someone you probably wouldn't find them. And I should know. She knows over a million emigrants went over, but she still thinks we all lived next door to each other.

She has her after-dinner cup of tea with me and she asks what everyone always asks, 'Did you do the right thing?' She wants to hear it was a ghastly mistake and old England's wind and rain is better than all that sunshine. But it wasn't for nothing that they called it The Ten Pound Cure. It was your escape from all that greyness and unemployment, it was an antidote to all the horrible things you'd seen in the war and that had happened to you. So I tell her what I tell everyone: if I had my time again I'd do it all again. Of course that's what I tell her – if you've made a mistake you don't want everyone knowing, do you? And hindsight is all very well but we were offered an opportunity – a whole land of opportunities - you'd have had to be a fool to turn it down. A complete fool.

Enid wants to know if I've got photos. I've got plenty at home but I don't like looking at them. Our last house was a bungalow, much like Enid's sister's, but bigger, grander. We were so proud of it. Built it ourselves. We worked all hours, knocked down the tumbledown shack that came with the land and started from scratch. Even Richie helped, or thought he did, collecting stones and bits of gravel in his little bucket. Of course that was much later. Bobby and Mattie had left home by then.

Enid wanted to know all about how we came to emigrate. I didn't want to be talking about that but since I've been in here it all keeps flooding back like water coming under the door when you haven't got enough sandbags to stop it.

'Such a big step, going all that way,' she said. 'I wish I'd been that brave. Just think where I might have ended up.'

'In here on 'nil by mouth', same as me,' I said, and we both laughed.

It was a Thursday. I remember because that was the day we always had liver but I hadn't started cooking yet. All the time I was talking Len was saying, 'Get a move on, I'm starving'.

Len was leaning on the table, his sleeves were rolled

13

up and his braces stretched tight across his shoulders. He was wiry, you touched his arm and it was hard as metal, but warm. Sexy that was, I can tell you.

The army had done that for him but that was the only good thing they'd given him. When he joined up he was barely more than a school boy, he had rosy apple cheeks and he was always laughing. Now the skin on his face was tight over the bones and he jumped when a door slammed. He never talked about the war but sometimes he'd shout out in the night.

There was grease on his wrist from where he'd been fixing Mum's mangle, he must have missed it when he washed his hands.

'What have we got to lose?' I said and I waved my hand at the scullery where the lino was lifting up, the mildew marks on the wall, the rain outside that was making lines in the dirt on the window.

He lifted his chin up, the way he did when he didn't want to do a thing. Len's dream was to have a farm, but how was that was going to happen? Jobs were like gold dust, and a job that had a farm with it – that'd be gold dust with knobs on.

I told him about the poster on the notice board at work. Immigration officers were coming round the country to talk to anyone interested. It was a good deal; you just paid your ten pounds, that was about a week's wages then, and the government would pay the rest. You went on a ship, all paid for, meals and entertainment and everything, which was a holiday in itself. I'd never had a holiday. We had a lovely weekend away for our honeymoon but we couldn't afford the time off work for any longer. Mum once took Joanie and me to Brighton for the day but that was to visit Auntie Marie who ran a guest house down there.

Len opened the newspaper and spread it over the table. I could see he wasn't having any of it. 'Why do they want us lot to go there? Hasn't Australia got enough people of its own?' he said. But apparently it hadn't. Jack, at work, knew all about it. Australia wanted to increase their population while Britain wanted to get shot of a few, so they were paying for the scheme between them. The Aussies were scared they'd get invaded if there was another war and that they didn't have enough people to fight.

Len wasn't even listening. I had another go. 'And the best of it is,' I said, 'It'd be dead easy to get a farm. There's loads of land and hardly any people. They say there's only two and a half people to a mile. Think of it!'

'Blimey,' said Len, 'we've got more than that to our privy.'

There was a crash and a yell from next door which was probably Mrs Locke throwing something at Mr Locke. It seemed like another reason to go, the chance to escape neighbours and family and all the other busybodies you'd be better off without. In Australia in the sunshine, everyone would be too busy swimming and playing on the beach to care what anyone else did.

I told him what Jack at work had said, how we'd never be able to get on in Britain, what with having left school at fourteen. The war had been over for six years but still work was hard to come by and women like me who had done well with the men away weren't keen to give our jobs up just because they'd come back.

But Australia was the land of opportunity and Jack said they were desperate for people to help run the country. 'Run a country?' Len said. 'Jack couldn't run a bath!' He was laughing but I could see it had got him thinking.

Outside there was a grey slush on the path that the rain couldn't shift. It had been there for weeks, thawing and freezing again, and down the road Dad would be coming home drunk and my brother would be taking a swing at him while Mum tried to break them up....

Mattie came in then from the living room where she'd been playing with Bobby. She was always earwigging, thinking she might be missing something.

'How would you like to live somewhere hot and sunny?' I asked her. 'Big house, garden to play in.'

She hesitated. 'Would I have a rabbit?' A girl at school had got one for her seventh birthday, she'd been going on about it ever since she'd been round to play. 'Dog, cat, cow, sheep, you can have what you like,' I said. 'There'll be room for everything.' Mattie yelped with delight and squeezed on to Len's lap so that he had to move the chair back from the table.

'Then I'll have a rabbit,' she said, snuggling. 'Snowy white with long floppy ears.'

He caught my eye and we both laughed. Neither of us said anything, but Mattie's excitement was catching.

There were quite a few of us from the engraving factory went for the interview. They were held down the local employment exchange and only took half an hour. It was only a character check and they did the medical while you were there. They called us The Ten Pound Poms because that was all it cost. You had to send your money in once you heard you'd passed and you didn't have to pay for the children at all. Then you could be off in just a few months. I said it was easier to get a new life than a new job, and we joked that they'd need a whole ship just for us lot from the factory, but in the end the others dropped out and it was just Len and the kids and me. Len would go first and find a house and a job and we'd follow in two years' time.

People said we were brave, or else daft, but I thought they were the barmy ones. What was there to stay for? We'd all thought once the war was over and our men came home life would get back to normal, but there were still lots of things you couldn't get, and half of what you could was still rationed. And London was a right old mess, derelict houses wherever you looked.

I had to pass two at the end of our road when I got off the bus. Most of the time you didn't notice them any more, but sometimes it would all come back. Moira Pettit's family went down the tube station one night when the air raids sounded and when they came up next morning, they walked round the corner and their house was gone, all completely flat. Then there was Pat from work, we were going dancing but I had to come home to change first. A bomb went off and blew the windows out, right outside the shop where she was waiting for me. If I'd been earlier, maybe that would've been me done for too. Or maybe if I'd got there earlier she wouldn't still have been waiting, and she'd be here now. You'd try not to think about it, because there was no point dwelling on it, it could be you the next moment, but you'd see kids playing on the bomb sites, completely oblivious and you couldn't help but remember. But in Australia there'd be no reminders, and no one to remind you either.

Len said he didn't envy me telling my mum. But you can't live your life for other people. I waited till we'd got all the papers through, no point in upsetting her for no reason, but once they came I felt excited.

Mum was helping Bobby down from the table, she'd just given them their tea as usual. I don't remember my exact words, but I wanted her to see it was a good thing. The best thing for all of us. Actually I do know what I said. I just came right out with it: 'Guess what, Mum, we're off to Australia! What do you think of that?' Well, no point beating about the bush.

She stopped dead still with one hand on the chair and one on Bobby's shoulder. The knots in her varicose veins were standing out like bicycle inner tubes. Bobby looked up at her, thinking he'd done something wrong. I lifted him down and sent him out to play in the garden with Mattie.

When he'd gone, Mum said, 'You're going *where?*' and her face was fixed and white, and she pursed her lips so hard all you could see was a line of purple, the way she did when Dad said he was just going out for the one. I felt a pang of pity but only for a moment.

'Well, I hope you know what you're letting yourself in for,' she said, and her voice had that edge that it got when she was determined not to be upset by something. I remembered that from before and it made me angry, and being angry made me strong.

'A land of rich and plenty, by all accounts,' I said. 'You should be pleased for us. All that fresh air and sun. Better than here any day, you can see that. Good food, good prospects.'

'There's nothing wrong with my food,' she said.

Trust her to take it personally.

'Mum, we've still got rationing.

'The houses will be done up soon enough,' Mum said, carrying dishes to the old stone sink, but she knew as well as I did that if you wanted to rebuild or renovate you had to have a government permit and that could take ages. Bureaucracy was one thing the bombs hadn't made a dent in. Jack at work had applied ages ago to build on the back of his place where a wall had fallen down in a blast, and he was still waiting. Australia wasn't like that. It was all too new. They were too busy to sit about thinking up regulations for catching people out.

Mum said what a mistake we were making, I'd have to be mad giving up my job, how would the kiddies manage. All the things you'd expect.

'Fred, have you heard all this?' she said, when Dad came in from feeding the chickens. 'Emigrating! I did think Len had more sense.'

But Dad said it might turn out to be the making of us and then Mum went sniffy, she must have thought this was one time they might have agreed on something.

After that if I mentioned our plans she would walk out of the room. Once I came home from work and her eyes were red, and another time I saw her in the garden hanging the washing out, wiping her eyes on a pillowcase. She must have thought if we didn't discuss it, it wouldn't happen.

Mattie

Nanny brought some empty biscuit tins home from work. Auntie Joanie made a hole in the side and threaded string through and hung them round our necks. Then she gave us a wooden spoon each and Bobby and me played soldiers marching up and down beating our drums. When Nanny came in she said the lady upstairs had come out to complain about the noise and that Auntie Joanie didn't have the sense she was born with. We tried to look very sorry even though it was hard not to laugh. When Daddy came home Auntie Joanie told him what had happened and did an impression of Nanny being cross. Afterwards Uncle Michael came round and said we should give him a song. Daddy played on the piano while Uncle Michael drummed on the table with his fingers and Auntie Joanie sang the rabbit song. I did the chorus all by myself.

Auntie Joanie says when she and Uncle Des get married I can be their bridesmaid! It won't be for a long time because they have to save up but when they do Auntie Joan says she will have a wedding dress like Cinderella is wearing in my storybook and my dress will be in pale blue with puffed sleeves and a sash tied in a bow at the back. She would have a headdress with a veil thrown back, and I would have an Alice band with blue satin flowers on it and blue satin shoes to match. I would be very important, maybe the most important person there apart from the bride because it would be my job to carry her train which would stretch right back up the aisle of the church.

I drew a picture of me being a bridesmaid and Nanny put it on the wall.

Chapter 3

Rose

If I was in prison I'd get more freedom than in here. At least there they let you out for exercise once a day. The best I get is a hobble down the ward to the toilets, and that's no joke on a zimmer. Mary has got one on wheels which would be better but they say I have to wait to see the physio. You could die waiting in here. Enid says that's the idea, it's a money-saving strategy.

They used to have a telly, in a little room down the end. I liked to sit in there with Mary, and Kathy who was brought in for investigations because she'd had some sort of a turn. We used to watch Corrie at night, and whatever was on in the afternoon, there wasn't much choice because you could only get the one channel, someone had broken the knob off and the remote didn't work, but it made a change from the ward. Then last week we walked in and there were no chairs and the telly was gone. Sister said they needed the space to put more beds in. They haven't put any more beds in, but there's still no telly.

So now the only place to walk to is the toilets but you don't want to linger in there. It smells of wee and disinfectant and they're not that fussy how they clean up when someone's had an accident. They have a raised seat thing looks like scaffolding which I don't need but it's too awkward to move out the way, what with the zimmer frame and everything. I try and wipe the seat over before I sit down but I have to be quick or I'll be having an accident myself. Sometimes I sit there and I think: what's happened to me? How have I come to this?

We did the home visit yesterday. I've lived there five years, know every nook and cranny, but it looked different, being wheeled into it in a great lumbering chair with a blanket over me like I was some sort of invalid. When I come in from the shops I always think how bright the hall looks, with the little plaque Bobby's girls gave me on the wall, and the brass mirror that was a present from Len one anniversary. But coming in with the O.T. and the ambulance men bashing the paintwork on the doorframe, it looked shabby. Faded. I could feel them looking round, forming a judgement. I'm pernickety but there was a furry layer of dust over the bureau, and the coffee table in the lounge had a matt finish where it should have had a Mr Sheen gloss. The pattern was fading in the middle of the carpet too.

'It's nice to be home, isn't it?' said the O.T. and I thought yes, but not as nice as it would be if I didn't have you lot in tow giving my bits and pieces the once over. And knowing I was going straight back to the ward didn't help either. My TV was crying out for a nice little murder.

'Now let's try the stairs,' she said, 'see how we can manage.' I didn't go much on the royal we, but I got out of the chair and I was up those stairs faster than you could say 'mind your step' just to show her. Of course I was collapsing with exhaustion and my legs were like jelly by the time I got to the top, but I hung on to the banister and I don't think she realised. I said I'd have a little sit down on the bed just to remind myself how comfortable it was, but that was just an excuse because I was going to keel over if I had to stand up much longer.

Fortunately she went poking about checking what other stairs there were and whether my cooker was safe or whatever, so I had a little rest and by the time she came back I was fine again. Then I had to show her I could get in the shower which of course I could, the step being only a few inches high, and she said she'd get me a seat fitted and a grab rail. I said there was no way I was having my bathroom cluttered up like an old people's home but she pulled a face and said we had to be practical at my age, and had I thought about a stair lift, she didn't want me taking another tumble.

These people have got it all wrong, trying to make everything safe so you live forever. Once you get to a certain age, what are you saving yourself for? You might as well have a quick death and save yourself the time and trouble of a slow one.

I didn't sleep well last night. It upset me, being taken home and then brought back again, and then Enid went on because I hadn't brought any photos back. She keeps on asking questions and it's upsetting. I don't want to be thinking about all that, it was a long time ago. But I shut my eyes and there it all is...

The kids were just putting their coats on ready to go to Mum's when I heard the postman and the next minute Len came rushing in, red in the face with a letter in his

23

hand. It turned out he'd got an interview for a job. It was for a tenant farmer in East Anglia. I didn't even know where East Anglia was but it hadn't seemed to matter when Len was applying, seeing as nothing ever came of his applications. He'd sent this one weeks before, we'd forgotten all about it.

'That's just typical,' I said, doing Bobby's buttons up. 'You wait all this time and an interview only comes up when you've stopped needing it.'

'But think, if we got our own farm...' he got a dreamy look on his face, and I thought, what is he talking about, because we'd had the emigration interviews, passed the medical and we were just waiting to hear when he was due to sail. He was going ahead of us to find work and get us a lovely house. They said you could get a house in six months.

I said, 'Well it's too late now. Get a move on, and find Bobby's mittens.'

Mattie was sitting on the stairs sucking her thumb. She loved school and was always first to be ready. Now she got up and started hunting for the mittens. She said, 'Is that the farm where I can have my rabbit?'

'It could be,' Len said. Bobby was pulling at Len's trousers and he picked him up. I was going to be late for work if I didn't get the kids out of that door and round to Mum's in the next three minutes.

'If I get this job we won't have to emigrate,' he said, like that would be a good thing. 'Think about it. Living in the country, and on our own farmland.'

I said, 'But it's all arranged!'

'We were only emigrating to get a better start – get our own farm. What's the point if we've got it all here?'

24

I was half way through tying my scarf but I stopped and looked at him. 'I thought we wanted to go.'

Len didn't answer, just picked Bobby up and started swinging him round.

I thought about Len and this new job all that day. I shut my eyes and tried to see myself in East Anglia – which wasn't the cleverest thing to do in the middle of engraving. Jack thought there was something wrong with me, I never made mistakes as a rule. But I tried to see myself in East Anglia, in a cosy farmhouse kitchen baking a pie, with Len bringing the cows in to the cowshed for milking. He'd come in for his dinner, wiping dirt off his boots. In time we'd have people working for us.

But I also thought about Australia and learning to swim and cooking our dinner on the beach and boiling up what they called a billy. I'd read all the pamphlets, I knew that was how it was. There was no class system, anyone could do anything, you didn't need qualifications or money to get started. Yes, it would be hard to be apart from Len for two years while he went on ahead, and even harder packing up all our things and moving in with Mum with her long suffering silences. But not as hard as staying here forever. We were going and that was definite.

Len was late bringing the kids home from Mum's and when I went round to see why, I found him telling Mum and Joanie all about the job in East Anglia. The kids hadn't even got their coats on, they were still playing out the back. Len was full of it and Mum had such a smile on her face, you'd have thought Dad had had a win on the horses and actually shared it with her. She said, 'At last, I knew you'd see sense.'

I meant it to sound like a joke but it came out harsher than I intended. I said: 'We have seen sense and that's why we're going to Australia.'

Len said, 'Not if I get this job.'

'I'm sure Australia would be lovely,' Joanie said, trying to smooth things over. 'But there's no point dragging the kids right round the world if you don't have to.'

'There's no 'have to' about it,' I said. 'We bloody well want to.'

Mum said, 'Rose, the kids!' But Mattie was up the end of the garden, I could see her bouncing her ball on the path, and Bobby was digging in the vegetable patch, they couldn't hear me.

Mum said, 'Well, I call it cruel. Taking them away from everything they know.'

'Cruel? To give the kids a better start in life?'

'Taking them away from all their family! They've lived half their life in this house. It's wicked.' Then her eyes started filling up.

But you can't live your life for other people. And if she really loved us she'd want what was best for us. Isn't that what she'd said to me before? 'I only want what's best for you?' Isn't that where all the trouble started? Well, now I was doing what was best. She should have been pleased for us. I said, 'Len, get the kids, we're going.'

Len didn't answer and I saw he was looking towards the door. Mattie must have come in while were talking and now she was standing there. She said, 'Why is Nanny crying?'

Joanie said, 'She isn't crying, lovey, she's just got a speck in her eye.'

Mum nodded without speaking but Mattie ran to her anyway. 'It's all right, Nanny,' she said, 'I'm here.' Mum's face twisted up then trying not to cry any more and she bent down and hugged Mattie to her, wrapping her pinny round her like a blanket so she wouldn't see. 'My precious, my precious,' she was saying.

I could have given in then, put my arms around them and sobbed with them and said it's all right, we won't go, we don't have to go. It will all be all right. And then we wouldn't have gone and it would have all been different. Len would have got his farm, I'd have made pies in the farmhouse in East Anglia. I'd have ended up like Mum was now, with my grandchildren's arms round my neck, holding on to me like I was the most special, the most loved, in their little lives.

But my mum's tears just reminded me, all that time before. I thought of how she must have looked at me as I sobbed and begged, and I thought maybe she wondered just for a second if she was doing the right thing. And then I remembered, oh I remembered, her voice, cold as the ice on the pavement that winter. Her mouth set in a line when she looked at me, and I knew she must have hardened her heart against me. And now I did the same, and it was easy, satisfying. I was her daughter, I was only doing what she'd taught me. 'I'm just doing what's best for everyone,' she'd said and now I said the same thing.

'I'm just doing what's best for everyone,' I said. 'Now Mattie, get your coat on. And go and fetch Bobby'.

Mattie

I was licking the icing off a bun when Auntie Joanie said, 'So it won't be long and you'll all be living by the seaside.

27

You must be very excited.' We were in a teashop with
Auntie Joanie and Uncle Des.

I guessed she was talking about the place Daddy said
was hot and sunny and how I was to have a rabbit when
we got there. I'd forgotten about it up until then. She had
a strange tone to her voice as though she was trying to
sound happy but wasn't really. She said to Uncle Des,
'Did you know they're going to be Ten Pound Poms?' He
said being a Ten Pound Pom sounded a lot of fun.

I knew how to make poms, or pompoms as they
were really called. You cut out two small circles of
cardboard with a hole in the middle, then you wound wool
over and over until you couldn't thread any more through
the centre. Then you cut in between the two circles of card
so you could thread wool between them, and then you
pulled it tight as tight and tied a knot. Auntie Joanie had
to help me because we weren't allowed to touch the
scissors. When you took the card away you were left with
a pompom. Auntie Joanie had sewed the last one I made
on to my woolly hat. It was on the seat next to me and I
ran my fingers over the yellow tufts.

I said, 'How can we be pompoms?'

Auntie Joanie laughed. 'Not a ten pound pompom,
silly. That would be either very heavy or very expensive!'
Uncle Des laughed too and I felt my cheeks go hot and red
but she put her arm round me and gave me a squeeze. She
said that a Pom was what they called an English person in
Australia but it was a joke and we mustn't mind.

I said, 'But we're not going to Australia.'

Daddy had only said we were going somewhere hot
and sunny, no one had mentioned it was Australia.
Although now I remembered that I had heard Mummy

talking about Australia but I didn't know it had anything to do with us. And Nanny had been whispering about something that sounded like that. I had wondered why she stopped when I walked in.

Auntie Joanie sometimes let me look at a book she had with countries of the world in it. I knew Holland was where the girls all wore wooden shoes and white hats with the sides turned out, and Africa was where the people had brown skin and didn't wear much of anything. If you lived in France you had to wear a striped sweater and a beret. Australia was koalas and hats with corks on them. It was a long way away.

Uncle Des said, 'I hope they won't make you swim all the way.' He was laughing but Bobby was looking at me and I was looking straight back.

'Are you coming as well?' Bobby asked Auntie Joanie.

She laughed, but she was really just pretending to laugh. 'No, not me. Well someone has got to look after Nanny and the chickens!' We didn't say anything and she hurried on, 'You'll have a gay old time. Your daddy will go ahead and get everything ready for you and in no time you'll be out there playing on the beach.'

'I'm going to have my own bucket and spade, Daddy said so,' Bobby said.

Uncle Des said something then and Auntie Joanie explained that Daddy was going in advance to get a job. Then they discussed what sort of job he might get. I didn't understand what they meant. I thought when they said he was going on ahead it was to get the boat tickets, and then in a few days we'd meet him and all get on it together.

Auntie Joanie laughed again. 'No, your dad will get a

job and find you somewhere lovely to live and then when he's all ready, you'll go too and then you'll all be together again.'

Bobby had been looking from one to the other, and now he suddenly opened his mouth and howled. Bits of bun came flying out. He said he didn't want Daddy to go away.

'Bobby lovey, it won't be for long. And then you'll all be together again.'

'How long?' said Bobby, stopping crying. 'A day?'

'Well maybe a bit longer than a day…'

He cried again, and then Auntie Joanie sat him on her lap and I could see she wanted to cry too and now I had a bad feeling about it. I remembered Nanny with the speck in her eye and wondered if this had something to do with it. I didn't know exactly what I was frightened of, only that something was coming towards me and it was bad and it was going to knock me down, and I couldn't get out of its way. I felt so sick I couldn't finish my bun. Uncle Des said if it was going to waste, he'd have it.

Rose

Len went for the job in East Anglia but he didn't get it. Of course I was relieved, but I was sad for him too. I didn't want him to have any more knocks, there'd been so many, and he wasn't the same man who'd gone into the army. He never talked about the war and I knew that was a measure of how bad it must have been. So if he'd got the farm job, I wouldn't have argued, not if it was what he truly wanted. No, really I wouldn't.

But he didn't get it so three weeks later there he was waiting at the front door with his case packed, in his best suit, all ready for the taxi to arrive. It was a big thing, to go on a journey in those days. You wore your Sunday best for travelling. You didn't have a load of clothes, not like now. You had your work clothes or your Sunday best, so you wore your Sunday best. It was all about looking respectable, worrying about what everyone thought. That's been the story of my life really, worrying about what everyone thought. Or having Mum worry about it for me.

But this was a fresh start. I felt sick but excited too. From now on it was up to us to make a new future for ourselves. I wanted to laugh at the likes of Jack at work, all talk but too much of a coward to strike out for what they wanted.

The taxi had just pulled up when the postman arrived. We'd got to know Charlie well and he wished Len all the best and all the usual stuff, while Len was opening his letter. I saw Len's face change, and I thought it must be bad news. Perhaps they'd changed his sailing date and we'd have to unpack again. For a fleeting moment I felt relief that maybe we were getting a few days grace. I still wanted him to go but maybe not now, not right this minute.

'What is it?' I said, as Charlie walked back down the path.

Len was screwing the letter up. He tossed it at the dustbin with a laugh, saying it wasn't anything, and went to put his case in the taxi. Then he turned and looked at me. He was such a good looking man, those dark eyes.

'This is it then,' he said, and we stood there like two awkward strangers. I put my arms round his waist and he was warm under his jacket, and I thought this is madness, what are we doing, and then he was pulling away from me and he squeezed my hand but he didn't look at me and then it all happened so fast, he bent down and hugged Mattie and Bobby, and the neighbours were waving and then he was in the cab and it was pulling away. Mattie said, 'Don't cry, Mummy,' and Bobby was saying, 'Why has Daddy gone away in a car?'

It was only much later, after the children were asleep and I was washing up, thinking how quiet it seemed, when I remembered about the letter. I wiped my hands and went out to the bin. The letter was on the ground at the side of it, he never was much of a shot.

It was about the interview for the farm tenancy. The chosen applicant had withdrawn and they were offering the position to Len.

My poor lovely Len, down all the years he never mentioned it. But he must have always wondered how things might have turned out if he'd taken it. I know I did.

Mattie

I gave daddy a pompom to take with him. It was pink with a yellow stripe round the middle. Joanie unpicked her old jumper to make a new scarf and she gave me some of the wool. Daddy said he'd keep it in his pocket and every time he looked at it he would think of me.

After he'd gone I went and sat on my bed with my book. Mummy came in and said there was no need to look like that, we'd all be together again before we knew it. At teatime we went to Nanny's and Auntie Joanie baked a steak and kidney pie. I helped roll out the pastry. She said I didn't have to eat the kidney, Grandad could have it.

One day, not long after we'd all moved in to live at Nanny's house, I brought a painting home from school and Uncle Michael said it was as good as a real artist could do and we should hang it on the wall. Auntie Joanie found a drawing pin in the drawer and put it on the door in the scullery.

Rose

Enid is due to go home on Friday but I'm hoping it'll be delayed, which is always on the cards in this place. She has to go home by ambulance and if they forget you, which they did with Mary, well that's that, you just have to wait. Enid plans to go out to see her sister in Australia, just as soon as she gets over this. I said maybe I'll go with her. Be nice to see Bobby and the family. Bobby's youngest is about the age I was when I met Len.

The day I met Len, I remember it like it was yesterday. Not that that's saying much, I remember most things better than yesterday. Anyway, I was just coming out of the newsagents with Dad's tobacco and the racing paper when a dog comes flying round the corner, snarling and growling with its teeth on show and when I try to shoo him off he goes for me. I hit him with the paper and before he could try for a second nip, this boy comes rushing over. He was a year or two older than me, about fifteen, skinny lad, with a nose too big for his face but somehow attractive with it. Very dark hair, almost as black as mine. I was so busy thanking him for yanking the dog away, that I didn't realise straight away that it was his dog. He brushed the mud off my coat where the dog's paws had been and his face was red from his collar right up to his hairline. I told him not to worry because we kept a greyhound at home and King (or Fanny's First Love as he was known at the track), was always getting mud all over

33

us. So we got talking. Afterwards Len always said meeting me was love at first bite. He could always make you laugh.

We didn't start courting for another year though and I was at work by then. I started work at fourteen – tell people that nowadays and they look at you like you were being sent up a chimney. But it was a nice little job, in an office in London. I didn't start till 8.30 but you had to arrive in London by eight if you wanted a workman's ticket, which was a shilling and a lot cheaper than if you travelled later. I had to wander around for half an hour waiting for the office to open. You got a bit cold sometimes but I liked it, time to yourself to just think your own thoughts and no one to order you about. I had to pass a butcher's shop and when the butcher saw me he'd come out and say, 'Rosie, would you like a bit of pork?' And if I said yes, he didn't come out with some mucky retort like they would these days, no, he'd give me a nice chop or some sausages to take home to Mum.

Once we were going out, we were inseparable, Len and me, he never even looked at anyone else. Everyone liked him, even Mum. The first time I introduced him, he had a bag of toffee for her and admired her dress even though you could hardly see it under her pinny, and she was eating out of his hand before the kettle had boiled.

If he walked into a room you wouldn't exactly swoon, he didn't have good looks in that way but when he talked to you and turned that gaze on you, with his brown eyes that were so dark you couldn't see the pupils, well, then he beat every other bloke in the room, hands down. He was a good listener, and he had lovely manners, he always stood up when a lady walked into a room, even Mum.

Naturally, Dad didn't like him, especially as Len got older and less in awe of him. Once Len went in the army he wasn't afraid of anyone. They had a terrible row over my coat. I'd started at the engraving factory by then and I'd bought it on coupons, so you can imagine how long I'd been saving, and it was only its second time on. Dad was in a temper, he'd probably had a bad day at the bookies, that was the usual reason, and he'd already had a go at Mum and she was in a sulk. I said I was going out with Len and Dad said not till I'd put his dinner on the table and I said it wasn't my job, and just like that he picked up the bottle of milk off the table and threw it at me. When Len came round to take me out of course he wanted to know why I wasn't wearing the new coat. I made some excuse because even though Dad was short he was tough, and I didn't want Len trying to take him on, but Len could see I'd been crying so he asked Joanie what had gone on and she told him. The blood rushed into his face and his brows came right down over his eyes, I'd never seen him look like that before. He said, 'Where is he?' and his voice had a tight strangled sound to it. He could never abide drinking and he was that angry he got Dad down on the floor and there's me trying to pull Len off him and Mum shouting, 'Give him one for me!'

Len was wasting his time, Dad had always been the same and a good hiding wasn't going to change anything. But Len always did his best for me.

We were all set to get married but then Len got called up and he said if anything happened to him he'd rather know he'd left behind a single girl who could start again than a grieving widow. That was him all over, always thinking of the other person.

Still, I did grieve. Len's mate got invalided out after Dunkirk and told Len's mum he'd seen Len mortally wounded. It was terrible, those few months, every day dreading to have it confirmed. It got so you almost wanted it confirmed just so the pain of waiting would be over. You'd do anything just to take your mind off it. And then out of the blue I got a letter from him, and the next month he was home on leave right as rain. Len was always the only one for me.

When he came home for good, I moved in with Len and his parents until we could get married. Of course moving in didn't mean what it does now. Len slept on the sofa and I had his room. But his mum and dad liked to go out of an evening so we had time for a cuddle. I did love him, my Len.

In those days you had to apply to the local authority to get extra coupons for a wedding. And there was still clothes rationing so Mum and Joanie helped me out for my dress. Both families chipped in with their food coupons for the wedding cake, and some of our mates from work too. It was the only way, you couldn't get the ingredients otherwise. Dad said over his dead body but Mum had hold of the food coupons so he couldn't do anything about it. Len looked so handsome. You should see him in the wedding photo. Both of us so happy, everything ahead of us

Mattie

My school was just down the road from Nanny's house. My teacher was Mrs Miller. Once I wrote a story and after I'd read it out to my class, she sent me to the class next door to read it out to them. When I'd finished they all clapped. I could feel my face going red, but I was pleased all the same. Auntie Joanie said maybe I'd grow up and write children's books.

I came out of the school gates, and there was Nanny with Bobby in the pushchair. When I got home Auntie Joanie had made a new pinny for me out of the same material as Nanny's. She had made a little pocket on the bib so I had somewhere to keep my hankie.

My best friend Denise invited me to her party and Auntie Joanie made me a new dress to wear. It had a paper nylon petticoat that made the skirt stick out and rustled when you walked. All the girls were jealous.

Mummy and Daddy liked to squash up on the sofa canoodling, as Mummy called it. I'd come in wanting to play with Daddy and she'd say, 'Go away, we're canoodling'. Daddy would say, 'Come on, room for one more on top,' and he'd budge up so I could get on his lap, but Mummy didn't like it. Sometimes she'd get in a huff and he'd say, 'Don't be like that, Poppet, she only wants a cuddle,' and she'd say, 'Just five minutes then,' and before I'd even got settled she'd say, 'Time's up. Your dad's tired, now you go off and play.'

Rose

Why is it that a cafe can cook lots of different food and it all smells lovely and in hospital they cook lots of different food and it all smells like cabbage?

Not that a bit of cabbage is a problem really, not when you've lived with the reek of the dustbins and the toilet on the landing in that tenement in Adelaide. Made your eyes water. Didn't matter how you tried to clean that privy, you couldn't shift the smell. Years of men losing their aim and hitting the floor, it had seeped into the floorboards.

In here everything reminds you of something. Too much time to dwell on things, that's the worst bit, worse than the food and other people's visitors all rolled into one. The woman who brings the dinners round, she reminds me of our landlady in Darwin, with her weasel face and crafty eyes. The doctor reminds me of Bobby – a bit slow on the uptake but very patient. And the volunteer who comes in and chats to anyone who's not got a visitor, she reminds me of my mother. Mum would have loved that – volunteering – having everyone think what a good person you are. Impressing all the neighbours with your good works. Poor old Mum. All she could impress the neighbours with was her doorstep. Kept it polished to such a gleam you daren't stand on it in case it reflected your knickers. Not that you could have stood on it. It was as slippery as black ice, you had to step over it or risk breaking your neck.

Oh Len. I missed him so badly once he sailed. It was like having your arm chopped off, whatever you did you knew something was missing. I kept thinking, what have we done it for? Two years that we could have been together and we've volunteered to be apart. But what else could we do? They said it was a paradise out there, we had to make it happen. And we knew from what they'd told us that it was harder to start off with the whole family in tow, and the best way was for him to go on ahead and get a home ready for us. We convinced ourselves two years wasn't long, we'd be busy, it'd soon pass. Or maybe we didn't convince ourselves, just tried to convince each other. But two years is a long time in nights and days, and hours and minutes. So many tears before bedtime and after bedtime too if you want the truth.

At work I was the same as ever, and I tried not to think about him, where he was and what he might be doing. But at night, in the single bed at Mum's I'd turn over, feeling for him, to put my feet on his legs and I'd wake with the sheets wrapped around me like bandage, reminding me I was celibate now. When I reached my arm out to touch him, my fingers would scrape the wall. Len was a passionate man. Lying there in the dark, feeling that old tingle starting up, I'd think, Len – if this is how it is for me, how must it be for you? I used to burn so hot it could've set my knickers alight.

I'd see him everywhere - as I walked to work I'd catch sight of the back of his head, or that jaunty walk of his, like he'd just had a win on the dogs. Sinewy shoulders, those arms.

I lived for his letters. They took a long time to come but they were worth the wait. It was a comfort to know that he felt the same as me, the being alone. And I didn't mind if he had a bit of life. On the voyage out it was all fun and games – well, six weeks at sea you'd have to pass the time somehow. One night he and one of the other men dressed up as women and did a comedy skit. He had to wear a blonde wig and a long skirt and to pretend he was Nell Gwynne. I'd have liked to see him in that wig, with all his muscles bulging, he must have looked a sight. It reminded me of when he used to play honky tonk on Mum's piano and she'd tap dance in the scullery. He always knew how to have a good time.

They could only post letters when the ship got to a port, and once he arrived in Australia we knew there wouldn't exactly be a post box on every corner, but he wrote as often as he could. After he arrived his letters were short, but then he was busy, I knew that. And they didn't say much. Mostly he wrote about how hot it was and that finding work was harder than he'd expected, and he might have to travel a bit to find it. Now I think about it, it was all a bit vague. Not much about where he was staying or people he'd met. And what of the wonderful country, the sea, the landscape? What of all the waiting opportunities? I should have known he was unhappy. But how could he be unhappy, he'd gone to Paradise? He was just working hard, and I knew that because he was sending me money, regular as clockwork.

But then there was a long gap with no money arriving. And then when it did arrive, it wasn't as much as before and no letter explaining. When more than two months went by with no money and no letter either I knew something was wrong. The post might get delayed or even lost, but it wasn't likely it would go on getting delayed or lost. He must be ill, or injured. What if they didn't have proper doctors out there, or he couldn't afford one because he'd sent us all his money? You couldn't just ring a phone number, you didn't all have phones in those days. And he was travelling around, I didn't even know if he was at the same address. I felt sick with worrying and every day the post brought nothing I felt sicker. The only way to find him was to go to the emigration people. I put it off and put if off but in the end there wasn't anything else I could do.

I didn't want Mum coming with me, but she was insistent. 'Better to have someone with you,' she said, making me feel I had something to worry about, even more than I did already.

Still, even though I didn't want her knowing my business, I was glad to show Australia House off, let her see it wasn't some tuppenny ha'penny affair we'd invested our future in. It was one of those old buildings you go past on the bus but never know what it is and never get to go inside either. Very grand what with the high ceilings, the big windows and the fancy staircase, you'd feel like the queen coming down that. You felt you were somebody just walking in the doors. And we did, we'd felt important, Len and me, marching in there, and getting a welcome too because they wanted us Ten Pound Poms, all they could get.

But today that feeling didn't last long. Once we got inside we were directed into the big hall and we had to wait there with all the other nobodies.

There was a long queue to see an official. One of those women who think they're better than you just because they're sitting behind a desk and you're standing in front of it.

'We get a lot of this sort of thing,' she said when I explained that I hadn't heard from Len in almost three months.

I said 'What sort of thing?' and for a second I swear I had a vision of hundreds of men like Len, all terribly injured or weak with fever, crawling along the ground to get to a post box.

She opened a drawer and got a form out and said not to worry, men weren't allowed to disappear, it was part of the emigration agreement, if they had registered as part of a family, then that's what they were and the authorities would make it their business to find them.

It was such a relief to know they could find him. But I didn't much like what she seemed to be implying. Especially with my mother sitting there taking it all in. I said, 'My husband is a good man, if he hasn't been in touch it's because something has happened to him.'

She stopped writing and gave me a hard look. I could see she was thinking, 'That's what they all say,' and I hoped my mum couldn't see it too. 'Don't worry,' she said. 'I'm sure he'll be fine. Communication can be very difficult in some areas.'

I thought she'd arrange to phone someone there and then, and be writing letters and making out reports. But once she'd recorded Len's details that was it and we were out the door.

The train was crowded coming home and we had to stand in the corridor. As we pulled out of the station Mum said, 'What do you think she meant: a lot of this sort of thing?' I said I didn't know. But I knew that she was thinking it had nothing to do with men being too ill to stick a stamp on an envelope.

'I'm not surprised men go off the rails when they get out there,' she said. 'All that freedom.' I said she was probably right but Len wasn't one of them.

'All men are if you give them half a chance,' she said. 'Now I know you think you know everything,' she said, 'but let me give you some advice.'

As if I'd take advice from her! I leaned forward against the window and concentrated on looking out. Some of the houses had their lights on. I saw a woman setting the table. I thought, you lucky bitch, you must be expecting someone.

'I'm just saying bear it in mind. If you should ever find out that Len – you know...'

'No, what do I know?'

'That he's been carrying on or something, all I'm saying is, it's best not to make a big scene about it'. She said if you embarrass them or make them feel stupid their pride won't let them come back, whereas if you turn a blind eye they would come running back home again with their tail between their legs. I said I wouldn't be having anything to do with Len's tail if that was the case. She gave me a look and said she'd learned all this the hard way. As though it was a good thing Dad had been living with us making our lives a misery all these years.

She reached into her bag and offered me a packet of boiled sweets, a peace offering. I shook my head but she unwrapped one for herself. 'I'm only trying to stop you making the same mistakes I did,' she said.

Mothers. Isn't that what we all try to do? But one person's mistake is another person's right action. If she thought I'd forgotten she was sadly mistaken.

The next month a letter arrived from Len. It was a Saturday and Mum had called in to take the children to the park while I did the washing. I felt so relieved when I opened the envelope I could have hugged her, and I hadn't felt like doing that in a very long while.

'What did I tell you?' I said, as I buttoned up Bobby's coat. 'Len's been poorly, poor old love. But he's fine now. I knew there'd be a good reason we hadn't heard.'

Mum stood up, smiling, and of course she was

relieved too because she was fond of Len. But then she said, 'Good, that's all right then,' and I could hear in her voice that she didn't believe a word of it. She thought he'd been led astray like all the other men the clerk at Australia House had lumped him in with and if he'd written now it was because the authorities had made him. I felt myself bristle.

I turned to open the front door. 'Yes, it's really good news,' I said. Something about the letter wasn't right but that was my business not hers. She'd hurt me in the past and this was payback.

'He needs looking after, poor old love,' I went on, and then I went in for the kill. 'So the sooner we're on our way the better.'

The smile had faded from her face before I'd even let go of the door handle.

Chapter 4

Mattie

It was still dark when we got to the station. Everyone had come to see us off. Nanny and Grandad, and Auntie Joanie, even Mummy's sister Auntie Marian, though she was married and I hardly knew her. Nanny was crying, and Auntie Joanie, though she was trying not to. Mummy was chivvying everyone along, the way she always does. She kept saying to me, 'Anyone'd think you didn't want to see your father.' But she was just covering up because underneath she was upset too. Nanny said, 'For goodness sake will you stop going on at the child.'

Everything we had was packed up in two cases. I thought: what happened to all the furniture we had before we moved in with Nanny? And then I thought – where's my bike! I said, 'Grandad, Grandad, where's my bike?' Mummy had said I'd be grown out of it before we went to Australia, but that was when we thought it would be two years before we went. It wasn't long since I'd got the stabilisers off.

Grandad looked unhappy, and I thought no, no, we can't leave my bike, I love my bike.

Nanny's eyes were red and she said she'd keep it till I came back. Mummy said, 'For goodness sake, mother!' Then she told me she'd given my bike to the girl next door and I should be pleased it had gone to a good home. 'And they have bikes in Australia, the same as everywhere else. We'll get you a better one when we arrive.'

Auntie Joanie bent down and put her arms round me and I clung on to her neck. 'Don't strangle me!' she said, trying to make me laugh. Then she pressed something into my palm. It was wrapped in tissue paper and when I opened it there was a silver chain inside. It was the same as the one she always wore. I used to like holding it when she sat me on her lap. But this one had a tiny charm on it, a rabbit.

She said, 'It's to remind you of our song. My bunny lies over the ocean.' Her face started to screw up then with how hard she was trying not to cry. And that made me cry more, thinking of everything we were leaving behind: Nanny, Auntie Joanie, my bike... She was clutching my hand tight as we walked towards the train. They weren't coming with us to the port. Then Mummy started hissing at Auntie Joanie that it was her fault I was getting upset. She pulled me away from Auntie Joanie and suddenly we were rushing along the platform and on to the train and Grandad was heaving our luggage on. Then the whistle blew.

I hurried to get to the window to wave but there were people in front of us and luggage in the gangway, and then the train was pulling out. By the time Mummy found us a seat we were far out of the station.

There were crowds at the port. They were playing 'Hearts

of Oak' as we climbed up the gangplank. For a long time afterwards just hearing it made me feel sick.

Rose

Lord but the cabin was small. When I saw there were two spare bunks I thought thank God for that, at least we'll have somewhere to sit down. I took my coat off and threw it over the top bunk and the cabin looked full already but at least we were on our way.

I said, 'This is just like living in a dolls' house! We're going to have such an adventure!'

They both wanted a top bunk. Mattie climbed up and put her teddy on the pillow and Bobby put his toy car on his. I was thinking, yes it'll be fun. Six weeks with food all laid on. Entertainment. No job to go to, time to spend with the kids, no Joanie or mother to interfere, just me and them. I thought, it's not small, it's cosy. We're going to make the most of this.

Then the door opened and a woman walked in dragging a case and behind her was another woman and she was holding a baby. You have to laugh.

Mattie

When we got on the ship there were lots and lots of people there, all excited they were starting a new life just like us. They were all up on deck waving but most of them were also crying. Then there were all the other people who had come to see them off and they were waving and crying as well. I thought it would have been nice to have someone to wave to but it would have been very sad so I was also glad that we didn't. I asked Mummy could we watch while the ship pulled out, because I could still wave goodbye to England and the other people wouldn't know I didn't have anyone, and she said yes. But we couldn't get near the rail to see over, there were so many people. Then I saw a lady run down the gangplank crying and a man ran after her and pulled her back. I think Mummy saw that too because right away she said, 'We don't need any of that, thank you very much,' and we went down to our cabin to start unpacking.

Before we left Auntie Joanie said, 'Don't fret, darlin', if you don't like it you can come home in two years.' She said two years isn't long but it is, it's two birthdays. I will write Joanie a letter every week so when we go home she will know everything that happened and I won't forget anything.

I had never heard of a buffet before. Mummy said it's where you can eat as much as you want and when you've finished you can still have seconds. We thought she was joking, but it was all laid out on big tables, jellies and puddings like a banquet in stories. Mum had slices of chicken and beef and lots of roast potatoes and then when she'd eaten it she went back and got some more. We all had two lots of cake.

One of the ladies in our cabin has a baby. He's called Gary and he can't walk yet but Mummy says he can cry to wake the dead. Mummy says it shouldn't be allowed. When the ladies arrived Mummy said it was a mistake and they had come to the wrong cabin. One of them had a little cry then because she said Mummy was being horrible and it was bad enough that her husband had to sleep on a different deck with all the other men and not in the same cabin as her and Gary and no one had told them and it wasn't fair. The other lady said, 'There, there, don't upset yourself' and put her arm round her. But Mummy said her husband was having to sleep in a different country and that wasn't fair either and don't start getting uppity with me, my lady. Then Mummy told me to look after Bobby and she'd get someone to come and tell them they were in the wrong cabin and it was a mistake. But when she got back there was a man with her and he didn't tell them there was a mistake. Instead he got another man to bring a cot for Gary and they put it up in the middle of the cabin. Sometimes when Gary cries I let him hold my teddy.

They have a library on the ship. Most of the books are about Australia and are for grown ups but there are some for children. I'm reading Heidi and I'm going to read Alice in Wonderland next which Auntie Joanie gave me when we came away. They have activities for children and games like Blind Man's Buff and fancy dress competitions. Mummy keeps trying to make me go.

Rose

You should have seen Dorothy back then, hair all anyhow, thin as a rake. I mean, we were all thin in the war, with the rationing but, well, arms like twigs and legs like two sticks of Brighton rock. Thin face and dry blonde hair that she wore pulled back, about as unflattering a look as you could come up with. I cut her hair for her when I knew her better, just took a bit of the length off. She was what you'd call genteel, but very poor. That's the worst of all worlds, you feel inferior to the rich people and intimidated by the poor people, who are poor and proud of it. Not that I was poor. And not that she was intimidated by me. Or maybe she was. She was such a mouse it'd be hard to say. She was the sort who can walk into an empty room and it'll still be empty. She looked like all her get up and go had got up and gone. But when I got to know her I realised she was just exhausted. Inside she was determined, as determined as I was. Maybe that's what drew us together. That and being in the same few inches of cabin, didn't have much choice but to be together.

Mattie

The lady from our cabin who is called Auntie Dorothy came and sat on the deckchair and I crawled further back under the lifeboat so she wouldn't spot me. I didn't want her sending me back to the others to join in their stupid games. Mummy said there was something wrong with me that I never wanted to enjoy myself, but how could I when you knew the ship was moving on, taking us further and further away? Sometimes I dreamt about hiding on the ship after we docked, and no one would find me until we'd already set off to go back home when it would be too late. But I knew that was just stupid. There was nowhere to hide. And even if there was Mummy would just keep looking until she found me.

The lady stood up and went to the rail and I picked up my book again but I wasn't even half way down the page and she was back. I could see her shoes, flat and ugly like some Mummy had, not neat with a heel and little bows like Auntie Joanie wore. She got up again and wandered along the deck and I thought, good, she's gone but then she turned and came back again. She pulled the deck chair right up to the lifeboat and sat down, right in front of me. If I'd stretched my legs I'd have touched her. I drew my knees in tighter. She leaned back and her shadow made it hard to see the words in my book.

I kept very still and when I saw she wasn't going to move, I turned the page over. I knew she wouldn't hear me over the hum the ship made but then I started to get stiff and when I moved my book fell off my lap and that's when she turned round.

Her eyes were red and watery and she was clutching a white hankie in one hand, and her glasses in the other. We looked at each other.

'What are you doing here?' she asked, suspicious, as though I was the one spying on her! But then she saw my book. When she smiled she had a kind face.

I didn't answer and she said, 'I bet you're hiding. Same as me.'

I thought, what did a grown up have to hide from? They could do whatever they wanted. If she wanted to sit and read a book she could stay in the cabin, no one would turf her out and threaten to take her book away if she didn't join in Monopoly or Grandmother's Footsteps.

'I wanted to read. By myself,' I said.

'And now I've come along and spoiled it. I'm sorry. Is it all right if I'm really quiet?'

I said it was all right and she said that if anyone came looking for me she would say she hadn't seen me. She reminded me of Auntie Joanie even though she wore funny old glasses and wasn't a bit pretty. Then she said, 'Do you like cake?' and she pushed something along the deck for me. It was wrapped in a serviette. She must have smuggled it out from the buffet at lunchtime. Even though you could eat all you wanted Mummy said you weren't supposed to bring food away. It had white icing on it. Nanny sometimes made cakes but she never iced them.

'My Sophie likes cake,' she said. I thought she was saying 'sofa' and I laughed, I thought she was teasing me. But then she went on, 'She's seven, nearly eight, almost as old as you. She likes reading too.'

I knew she had children, I'd heard her telling Mummy, and it would be nice to have a friend, someone who didn't want to play Blind Man's Bluff and Hide and Seek any more than me. I hadn't realised they weren't with her on the ship, I'd imagined there was a special part of the ship where lots of children were if there wasn't room in the cabin for them to be with their mum. Whatever other reason could there be? But she said they were in Australia already and she was going out to find them. Her son was ten.

'Whereabouts are they?' I asked. Because if they were where Daddy was, I might still be able to have So-fee as a friend.

Her eyelids turned pink although she didn't actually cry. 'I don't know,' she said, and she was looking over my shoulder as though she could see something in the distance. But there was nothing behind me, just the wall and the lifeboat. 'I'll just have to keep looking till I find them.'

I wondered then if she was odd in the head, because even I knew that Australia was a very big country, and even in a town like at home you'd have had trouble finding someone if you didn't know where they lived. But I liked her, her sadness made me feel strong, as though I was the grown up, and she was the one who needed looking after.

'Don't worry,' I said, standing up, and it wasn't like me at all. 'I'll help you look.'

She pulled me to her in a great hug. It felt strange and I didn't like it at first, but then I thought of Auntie Joanie and how long it might be before someone would hug me like this again. I moved Auntie Joanie's rabbit necklace that was digging into my neck.

Rose

They had dancing several nights a week, themed sometimes – Pirates nights, Arabian Nights, you name it they had a night for it. I went once or twice with Dorothy, just to get out of that cabin, breathing in the same air the others had just breathed out. Dorothy never wanted to go but I said to her, what's the point sitting around moping? That won't get you there any quicker. And she needed to keep her spirits up, poor old thing. She'd lost her husband in the war, never got over it. And then to lose your children like that. When she first told me I thought she meant they were dead. So one way or another I suppose it felt like we had a certain amount in common. Even though we hadn't.

It was hard for both of us, watching the couples, seeing them laughing and hugging, and dancing to the same music we used to. Too much time on that long old voyage to think, to wonder about what we'd got ahead of us. Or in my case, what Len had got himself into. Wondering what he'd found that had taken him away from me. But we'd soon be with Len again and it'd all be explained. The authorities had written to him, he'd be meeting us at the port.

If I was a bit fed up Dorothy would say, 'Come on,

Rose, buck up!' So I was lucky to meet her because when I was up, she was down, but if I was down... No actually she was nearly always down! But we jogged along.

I wasn't so keen on Trudy. Always fussing round Gary, picking him up the minute he cried, thinking she knew everything. She was at that age when they think they're the only ones ever had sex, even though you've got kids yourself to show for it. One day she said, 'It's not fair they separate the husbands and wives. Weeks and weeks and no chance of marital relations.'

We were on 'A' deck and her husband was on 'D' deck and that upset her too because it was below the waterline but someone had to be below the waterline or we'd all tip over.

'It's not right,' she said. 'They should let couples be together. We have needs.'

'Don't tell me about needs,' I said. 'I've gone months and not so much as a kiss. It'll be healing over soon.' You should've seen her face. At the factory that would have had them falling over. No sense of humour, that one. Anyway, I thought, where's your initiative? Len and I would have just got on with it, we'd have found somewhere quiet to have a cuddle when we wanted one. You always can if you make your mind up.

I liked the film shows. They put them on in the daytime and I used to sit there thinking of Jack and the others back at the engraving factory hard at work and here was me on the holiday of a lifetime, sitting here watching a film show in the middle of the day. Wish they could've seen me, that'd show them. With their clever remarks about the mistake we were making and all of that. Course they weren't films with Clarke Gable and that sort, these were all about Australia and the way of life. I went to all of them. This was the first we'd seen of Oz really, no one had a telly in those days, or no one we knew, so we only knew what Australia House had told us. Some people said 'We'll find out what it's like when we get there,' but I wanted to know all I could. When I found weevils in the raisins I wouldn't have known what they were if we hadn't been warned about them in those films.

It was at one of them film shows where I ran into Eddie. I'd known him from school. Who'd think you'd travel all this way then meet someone who'd lived in the next road? He moved away after the army when he got married, but now he was divorced and looking for a new start. He said to me, 'What would people think if they knew – you, a married woman sitting with her fancy man in the back row of the cinema!' Of course it wasn't a proper cinema, and he wasn't my fancy man and even if he had been – anyway he wasn't.

In the evenings once the children were asleep, Dorothy and me, we'd sit up on deck, have a cup of tea. Once my children were asleep, that is. Who knew where hers were. I used to think how hard that must be for her, seeing me with my two every minute of the day.

She didn't talk much about them usually, it'd set her off, but we'd had a laugh that day, it was the Arabian night theme and the skits had been silly but it took your mind off things. We were sitting on the deck, the evening breeze in our hair.

'I'm all right for weeks on end, and then it just

sweeps over me,' she said. 'It's brought it home to me, now we're on our way, just what a task I've set myself. All those film shows showing how vast the country is.'

She opened a small wallet lying in her lap and took out a photograph. Two little kiddies: a curly headed boy, about Bobby's age, though he'd be older now. The girl looked about six, she had a white dress on, she was smiling, not a care. She'd shown me them before, it was before her husband went off to war. She showed everyone, in the hope it'd mean something to someone somehow.

She'd told me what had happened already, that she'd had to put her children in a children's home after her husband was killed because she'd had a breakdown and couldn't look after them. It was supposed to be temporary, as soon as she was on her feet and could get a job she'd get them out again. But although she'd told me I hadn't really taken it in. I was too busy with my own worries. But after a while on that ship it was like being in limbo. Your worries didn't go away, but you had a holiday from them knowing there was nothing you could do till you got off. So now she was talking and I was listening.

She said one day a woman phoned from the children's home wanting to discuss the children's future. She thought she was ringing to ask when she was going to take them out of the home. But it wasn't that.

'She said they could pay for them to go to Australia. They'd go to a private boarding school, have a good education and they would send me a ticket to follow on in the next few months.'

It was all I could do to stop myself saying, 'And you fell for that?' But on the other hand, why would a children's home make up a story as barmy as that? But I guess you could end up clutching at straws if you were widowed, you'd had a breakdown and you were on your own with no money. Yes, I could see that. And we'd had it drummed into us that Australia was looking for young blood, so there was a kind of logic to it.

'She said they'd have a better life, what with all the sunshine and the freedom, and they could stay at the boarding school during the week so I could work. I was over the breakdown by this time but I couldn't get a job that paid well enough to cover for someone to mind them. So a chance like this, and for them to go to a good school... and there's lots of jobs going in Australia, not like back home. Everyone knows that. So it seemed like the answer to my prayers.'

But her own ticket never arrived. When she enquired she found the woman she had spoken to had left and they said there was no scheme for the parents to go and never had been. When she finished speaking she turned her face away, but you can tell if someone's crying even without them looking at you.

All the same, all the same, it did seem a bit far-fetched. If it was true, wouldn't it be in all the newspapers? There must be loads of mums like her wanting their kids back, and probably just as many wanting to get shot of them. I thought of my friend Maisie with her eight – she'd have jumped at the chance to send off the older ones to a bright new future, no cost, no questions asked. And Dorothy didn't seem the sort to make things up. Not like Len's sister-in-law, who never went out of the house without seeing Humphrey Bogart crossing the road or Dean Martin on the bus. She once said Frank Sinatra stopped her in Parliament Square to ask what the time was. As if Frank Sinatra wouldn't have a watch, and with Big Ben right in front of him.

She picked her cup and saucer up from the deck and her hand was shaking. But there were bound to be people who could help.

'Have you spoken to the welfare officer?' I asked. 'Once you tell her where you have to get to, she'll help you plan the journey. She's got lots of maps and things.'

She looked at me as if I hadn't been listening. 'But I don't know where they are.'

'But you've got an address,' I said. 'You know the general area.'

She looked at me like I was half daft. 'I told you. They didn't keep records of where the children went to, only that they'd gone. Once they'd put them on a ship, they thought that was their job finished.'

I obviously was half daft because I hadn't taken that in before. Too busy with my own worries I suppose. I took my handkerchief out and wiped my nose while I thought what to say.

'It'll be all right,' I said at last. Well, what else could I say? And I went on, 'Things have a way of working out for the best.' Which I didn't believe for one minute and never had. But it was worth the lie for the hope on her face. Truth is over-rated if you ask me.

She leant back in the chair and closed her eyes. I sat back too, taking it in. It was almost easier to believe the story about Len's sister-in-law and Frank Sinatra.

She turned to me, and laid her hand on my arm. Her pale eyes were watery again. 'Do you really think I'll find them again?'

I drained my cup and leaned down to set it next to

hers. For all her weariness there was determination underneath, and where your flesh and blood is concerned, you don't ever give up, however hopeless things seem.

'Without a doubt,' I said.

I suppose it's no surprise she took a shine to Mattie. Sometimes I'd be wandering round the ship looking for Mattie, thinking that at last she'd found someone to play with and thanking God for it, and where would I find her but back in the cabin with Dorothy's arm round her, both of them sitting there sobbing.

Mattie

Bobby had a birthday while we were on the ship, he was six. They did a special birthday tea for him with a cake, almost as nice as Nanny made on my birthday. He had a toy car from Auntie Joanie and marbles from Nanny. Mummy said she had kept them hidden in our suitcase. I sat next to Uncle Eddie at tea.

'This is the best birthday party I ever went to,' he said. 'We're going to have such a lovely time in Oz. Just wait till you see a kangaroo with a little joey in its pouch. Or a koala. And it hardly rains, and it's always lovely and warm, no more chilblains.'

I liked the sound of not being cold, and not having chilblains, they were always so itchy. And seeing a little joey. He pointed at Bobby's birthday cake, and he said, 'You think that's good, that's nothing to what Australia's got in store!'

He took another bite of cake and a crumb stuck in his moustache. It reminded me of Grandad who always got crumbs stuck in his moustache and I thought how good it would be to tell him and Nanny I'd seen a kangaroo with a joey in its pouch and I wondered how long I'd have to wait. I knew we could go home after two years and we'd been on the boat for ages already so it might be nearly time to go back anyway.

'Why are you thinking about going back?' Uncle Eddie asked, and the crumb fell off his moustache and on to the cloth. And when I explained, he said that they counted the two years from when you arrived, not from when you got on the boat. If you wanted to go home earlier you had to pay all the money back. And it was a lot of money so no one did but anyway why would you want to because Australia was lovely, or why would we even be going?

Uncle Eddie was very funny. When they did the crossing of the line ceremony he went as King Neptune. He had a green silky robe and a long green beard. He isn't really our uncle, just as Auntie Dorothy isn't really our auntie. Mummy says she was in the same class as Uncle Eddie at school.

One day we stopped at a place called Port Said. You weren't allowed to get off but a lot of little boats pulled in near us and you could buy things from them. They were called bum boats which I thought was very rude but made Bobby laugh. They put your purchases in a basket and you had to haul it up, and send the money down the same way. Auntie Dorothy bought a bracelet for So-fee. I asked Mummy if I could have one but she said she wasn't made of money. But Auntie Dorothy bought one for me and a little leather ball for Bobby. My bracelet was silver with a blue stone in it.

Auntie Dorothy has a posh voice and I thought she must be very rich because she used to live in a crystal palace. But when I asked Mummy she laughed and said Auntie Dorothy was even poorer than us and she used to live at Crystal Palace, not in one, and that's what you get for ear-wigging.

When we arrived at Melbourne, where we were getting off, it was raining. I looked for the kangaroos but I couldn't see any. I asked Uncle Eddie where they were and if they only came out in the sun and he said, yes, they'd be sheltering somewhere under their umbrellas. But he laughed when he said it so I knew it was a joke. But I still didn't know where they were.

It was strange to step on to dry land, not that it was dry, with all the rain. You were used to the ship rolling, and the engines humming, you hardly noticed it, but you noticed it when it stopped. It was as hard to balance on dry land as it had been on the ship when we got on. But then you got used to it.

I was sad to say goodbye to Auntie Dorothy but I knew Daddy was coming so that made it not so bad. We had to wait in a big hall with crowds of people while Mummy tried to find out where he was.

Only Daddy didn't come.

Chapter 5

Rose

Say one thing for hospital, it makes you appreciate being home again. I'd have discharged myself before but Joanie hadn't brought my clothes in and if they see you walking out just in your nightie they think you're gaga and bring you back in again. Which I know for a fact because that's what happened to Ida. Even though you'd have to be gaga to want to stay. Of course Ida is gaga.

Joanie brought me my blue cardigan and my good dress with the belt, and once I was dolled up again you'd have taken me for Kate Moss. Kate Moss's fat old granny anyway.

Lovely to be home. Have a cup of tea when you want it, telly on with something you actually want to watch.

The occupational therapist came this morning. Nice girl, well, I say girl, she must have been fifty. They're going to put in a handrail by the front step and a seat in the shower which folds up when you're not using it. I'm not keen but she says I should have one so I'll be able to reach to my feet with the back scrubber. Not that I'll need it,

I'm getting better all the time.

After she'd finished inspecting we had a cup of tea and got talking and she said had I considered one of those baths with the door on the side? Saves having to climb in, she said. I could guess the one thing it wouldn't save was money – bound to cost a bit, something like that. And what happens when you don't shut the door properly and all your bathwater is coming through your kitchen ceiling? She said they have safety precautions. I said rockets to the moon have safety precautions and look at what's happened to some of them. She didn't have an answer for that.

Anyway I wouldn't have one of those baths on principle. There was one in my magazine. Full colour picture of some twenty year old posing in a swimsuit. Or at least the body was a twenty year old, the face was an actress who's even older than me. They must have stuck her head on someone else's body, it'd take more than liposuction and organic vegetables to make her look like that. I wouldn't mind having a young girl's body again. Twenty four inch waist and my bosom up where it used to be. Though I wouldn't want my old face either, come to think of it. Unless I was an actress posing for adverts for baths with the door on the side. And I expect there's only a limited amount of that sort of work around.

The O.T. woman gave me a funny look and I wondered if I'd been talking out loud because she said, 'You look very good for your age.' Which was very nice of her but once you've been categorised for a walk-in bath, who cares whether you look eighty, ninety or a hundred and fifty.

We had a nice chat then and turns out her parents used to live in the road next to Mum's and they'd thought of emigrating, but they fancied New Zealand or Canada. She remembered her dad coming home with the brochures and spreading them all out on the table.

'He said, now which one do you fancy? We'd never been abroad. It was ever so exciting. But in the end we didn't go anywhere.'

'That's a shame,' I said. 'It's good to see a bit of the world.'

'Yes, but we see it anyway now with holidays, don't we? We're going to Sydney in September.'

That put me in my place. It changed everything forever for us and now it's a hop and a skip and back in a fortnight. We were naive, Len and me, but in those days we all were. It wasn't like today where they're born knowing everything. Hardly anyone had been overseas, unless it was in the army. And the emigration happened so quickly - just a few months between applying and finding yourself on board a ship. No time to investigate what the new country was like. We just knew it was an escape from wet weather and bomb sites. We never thought about whether there were council houses, or health care or social security. We assumed it was the same as at home but with sunshine. But Australia was a different society from what we'd been used to. They didn't have the structure for a lot of government support, and they didn't believe in it either. We didn't think about any of that. Or if we did think about it, we thought we'd get rich so quickly we wouldn't need it anyway. More than a million of us went over in total and in the early days each batch must have had the same shock we did. I heard people who had friends come out before them complaining that they hadn't warned them about the hostels but how could you risk your family back home finding out what it was like? And when they'd probably been telling you, right up till you waved goodbye, what a mistake you were making and it wasn't too late to change your mind?

Of course I didn't tell it like it was in my letters, I'm not stupid. But I didn't ever lie, not about anything, whatever people might think. Not telling the exact truth isn't the same as telling a lie, just ask a politician.

When we arrived at the harbour the rain was bucketing down. All that way and weather worse than at home. But I told Mattie and Bobby it was lucky we'd arrived in the rain because that cooled the temperatures down, otherwise the sun would have baked us alive. I believed it too – I didn't know then that Melbourne could be as cool and grey as an English summer. But I'd have said what I said anyway, just trying to cheer them up only then Mattie starts worrying about how hot it will be when the rain stops. It seemed whatever I did or said was the wrong thing. I thought she'd be different once we arrived, call it the triumph of blind hope over bleeding experience.

As the ship pulled in, we saw a crowd of navvies in vests with hankies over their heads along the side of the wharf waiting to help. They were just working men, I suppose, same as you'd see anywhere, but they looked like bandits or pirates and not in a sexy swashbuckling way either. It felt threatening, not welcoming. I thought if these are Australia's best, I wouldn't want to see the worst.

But it was England's best example of manhood I was looking out for. Len would surely have got our message by now and even if he hadn't he'd have been contacted by the authorities. If you had relatives out there, they notified them for you because they knew there was a better chance of families staying and settling down if they had relatives to go to. So Len should be here somewhere.

Dorothy picked Bobby up so he could see over the side of the ship. 'Is that Daddy?' he cried. Then, 'Is that him?' I hoped it was that the men were too far away to make out their faces, not that he might've forgotten what Len looked like. But it was over a year since Len had left, maybe he wouldn't recognise him.

As we waited to get off, baggage was being winched over the side, but suddenly there was a crash and a splash as a huge crate came loose and fell in the water. We all gasped, even though us Ten Pound Poms knew it didn't belong to any of us because only stuff like furniture would go in a crate that size, and only full fare paying passengers could bring big items like that. Then we heard a woman crying because the crate had her dining room chairs in it. It had been hard, having to get rid of all our stuff but now I was glad I didn't have it to lose.

I took Bobby's hand as we came down the gangplank, and Dorothy held on to Mattie. Mattie was hanging back and I heard Dorothy chivvying her on. 'I said, Come on, Mattie! First one to spot Daddy wins a prize!' but I felt scared myself for a moment. The ship had been a kind of haven, protecting us all, and now we were on our own.

'This is it, then,' said Eddie as we stood at the dockside to say our goodbyes. Dorothy's eyes were filling up, and we had a bit of a hug. Funny, until that moment, it hadn't really thought of her as my friend, she was just someone in the same cabin, like Trudy only less irritating. But still a bit irritating, always sitting on her bunk with

Mattie, having a little grizzle together. But suddenly it struck me that Dorothy was my friend. I hugged her again, and for a moment I thought my eyes were going to fill up too, thinking of her all on her own, in this weird old country, hunting God knows where for her children.

But there was no time to dwell on things, people were shoving us trying to get by and get their new life underway. Eddie took my hand and squeezed it but I let go and bent down and started straightening Bobby's shirt. Eddie had been good company but you have to know when to call a halt to things. He told me he'd write and I said I would send him our address care of the reception centre, same as I would do for Dorothy. I didn't have much faith in them to send letters on, but then I didn't plan to write to him so that wasn't a problem. I could feel Eddie's eyes on my back as we walked away but I didn't turn around.

All the people going to hostels went in one direction, and all of us being met by relatives went in another. We stood with all the other families where we'd been told to wait. Bobby was dancing about, and Mattie sat perched on a suitcase hugging her doll. It was thrilling to see other travellers' friends and relations pushing through the throng, eager, and so excited. I thought: *This is It.* Our new life starts today. Even some of the men had tears in their eyes. I thought about the tears they'd all shed at leaving England and I recognised the woman who had tried to run back down the gangplank as the ship was about to leave. It had made me gasp and I'd hurried the children away so they wouldn't see. It was different now; she was smiling, it must be her sister or a friend who had her arms round her neck. 'It's worth it,' I thought, some things are hard but you have to see them through. And I looked up because it seemed the cue for Len to appear.

'Where is he?' Mattie kept saying, like a blooming record stuck in the groove. 'Where's Daddy?'

A young man came to greet the family we were standing next to, and then suddenly there was hardly anyone left. I joked with a woman who was also still waiting that we'd been forgotten, but then her uncle came for her and that left just me and the children.

What if Len hadn't got my letter? What if the authorities had forgotten or they had got the address wrong? Supposing he had already moved on?

I left the children with our luggage and went to look for help.

The woman at the information desk switched on a smile but it wasn't so much for me as because I was last in the queue and after me she could probably pack up and go home. I wished I could do the same. She had a nasal twang to her voice that only reminded me how far from home we were.

'Don't you worry,' she said when I'd explained. 'Delays happen all the time what with the distances people have to come. Communications can be a bit erratic, or maybe your husband didn't get the notification when you were coming. It happens sometimes. Or maybe he sent word he couldn't get here and that's got lost. Nothing to worry about.'

It sounded like quite a lot to worry about. What were we supposed to do? When I spoke my voice came out squeaky and high pitched. I was glad the kids weren't around to hear it.

'You got a phone number?' she said. I had a contact number but I wasn't sure how near that was to where he was living. Besides, he shouldn't be there, he should be on his way to meet us. If he wasn't we were in even more trouble.

'He'll be along,' she said. 'These things happen but it all works out in the end.' She said she'd leave another message at the contact number he had given. I wasn't to worry.

'Is Daddy here?' Bobby asked, when I got back, looking off into the distance, as though he might be hurrying along behind me.

'He's been held up,' I said brightly, with all the acting skills I could muster. 'He wants everything to be just right for us. In the meantime, we're going to a lovely hotel.'

Mattie looked doubtful. She knew I'd felt sorry for the people, like Dorothy, who weren't being met, and were going to a hostel instead of being whipped away to a lovely home like the one Daddy had got ready for us. But a part of me had been envious of those people who would be going to the hostels we'd heard about from the film shows which would be like smart hotels and with delicious food, like on the ship. So if we had to wait, there would be worse places to do it.

'It's a special hotel called a hostel,' I explained, and knowing how Bobby had liked the ship I added, 'it'll be just like the boat, but without the seawater!'

'Will there be a captain?' he said.

I said no, there wouldn't be a captain but we wouldn't need one. Bobby was happy with that but Mattie caught my eye and she must have seen something in my expression, for all I tried to hide it. She squeezed my

69

hand. 'It'll be all right, Mummy,' she said.

Bobby was nearly asleep by the time our bus arrived. 'Soon have you tucked up in bed,' I said as I helped him off the bench but it turned out that first we had to be driven to a waiting area to be allocated a hostel. We piled off the bus with a crowd of other weary travellers. The man behind me shoved Bobby as he pushed past and I snapped at him to watch where he was going, and Bobby clung to me frightened. The man snapped back, and his wife joined in. I let it go. We were all bad tempered, and maybe it wasn't just tiredness, maybe we were all a bit scared.

We were ushered along and suddenly we were inside what seemed like a vast exhibition hall but with us as the exhibits. Officials tried to direct us but we were like old rags for sorting, this one over there, this lot over here. We looked like a jumble of old rags too, some of us, our clothes all screwed up in the damp. It was bare inside the hall with just some benches to sit on and I thought, well now I see the difference between us and the full-fare paying passengers, and it's not only that they get to have their furniture dunked. Everyone was milling around wondering what was going on, and no one to ask and when you did see someone you couldn't get near them for all the others trying to do the same thing. I saw a woman I used to chat to at breakfast and she bustled over, glad to recognise a face. She told me she'd spoken to an official but it was a waste of time, you couldn't understand them, with their funny accents. She kept repeating, 'What have we come to?' and 'You wouldn't get this sort of treatment back home.' I said, 'What you mean is: If we'd wanted this sort of treatment we could've stayed at home!' I meant it as a joke, but she nodded like it was the truth. And it was a bit.

Bobby said, 'I can't see the buffet,' but then I saw something almost as good. 'Auntie Dorothy!' Mattie cried. 'Over there!' Dorothy was, huddled up on a bench by the wall with Eddie next to her. He had his arm round her and she was crying into his shoulder. There wasn't anything between Eddie and me but still I had a pang seeing them. He would have said he was only giving her a bit of comfort, but then that's what he'd said to me. Eddie saw me first. 'You just can't keep away,' he said, laughing, but he eased Dorothy off him so I guessed he felt a pang of guilt himself. Mattie went flying over and threw herself on to Dorothy's lap.

I told them what had happened while Eddie played one potato two potato with Bobby. I said the telegram to Len hadn't got through so we'd be waiting for a few more days yet which was true or good as. Eddie tutted and said that was typical, the organisation was all to pot, and a lot of other things which I had to shut him up about for the sake of the children, and for me too. It was bad enough feeling it was all going wrong and you'd made a terrible mistake without people rubbing it in.

It turned out we were to spend the night right there in the hall. I made a little nest of clothes from our baggage for Mattie and Bobby to lie on the bench and Dorothy and I sat at either end so the kids could get between us and lie their heads on our laps. I can't say it was the best night I ever spent but as I said, 'One thing about starting off like this – it can only get better.' And we both laughed just as though it was true.

Mattie

When we got to the camp Auntie Dorothy said, 'Would you credit it, it's just like being in the army,' and Mum said sssh as though she didn't want us to hear, but I couldn't see what was wrong with being in the army. Daddy used to be in the army. Everyone had to stay at the camp until they got a job but Daddy already had a job so Mummy said we'd only be here until Daddy came to get us.

Everyone was given their own hut and Mummy said flies and spiders were nothing to get upset about and the creepy crawlies were more afraid of me than I was of them. I thought they must be very frightened indeed, then.

You had to talk quietly because the huts were divided down the middle long-ways so if you talked too loud everyone else could hear you. They were called Nissen huts. There were lots of foreigners, so there were lots of different languages and shouting. Mummy said that was what foreigners were like but Auntie Dorothy said we were all foreigners now. I knew she'd made a mistake because everyone knew Australia was just England with hot weather and they were crying out for us to come and live here, and anyway Daddy was here, so it was ours already. It was just a case of whether we would want to stay. Mummy said of course we were staying, but Auntie Joanie had said we had a choice.

You weren't allowed to keep any pets in the huts, or do any cooking and you all had to eat in the canteen. When you were in the queue you could hear people saying, 'Not more foreign muck,' but it was horrible even if it was English food. Mummy said we'd like it when we got used to it. It could get very noisy in there with children running around and throwing food because a lot of parents didn't eat at the same time as their children. Sometimes Mummy would tell them off but as soon as she wasn't looking they'd start up again, and one time a man came over and said who did she think she was, shouting at his kids, and Mummy had a row with him. We always tried to get in early for our meals because after half an hour the place was disgusting. One of the mothers started taking the meals back to the hut for her family, which wasn't allowed and she got in a big row but she didn't stop and Mummy said she didn't blame her. She said she'd have done the same but it meant buying your own crockery and she didn't want to spend our money on that. Mummy said the first thing she'd do when we got a place of our own was cook us a proper dinner.

We had to get up at six thirty in the morning to go to the toilet because that's when they cleaned them and after that they were dirty and horrible. She said you couldn't blame the authorities, it was the people that used them, they must have been dragged up. She got us a potty and the rest of the day we all had to use that, and then she'd empty it. It got a bit smelly in the hut but not as smelly as in the toilets.

Even though I hated the camp, mostly I preferred it to the ship. On the ship I was the only one who was unhappy, but in the camp it was nearly everyone.

Rose

We'd all thought it was hot all the time in Australia, it's what they'd told us. Or maybe they hadn't told us but it's what we all thought. But it was so cold in those Nissen huts, every night we woke up shivering. I made a joke of it

73

to Dorothy, saying I was going to write to the rag and bone man who I'd given our woollies to and ask if I could get them back again.

After breakfast that first morning – noisy affair, everyone queuing up in a canteen the size of an aircraft hangar – I left the kids with Dorothy and called at the office to see if there was any news of Len. The woman at the table brushed her hair from her face and looked up. She had the look of someone who knew what you were going to say before you'd even opened your mouth. 'Someone will have contacted him,' she said, 'he'll be on his way.'

She put my back up right off. 'But what if he isn't?' I said. And besides, there was a notice outside saying that the bus to town only ran once a week. Unless he had a car, how would he get here?

'Just be patient,' she said, with a smile that looked glued on. 'Why don't you enjoy the rest? Your kids can join the school, or there's the free child-minding service if you want to get a job.'

A job? Just how long might we be waiting?

'Give it a few days,' she said, 'then call in again if there's no news.' Her eyes flicked to the person behind me in the queue. 'Or maybe a week or so.' And that was it, I'd had my turn. It was like being back at school with the teacher saying, 'Sit down, Rose, and stop being a nuisance.' It wasn't like me to give in without a fight, but I did anyway. We might all speak the same language, but still we were the foreigners. The pamphlets and the leaflets had told us Australia was crying out for us, but I wasn't sure the Australians had read them.

The woman in front of me in the dinner queue was in a hut near ours, I'd seen her earlier playing with the toddler who was wriggling about on her hip. He looked a proper handful. Snot running down like a waterfall but each time she tried to wipe it off he turned his face away. I was glad my two were older.

'Not easy to keep them occupied, is it, with all this queuing,' she said, but she wasn't talking about her toddler, she nodded towards Bobby who was pretending to poke Mattie with his finger. At every pretend prod Mattie squirmed and whined, 'Mummy, he's touching me!'

'Have you been here long then?' I asked. I guessed she'd know I wasn't referring to the dinner queue.

She hitched the toddler higher on her hip. 'Three months next Saturday.'

'Three months?' We'd been here three days and it felt like an eternity.

'Three months is nothing. There's people been here more than a year, just waiting till they can go back home without paying all the money back.'

'Shame on them for not getting a job then.' You get the shiftless and work-shy wherever you go, and hadn't the woman in the information office told me there was work available?

'Yes, there might be work around but it's not the getting it, it's the keeping it. My Geoff has had three, but it's a ten mile walk into town. You can't keep that up every day. And until he can earn enough for a flat for us, we're stuck here on the camp.'

The little boy pushed his fingers into her mouth and she nibbled on one making him laugh. I told her my husband was coming and would have a home organised for us, and she didn't even try to hide her envy.

'You lucky beggars,' she said. 'That's what we should have done. But we didn't want to be apart. We thought work would be laid on and everything. That we'd be on our feet in no time.'

'The bus will have to start running more often,' I said. 'You can't be the only one in this position. Maybe you could start a bus company yourself – sounds like you've got a readymade market.' I was pretty pleased with my money-making solution. Len always said I had a head for business.

'And where would we get the money from?' she said, bemused. 'I don't suppose banks would be queuing up to lend us the money.' She paused. 'Come to think of it, not sure where you'd even find a bank.' Her little boy started to struggle and she set him down on the ground. 'And if we did manage to save a bob or two, I'd rather spend it on the fare home,' she said.

The school was just a few tables set under an awning but I liked the informality of it, you don't need a building to be learning something. I was standing round the side of one of the huts, where the teacher couldn't see me but where I could hear what she was teaching about the geography of our new country, when Dorothy spotted me. She had colour in her face now, it suited her. Not the pasty white she used to be. She came hurrying over and pulled me to where we could talk more easily.

'I've got a job,' she announced, 'and no ten mile walk involved either'. One of delivery drivers had taken a shine to her and was going to give her a lift into town. He'd fixed for a mate to give her a lift back.

I was pleased for her but maybe my face gave me away. I wasn't jealous exactly, but she was moving things on, while I seemed stuck.

'Your Len will be along soon,' she said, 'I don't suppose he can drop everything at a moment's notice.' He'd already had a few months' notice, but she was trying to be diplomatic.

I told her about two immigrants I'd heard about who had had nervous breakdowns and had to be repatriated.

'Apparently it's common knowledge that women are more likely to have a breakdown than the men because they're mostly the ones stuck on the camp all day while the men can get into town and get jobs. So lucky you've got a job.'

'Oh I know,' she said, 'homesickness spreads quicker than flu, we'll all get it if we aren't careful.'

The next day as I waited to speak to the woman at the desk again, it was there in the people waiting behind me, the homesickness, the disillusion. 'We didn't sign up to go looking for jobs in the middle of nowhere,' said one. 'Didn't sign up to find our own jobs at all,' said another. 'They told us jobs would be waiting. Isn't that what you thought? It's what we thought.'

I didn't join in, but it was what I thought too, and what Len had thought. Had he done the ten mile walk looking for work? Had he caught the homesickness bug, was he too depressed to come for us? Or was it such a struggle he no longer had the strength?

It was a different woman at the desk, but she had the same toothy smile and the same answer. Just be patient. It'll all work out.

I took a decision then, as I walked back to our hut. I

could sit around moaning and moping like these other women, or I could get up and fight back. I waited a week, just in case he might still show up, then I took the kids into the little school early and got a lift to town with Dorothy's new mate, the delivery driver.

The man at the bus station ticket office raised an eyebrow and leaned back in his seat. 'Do you realise how far away that is?' he said. 'It's right up the top of the country. You'll never make it.' He had that nasal twang that I was going to have to get used to. I didn't answer. 'And a woman travelling alone,' he went on, 'it's not good.'

'I won't be travelling alone,' I said, 'I've got my two kids with me.'

He raised the other eyebrow and said did I know how far it was? 'You'll be days and days. And a bus isn't like the lovely ship you came in on. And you'll be going right through the middle of the country. It's hot up there, ya know, sweltering. Aussies find it hard sometimes and we're used to it.'

But we'd be glad of a bit of heat, that's what we'd thought we were coming to. And I did know how far it was, I'd worked it out from the map on the wall in our hut. It was further than Britain was from Spain, maybe a lot further, but seeing as I'd come half way round the world already, that felt like a skip and a jump. But anyway what choice was there? The hostel had to be paid for and we'd be running out of money soon. The biggest risk was that we'd pass Len en route but I'd leave a message at the camp that I was heading for his last known address, a small mining town near Darwin. I'd ask them to contact him again and let him know we were on our way. I didn't know if he'd got the other messages I'd left. Maybe it was a fool's errand but what else could I do?

I told the station clerk I'd have a single adult fare and two children. He just looked at me. But he sold me the tickets.

Dorothy came to see us off. She said it was like leaving family, and we had a laugh about that because I said leaving my family was more likely to make me laugh than cry – course I meant family back home, not Len and the kids. I was glad I could brighten the moment but it didn't last because the next minute Mattie had her arms round Dorothy's waist and was crying her eyes out.

Mattie

On winter evenings Auntie Joanie liked to toast bread on a toasting fork at the fire. Nanny would put Bobby to bed and then she'd bring in a pot of tea and we'd all sit round watching the flames. Auntie Joanie called me 'Joanie's special'. She didn't call Bobby that.

Once Auntie Joanie put a potato in the coals to cook but when she took it out later it was charred and black. She said it was lovely but I wouldn't try it, but then I did and I liked it and she let me have it.

When I closed my eyes I was back at home. But each time I opened them again we were still on the bus.

Rose

We passed so many dead trees I thought we must be in a tree cemetery. The road cut straight through that drab arid landscape, and wherever you looked it was all the same: dust and heat and more dust. And another dead tree. They'd shown pictures of what Australia would be like, course they had, but those photographs were of green grass and sunshine and people laughing, or sand and sea with people swimming and having a lovely time. There were no people here, nothing could survive in this damn heat from the fireball in the sky that seemed set on burning everything up. Len, I thought, why didn't you warn us? Why didn't you just come back home?

We were on that coach for days, stopping at scruffy little roadhouses where you were frightened in case something bit you or stung you or climbed on you and that included the owner. I'd have given everything for a grey sky and a bit of drizzle. You go into a trance after a while, you don't know anything apart from the dust cloud around you and that blinding light that made your eyes ache. You lose track of how long you've been travelling, can't remember where you're going. Or where you've been, come to that.

Bobby was travel sick, Mattie dozed or looked out of the window in a daydream or made up little games. There were a few other passengers but none going as far as us. I got talking to a woman who was travelling home to see her mother and even though I wouldn't have wanted to be travelling home to see mine, still I was envious that she knew what she was going to and that there would be a warm welcome when she got there. Her kids were noisy and boisterous, chasing each other between the seats until the driver turned round and shouted at them. Her toddler had a bad heat rash and cried with the itching.

Dorothy had given Mattie a book she'd been keeping for her daughter but the ride was too bumpy for reading. She said the book was just on loan, which was Dorothy's way of keeping her own hopes up that she was still going to find Sophie and that we'd all meet up again. I started a game of I-spy but we soon ran out of variations on sand, dirt, trees and sky. We sang songs though, and played Old Maid and Mattie turned out to be good at 'My auntie went shopping and bought...' and she was nice with Bobby, helping him out when he got stuck. I was the one who needed help. My life had been making lists – what to take, what to leave – since before Len went and my head was too full of that to find it much of a game. Bobby kept asking what the place was like that we were going to, but how was I to know? I just kept saying I wasn't sure but it would be very nice. Mattie kept on, 'But how do you *know?*'

The bus dropped us at a hotel near the mining town where Len was staying. In fact it wasn't near the town but I didn't know that. And it wasn't a hotel and I didn't know that either. I didn't know that when Australians say 'just up the road' they can mean it's hundreds of miles away. Or that hotel means bar. But this one had rooms where you could stay and there was a phone which the lady behind the bar let me use. I called the number the immigration camp had found for me. The person who answered the call said they'd seen Len only that morning and given him the message that we were on our way. I was almost sick with relief.

I told her where we were staying and booked a room for us while waited for Len to come. We were exhausted. Uncertainty tires you out. But at least we hadn't missed him, I'd been worried he wouldn't have got the message and he'd have set off to meet us at the camp.

But I also thought: why hadn't he set off to meet us at the camp?

TWO

'My bonnie lies over the sea'

Chapter 6

Mattie

Daddy didn't look how I'd remembered. He had a moustache now. I didn't like it. He had always seemed special, better than other dads. He was always laughing and you knew things would be all right if he was there. Whatever mood Mummy was in, she always cheered up if Daddy was around.

When he walked in he was smiling, but not the old smile, the smile without the moustache, and he was different around the eyes, they had creases under them that they didn't used to. I thought, 'something's happened' because when he went to hug Mummy they both seemed stiff like when someone is cross with you. But when he put his arms out to me, I felt awkward too, so then I thought feeling like that must be normal when you haven't seen someone for a long time. Bobby stood very still, not knowing what to do, but then Daddy took a toffee out of his pocket for me, and for Bobby a little ship that he had whittled out of wood. Bobby was so excited with it and then Daddy picked him up and they were both laughing. I thought, I'm not going to be the favourite any more. I'm not anyone's favourite any more.

We had to get on another bus to go to where Daddy was living. It seemed like we had been travelling forever and you were so hot all the time, it seemed like you wouldn't ever cool down. Bobby and I sat behind Mummy and Daddy on the bus and I tried to hear what they were saying. They looked as though they were arguing.

Mummy had said it was a mining town but it wasn't a town at all, not one with streets and houses and gardens. They didn't have paths at the side of the road and the road wasn't a proper road even though it was the only one. It was made of dirt and stones. I wondered where the proper houses were, I could only see big sheds and caravans, all set out higgledy-piggledy on the dirt. Daddy said they weren't sheds they were the houses and there was nothing wrong with them just because they were different from what we'd been used to. He said the shops might look different but you could get everything you needed.

I couldn't see any shops but when I asked Mummy she said of course there would be shops because everybody had to buy things, but later we found out there was only one and it was just a shack with a counter and some shelves with a few things in boxes. There was no Woolworths or anything like that. All around everywhere was dry and dusty. And hot. It was very hot.

We were to stay in one of the other shacks, where Daddy had been living before we came. There had been other men there too but now they had moved out into caravans. The lady our shack belonged to lived in a caravan too.

When we got to Daddy's lodgings Mummy went very quiet, and Daddy said that it was much better inside than it looked, and we must all muck in and anyway it was only temporary. I wished Auntie Dorothy had been with us, because then she and Mummy would've had a joke about it and we'd all have ended up laughing. But Daddy led us all in and Mummy moaned at Bobby for dawdling and Daddy told her Bobby was only a scrap and not to go on at him. He said it with a smile but I could see Mummy didn't like it.

While I looked around I could hear them talking but quietly so we couldn't hear but then suddenly Daddy said, "Rose – it's a job. Don't forget it's not like back home, there's no welfare and all that. And it's good money.'

Mummy said, 'So you'll have a fair bit saved then.'

Daddy didn't answer. He picked Bobby up and plonked him on the bed. He said, 'This is where you'll sleep, young man.'

I said, 'Where will I sleep?' because there was only the one single bed, the other was a double. There was a curtain across the room to separate it off. At home I only had to share a bed with Bobby if Daddy's relatives came to stay. When we'd stayed with Nanny I had slept with Auntie Joanie but I liked that.

Mummy said, 'Don't worry, sweetheart, we can buy another bed out of all this money your dad has been saving.'

I was pleased because she hardly ever called me sweetheart. I thought, maybe this really will be a new start. And to be getting a brand new bed too.

For cupboards, there was a tea chest with its back against the wall that Daddy had piled his clothes up in. There was a shelf on the other wall. I guessed we'd be getting new cupboards too.

Mummy pointed at the shelf, which was a bit wonky. 'Don't they have spirit levels here then?' she said.

Daddy said, 'Don't start, it's not easy getting accommodation, we were lucky to get it, it's only because I knew the landlady.'

I thought of Auntie Joanie's bedroom, and the wardrobe with the mirror on the door, where I slept after we moved in to Nanny's house. If you sat up in bed you could see yourself in the mirror. Auntie Joanie used to cuddle up to me. Her skin smelled of flowers and talcum powder and her hair smelled of pure Auntie Joanie. She used to wear her silver chain in bed, like the one she gave me. I used to try to stay awake until she came to bed and sometimes she'd tell me about Uncle Des and how nice he was and what they'd seen at the theatre.

I needed to go to the toilet and Daddy came with us to show us where it was. You had to walk along a track and then there was a shed like at Nanny's but instead of a toilet there was a board to sit on over a can. It smelled horrible and there were a lot of flies. Daddy said now and again someone would take the can away and bury everything that was in it. They called it the thunderbox. Daddy said this was what it was like living in the country, and that it would have been just the same in England if we'd lived in the countryside instead of a town. I thought he was making it up, but Mummy said that was true. She said Daddy's auntie's cottage used to back on to a river and they used to empty their toilet bucket into it. They used to swim in the river but always made sure it was upstream of where they were emptying their bucket. Mummy and Daddy had a laugh because his auntie didn't think about her other neighbours upstream emptying their buckets.

Back in our room, Mummy said, 'Know the landlady well, do you?'

Daddy said, 'She's been very good to me while I've been ill,' and Mummy said, 'Has she indeed."

Mummy was looking around and for a moment she looked sad, and she said what a shame they'd had to sell their furniture especially as she had to let it go for a song. But then Bobby asked what song was it, My Bunny Lies Over the Ocean? Mummy laughed and Daddy gave me a hug and said, 'Don't cry, Mattie. We can have a sing song later if you like.'

'Well, there's plenty to do here,' Mummy said. 'So let's get started.'

Daddy walked over to her and put his arms round her. 'Rosie,' he said, 'you're a marvel.'

'At least we're agreed on something,' she said. Daddy laughed but Mummy didn't. I could see her face over his shoulder and she reminded me of Nanny and how she looked saying goodbye to us at Waterloo.

Rose

Dear Dorothy,

I am sending this to the reception camp and have asked them to send it on if you've left already. I am hoping you will have got some help with finding where your children are. I think about you often, it must be terrible for you, not knowing where they are and what's happened to them. Still at least they are old enough to know it wasn't your fault, and you'd have kept them if you could. Be much worse for a little one, not knowing where its real mum was.

We are back with Len at last. He has been very ill which is why he couldn't come to meet us but he is much better now. He'd left messages for me at the camp but they must have lost them. He has got us rooms with the landlady he'd been staying with. Len says deep down she's got a heart of gold – it must be very deep down if you ask me. But he's working down a mine now so maybe he knows what to look for. I think she's got it in for me. Every time I cook anything she says I make the place smell, which you'd think she'd be glad of, a change from her own stink which is of cigarettes and dirty washing. Len has put his name down with someone to get a caravan for us when some people he knows move out. Who'd have thought that having a caravan could count as progress. When I think of our nice little rented house back in Croydon. We wouldn't have dreamt of putting up with the place we're living in here. But it won't be for long, once Len has saved a bit we'll be able to move on. What are the insects like where you are? We're covered in insect bites and we've got spiders the size of a dinner plate, and they say some of them bite. And there are frogs and snakes. And to think back home people moan about mice!

Len hasn't been able to save as much money as I'd hoped. They have a strange way of going on here. If you're off sick, they dock double your wages because that pays for the man who fills in for you. Len was off for a while because he hurt his arm, so he used up what he had put by. Course he went back as soon as he could, but now he gets pain in his arm which he probably wouldn't if it had longer to heal. I must say I wish you were a bit nearer, I could do with a laugh. I've made a few friends with the Aussie women here but we don't always see eye to eye.

They don't mind their husbands going off drinking, they say it's their right after a hard day's work. I don't hold with drinking and I didn't think Len did either, but it's all different here. He keeps saying he'll stop but he doesn't say when. They don't call it down under for nothing, seems to me everything's got turned upside down. I'd like a job myself but there's not much around here, we're a bit cut off from things. It's the same with some goods, we're so far away from everything they can't get the goods in so you can't get a lot of things – still, after rationing, at least we're used to all that!

Hope we can meet again one day.

Your good friend

Rose

Mattie

The kitchen table is a board on some bricks and that's where we make the bread. Mummy sends Bobby out to play while I help with the kneading. There aren't any scales but Mummy measures out what she thinks in a mug, and it turns out all right. It's nice having her at home and not at work like it used to be.

I also help with the washing. Nanny used to do it in the sink and then put it through the mangle in the yard outside but we don't have a sink or a mangle here. Mrs Donnelly, the landlady, let Mummy have some old kerosene tins and we boil them up on the stove with the washing in, and then Mummy squeezes the water out by hand. The washing used to come out of Nanny's mangle almost dry, and stiff as a board. Mummy's still has water dripping out of it but the sun is so hot that it all soon dries.

We have to be very careful with water, and everyone collects rainwater. When something got in the tank and died we had to empty it all out. Mummy said she couldn't bear seeing all that water running away but she said we would get a disease if we drank it.

While we are working Mummy talks about where she used to work, at the engraving factory, and about Daddy and what he was like when they were courting. When I ask her if she likes it here she says it's just a matter of getting used to it, it's an adventure and you have to get the most out of life. I don't see why we couldn't have got the most out of life with Nanny and Auntie Joanie back home. It's different for Bobby. He likes running about outside and digging in the dirt. But I like drawing and reading my books and now there's no library and anyway there isn't any time because there are always jobs to do.

I asked if I could have some paper so I could write to Nanny or do her a drawing but Mummy says she isn't made of money and anyway the shop probably wouldn't have any.

Cattle and horses wander about wherever they like in Australia. In England there were only dogs and cats and the chickens Nanny kept and you had to go to the country to see sheep and cows. I saw cows once when we had a day out with Nanny. On the journey here we even saw kangaroos and wallabies. A kangaroo jumped right in front of the bus and the driver had to swerve. Bobby gets very excited about the animals and Mummy says he gets that from Daddy. Bobby said could he have a parrot for a pet and Mummy said, 'You must be joking'. I haven't asked about the rabbit Daddy said I could have. We might not be able to take it home with us when we go back to England, and that would be cruel.

Mummy says the time we've all been apart has changed Daddy just as much as the army did. She says at least in the army you had your mates, but here he'd been on his own, dumped in the middle of nowhere and it was very hard for him and he had been very ill and we must make allowances. She tells me all sorts of things when we are doing the cooking.

She said, 'Your dad says Aussies are used to immigrants but they prefer any of them to a Pom. He says the Aussies think we think we're superior and we want them to change to our ways.'

I said, 'And what did you say?'

'I told him, more fool them if they don't want to learn any better.' And she gave the dough a slap and turned it over on the table. I liked it when she talked like this, because if there were enough things she didn't like, we'd soon be going home. Mummy always gets her way with things.

But then she said, 'Your dad says their ways are fine, and it's just a case of getting used to them. Now he's grown accustomed he likes it. And we'll all be the same.'

'We might not,' I said. 'Not everyone likes the same things. Bobby likes rice pudding but I don't.'

'You're lucky then aren't you,' she said, 'we won't be having rice pudding in all this heat!'

I said, 'Maybe we won't ever fit in here.'

She picked up an old can which she'd washed out and which the dough was to go into. 'You don't come all this way and then pack up and go home again just because it's not all handed to you on a plate. What would everyone back home think?'

'Nanny would think: Hurray! They've come home again.'

Mum snorted. 'She'd say 'I told you so' and I'm not having that.'

I said, 'But –'

She wouldn't listen. She said, 'We've made our bed and we'll just have to lie in it,' and we both glanced through to where we could see her bed. The sheets were rucked up where she hadn't made it yet and it was wonky because one of the legs was missing and the block of wood they propped it up on had fallen over. 'Maybe not that bed!' she said, laughing.

My teacher gave me some paper so I could write to Nanny and Auntie Joanie, but they haven't answered yet. Mummy is sending a letter this week so I am doing another one that she can send with it.

I am writing at the table which Daddy made out of a board and some wood he found for legs. When Nanny wrote to Mummy she said she hoped I was working hard at school. But it isn't a proper school. There's only one class, and we're all different ages, so Bobby is in the same class as me and that's not fair. And our teacher isn't a proper teacher, she spelled 'quarter' as 'quater'. When I told her she said I needn't think I was anything special, with my fancy Pommy ways. And she didn't change it. But then she gave me the paper to write to Nanny, so she is nice sometimes. And I feel sorry for her because she hasn't got a proper classroom, we all sit at tables outside. If it rains we sit in her shack. She calls it a house, but it's not a proper house either. Mummy says we'll move to a town soon with a proper school.

I loved my old school. Mrs Shaw was my first teacher, then I had Mrs Lint, then Mrs Miller. I was a good runner. When they were picking teams, I was always first to be chosen. My friend Janice always moaned if the other team picked me. At the start of term when you had to find a seat in class, the girls used to shove each other out of the way to sit next to me.

When we left England, we were learning about Boadicea and I liked hearing all about her but here it's all Van Daemon's Land.

I asked Mummy, 'What's a guttersnipe?' and she said it's just ignorance, take no notice of them. Dirty Pommies, was another one. Mummy said they were only repeating what they'd heard their parents say. But why would their parents say that?

I've got fifteen mosquito bites. Bobby only has four. Mummy says not to scratch them because it will only make them itch worse. It does make them worse but I can't help it. We've got mosquito nets for over the beds which I am glad about because we get frogs in the house and I'm scared one will jump on my face. They jump about and climb the walls just as though they think it's their room.

Some of the spiders are very big but Daddy says the worst ones are very small, and some of them bite and some are poisonous. Bobby keeps creeping up behind me and tickling my neck, then he yells, 'Mattie! There's a spider on you!' He thinks it's funny when I scream. Mummy says not to make such a fuss.

Bobby has made friends with a boy who lives in one

of the caravans. There are eight children in the family and
the older ones go to the same not-proper school as us, but
sometimes they don't come and then there are only five of
us in the class. Sammy, who is the youngest in the class
and is Bobby's friend, doesn't have any shoes and has
never been to the town. Mummy says there are families in
England just the same, it happens anywhere where people
are a long way from a big town but I never heard of
anyone our age not having shoes. In 'Heidi' they didn't
have shoes, but I thought that was just in a book. Mummy
says just because people don't have shoes, that doesn't
mean they're not happy. Mummy says when Nanny was a
girl she didn't have shoes and had to go to a charity soup
kitchen for her dinner, and had to clean other people's
steps before she went to school, and think how much
worse that was than here because of the cold and the wet.
She said Grandad's family had more money, and his
mother was one of the women serving in the soup kitchen.

Daddy works very hard, he is hardly ever home. Mummy
says what he works hardest at is drinking but he works at
the mine so I'm not sure what his job is really. At night he
doesn't come home until after we are asleep. At the
weekends he goes fishing with other men from the mine.
It would be nice if Daddy was home more because then
we could go out somewhere or he could play with us.

I've made friends with a girl at the school. Her name is
Susan and her mum and dad run the shop. She's older
than me. I lent her my Alice in Wonderland, and she lent
me What Katy Did. She turns the corners of the pages
down to mark where she has got up to so at the end of

every chapter the page has a crease in it. Auntie Joanie always says you should use a bookmark.

I can't get used to his moustache. And Daddy has grime in the lines of his hands from the mine and it stays there even after he has washed. When he comes in from work even if we're still up, he just wants to sleep in the chair. He used to make up stories at bedtime but now he mostly isn't home at bedtime. Even though I can read, I liked him making up bedtime stories, they were very funny. Bobby liked them too. But now Bobby is shy of him and a bit scared because Daddy's voice is very loud when he shouts.

Bobby and I were in bed but I was still awake and I heard them in the living room quarrelling again.

Daddy said, 'I was ill!'

'Too ill to lift a pen? I bet you weren't too ill to lift a glass.'

'I wrote to you as soon as I could.'

'As soon as Immigration made you. And if you were so ill, why didn't you get Dirty Dinah to write for you? She's always eager to please where you're concerned.'

'What are you getting at?'

'I'm not stupid. Or at least I am – or I wouldn't have come all this way to get you. But I'm not as stupid as that.'

He started to answer and then Mummy hissed, 'Keep your voice down!' even though hers was the louder. There was a lot more mumbling and I had to sit up and keep really still to hear.

And now Mummy's voice was different. 'We can still do those things, if we work together.'

'You weren't supposed to be working at all,' Daddy said. 'Do you think I wanted to bring you to a dump like this?'

I was sorry now for how I'd moaned about the dingy room and the flies and the heat and the smell from the thunderbox. I thought Mummy and Daddy didn't mind those things because they made a joke about them. I hadn't thought that maybe they were just pretending so it wouldn't seem so bad.

Daddy said, 'Life is hard out here. People are hard, they fight for what they want. You toughen up or go under. I've toughened up. That doesn't mean I wanted you to.'

I held my breath then, because this was Mummy's chance to say he was right and she didn't want to toughen up or for us to live where life was hard. It wasn't hard in England. We could go back.

There was a long silence and I wondered what was happening. I slid out of bed and crept to the door and as I got nearer I could hear they were still talking but their voices were very quiet. I opened the door a bit more, just enough for me to see them. They were standing up, they had their arms round each other. They were kissing.

Daddy murmured something I didn't hear and she laughed. He pulled a kitchen chair over and sat down, pulling Mummy on to his lap. He said, 'Okay, so I'll cut down on the drinking. But we have to fit in. And that means doing what Aussies do. So I can't give up entirely.'

Mummy said something into his ear or maybe she was kissing his face. He went on, 'So if we're going to fit in, you can start by doing what other wives do, and stop nagging every time I'm late home or want a drink with my mates.' He said it with a laugh in his voice like it was a joke. But Mummy got up off his lap.

He said, 'Rose - ,' but she had seen the bedroom door ajar and was coming over. I hurried back into bed and pulled the covers over. She shut the door and I couldn't hear any more

Rose

Dear Mum and Dad

Hope you are in good health. We are all well and Len sends his love as do Mattie and Bobby. They love it here, all the fresh air and sunshine, and it does make a lovely change from all that smog back home. Everyone is very friendly here and Len has got a good job, very well paid, and I'm hoping to start work soon. Len had been very poorly as I thought, hence his not being able to write (he had also broken his arm) but he is well again now. He was delayed meeting us off the ship but now it's like we were never apart. Mattie and Bobby have started at the local school. It's very small but that's a good thing as the teacher will have more time to spend with them. They've made a lot of friends and are loving the outdoor life. They are brown as a berry, well, we all are!

We get lovely fruits out here, things we hadn't even heard of at home, like pawpaw and guava. Nothing keeps for long in the heat though – and to think you used to complain your meat safe didn't stay cool enough. Our meat went off last week, and I thought I'd been so careful. It was a smashing joint too. But it's lovely to be warm instead of cold all the time like at home. Love to everyone.

Your loving daughter

Rose

Mattie

Nanny sent us a parcel! In it there were three comics for me and one comic for Bobby. Mummy said Nanny had been given the comics she was sending me, but she had to buy the one for Bobby. Mummy said it was typical of Nanny, and that I could have bought three times the number of comics for what she'd spent on postage. I bet Nanny knew even if she'd sent me the money, I wouldn't have been allowed to buy comics so it was clever to do it this way. She didn't put a letter in for me. I expect she is too busy to write to me or perhaps it makes her sad because I am so far away.

Bobby's comic was The Dandy. Nanny bought it for me once and Auntie Joanie and I had sat on the sofa and read it together. The ones Nanny sent me were called Romeo. They weren't funny like The Dandy. The stories were all about how a girl loved a boy but he didn't love her, or he did love her and they were going steady but then a friend would see him with another girl. The other girl would turn out to be the boy's cousin or something, or it would turn out he had a twin and so it was all a misunderstanding. The last drawing would be of him with his arms round her.

It made me think about Auntie Joanie and Uncle Des. I wondered how long it would be before they got married. I thought it couldn't be very long because Auntie Joanie and me had done all the important things already. She had found a picture of the dress she would have, and another one of the dress I would have. Mine was blue and hers would have a very long train which I would have to carry. I would have blue satin shoes to match.

The girls in the comic didn't look like Auntie Joanie

but they were still pretty. They were usually blonde, with thick yellow hair down to their shoulders. Their lips were pink, and when they were sad their lips would be parted while a fat tear shaped like a pear would trickle down their cheeks. Even when the drawings weren't in colour, you knew that was what they would look like. There was always a best friend that the girl could tell her problems to, and she usually had short black hair and would be less pretty but still quite pretty. If there was a girl trying to steal the first girl's boyfriend, then she would be haughty and other people would call her 'stuck up'.

On one page there were beauty tips, such as if you were asked on a date and didn't have time to wash your hair. They said you should use dry shampoo. I couldn't imagine what that would be like or how it could work but they said you had to part your hair into sections and then spray along the partings. Then brush out for a glossy finish just like it was freshly washed. I thought that would be useful here, with water being in short supply, and wondered why everyone didn't wash their hair that way. It would have been a good idea at Nanny's too – she used to make us lie on the draining board with our heads backwards over the kitchen sink until I got too big. It had to be done in the morning or my hair wasn't always dry by bedtime. It's easier now because it dries in the sun.

Mummy has started working in the shop. What happened was Susan's dad had a heart attack and her mum had to drive him to the hospital which is a long way off. Mummy was in the shop the day it all happened and said she would stand in for them for a few days till they got back, so she did and when Susan's dad came home he was still poorly and they asked Mummy to stay on. Mummy used to tell Daddy that running the shop was a mug's game but I never saw her playing any games.

While she is serving in the shop Bobby and I play with Susan, or if Susan is helping her mum I sit on the seat by the counter with my book. Mummy says I'm not really reading, I'm earwigging, but I like listening to what people say when they come in. It is mostly ladies from the caravans. They often talk about Mrs Donnelly, our landlady, whose name is Diana and who Mummy calls Dirty Dinah, and whenever she says that the other women laugh. They say things like, 'She's dirty right enough,' or 'She's desperate for a husband – and she doesn't care whose husband,' and then they laugh some more.

I heard one lady tell Mummy that Mrs Donnelly had a little boy and a husband once but she left them for her boyfriend only then the boyfriend ran off. I think perhaps Mrs Donnelly is only horrible because she is sad and lonely because she hasn't got a husband or a boyfriend any more but when I said that to Mummy she said, 'For goodness sake, Mattie!' She said there was something wrong with anyone who would walk out on a little kiddy.

Mummy says Dirty Dinah is always having little digs about Pommy ways and saying things like if people think England is so great why did they come, and Mummy says to them, 'If we'd known she'd be here we wouldn't have!' She can always make the customers laugh.

Mrs Donnelly never knocks, she just walks in and says, 'Not interrupting anything, I hope.' She always has a cigarette in her fingers. Mummy says she doesn't knock because she forgets we're paying rent to stay here and thinks she can do as she likes. She came in today looking around, as though she was checking everything was as it should be. She said, 'I was after Len to shift a kerosene can for me. It's in the way and I can't shift them when they're full.' Her neck was craning round, trying to see if Daddy was in the bedroom.

Mummy said he was working late and she'd ask him when he came in. I was still awake when he came home and I called out to Mummy to remind him but she said to go to sleep and not bother him.

I woke up and they were shouting again. Mummy was saying, 'You're worse than my father', but I couldn't see what was wrong with that, Grandad was always fun to be with. Daddy isn't at all like Grandad. Grandad would always play a game of draughts with you when he got in from work, and give you sixpence if you won. Daddy is always at work or out with his mates or else he is asleep. So maybe that was what she meant, because if 'worse' meant not so nice or so much fun, then that was right. Daddy likes going fishing but it makes Mummy cross.

'I've told you,' he said, and I imagined his face going rigid like it did when he got in a temper. 'Women don't come fishing and that includes you.'

'Well maybe they should. We came here to be a family, not to be left on our own every night and every weekend. We might as well have stayed at home.'

'Trailing after me, tracking me down, like a criminal. Sending the authorities after me.'

'Keep your voice down -'

They went on and on. I was frightened. The next day as we came out to go to school, Mrs Donnelly saw us.

She told Mummy she would have to leave if they kept up that racket all night, this was the third time in a week and Mummy said she didn't know she was counting but it would be her pleasure and she didn't know why she put up with a flea pit like this anyway.

Bobby and I looked at each other. I'd never heard Mummy talk to anyone like that before.

I thought now we would definitely go home and when we called at Mrs Donnelly's caravan on the way home from school I thought that's what we were going to tell her, but when Mrs Donnelly came out of her caravan on to her step, Mummy said she was sorry and it was just with being in a new country and everything so different. Mrs Donnelly looked at her for a minute, and then she said men could be a trial couldn't they, we needed the patience of saints, and Mummy agreed, and that was the end of it. I pulled a face at Mrs Donnelly behind Mummy's back but she didn't see.

Last night we were asleep when he came in, he woke us up making a lot of noise. I think he must have fallen over a chair in the kitchen because when I got up this morning, a leg had broken. I felt sorry for Daddy having to work all day and then some of the night as well. Mummy said the sort of work he did only took one arm. I thought he was lucky to have found a job he could do even with a bad arm. Mummy was still cross with him when he came home from work early the next day but Bobby and I were glad because he played five stones with us on the floor.

I have started reading Jane Eyre. Auntie Dorothy lent it to me. It is hard and the print is very small, and I was afraid of the bit in the room where the dead person was. But I liked the bit about the horrible school. I feel very sorry for all the girls there. I have decided I will try and read as many books by English writers as I can so I will go on talking like an English person and not Australians who say things like tucker for food which isn't proper English, and veggies for vegetables and mossies' for mosquitoes. Then when I go back I will fit in. Mummy thinks if we go home again people will laugh at us but Auntie Joanie won't be able to get married until I'm there to be the bridesmaid. So we will have to go back.

We were in the shop and Mummy was putting some cans on the shelves when a lady came in. Her husband was one of Daddy's friends. Mummy didn't like her because once they'd had an argument. Mummy had said something about it not being right for the men to go fishing all weekend and the lady said the men worked hard and it was their right. Of course this hadn't gone down well with Mummy. But I could see Mummy trying to be polite, and she asked if her husband caught much last weekend. The lady said did she mean the weekend before, because they didn't go fishing last weekend because the truck was broken. Mummy said, yes, she meant the weekend before.

After she'd gone I said, 'But they did go fishing, didn't they?' Because we'd gone down the track to meet Daddy when he came home and he'd made a joke about not catching anything. She said of course they went fishing, and it must be that the men didn't want that lady's husband to go so they hadn't told him. She said we shouldn't mention it to anyone so as not to make trouble.

Then she sat down on the chair by the counter which was where I usually sat, and asked me to get her some water. When I came back she had her head resting on her hands. I said, 'Are you ill?' and she said, 'No', but when we went home she made us play outside so she could lie down and be quiet. I was worried because Mummy was never ill but when she got up later to cook dinner she seemed all right again.

It was a bad row, worse than the others, even before the knock at the door. Mummy said Mrs Donnelly was always passing remarks and now she knew what she meant. Daddy said it was nonsense, and Diana was just a troublemaker and Mummy said oh it's Diana now, is it? I guessed the problem was having enough money for the rent which they had quarrelled over before or that Mummy was complaining again about him going out on the town which didn't make sense because the town was a long way off and he wouldn't have had time to go to work and go there as well.

When there was the knock at the door they both stopped. I thought it might be Mrs Donnelly complaining about the noise again.

Daddy went to answer the door. But it wasn't Mrs Donnelly.

Chapter 7

Len

When I first got here I missed Rose the way you'd miss your arms if they got chopped off. But I was going to make a better life for us, so it was a noble kind of missing, because I was doing the right thing.

I rented a flat when I arrived in Fremantle. I'd expected to be excited making a fresh start but instead there was this terrible isolation. I'd wake up in the morning and think, 'What have we done?' The weather was bad that first week, so it didn't make sense that we'd come for that, and already I was finding that jobs weren't ten a penny like I'd been told.

A few times I went down to the docks and watched the English ships leaving for home. There were always a few other Brits down there and we'd talk about the people we'd left behind and have a few beers and get maudlin.

The first interview I went for I felt a proper Charlie. I put my suit on and a shirt and tie like you would, and I followed the directions they'd said not realising part of it would take me right by the beach. Everyone I passed was in shorts and I didn't think anything of it, but then I got to the works and they were in shorts too, even the manager who was interviewing me. He said, 'Take your tie off, mate, you'll be boiled alive.' I was too, the sweat was running off me. I took my tie off but it didn't feel right, everyone dressed up like they were on their holidays. How can you run a business dressed in shorts? I didn't feel I could fit in somewhere like that even though I didn't say so. I didn't get the job, nor the next one. I put my suit on each time because a suit gives a good impression, there's no getting away from it but they all dressed the same as the first lot. I gave it up after a bit.

I think the suit even counted against me because the first jobs I went for they all wanted to make it clear however good I might think my experience was it didn't count for much with them. I learned a lot of skills in the army, and I'd done my apprenticeship before that, and back home if you have a skill you're proud of it. But here you were no better than a handyman, being an apprenticed tool machinist like I was didn't count for anything. And the machinery they were using was obsolete, you couldn't do the fine work I'd been used to. They'd want you to sweep the floor and tidy up, like you were a dogsbody.

But I needed to work, so I decided if they were paying, I'd do it, whatever it was. What's the point of standing on your pride? The ones who did that made themselves miserable, and poor with it. I reckoned if Aussies liked to do things their way then that was up to them, it was their country.

I got talking in a bar one night and someone told me there was work if you travelled into the outback. I decided to risk it – not like I had a choice, there wasn't anything else. It was pretty grim but they took me on straight away and I decided to stick it out because if I had regular money coming in I could start looking forward instead of back. And the sooner I could start saving for a house, the sooner Rosie and the kids could come out to me.

But then I got a letter from Rose and I remembered the good job I'd thought I'd get, and the farm we wanted and it all seemed so out of reach. I didn't have the heart to tell her.

And then one of the blokes I was working with said he and some mates were going out and invited me along for the night. I thought we were going to a bar, or hotel as they call it, but when we set off they said it was a special treat, only happened once a month and I was lucky I'd tipped up in time for it. They were laughing and joking like we were all going to have a high old time. Suddenly I saw a queue up ahead of us, maybe twenty blokes waiting in line. We joined on the end of it. I still couldn't make out what it was – I hadn't come across a bar you had to queue for and they didn't have picture houses there or that sort of thing. There wasn't much of anything around there, just scrubland and more scrubland. Every few minutes someone from the front of the queue would go round the corner and we'd all move up. I said, 'Come on, what is it?' but my mate just laughed and said I'd find out soon enough and then I'd be glad I came, and they all laughed some more. When we got up to the front of the queue, they pushed me to go first. This bloke came up to lead me off and he took me round the corner and up to a van a few yards ahead. The back doors were open and a man was coming out buttoning himself up. There was another man waiting and he went in, and the bloke waved me to wait where the last man had been standing.

I thought I must've got the wrong end of the stick. I couldn't see how it could be what I thought it was. Then the bloke who had led me off from the queue came back and told me how much it was. I said I didn't have enough and he looked mad and said what was I wasting his time for, only they weren't the words he used. I went back to my mates and told them I was a bit short this month and I'd have to leave it. I could hear my mates laughing, they knew I just didn't have the stomach for it

I thought there must be a team of women for all those men but they said there was just two. They came from a town up the road and were driven round here once a month. It made me sick to think about it.

That's when I stopped writing to Rose. I didn't want her coming where something like that went on, and people you worked with and thought were mates thought it was all right.

I shouldn't have stopped sending the money. But when I met Diana, it seemed the easiest thing, to sever all connections back home. She was on her own, struggling for a living like me. I didn't want to have to go back and tell everyone what it was like.

There was a knock at the door and when I opened it it was Jed, the bus driver. He's another of Diana's tenants, lives across the way. If you want to travel anywhere out of this place, he's the one you have to book with. He said there was a change to the timetable, the bus had to leave an hour earlier than planned. I couldn't think what he was telling me for. Then Rose came forward to speak to him. I could hardly believe it. The bitch.

Mattie

Daddy slammed the door and then he picked up a chair and threw it across the room. Bobby had to jump or it would have hit him. Mummy said don't you lay a finger on my children, and he said they're my children too, where are you taking them, and she said what was it to him, and it went on like that right up until bedtime.

The next day Mummy and Daddy were friends again but the day after we had to get up really early, straight after Daddy left for work. Mummy said it was a big surprise for Daddy and we were going to get packed up and go on a long coach ride like before. We weren't to make a noise because if anyone found out and told Daddy that would spoil the surprise.

When we got up we found our things were already packed and then Susan's mum drove up and she and Mummy put our case in the back of their truck. They had a conversation and Susan's mum said Susan's dad had tried to stop her coming but she said all Mummy was asking for was a lift to the bus station and Susan's mum said she'd told him that as far as she was concerned they owed Mummy that. Then we all got in and she drove us there.

It wasn't really a bus station, just a shelter where the bus waited. We stood there, shivering because it was chilly before the sun came up, and I was thinking it wasn't very nice not to have said goodbye to Daddy. But then he might have stopped us leaving so perhaps this was the best thing. Bobby asked if Daddy was coming and Mummy didn't answer. I thought of him getting home from work and us not being there. I felt sad but only a bit because I was glad we wouldn't live there any more.

'Where are we going, Mummy?' I asked, and my heart

was beating with what she might say. I could see Nanny at the dock come to meet us. See Auntie Joanie waving. Grandad would pick Bobby up and put him on his shoulder. And then she said it, what I wanted to hear most of anything.

'We're going home,' she said. I flung my arms round her and she hugged me back.

When the bus pulled up and opened its doors Mummy hurried us on while the driver climbed down and helped put our bags on. Mummy sat in front and Bobby and me were in the seat behind. She kept peering out of the window and looking at her watch. I said, 'Why aren't we going?' because we were the only ones on the bus and Mummy said, 'Any minute now.' And then at last the driver got on and started the engine. The bus pulled away and I was so glad to say goodbye to this horrible place with its smelly toilet and spiders and fat green frogs.

And then suddenly Bobby jumped up and pointed out the window and I looked out and in the distance there was a figure. He was running. Mummy had seen it too, and her mouth was open and then she said, 'Come on!' and I think she was calling to the driver, but he had seen the person running too, and now the bus slowed and stopped. He opened the doors and Daddy got on.

Mummy was sitting with her bag on the seat next to her, and she held it there so there was no room for him to sit down. He took the seat in front of her, and gave us a wave just as though everything was normal.

Bobby whispered to Mummy, 'Did Daddy spoil our surprise?' and she said, 'Seems like he decided to surprise us instead.'

'Is he coming too then?' I asked.

'He's just teasing,' she said. 'He'll get off in a minute.' I felt relieved about that. Nothing had gone right since we'd been back together.

But Daddy didn't get off.

We were travelling a long time and she stayed not speaking to him. We had to stay overnight at a roadhouse and when we got on the bus the next day, Daddy got on too and sat next to her and she let him and later I saw she was asleep with her head on his shoulder. I thought maybe they were friends again and Daddy was coming with us back to the port and it would all be like it used to be. He would play piano in Nanny's parlour and Auntie Joanie would dance with me.

Auntie Joanie would be so excited because now we were home she could get married. We would choose the material for my bridesmaid's dress and after she had made it we would go to a shop and buy the blue satin shoes and the Alice band with the flowers for my hair.

That was the best time of all, thinking about Nanny and Auntie Joanie and being a bridesmaid, even though it was hot as hot on the coach and Bobby was sick over me again and it was ages before we could wash it off. I thought we were going home. For a few hours it felt so close I could almost smell Auntie Joanie's perfume, even over the stink of Bobby's dried on vomit.

Chapter 8

Rose

The chiropodist came this afternoon, there's always someone calling in, never a minute to yourself. Nice woman though, coloured, with a bosom the size of a pillow. Joanie says we're not to say coloured any more, it's Black or West Indian or whatever. It used to be rude to say black and polite to say coloured. It's very hard to keep up. I said how do you know when it changes and Joanie says she relies on her Sian. She works in social services and they're very hot on all that sort of thing.

The chiropodist – Olive – has got an accent as thick as pudding, and a warm rich laugh like custard to go with it. I thought, this is more like it, someone with a bit of life about them, not like those miseries down the computer class thinking they rule the place. She cut my toenails, which I can't get down to since my fall even though I can walk about and do everything else just as good as before. I said to her, 'Will I be able to dance again?' and she said she didn't see why not. And I said 'That's good, I couldn't before'. She laughed just as though she hadn't heard it a dozen times.

Olive rubbed some cream in and then she said, 'All you need now is a coat of polish and an ankle bracelet.' I asked her to bring them for me next time – 'And get me a nipple ring to go with them!'

She had a bit of time before her next appointment so I made a pot of tea and she told me all about her three children and her husband who is a district nurse. She said they met on a geriatric ward when he was a nurse and she used to come in to do the old people's feet once a week. 'Our eyes met over a bed pan and that was it,' she said and she gave such a laugh the picture of Bobby and Donna on the mantelpiece fell down. She set it up again for me and I told her all about Bobby and his pharmacy. She was impressed.

'He must be very clever,' she said. 'With all that training it's almost like being a doctor.' I agreed. Well, there was no need to say it's his wife who's the pharmacist. He's just as good as her, after all these years. You'd never have guessed he'd end up behind a counter all day but then if things had turned out different I don't suppose he would have done.

I might get myself a cat, I miss having someone to look after. One with short hair, I don't want to be cleaning up cat hairs all day. Joanie thinks I should get a little dog, she says they're more company. I'll think about it. They need to be walked but it seems unnatural to put them on a lead after you've been used to them roaming. I used to walk for miles with ours.

I got the bus into town again yesterday. I've started a computer course. It's very good, you phone to say you want a session and they book you in, and when you get there, there's your computer all set up for you. You sit down with the headphones on, which flatten your hair down a bit but it's not for long, and then you listen to the instructions and do what they say. It takes me a long time to do each section because I'm learning to type as well. Joanie's been going for a year, she's very good, she can send emails and everything. She says you're not supposed to look at the keyboard when you type – I said to her, well how do you know where the letters are then? ESP?

We could have done with a computer back on the farm, especially one of the ones that does the accounts. I had to do all the paperwork but if we'd had a computer Len would have wanted to do it, I'm sure. Technology. He'd have liked all that. I'm not sure we had technology when he was alive.

After the computer course I went for a coffee with Joanie in the department store. We're going to book our sessions for the same time so we can have a chat or a wander round the shops afterwards. Some of her old waitress friends work there and they brought our coffee right over to our table instead of us having to queue up. It's strange being able to go in and buy a cup of coffee and not even think about the cost. Joanie feels the same. It's the way you grew up, you got used to having to be careful. Bobby's Tamsin said to me one day, 'We're not like your generation, Gran, make do and mend.' I thought, no you're not – she got a stain on her tee shirt and she threw it out! I said, 'Why do you think they invented washing powder?' Bobby should have told her, you don't get rid of a thing when there's nothing wrong with it. Course his wife's not much better, she buys her dusters. What does she think old knickers are for?

Joanie's grandson Steven, the eldest, has given me his

computer. Nice boy, he set it all up for me in the bedroom. When I've got on a bit further with my course I'll try switching it on. Joanie says we'll be able to email each other, but I don't know why we'd need to do that, she's on the phone every minute.

When she sipped her coffee I noticed the row of little lines running up from her top lip. Mum had those and I've got them. But looking at Joanie, I can still see the young woman she used to be, how she looked before we set sail.

We had to travel down to the port the day before we sailed and Mum and Joanie wanted to come and see us off, but I said just come to Waterloo and see us onto the train and let that be enough because otherwise we'd just be dragging out the goodbyes even longer. I was glad I'd said that too, the way Mum cried her eyes out. It's not like you don't know that leaving will be hard, so why not just get on with it, instead of making a big song and dance and upsetting the kids? And of course, even hugging me goodbye she couldn't give up, still going on right up till the last minute.

'Something is up with Len, you know it,' Mum said. 'Give it some more time. Let Len come back here.' I stepped back and knelt down to check the luggage labels on the cases, not that they needed checking but if I heard any more I was going to scream. She bent down to me in case I couldn't hear her. 'It's not too late to turn back,' she said. 'No one will think the less of you.' I didn't even answer, just gathered the kids up and got on that train.

Mattie cried because she missed waving goodbye while we were looking for somewhere to sit. I said, 'Buck up, you'll see them again soon,' and the minute I said it I realised that wasn't true at all. Chances were she'd never see Mum again. For a minute I could have cried myself.

When we got to Southampton there was a long wait to go onboard. We had to sit on the kerb with all our stuff and just wait. Bobby was irritable and tired, and Mattie was pale and silent. Exhausted with all the crying. And we were all cold, it was a chilly morning, you could see your breath on the air. As for me, well, I like to be busy. Sitting about with time to think doesn't suit me. That was the worst of it, really, the waiting. And I did think: 'What have I done?' What if Len didn't want us? It wasn't too late. I could have swallowed my pride and turned back. I don't mind admitting there was a minute when I wavered.

And then suddenly we were getting on the ship and that was that, we were on our way.

Joanie stirred her coffee and said, 'They're very different from us. They take it all for granted.'

I blinked at her. I'd been so far away remembering it all, I couldn't think where I was for a minute.

'Kids today. Take it all for granted,' she said again.

'Oh I know. They think the world owes them a living.' We were on safe ground with 'kids today'. It was one of the things we agreed on. I liked our coffee time after the course. Ladies of leisure, who'd have thought I'd ever have time to sit about in a café? We rub along despite our differences. She added cream from a carton the size of a thimble to her cup. At Joanie's house now she always uses a milk jug. All that waitressing has made her very genteel.

'Far too easy.'

'Is your Richie the same?'

'The same as what?' That's the only drawback with

all this sitting about. It lulls you into a false sense of security, you can let your guard down. I always hear alarm bells when Richie's name comes up. Joanie likes to do a bit of fishing in that particular pool.

'Is he wasteful? Or does he take after us?'

'Oh Richie's not like them. He looks after what he has and he doesn't buy anything unless he's one hundred per cent sure he wants it. Bobby's the same, but then there's only fourteen years between them, I suppose Richie is mid way between their generation and their children's. '

'Have you heard from him lately?' There she goes, fishing again.

'He's not easy to get hold of, but he'll call when he can.' I'd told her he worked for the government and had to keep his work and his whereabouts secret.

'But you think he's in Adelaide?'

'He could be. He goes all over.' His best friend had moved to Adelaide and we'd heard he was there. But that was a few years ago.

'He's good then, isn't he, ringing. Not like some sons you hear about.'

'Bobby rings as well,' I said, in case she was having a pop at him.

'No, I was meaning my Karen's husband. He doesn't call his mum from one month to the next.'

I thought of Len, who had never called his mum much either. Too busy with his girlfriend. Maybe Karen's husband was the same. But that was just men, really, they don't think about phoning, it doesn't mean to them what it does to us. It doesn't mean they don't care about you, it's just their way. Richie would call if he had my number. I said it was time I was on my way and we agreed we'd meet

119

at our next lesson on Friday.

My sister Marian came last Monday. Nice little suit she had on, pale blue and a white shirt under. I felt a bit down at heel sitting here in my slippers which have seen better days, though they only came from the catalogue so the days they did see were never that good. Marian had come from a bridge session. Since she was widowed a few years ago she plays every week. She's had a whole new lease of life since her Reg died. Joanie said she was tireless caring for him, and he was ill for years. That's how I was, nursing Len. Tireless. Everyone said so, so it must be true. Though I'm not sure what tireless means, now I come to think about it. Tired is what I was. Tired of the farm, having to do his work as well as mine. Not getting anyone permanent in to cover because we were all pretending he was getting better and he'd be back on his feet soon, even when he took to the wheelchair and could hardly walk any more. Tired of changing his sheets, and his soiled pyjamas and him getting thinner and thinner. Poor Len, he shouldn't have had to suffer like that. They say the good die young but what a load of rubbish that is. If you're good and you don't die young, what you get is pain and suffering. Len made his mistakes but he had a good heart. Whereas Dad, who made Mum's life a misery and ours, and deserved a bit of suffering if anyone did, died peaceful as a baby aged ninety-two, in his sleep one Boxing Day. Mum there and my brother Michael and my sisters and all their kids, Marian crying because he is your dad, even if he is a toe rag. Not like poor Len, alone on a ward with the screens round because the doctors had said it would be hours yet and I'd popped home for a change of clothes and Mattie wasn't coming in till the evening.

And me, what sort of death will I have? I was obviously not good enough to die young, but have I been good enough to get pain and suffering? I hope not.

Marian was going on about something but she'd reminded me of Len and the bus, and now it was all coming back so vivid it was virtually blotting her face out.

We almost came home. We were that close to it. Five minutes later and we'd have done it. Just five. Or if the coach driver hadn't changed the time, or if Len hadn't come home early, or I'd picked a different day. If I hadn't, or he hadn't, if they hadn't, if we hadn't…

For some reason the bus had to leave an hour earlier than the driver had said. That's how it was then, timetables weren't cut in stone, and I don't suppose Jed thought it was any big deal when he came to tell me. He was staying in one of the rooms Dirty Dinah rented out so I knew him and it wasn't exactly out of his way.

As soon as Len opened the door and I saw him I knew it meant trouble. Len was furious, shouting at him like it was his fault I'd booked, and carrying on, slamming the door and kicking at the chairs.

Len said why was I going, why, like there was some great mystery, like it wasn't as plain as the black ring round his neck and the bristles on his chin. And I felt the blood rush up into my face and I let him have it then – how could he let us come out to a dump like this, how was this a better life? How was working down a mine better than what he could have got at home? How was being eaten alive by insects and having to shit in a hole in the ground a better life? On and on it went, me giving him what for and him with his pathetic answers – I said why didn't you just write and say it's a nightmare, we made a mistake, I'm coming home. Why didn't you tell the truth? Why didn't you? But he just had more lies.

And then suddenly I'd had enough. I looked round and Bobby was standing there, white as a sheet and Mattie was sobbing and screaming, 'Stop it, stop it!' and I hadn't even heard her. So I said all right, all right, if he'd stop drinking I'd stay. Anything to shut him up and stop upsetting the kids. Anything to stop the row before Dirty Dinah came hammering on our door poking her nose in.

He said he would stop drinking and when we went to bed he tried to give me a cuddle, and in the end I had to let him so he wouldn't think I was still angry. He was affectionate, stroking my hair and whispering to me, tender even, but it was too late for all that nonsense.

When we got up in the morning he said he knew I hated him going fishing all weekend, but it was all arranged, didn't want to lose face, would be just one last time, and would that be all right? I said, of course darling, if that's what you want, and I'm not often sarcastic so he didn't see it at all, and he was pleased as punch thinking he'd got away with it. I had a little laugh to myself, because it wouldn't make a jot of difference to me if he went fishing once or every weekend for the rest of his entire life.

He came in from work on time that night, and the kids were so pleased to have him to play with but he wasn't getting round me as easy as that. I'd made my plans. The next morning I watched him go off to work but even so my heart was banging as we packed up to leave, and it didn't let up till we were on that bus and it was pulling out.

That's when I heaved a sigh of relief so big I thought I'd never breathe in again. And that's the exact moment I saw Len come running down the track.

The bus was already moving, and I willed it to pick up speed, and it did, gradual but getting faster, but Jed had seen him and I thought no, no, no, but he had, he'd seen him. He slowed down. The bus waited. And Len caught up and climbed aboard, laughing like he and Jed were old mates, and the bus set off, just as though he was coming too.

Len wasn't a violent man, or didn't used to be, but I went cold all over and the sweat came out on my forehead and I could feel rivers of it running down my back. I was frightened. My own husband, and I was frightened. Me, who would take anyone on and not be scared of losing.

Still I faced up to him. When I was a girl and that dog of his bit me he'd told me, 'Don't ever let an animal see you're afraid' and I thought of that now.

'Don't go, Rosie,' he said, and I saw then that he was the one who was scared. It made me strong.

'Too late, I've gone,' I said. I was still shaking but you couldn't hear it in my voice.

'I can make things better,' he said. I didn't answer him. I didn't want a conversation, it was all too late. But I couldn't help myself. I wanted to hurt him, rub his nose in it. 'Then why haven't you? Made things better?'

He tried again. The bus was bumping over the uneven track, but Len kept hold of the grab rail and stood his ground. 'We'll move. Wherever you want to go. Back to England if it's what you want.'

He said Diana – *Diana!* - was a terrible mistake and he'd been stupid. As if I didn't know that! And a part of me had known about Dirty Dinah from the outset, truth to tell. There was something in the way she said his name, and in her instant dislike of me. She didn't even like the kids and everyone loves Bobby. But I didn't have the strength to face the truth before now. Or maybe I was more like my mother than I knew. Didn't she always say if you kept quiet, a man would come back when he was ready with his tail between his legs? And wasn't he doing that right now? Though might be better not to think about what his tail had been getting up to.

'It didn't mean anything,' he said, looking like he might cry any minute, and gripping the handrail so hard I expected it to come off in his hand.

She wasn't even attractive, it was an insult. Her feet were always dirty, and her fingernails. She wore her hair scraped back in an elastic band.

He was mumbling, 'I'm so sorry,' as if that made any difference. I'd travelled from the other side of the world and for nothing. He started to cry. I've always despised weakness.

Len left everything. His clothes. The bits of furniture he'd bought before we arrived. He didn't have anything above the clothes he stood up in. Fortunately he'd had the wit to bring his money from the jar on the shelf where we kept it, though there wasn't much left in it, after I'd taken what we needed.

When I'd got on that bus with the kids I thought we'd never see him again. He'd made his bed and he could lie in it with whoever he wanted, just so long as it wasn't me. The kids and me were on our way back and the only thing that had stopped me booking our passage already was that I didn't have the money and Ten Pound Poms who went home within two years had to pay the full fare back. But I'd reckoned that with a few months work I'd raise that, and if I was desperate I could see if my brother Michael could lend me the fare – though that was only if we were really in trouble. I wasn't about to go shouting my mouth off back home about how things were turning out.

'Rose,' he said, 'Rose? Are you listening?' But I turned my face to the grimy window thinking goodbye and good riddance and that went for Len as well as this miserable apology for a town that he'd brought us to. We'd been there three months, that was all. Three months! And it felt like a bloody lifetime.

'Rose, are you listening?' Marian said.

I said I was. No point adding that what I was listening to was the thoughts in my own head which are mostly more interesting than what anyone else has to say.

I had plenty of time to think on that coach journey which also felt like a whole lifetime, except that you were too tired to think, what with the heat and the glare of the sun, and Bobby vomiting over my handbag and down Mattie's dress, too busy wishing, wishing you'd done things different, listened to your mother because maybe she was right for once in her life. And Len took advantage of that, he knew what I was feeling, and he kept on, over and over, about how I was no worse off if he came with us to Adelaide, and I could still go back home when I had enough money, and with him around it'd be easier to save, I'd be no worse off, and we could try again and if it didn't work out I was no worse off, and however you looked at it I was no worse off. He cleaned Bobby up and washed Mattie's dress at our overnight stop and he brought me a drink and settled the children down in the dingy little room and told them a story which made it seem not so dingy after all, and when I woke up in the morning he was getting them up already and dressed and teasing Bobby about something and making Mattie laugh. Back we went on the bus and still he went on, over and over: no worse off, you'll be no worse off. He said I could look at it as a purely practical arrangement. And I was too exhausted to look at it at all.

By the time we arrived in Adelaide, for the first time, I felt that perhaps the old Len was coming back again. Strong, protective, the man I used to love, and a good dad to his children, a family man. I agreed we would try again. And if it didn't work, well, I'd be no worse off.

When we got off the bus it was already dark. We had to leave the kids at the bus station with the luggage while Len and I split up to go and look for lodgings. Mattie was scared but what else could we do? When I got back Len was yelling because Mattie was eating an apple someone had given her and he said she shouldn't accept things off strangers.

It wasn't like him to shout at her, but I understood it when I saw the place he'd found for us. I couldn't complain, I hadn't found anything at all. When I saw it I knew then, it wasn't Mattie he was shouting at, it was himself.

It was a filthy little room in a tenement, well, two rooms but it made the last place look like Buckingham Palace ('No worse off?' I said. 'We're already worse off!'). Filthy sink on the landing to share with six other families, no one else with a word of English. Cockroaches, beetles, and the smell of cooking every minute of the day. The stains on the mattresses… I told Bobby people must have spilled cups of tea on them. But we were lucky to get that. Everywhere you went there were signs up: 'No coloureds, no kids, no dogs.' I thought with Adelaide being like a proper town with proper buildings we'd find somewhere better. But we were short of money. Wherever you are in this world if you haven't got money you haven't got anything. I made my mind up that was the last time I was ever going to be poor.

We got the kids into bed – we all slept in our clothes we were so tired, and our boots were cleaner than these beds – and I thought, what have I brought my family to? A couple was quarrelling in a room upstairs, and there were people crashing pots and pans at the sink outside our room, jabbering in Greek or Italian or God-knows-what.

I thought of Dorothy, maybe she was staying somewhere like this, maybe she'd heard where her children were by now. I wondered if many other English families came here, couples with children maybe. As I pulled the cover over me, the cover that smelled of cooking fat and sweat, I thought I heard some English voices, there was a little boy crying, and a little girl, and a voice was saying, 'Don't cry, Mummy's here,' and the voice sounded like mine, and maybe it was.

'Well, I'll be off,' said Marian. 'I don't believe you've heard a word I said.'

Chapter 9

Rose

Marian's been round again, still banging on about these bridge sessions of hers. She says they're a good laugh and I'd like them. She says they take it in turns to have it at each other's houses. She says some people provide a sandwich lunch but she only does biscuits but no one seems to mind. She says a lot of other things and I say seeing as I'd have to go on the bus, I'd want more than a biscuit when I arrived. But to tell the truth I wouldn't mind a little outing once a week, someone else's home to have a nose round. The only down side would be having to play bridge when you got there.

'It'd take you out of yourself,' Marian says.

'I don't need taking out of myself. Anyway, it's not my sort of thing,' I said.

'How do you know if you don't try?'

'I don't need to chop my leg off to know I wouldn't like it.'

'We get a good mix, and some of them have had very interesting lives. Lived abroad almost as long as you, and husbands in the embassies and all sorts.' She was always one for glossing over the details. If you probed you'd probably find one of them once had a cousin who knew someone who had an uncle who once worked in an embassy. As a doorman!

'And it keeps your mind agile,' said Marian. 'You have to concentrate and keep track of what is going on. There's one of our crowd – Moira – and she's almost ninety. And she's as sharp as…' She looked around for a comparison and couldn't find anything even though there was a knife on the table right in front of her. So Marian's mind's not as sharp as all that then. Finally she saw it, 'Sharp as a knife,' she said.

'Marian,' I said, 'that's a butter knife. I'm sharper than that and I've never been to bridge in my life. And my mind is agile,' I said. 'I get all the mental exercise I need trying to work out who is sleeping with who in Coronation Street.'

She pulled a face. 'I don't watch television, you end up brain dead.'

'At least I've got an excuse then,' I said, 'what's yours?'

We had a laugh at that and then she made us another cup of tea and I cut us some more of the fruit cake that was on the table.

'Come to bridge just once,' she said. 'Or bowls. You'd like bowls.' The woman was obsessed. 'You'll make lots of friends.'

I said I didn't need more friends. What are friends but people trying to find out your business? And I don't see the point of card games. Or ball games. When you're finished there's still the chickens to feed, the cows to bring in, the milk to deliver.

'I'm sure it's all very nice for those with time on their hands,' I said, 'but I've never been one for sitting around.'

She took a piece of cake. 'And what are you doing now but sitting around?' she said. 'You're not exactly run off your feet are you?'

It was all very well for her in her nice little suit. She had a cream one on today with piping round the collar. But I didn't have a load of fancy clothes that would fit in with all her posh friends, and I didn't feel like spending my hard earned money buying some. Marian and Joanie were always boasting over bargains they found in charity shops but I'd spent my life scrinching and scratching, I wasn't doing any more of it.

'If you wanted to come, I could give you a lift,' she said. Rubbing my nose in it that I can't afford a car. 'Very nice cake,' she said. 'Where's it from?'

I said, 'You should know, you brought it!'

She said she hadn't brought it, she said I was getting confused with the scones she'd brought last time. As if I wouldn't know if I'd bought a fruit cake. Talk about mental agility!

I wonder if I did the right thing staying in this country. You get sick of the cold weather and it's not as if I'm close to Joanie or Marian. They're company and they've been very good to me but Joanie's got Des and Marian is, well… Marian. We didn't see eye to eye as kids and we don't now. She wants to improve me, with her bridge and her bowls club. Sometimes I call it her 'bowels' club just to annoy her. Last week she was on at me to join her book reading group or whatever it is she calls it. I ask you, who in their right mind joins a group to discuss a book. Books are for reading, I can't see why you'd want to be sitting round talking about them, you might as well be reading another book. When I said that to her she called me a Phyllis Tyne, whoever she is.

I miss the warm weather and the friendliness, and the big wide roads with hardly a vehicle on them. It's all hooting and exhaust fumes here. You go out for a healthy constitutional and come back exhausted from dodging the traffic and with carbon monoxide poisoning. I was on a crossing and a white van screeched to a halt and the lad called out, 'Take your time, Grandma, I've got all the time in the world.' Silly bitch that I am, I gave him a wave. I only realised when he gave me the finger. You don't get that sort of thing at home either. They respect their elders over there. They're known for it.

But that's the trouble with emigrating, you end up not belonging anywhere. When you're there you wish you were here and when you're here…. I know lots of people like that. Not me, obviously. I shouldn't have come back. It was much better over there.

If I'd stayed there I wouldn't have fallen off that bus. I might still be busying about the same as ever. Funny really, you carry them all with you, your memories, they're not like luggage that might get lost in transit, you turn around and they're all there right behind you. Or like stuff you shove up in the attic, and you've forgotten all about them, then one day you're looking for something else and there they are, you brush the dust off and they're shiny as yesterday.

'Rose? You were miles away!' Yes, and I wish she was miles away, coming round eating all my cake. Or her cake. Anyway she's had most of it, whoever's it was. She's telling me something, probably more fascinating facts about her bridge group.

I wonder if she knows about Richie. Joanie does, I'm sure of it. It's there in all the things she doesn't say. I look at Marian hard, trying to see into her head, but all I can see is a bridge table and a pack of cards.

'Do you want that magazine Joanie gave me?' I ask. 'I've finished with it. And I saved you the crossword.' I'm trying to smooth things over and it works because she picks it up and soon she's telling me about an article she read about a woman who had twins and one was white and one was coloured. 'Black,' I say. 'Joanie says to say black.'

'Oh no, I don't think coloured people would like that,' she says.

After she'd gone I put the news on but I wasn't watching it. I was back in the factory in Adelaide where we both had to work, while Mattie and Bobby had to be minded by Mr and Mrs Flint, that creepy couple in the flat downstairs and I had to send them for all Mattie cried, because where else was there? We had to work, you can't live on air. Poor old Mattie, forever asking when she was going to be a bridesmaid. I used to think: how can she still think she's going to be a bridesmaid? Does she think she'll sprout wings and fly back to England? But I put off saying anything, she spent enough time weeping and wailing, I didn't want any more tears than we already had. Always crying, saying I'd taken her away from everyone who loved her. Didn't she think I loved her?

Anyway I'd have gone back home if I could, I think that's why I couldn't bear it when she said it. It was hard on all of us. Poor old Len chasing up and down the country for a job, up and down like a whore's drawers.

The first place he got was at a mill but we'd no sooner found somewhere to live than they laid a lot of the men off and he was one of them. He heard of another mill with vacancies and he rode all the way there on his bike, even though it was miles and miles away, and all on dirt roads, not tarmac, but he didn't get the job and worse, he got caught in a storm on the way home and fell off his bike. Mattie screamed when she saw him coming up the track, limping and his legs all covered in blood. After all that journey I thought they should have given him the job anyway just to be fair.

After a bit he found work on a nearby farm but it was seasonal and it didn't last long. After that he got taken on at the mill in the very next town which was much better because it was regular work and he could get his shower there at the end of his shift which helped with the water situation. I was so relieved when he found a house at such a low rent, though I wasn't quite so pleased when we found the roof leaked and there was a rat's nest in the kitchen (not that you could call it a kitchen. It was just the place where I did the cooking). Still no running water and a tin can for a toilet. But it wasn't so bad and when he got a promotion I bought a proper chest of drawers and a settee.

Of course in the end he got laid off again, none of these jobs seemed to last five minutes. No reflection on Len, it's just how it was. He went off to try at a mill he'd heard of even though it was a hundred miles away. I told him I wasn't moving again, if he took it he'd be going on his own. He didn't get the job there either. I had a part time job cooking at the hotel by then and when we couldn't afford the rent where we were living I fixed it for us all to move into the hotel temporarily. The manageress was on a good thing because now I was at her beck and call, and she had a handyman in Len thrown in.

We only had two rooms at the back, but the kids liked being near the town and even though they had to keep out of the way of customers, there was always something for them to hear or see. I was run off my feet because now I was on the premises I had to take on the cleaning and washing as well as the cooking, and I didn't see much of Len either. He said the bar was as good as any employment exchange, and he said you often heard of jobs going from customers. Which was true though and he did pick up bits of work. 'At least it's work,' he'd say to me. 'It keeps the wolf from the door.' And I'd say, 'I'm more concerned about keeping the wolf from the bar!' He'd laugh at that and then I'd say he needn't think he could be in there drinking all our profits while I was working my fingers to the bone, and he'd put his arm round my waist and nuzzle my ear and say, 'Rosie, Rosie...'

Sometimes Len would try and add a little bit to the letters I wrote home. I'd tell him, 'Don't you mention you're still labouring, they'll only say: "He wouldn't have done labouring if he'd stayed here".' Len would say, 'It's all money, what does it matter where it comes from?' But it mattered to me. Like I always say, the truth is what you say it is. People only know what you tell them. So I never mentioned when we were living in the hotel. And when we were living in the shack with the leaky roof and the rats' nest, I didn't mention that either. Why would I? But I never actually lied about anything, not what you'd call lying. Emphasising the positive, that's all I ever did.

Dear Mum and Dad

Guess where we're living – a detached house! It's in half an acre, and very secluded and romantic in its way – lighting is by kerosene which is cosy in the evenings. It's ideal for while we save up for a deposit for our own place. We have mango trees in the garden – I bet you've never even heard of mangoes. When we first saw them we didn't know you could eat them. They are big juicy fruits and we all love them. You can have them stewed, or raw which Mattie likes, although it makes a mess peeling them. The town isn't far away – we were a bit remote before – and we have everything we want here so it's not so different from at home in many ways but better because of the sunshine. We'll get a car or a truck soon and then we'll be able to have trips out at the weekends. Mattie and Bobby are very pleased with the school. I'm working too in the town, I'm quite the sophisticated lady these days, and I don't have to get the bus because a neighbour gives me a lift in and if I don't mind waiting, which I don't, another neighbour brings me home after. I say neighbour, but he is actually just someone we met who lives nearby. Our house is up a track, very secluded and private, so we don't have neighbours in the way you think of them. What do you think of that? In England there would be a dozen families living on the same land that is just for us out here. We're doing much better than we could have hoped to back there, and everyone is very friendly here.

Send my love to everyone.

Your loving daughter

Rose

I should have been a story-teller, I had a definite gift.

Joanie said, 'You sit there and look out the window.' She meant: 'Talk to Des while I get the dinner.' We were out in their dormobile for the day, and she can't bear anyone around her when she's cooking. Mind you, there was no room to be around her. Des sat on the bench seat on one side with his legs stretched out and I sat opposite with mine bunched up and the table in between us, pushing into my belly if I leant forward. The kitchen was at the far end, and when I say far I mean near, because nothing was far. There was a wardrobe one side, and if you'd tried putting a coat in it would have been full up – and the kitchen sink and two-ring cooker were on the other side. And what was she cooking? A roast dinner. I ask you, and it was red hot out, well what counts as red hot for England.

'A corned beef sandwich would do,' I said, 'Don't go to a lot of trouble for me.' When they'd said come out for the day in the dormobile, I'd thought we'd be having a picnic, not all this malarkey.

'Trouble?' Des said. 'We always have a roast on a Sunday, it doesn't matter where we are.'

'I can't eat off plastic plates,' Joanie said. 'It doesn't taste right if it's not off china.'

She had a proper dinner service stacked in the tiny cupboard next to the sink. Side plates and china cups and saucers. Wouldn't drink out of mugs. 'The lips are too thick, tea doesn't taste right.'

I thought about the thick old mugs they gave us at the reception centre. The one plate and the knife, fork and spoon you'd had to queue up for. I looked at Joanie, she was happy as Larry. From the window over the sink she had a view straight across Beachy Head. I'd never been here before but it was one of their favourite spots to drive to. She stopped chopping and she was looking out, dreamy and content. I thought: was it better to have it hard and to learn to make the best of it like we had in Oz? We always said hard times make you appreciate what you've got, but Des and Joanie looked like they appreciated what they'd got. And they hadn't done so bad just by staying put. That's what was irritating me about their little dormobile, I knew that really. It wouldn't have suited me and Len but it suited them. And if they hadn't seen as much of the world as we had did that matter in the scheme of things? They'd been all over Europe in their dormobile, been to loads of places I hadn't – Venice and Rome and Paris – and they were happy with that. Were we any better off than them for knowing Melbourne and Sydney and seeing the Great Barrier Reef? I was glad we had but then if I'd seen Italy and France maybe I'd have been just as happy with that. You make your choices in this life, you can't do it all. And in the end who are you trying to impress? What's it all for?

I offered to peel the spuds but Joanie said that was Des's job, but when she put the bowl of water on the table with the potatoes, I got a knife and set to. I don't like to be idle, it's never been my way. But still it was pleasant, the quiet and the sun coming in the window, the only sound was Joanie whistling 'That Old Black Magic' while she chopped carrots. She whistles like a man, Dad taught her that.

We were quiet for a while just listening to Joanie. Then Des said, 'What's your Richie up to now?'

I was aware of Joanie stopping whistling. Her head turned just fractionally and I knew she was standing there waiting. I kept on peeling, didn't pause.

'Oh all sorts. Very high powered from the sounds of it. He travels all over.' I liked to keep it vague.

'How old is he now?' said Des.

'Thirty something.'

'Not a kid any more,' Joanie said, reading my mind.

'He was always a wanderer,' I said, 'and a loner. Right from when he was little he'd go wandering off. And we were so busy on the farm we couldn't always keep track, he got used to fending for himself.'

'So he's working then, is he?' When Joanie had asked before I'd fudged and hedged but it wasn't so easy with Des being so direct and sitting bang opposite looking me straight in the eye. And Joanie hanging on every word. I scraped a last bit of peel off the potato and put it in the water.

'Roast potatoes are nice but they're fiddly, aren't they?' I said. But there was no diverting Des.

'So he's working?'

'He's doing the same as before, as far as I know. We don't hear a lot of him.'

'I suppose that's the thing in a big country like that, it's not so easy to keep in touch.'

That felt like implied criticism – either that or he thought we were all so backward out there we hadn't heard of the telephone. But whatever it was I had to let it go. 'I think it's just boys. I know Bobby's always on the phone but he's not typical.'

'Is he always on the phone?' Joanie said, jumping in. Why couldn't they mind their own business and get on with the dinner? 'When did he last ring then?'

'Last week,' I said. 'Tuesday, I think it was. He was

worried because he hadn't heard from me.'

'Funny,' she said. 'You didn't mention it.'

'There wasn't much to report. They're all fine. He wasn't on the phone long, he was in a hurry.'

'How's that wife of his? Has she had her operation yet?'

I'd forgotten about Donna's piles. 'No, they put it off again. She's been too busy in the pharmacy.'

Joanie finished rubbing salt in the pork rind and put it in the oven. We were supposed to be going for a walk while it cooked and I was more than ready. I was getting stiff sitting here with my legs squashed up under the table.

'I thought it was urgent,' she said. 'Wasn't she supposed to be in a lot of pain?'

'They must have settled down a bit,' I said, 'he didn't say much about it. Anyway I must pop in the lavatory before we go out.'

Joanie opened the toilet door and took out the broom and the dustpan and brush, and the windbreak which all had to lodge in there, there being nowhere else. I squeezed myself in and perched over the bowl and I was glad to be away from their questions even though I was as squashed as a sardine in a can and the only thing between us was a door the thickness of sandpaper.

'Why don't you ask Bobby to come over?' Joanie called out. 'Or Mattie. They could stay with us if you're not up to it. They could come over for the millennium, we could have a party.'

I started pumping the flush and pretended I couldn't hear her.

Des says Joanie and me are thick as thieves, and it's true

we get along in a way we never did when we were younger, and we're always together, always having a laugh. But there's a bit of me can't ever really relax. She knows where the bodies are buried, some of them anyway, and even though Len is dead and gone where the truth can't hurt him, still we've all got things we'd rather keep to ourselves. Joanie thinks if she met the children she'd find out a bit more but Bobby can't afford to come and Mattie won't come on principle. She's over fifty and I do believe she's still not forgiven Joanie for having someone else as a bridesmaid. I used to tell her not to dwell on it, but whenever it came up her eyes would fill up. Poor little mite. I know it wasn't easy for her. I was hard on her, I know I was. But we had to stay strong. It was the only way.

I had a long wait to get on a computer today, the woman on the desk said I wasn't booked for eleven, she had me down for ten, so I'd missed my slot. She said it like I was making an excuse for turning up late. As if I'd have booked for ten!

Joanie was there already, she must have come early even though we'd agreed on eleven. But she didn't see me, she had her headphones on. I don't use the headphones now, not since I found you can get the instructions off the screen. I've never been good at listening. Mind you, I'm not all that hot at reading either, the way things are going with this course. Joanie says it's a matter of getting used to it, but I've been coming for weeks now and sometimes I still get stuck logging on. I've got my password, which is LEMONS, which I keep written on a piece of paper in my handbag because as soon as I sit down at that computer I can't remember whether it's supposed to be LEMON, LEMONS, or MELONS. Actually it could be MELONS now I think about it.

I told the woman I'd sit and wait for a computer because half the time people don't do their full session and I could go on then. She said that wasn't allowed but I pretended I hadn't heard and said, 'I'll just wait over here,' and sat at the table in reception where they have all the leaflets for if you don't speak English or you want to claim some more benefits.

I didn't have to wait more than ten minutes and a computer came free. The woman on reception said it was no good me starting because the next person would be in before I'd had a chance to get going, but I said, 'That's really kind, I do appreciate it,' like I'd thought she was saying something else, and that took the wind out of her sails. When they say age brings wisdom I think that's what they mean.

Anyway I should have stayed at home because even though I got logged on, I couldn't remember any of what I'd done last time even though it was only Wednesday and I'd passed the test they give you at the end of each *'module'* and everything. If it had been the usual woman on the desk I'd have got her to check it for me because I think the computer had a fault in its memory banks but I thought I better leave well alone with Face-ache on duty.

And I was glad I had because I did the *'module'* again and when I got to the paragraph where you had to cut a sentence out and then paste it back again, it all came back to me. The paragraph was about different kinds of cattle so naturally I wouldn't forget that. I got on fine after that but there wasn't time to do the test again. Sometimes I think the computer's not the only one with memory bank problems. But there are other things I remember just like they were yesterday.

Halfway between the house and the cowshed the land rose slightly. Usually I was in such a rush to get the milking done I barely noticed, but with the sun just coming up the land seemed to shine. Radiant yellow, but tinged with orange, and getting brighter every minute, the colour of hope I always think. It was so peaceful, hardly a sound but for the cows. I'm not a sniveller but there were tears in my eyes. And it was ours, all of it. As far as the eye could see, and as I stood there on that incline, I could see a very long way indeed.

I liked the milking, the smell of the cows, their different temperaments, and so trusting. They were like children, but children who didn't argue or answer back or cry because you'd taken them away from everyone they loved and who loved them. Some were bad tempered or touchy, but we had an understanding: they needed me as much as I needed them, and once they'd got what they wanted, they were content. When I was with my cows, with their soft brown eyes, and their rough tongues, I was happy too. I could have stayed in that shed forever – or out in the field, driving them to new pasture – and been completely content. Len felt the same. Not for the cows but for the land. He said the soil had a different feel to it when it was your own. For all the dirt in his fingernails and the smell of manure on him, he was an old romantic. We'd sit on the veranda at sunset and Len would say, 'It's ours and we did it all ourselves.' And I'd say, 'It's surprising what a Pom can do with ten pounds,' and then we'd both laugh.

That's what I wrote to Mum anyway. And it was true. Some of it. We did live on a farm, though we were tenants for years before we got our own, and there was a veranda though it was falling down and we were too busy to fix it let alone sit on it. But we were happy. This was what we'd come for and when you were feeding the animals or planting your own vegetables it didn't matter that it wasn't our name on the deeds.

In her letters Joanie would ask, 'But aren't you lonely?' She couldn't imagine what it was like living somewhere with no picture house, no newspapers at the corner shop. No shop. But that's what I liked, being far away. No one to judge you, no one but your family and your thoughts, and with no time to think them, your thoughts weren't a problem either.

I knew we'd turn ourselves into Australians one way or another. Not that it was easy. Sometimes in those early days I'd wake in the night and lie there listening at the sounds outside and I'd realise Len was doing the same thing. I'd see something moving on the wall and I'd pray it was just my eyes playing tricks and not something that would bite or sting or make your face swell up, or give you blood poisoning. Aussies loved to scare you with their horror stories and then they'd say, 'That's really rare though, sport, never known it happen round here.' And you didn't know whether they'd been pulling your leg all along, or it was all true and now they were trying to stop you worrying.

But if everything wasn't perfect, well it hadn't been perfect back home, that's why we'd come. Sometimes you'd run into other Poms and they'd be complaining they missed their family, or they didn't like the area, or it was too hot, and I'd just walk away. How would it look to all your family if you went running back home again, crying that you didn't like it? They'd just say, 'I told you so'. I'd come *that* close to doing that myself. But I'd soldiered on and I was glad. I was never going to have that said to us.

Aussies thought you were a failure if you didn't own your own place but how could we, when we'd arrived with nothing and no one to help us? We got on the list for a housing association, but we had to move on – never did find out if we ever got to the top of it. And all that time Mum was going on in her letters about the nice cosy flat Joanie was renting, and how well Michael was doing, and the little terrace Marian and Reg had put a deposit on and there's us living in squalor and thinking we we're lucky to get a roof at all.

I used to read Mum's letters out over dinner, but I had to miss out all the bits about how well everyone was doing back home and about Joanie's wedding plans. I always meant to mention it when the time was right, but the time was never right, Mattie found enough to complain about, she didn't need any more ammunition. Always going on about being Joanie's bridesmaid and when would that be. Then the sun was too hot, the rain was too wet; she didn't like this, she hated that. I used to say to her, it's not as if living in England was a bed of roses, Miss, but you don't get damp out here like at Nanny's house. I can remember getting into bed and thinking the sheets were wet. You'd be grateful for the heat if you'd known cold like I did, I'd say. Middle of winter and no heating in the bedrooms. If we were ill, Mum would light the gas lamp to take the chill off! And being ill was the only way to get a bed of your own. I shared with Joanie until I left home, well, I did sometimes anyway, never thought anything of it. When have you ever had to share a bed? Well, all right, but we weren't there for long, were we? Think about that, my lady, before you start up with your complaints.

Bobby was good with the animals, but Mattie wasn't interested unless there was an ailing one that needed nursing, and then she'd treat it like a doll, playing doctors and nurses. Otherwise it was '*Ooh, she smells, she flicked her tail, she looked at me*'. I showed her how to milk but she couldn't get the hang of it and she must have startled Jessie because suddenly I heard her yelling and when I ran back Jessie had kicked the bucket over and there was milk everywhere.

I should have told her about Joanie's wedding, of course I should. I blame myself. But we'd been in Oz a year by then, you'd think she'd have put two and two together. Poor little thing, she did cry.

I wonder what she did with that rabbit necklace? I never saw it again.

Chapter 10

Rose

The party was in the garden of one of Marian's bridge ladies, and the house was a three bed semi with an extension that they called a conservatory even though it was really a lean-to. Luckily it was a nice day so we could spread out into the garden and she had it very nice, say that for her. In the garden she'd set out a dozen tables and chairs, mostly white plastic or they'd been white once. There was a cake stall and a jam-making competition, and if you weren't almost dead of excitement already, there was a slide show of someone's coach trip. But I wasn't complaining, you've got to make the most of things when you're well enough to do them. Even when those things only amount to watching old biddies even older than I am arguing about who makes the best jam.

Marian and I sat down with our cream scones to watch the jam tasting. A woman in a lot of face powder stood on the far side of the stall picking up each jar and dipping a teaspoon into them. By each jar they had a saucer with a clean spoon, and a napkin for her to dab her lips. Very genteel.

'Sweet,' she said. 'Too sweet. And too much pectin. Look - ' she tipped the jam upside down. 'It's as solid as a jelly cube. You could cut it into slices.'

I heard a gasp of indignation behind me and felt a rush of air behind me as someone walked off.

'Ruby didn't like that,' said Marian, with a certain satisfaction.

'Who's the judge?' I asked. 'Is she a cookery expert?'

'It's Iris. It's her turn,' Marian whispered. 'Ruby was a bit cutting about her lemon curd last year, so she's getting her own back.'

I'd never been to this kind of thing before, never had time for it. I'd always made my own jam and then we'd eaten it, not sat about discussing it.

The highlight of the afternoon was a performance by the Four Blind Mice. Actually only three of them were blind, they had to have someone who could see to drive them. Marian said we were lucky to have them because they were in great demand locally, in old people's homes and day centres and the like.

They introduced themselves with a song – 'Four blind mice, four blind mice, Hear how they sing, Won't you please join in – ' I forget the rest but they weren't very good. On the other hand they were better than the jam-making woman. I clapped as loud as I could so they knew at least someone was listening.

Marian said the woman singer was married to the chap who played the piano accordion but then I saw the male singer who wasn't blind, give her a squeeze. I nudged Marian.

'What the eye doesn't see,' she said.

'Dirty devil,' I said. 'Why doesn't someone tell her

147

husband?'

Marian laughed. 'Go on then!'

But she was right, what people don't know can't hurt them. It's when they find out, the trouble starts.

At the end we all clapped hard, though the sound was lost in the garden, but I clapped hardest of all for the one on the accordion. I hadn't touched my cream scone and I sent a kiddie over with it to give to him.

'I suppose it's going on all the time, people carrying on,' Marian said. 'I could never be bothered myself. I expect you were the same, weren't you?'

I felt the flush rise up my face but she was dabbing at her mouth with a paper napkin and didn't notice.

'Too busy,' I said. 'When you're working flat out every hour God sends, fluttering your eyelashes seems just like more hard work.'

'If you're fluttering your eyelashes, I hope it's for me,' said a voice. I knew that voice but it took me unawares, out of context and all, and I couldn't place it for a moment. Then it hit me, right in my stomach.

I hadn't seen him since we left our farm. He looked shorter and fatter but it was unmistakably him. I blinked at him, for a moment I couldn't think of a retort. Then I said, 'What are you doing here?' Well, what else was there to say?

Eddie laughed, that same old deep-throated sound that comes with a sixty-a-day habit. 'Same as you. Getting stung for the raffle and keeping out of trouble.'

'Causing it more like,' I said. 'Talk about bad pennies, you're like an entire purse full.' I said it like it was a joke, though really it was what I'd always thought. He'd never been good news though he still had that knack of making you glad to see him despite yourself.

'Aren't you going to introduce me?' said Marian.

'You know him already,' I said. 'He was at our school. Used to live round the corner when we were kids.' Marian's expression changed ever so slightly. If Eddie had grown up near us then obviously he wasn't really posh enough for her. She said there was someone she had to see and excused herself.

We got ourselves a cup of tea and he told me he'd moved back to England after his wife died, and what he'd done since he'd worked for us on the farm. He was shaken to hear about Len. Then he asked after Mattie and Bobby and Richie. 'And do you still hear from Dorothy?' he said. He chatted on but to tell you the truth I was hardly listening.

Eddie ran in wiping his hands on his overalls and shouting 'Dotty's here!' which I could have guessed what with the dozen toots she was giving on the horn and the chickens squawking in the yard with the noise. Dorothy was so pale and drawn when we met on the boat, and with that pointy little nose and chin, you could have taken her for a witch if it wasn't for the blonde hair. But now her cheeks had filled out, and her skin was as dark and glossy as if she'd been dipped in treacle.

She was just half a day's drive away but we were always so tied up on the farm there was no time to visit. But she had her own catering business now and occasionally she could get away to come to us.

She came towards me, arms outstretched, and Dan unfurled himself from the front seat. He seemed a head taller since we'd last met, although it could only have been six months ago. He was blonde, like Dorothy, and with a warm friendly smile. Sophie was more reserved, she stood hesitantly by the truck while Dan lifted out the tray of bread rolls she'd brought us.

I gave her a hug. 'You're looking very well.'

'A bit too well, I know what you're saying. That's the trouble with catering.'

'Well, you have to sample it all or there might be something wrong with it.'

She nodded. It was a joke we always had. 'At least you've got an excuse, I don't know what mine is.'

'Oh Rose, you're as sylph-like as ever,' Eddie said, coming over. He nodded to Dan and Sophie and put his arms round Dorothy. 'You're like two goddesses. And anyway a man likes something to get his hands on.'

'Just as long as you're not getting your hands on anything of mine,' she laughed, pushing him away. Eddie had a soft spot for an attractive woman, or a hard spot as Len liked to say.

He went over to where he had left his barrow and pushed it across the yard.

'He's still here then?' Dorothy said.

'It's been three months. His last job didn't work out. He really thinks he's got his feet under the table this time.'

'As long as that's all he's got.'

'Dotty!' I gave her a push.

Eddie had stayed now and then ever since we had lived here and he was handy around the farm. Good company too, always willing to drop Mattie off or collect her wherever she was going. Sometimes I thought he was a bit too willing. Mattie was fifteen now and more than once I'd said to him, 'That's my daughter you're looking at, if you don't mind.' He'd laugh and say, 'And a beautiful one at that. Takes after you.' He always had an answer.

She came into the kitchen and I cut her a slice of cake. It was still warm from the oven. She looked at it before taking a bite. 'I bet your bakers don't give you anything as good as this,' I said.

'Too right. And if they did, I probably couldn't afford it.' She closed her eyes, savouring it. It was lovely to see Dorothy. She always gave you a boost.

'You've painted in here since I last came,' she said, looking round. I'd done it in yellow, and made yellow checked curtains to match. It was a dark kitchen but the yellow brought the sunshine in. Lifted your spirits.

Five years it took her to find her kids. She travelled all over, they hadn't kept proper records, the organisation that brought them out here. She had to keep stopping and getting work so she could afford to keep looking. And it was only a fluke that she found them. She met someone who knew about a children's home where there were foreign kiddies and she was lucky, and lucky too that they hadn't been split up. They could have been anywhere. Kids were sent all over, some went on to farms in the outback. You'd never find them then. Dorothy says they even changed their names sometimes, but I can't believe that, it'd be too wicked and anyway what would be the point? They were thin as rakes when she found them but she couldn't take them out straight away because she didn't have anywhere to live. She sent them some new clothes but when she went to visit them, other kids were wearing them, they weren't allowed to have anything of their own. They were training the boys to be farm hands and the girls to be domestics. This was the wonderful education they were getting. Even now she'd have a little weep if she started talking about it. If I thought too hard about it so would I.

Len took Dan and Sophie round the farm, and when Mattie came in from school she sat in the living room with Dorothy while I got dinner ready. They were like two old women when they got together, or else two schoolgirls, depending how you looked at it. Even though Dorothy had got her own daughter back, she never forgot how fond she had grown of Mattie. Last Christmas they all came over for a few days but Dan had changed since then, he was almost a man, he was going to be tall, as his dad must have been.

I made a joke about having to keep an eye on them all. Dorothy said, leave them alone, they're only having a bit of fun, and I thought, yes, that's what I'm afraid of.

'Don't tell me you're getting yourself a fancy man,' Marian said as we walked back to the car. She'd won a DVD in the raffle and even though we both knew she'd never watch it, she was in high spirits.

'Fancy man?' I said. 'He's got a face like a wrinkled raisin.'

'All raisins are wrinkled aren't they?'

'And he talks out of one side of his mouth.' I wasn't having her thinking anything was going on with Eddie.

'Robert Mitchum talked out of the side of his mouth. I always thought it was rather attractive.'

'Yes, but it makes Eddie look like he's had a stroke,' I said.

'Well, don't let him sweet talk you into anything,' she said. 'Freda from the bowls club met someone but once he got in with her it turned out all he wanted was his washing done.'

I tried not to think about what Eddie's washing might be like but seeing him had made me feel young again. He looked at me as though I was still attractive and no one had done that since Len died. Well, before Len died, let's be honest. For years I'd been no more than his nurse and not the sort like Suki with her button nose and legs that didn't have veins running up them like fat grey worms. I didn't mind at all if Eddie came calling, just as long as he didn't want any funny business. In my magazine last week it gave a statistic for all these women having sex in their eighties. I thought, why would they? Can't they find anything to watch on telly? What a life some women must have – isn't it enough you're washing their underpants without you've got to investigate what's in them? No wonder women live longer, you'd be putting ground up glass in his Horlicks just to get a bit of rest.

On the way home from the fete Marian gave Ruby and her grandson a lift. He turned out to be the kiddie I'd asked to give the scone to the organist. He gave me a picture he'd crayoned. The picture was of all the jam jars lined up for judging, and he'd drawn Ruby winning, even though she hadn't. He was only six. He reminded me of Richie at that age. I remembered him coming home that Christmas with a card he'd made: 'To Mum – Happy Xmas.' It was very good writing for his age. A Santa was on the front, with a wad of cotton wool stuck on for his beard and he'd drawn a lovely face. He was so excited to have made me something. I stuck it on the wall in the kitchen. Mattie cried when she saw it.

He was always good with his hands. He liked writing and drawing and at home Mattie got him doing sewing. He made a pin cushion out of felt, in the shape of a duck. Very even stitching round the edge. He was like Mattie in that.

I couldn't help thinking about that piano accordionist. What must it be like to find out that everyone has known something but you, even though you're the one it affects most of all? But after all, maybe he did know. You can't tell with secrets; the fact people don't talk about it doesn't mean anything. But if he had no idea, then what would happen if he suddenly found out? Would he be embarrassed that he was the only one who didn't know? Would he be upset? Would he be so mad he'd go haring off in his car, not a word to anyone and you'd never hear from him again apart from the odd Christmas card and not always that? Maybe he'd even go abroad. Somewhere far away where no one knew him or could find him again?

Suddenly Marian gave my arm a push. She said, 'Rose! You were miles away. Adrian wants his picture back.'

Mattie was pouring milk on her cereal. Milk from our cows. That would be something to tell my mother about. Put that in her pipe and smoke it. I said, 'I'm thinking of going back. For a holiday.'

Len said, 'Back where?' That's how much of a surprise it was.

I said, 'England, where do you think.'

'Well not there for a start.' Len put his knife down.

'Where's this come from?'

I laughed because I was going back and I was going to tell them all – Mum, Dad, Joanie - about how good our life was and they'd listen and have to admit they'd been wrong.

'I feel like a break, and we can afford it. And they can see how well we're doing.'

'You tell them in every bloody letter. They must get sick of hearing about it.'

'What do you mean? I'm only telling them the news. Anyway, I feel like going, what's wrong with that?'

Len raised his eyebrows and went on eating his breakfast. He looked mystified but then so was I. I'd woken up a few days ago and knew I had to go home. And 'home' meant England. South London. Which was a surprise because I thought I'd stopped thinking of it that way long ago. We'd been in Australia eight years now and everything was flourishing – we could afford help on the farm when we needed – the farm we owned. And the kids were doing well at school. The hunger that had brought me out here had eased now; it's true that time is a healer. There are some things you realise you will never solve. You don't forget, but over time the remembering becomes less painful. So why go back? It didn't make sense, but there it was. A part of me didn't even want to go but the rest of me knew I had to.

You heard of Poms going home, and I'd always laughed at them. Thought we were made of sterner stuff. But I suppose you can't spend decades of your life in a place and not have some kind of attachment even if you're not aware of it. I looked out of my kitchen window and the sun was too bright and the air was too warm and suddenly I didn't belong here as much as I'd thought. And I wasn't mad with Mum any more. Len's mum had died – she was only in her sixties, the same age my mother was now and I suppose in the back of my mind I knew if it could happen to her it could happen to my mother and I'd never see her again. And then she'd never find out how well we'd done! And maybe I had a bit more sympathy for her now too. When you become a mother you think only of your children, but as they get older and start finding fault with what you did, you start thinking about your parents and how they'd probably done the best for you too as they saw it, however wrong that turned out to be.

'What do you think?' I said to Len.

'Don't ask me, it sounds like you've made your mind up already.'

'It'd leave you with the farm to handle on your own. Can you manage with Bobby and the help?'

Len shrugged. 'Have to, if you're not here.'

I started clearing the table and filled the bowl for the washing up. 'Mattie can do the cooking while I'm away,' I suggested.

'Mattie could go with you,' Len said.

'When is this exactly?' Mattie said. 'Because you know I've got exams coming up.'

I should have let it go because I certainly didn't want Mattie with me. I could just see it: every time I told Mum how good something was Mattie would open her mouth about how hard life had been to begin with, the shacks with the rotten floorboards, the creepy couple I had to leave her and Bobby with when we worked at the factory, how hard up we'd been. All the things I'd been so careful to keep quiet about. No, there was no way Mattie was coming. But I was irritated at the way she was throwing Len's generous offer back in his face and I was never good at keeping my mouth shut.

'I'm not twisting your arm, my lady,' I said. 'If you'd rather do exams than go on holiday just say so.'

'It needn't be till after your exams,' Len said, 'Wouldn't you like to see Joanie and Nanny?'

She shrugged. 'They've never been that bothered about seeing me.'

She'd never got over not being Joanie's bridesmaid, even though that was years ago. And they say *I* bear a grudge.

Len said, 'Of course they'd want to see you. Just because they couldn't afford to come here doesn't mean they didn't want to. You were the apple of their eye.'

'Still are,' I said. 'Look at all those comics Nanny used to send you. Must've cost her a fortune.'

'You told me a neighbour gave them to her,' Mattie said. 'It's not like they cost her anything.'

'But the postage did, I told you that. She'd be heartbroken to know that's what you think.'

'I don't know where you're getting this from but I don't like it,' Len said to her. 'It must've broken their hearts when you came away, and the fact they haven't seen you for a few years won't have changed how they feel, even if it's changed how you do.'

She shrugged again, the way teenagers do. Bobby came in just then, late as usual and I was just opening my mouth to say, 'How would you like to come on holiday to England' when she got up, went over to Len and flung her arms round his neck – not round me even though I would be the one taking her.

157

'Thanks Dad,' she said. 'Of course I want to go. I'm a bit nervous about my exams, that's all.'

I could've kicked myself. I'd have to make damn sure Mattie didn't get too much time by herself with the family, and didn't raise anything I'd rather not talk about. But it would all work out and there might even be an advantage – Mum would say, 'They *must* be comfortable! All that fare and she's bringing Mattie as well.'

Of course, we didn't go. Len thought I should've gone by myself, but all the things I'd been looking forward to: telling them about the farm, how well everything was going, well, the gloss had gone off it. And mothers have an antennae for these things, she'd have known something was up. It was safer to stick with the letters. All they needed was a few hints in the right place and it'd all make perfect sense.

Dear Mum and Dad

Hope you are well as we are. We're busy on the farm at this time of year but it's much easier now we can afford to hire help. We have a few aborigines who come in regularly and they're hard workers so it takes a lot of pressure off Len. Bobby is doing well at school and Mattie too. She has a lovely little job at a local garage – they love her there and she's doing very well, always getting pay rises. Supposed to be just weekends but the garage owner's wife is expecting, so they need Mattie there to help out all she can. Mattie loves playing with their children so it's working out very well. Len still wants her to go to college after her exams but it wouldn't surprise me if she stuck with this job for a bit. She can always go to college later. It's very convenient so she could do worse.

How are Joanie's girls doing? From what she says they're growing up fast. Well, must close now as we want to watch the new television.

Your loving daughter

Rose

I referred to Mattie's job in a couple more letters saying that the woman at the garage where Mattie worked was ill and not able to look after her young baby and all their other children, so Mattie had brought the baby home a few times to help out. After a bit I'd say the woman was too ill to cope and the baby was going to come and live with us. Later on I'd say Len and me had adopted it.

Len said if she'd believe that she'd believe anything. (But not only did my mother believe it, she admired us, me and Len, taking the poor little thing in and giving it a home. She knitted a matinee jacket and a cot blanket).

Len was furious with me, he thought we should just come clean, but as I said, when you take a step like we did coming out here and everyone is against you coming, you have to keep up appearances, even if it means stretching the truth a little. It's a matter of pride. And you don't want everyone back home knowing there's been a slip up. In the end Len went along with it. It meant he couldn't tell his family either but there was only his dad and his sister back in England and seeing as it was me who wrote the letters, I told them the exact same thing.

As for people around here, no one would take any notice one way or the other. That was something I liked out here. Everyone was working too hard to bother about what other people did and with the farm being off the beaten track we weren't troubled with nosy neighbours wanting to know your business. I'd sent Mattie off to stay with Dorothy for the last few months.

Joanie wrote saying we were mad taking on a baby at our age and it was bad enough running around after your own kids without clearing up after other people's. Len said she had guessed and even if Mum was daft as a brush it didn't mean Joanie was the same. But I thought he was wrong. They were there and I was here and as long as we all stayed where we belonged, the truth was what I said it was.

I can be such a silly bitch sometimes.

THREE

...still lying

Chapter 11

Mattie

The bedroom ceiling needs painting, that crack is the length of the snake that used to live under the shack at Dirty Dinah's. Jeez, I could do without being reminded of that. Maybe I'll change the whole colour scheme, get some new blinds, paint the walls. A soft blue maybe...

Henry collapses across my chest with a grunt and a spasm that makes his legs shake. I ask if he's okay - we've had one heart scare already. But he mishears and hands me a bunch of tissues as he rolls off.

I don't mention the decor.

Amy at work says once the sex goes, that's the end of the relationship. She says sex should be hot and wild and passionate. But then she's only been married eighteen months. For Henry and me, sex is a compromise: how often he wants it and how often I don't. If it was never I wouldn't be sobbing into my pillow, but his demands are so moderate it'd be churlish to refuse. And he's not someone you can discuss these things with. For a literary person, he's surprisingly literal. When I told him I needed more space he thought I wanted a bigger bed.

It wasn't always like this. When we were first together his love-making was tender and sweet, with a healing quality which was what I needed. And he did heal me. I'd been knocked down hard and he built me right back up again. I'm grateful for that. But that was a long time ago. The sex is still the same but my needs aren't, I want what Amy has got. I could blame Henry and say he lacks imagination and inventiveness in the bedroom but actually, it's me who's the problem. I could have spiced things up myself but then he might have wanted it more often, and God, I don't want that! Henry is perfectly happy with things as they are so if there are any changes around here they'll just be to the decor.

We've lived in Brisbane since we got married, and in this bungalow for the last five years. We bought the plot then picked out the house and by the time we'd signed on the dotted line it was virtually built. They throw up these kit houses so fast, with their low roofs and wide drives. Three bedrooms, big kitchen, wide neat lawns, brown through lack of rain, and a pool that's shaded by a tree where a possum lives. Henry doesn't like it when I feed the possum, but I like animals. Maybe not so keen on the ones you have to milk or herd or send off for slaughter, but most others. We're not too close to our neighbours and they chose a different style of bungalow from the range on offer so we're not identical (only nearly identical). Everyone wants to be different, and everyone ends up looking much the same: manicured and neat, unobtrusive and acceptable. Mum would approve.

I don't think kit houses had been invented when

Mum and Dad came to Oz. They built their own house on the farm and we lived in a caravan for a year while it went up. They had help, obviously. But Dad was talented, he could turn his hand to most things. And Mum was the same, always a worker. The trouble was she wanted us to be workers too. It was fine for Bobby, he loved the outdoor life. Being knee deep in cow dung was probably his favourite thing. But I hated all that. I'd race through the chores so I could hide away with a book. But for Mum reading equated to laziness. Once Mum was so angry when she caught me, she tore the last two pages out and threw them away. I thought that was a peculiarly cruel punishment. But I saw her shove the pages in the bin under the potato peelings so at least I found out how the story ended.

Buying this house was my idea. These days I'd rather be where we used to live: an older house, more idiosyncratic. But just as some couples think a baby will bring them closer, I thought choosing new carpets and soft furnishings would do that for us. I wanted to leave behind the bedroom where we'd tried so hard to make the babies that would play in the walled garden, read the books we had selected so carefully, planning the evenings we would read to them as they lay snuggling their teddies in bed, cotton sheets pulled up to their chins. But I should've known Henry was never going to be interested in soft furnishings, and he'd liked the old house better too.

We've been happy enough. It was fun when Henry was travelling around the country, we even went to America once. It was exciting, prestigious. Now there isn't so much of that, and what there is doesn't feel prestigious or exciting. But that probably says more about me than about Henry.

Henry rolls over and flings his arm across my chest. I lift it carefully and he shifts his weight and turns away. I can't think why I turned down the chance to get a bigger bed. Poor Henry, it's not his fault. Nothing is his fault.

And he didn't always have that paunch and the grizzled beard. He was rather dashing in his way. It was the accent I fell for, you could hear the education in it, rich with English libraries and leather bound books. His parents had been Ten Pound Poms too but they came here in the sixties and they just got on a plane. It must have been strange, not having that period in limbo on the ship getting used to the change that was coming... Or maybe it was better that way, no time to worry, like having a plaster ripped off. Whatever, it wouldn't have cost ten pounds any more... But they didn't settle and they went back to England. Henry went to university there but came back for a visit and stayed. And now here he was, at my teacher training college. I was twenty-two, older than the other students and I felt it. Henry was twenty-eight though he'd seemed older. And clearly he was an intellectual and that was irresistible.

He said, 'Excuse me, but is anyone sitting here?' He sounded like a posh version of Uncle Eddie and Grandad and Dad all in one. Not that there was any education in their voices, but Henry was English and those early childhood memories, they'll get you every time. It wasn't love at first sight so much as love at first listen.

The college canteen was busy at that time of day and I'd got the last remaining table. I moved my bag off the seat and he set his tray on the rickety table. As he bent forward his shoulder bag slid down his arm and I caught it just before it hit the teapot en route to the floor.

'Thanks awfully, such a butterfingers.'

Butterfingers? Whoever said butterfingers? He was wearing brown cord trousers which must've been horribly hot and a white open-necked shirt in a heavy cotton. There was something arty, piratical even about it with its full sleeves and deep neck. There was an old tea stain on the front and a button was missing. His hair was dark and fell in soft waves to his neck.

He gave me a nervous smile as he sat down and I looked away, embarrassed to be caught looking at him. He drew from his bag a sheaf of papers and after reading for a short while began placing ticks or comments in the margin, peppering his actions with sighs and the odd shake of the head.

'I hope you're not being too harsh,' I said, with a nod towards the paper he was marking.

'I don't have to be, this one's pretty good. But some of them - .' He rolled his eyes to heaven. Then he stopped short and offered me his hand. 'Henry Armstrong.'

I was entranced. I'd never met anyone called Henry and his old-fashioned name threw up immediate literary associations: Henry Fielding, Henry James, Henry Miller. Intuitively I placed him as an authority on opera, art, literature, all the things I thirsted after. I was in my second year at college and aware only of the depth of my ignorance. In private he probably wore a smoking jacket.

I took his hand. 'Mathilda Marshall.' No one ever called me Mathilda. Even though that was my name, I blushed at my own pretentiousness.

He paused in mid shake. 'As in 'Waltzing Mathilda?'' He laughed and then stopped himself. 'Sorry. You must have heard that so many times before.'

It was too obvious, no one had ever said it, but then no one knew me as Mathilda. But I smiled intending to indicate that even if it was an old joke, it was okay coming from him. 'Are you visiting? I haven't seen you here before.'

'Visiting lecturer. There's supposed to be a study for me to use but the door is locked and I can't find anyone with the key.'

He looked so helpless I was almost tempted to say I'd look for it for him. Instead I said, 'I'm nothing so grand I'm afraid. I'm doing teacher training.'

'Poor you,' he said with a smile. I'd studied evenings and weekends to get here, and it had been a long road. I was proud of myself and had hoped, if not to impress him, at least to indicate that I was in an associated academic field. But he would know that; this was a teacher training college after all.

'It's a very challenging profession,' I said, on the defensive and sounding like it.

'It's challenging all right,' he said with a laugh. 'I'm not nearly brave enough, I'm afraid. I taught a class of eleven year olds once and ended up running out screaming. Little savages the lot of them. No, I like to keep a safe distance between the students and me. It's the cloisters of academia for me I'm afraid.'

The cloisters of academia! I almost clapped my hands with delight. He finished his tea and said he must leave – he was giving a lecture that evening on Dr Johnson and he needed to collect his notes from his digs. Why didn't I come? It was open to all.

'I think I've got something on tonight,' I lied, not

wanting to seem too eager. 'But I'd like to come. I'm interested in the Shakespearean period.' I spoke as though I was interested in many periods, but with a particular penchant for this one. I was rather proud of myself for knowing who Ben Jonson was even if I hadn't known he was a doctor.

Henry laughed. 'Wrong Johnson, and wrong period, I'm afraid. This is Samuel Johnson. The one who wrote the first English dictionary.'

'Oh, that Johnson!' I said, as though I knew after all, but I blushed with embarrassment, giving the game away. He said this wasn't his usual subject but he had a particular interest and had been asked to speak on it. He hoped his audience wouldn't make the same mistake I had. I joined with him in laughing at the foolishness of the ignorant and uninformed. He told me that ordinarily his work involved research into medieval documents; that was what his thesis had been about. Thesis? I'd never known anyone who had written a thesis. I said I'd come if I could.

I went to his talk, along with my flatmate though not from choice. Sonia was more attractive than me, with a throaty, sexy laugh that could hook a man from the other side of the room. This was not at all her ideal way of spending an evening but the only thing less appealing than that was spending an evening alone.

She wasn't impressed with Henry and even I could see he was not an enthralling speaker. He failed to convey why Samuel Johnson would be of interest now or ever had been and when he quoted him, with a fanfare to Johnson's wit and wisdom, he drained from the words any semblance of amusement, while the silent and embarrassed audience shuffled and fidgeted wondering what was supposed to be so funny. I blushed for Henry, but my sympathy brought me closer. And when he made a point and brushed his dark wavy hair from his face with the back of his hand, it had me quivering. The more dry and academic Henry appeared, and the more he used words I barely understood, the more captivated I was. Each time I found my attention wandering from his subject matter, his shaggy hair and sudden smile would drag it back. I envisaged us seated in a writer's garret, reading medieval manuscripts by candlelight or guffawing over Johnson's witticisms while Henry explained their significance or gasped in amazement at some undiscovered aspect I had suddenly espied. 'That's astounding,' he would sigh, 'these documents have been studied for centuries and no one has noticed that before.' His forthcoming book would be dedicated to me, or my name would be at the top of the acknowledgements page, accompanied by phrases such as 'with special thanks to' or a sentence with 'invaluable' or 'inestimable' in it.

Sonia was less convinced. At one point as Henry turned to write on the blackboard he tripped over the wastepaper bin. Sonia whispered, 'If he'd kicked he bucket instead we could all go home.' I smiled but I was mortified.

'Don't tell me you fancy him,' she said, when I wanted to stay behind to ask questions.

'I'm interested in Dr Johnson!' I objected. She raised her eyebrows. 'And I want to make Henry feel at home. He's a stranger here,'

'You're right there,' she said, 'they don't come much stranger than him.' She strode off, her bangles jangling as she walked.

So I stayed behind, feigning fascination in the subject,

and Henry said if I was truly interested I should come to his flat and he would be happy to lend me some books. I said I was and he did.

We were married within a year. A vacancy came up for a lecturer at the university and Henry got it. I wore white at my mother's insistence, and instead of a bridesmaid, I had Richie as a pageboy. He was seven, already a little too old for the role, and he had a sudden growth spurt between my making the outfit and the day itself. The trousers were too short and even I could see the little waistcoat looked ridiculous.

Henry's mother flew over for the ceremony (his father was dead and his brother couldn't afford the fare). There was a plan at one stage for Nanny and Joanie to fly over too, but it didn't happen. As I said to Mum, I didn't go to Joanie's wedding, so it was of no significance whether she came to mine. Mum said, 'That's no way to carry on, is it? They'd come if they could.'

I sent them two tiny slices of wedding cake, as thin as I could slice them, in a little box, the excess space taken up with shreds of paper napkin.

The alarm goes off and I turn over. The alarm is for Henry, not me. He's always awake by the time that irritating buzzing starts but he likes to wait till the third burst before he switches it off, reaching over and taking the covers with him. I feel the waft of cool air as he pulls back the duvet and swings his legs over the side of the bed. I pull the duvet over my head but not fast enough to block the sound of him blowing his nose loudly and thoroughly. There's a shudder in the mattress before he stands up, as he tosses the used tissue at the wastepaper basket by the

chest of drawers. When I get up in half an hour's time I
will pick it up from the floor and put it in the bin.

Henry likes to be at his office for 8.30 a.m. even if he
isn't lecturing until the afternoon. He is writing another
book and still at the planning stage, enthusiastic and eager,
coming home with snippets of information which is going
to take the literary world by storm. This stage will last for
a few months and then he'll start coming home morose
and despondent having discovered that a rival is carrying
out almost identical work but is more advanced or is
investigating an area Henry hasn't considered and which
now seems like a huge oversight; or perhaps an
assumption he has made is now being contradicted by
other facts... But he will have to continue the book
because he has a deadline, has created expectations, and so
his mood will darken along with the smudges under his
eyes.

He has written three books, and their sales while
modest remain surprisingly constant for academic books,
perhaps due to each fresh intake of students buying the
latest in the hope of pleasing their tutor. Such an
explanation would never occur to Henry and if his
students hoped to curry favour they would be
disappointed. He assumes his students share the same
passion for their subject as he does and besides he is far
too modest to suppose they care what he thinks about
them.

When his first book failed to be the sensation he
hoped, I was as agonised as he was, but by the time he was
working on the third, I realised that this was likely to be a
repeating pattern; that academic works are unlikely to
resonate beyond their own small field, that there is always

someone else investigating the same topic, perhaps someone with more flair or knowledge or, in Henry's case, better contacts. Henry's not what you could call a networker.

I must have dozed off because the next thing I hear is Henry at the coffee grinder in the kitchen, my own alarm call. I get straight up then and make for the shower. Lately it feels more important than it used to be that I wear some make up and do my hair.

When I get into the kitchen there's a letter for me, Henry must have brought it in from the mailbox. The envelope is in Mum's bold hand. On the aerograms she used to send family sometimes she pressed so hard her pen almost tore the paper. She says how well she is doing since she got out of hospital, and that she sees Joanie most days. Strange that Joanie should have become such a pal, given the way Mum used to talk about her. It's still a mystery to me why Mum has stayed in England at all. Hadn't we grown up hearing how much better everything was here? She'd given it a sufficiently bad press that I had no wish to go, ever. There was no one there who I cared about, and if I wanted grey skies and cold I could go to Melbourne out of season. People say that emigrants are never at home anywhere, and I can see that. Some people live in the same town all their lives, know everyone, would never live anywhere else, but when you move around as we did, you don't form those bonds. I could see that Mum might want to go back to her roots, she'd lived in the UK long enough to have some. But why had she stayed there? Bobby and his children are here, and me. Richie too, no doubt. Why would she leave us all behind?

I am still mulling it over as I get in the car. I try not

to think about Mum too much because I always end up getting worked up about it. I tell myself it was up to her if she wanted to live back in England, and that if she then fell off a bus and ended up in hospital, she couldn't expect me to come running. And anyway if I'd gone she would have been angry. She would hate the waste of the airfare when I couldn't do anything to help anyway. She would reason that if I hadn't visited when she was well then there was no point in my showing up when she wasn't, just to sit by her bedside drumming my fingers. I could hear her saying it. Could sense how she would resent my presence at the bedside, feel the gulf between us that our inevitable silence would only emphasise. Or our stilted conversation which would make it even worse. But I feel guilty all the same.

When I get to college Suzanne is gathering up some folders on the table in front of her. We've been friends since I started work at the college five years ago, and she'd heard the whole sorry story of my relationship with my mother over countless white wine spritzers. She was the patient listening ear I had failed to find in Henry. Today she was obliged to be patient once again. I told her Mum had written; it was a rare enough event to be worth mentioning.

'Don't tell me,' she said, 'She's sent you the air fare and she wants you to go and live with her.' We both laughed, she knew Mum was about as keen for me to visit as I was to go. If anything, her letter was to let me know she was fine so I wouldn't ever feel I had to. But all the same I felt guilty that I hadn't gone when she'd first had her accident. She had been in quite a bad way.

Suzanne pursed her lips with just the merest hint of

frustration. 'How many times do I have to tell you? Henry needed you. You decided to stay with him and that was the right thing.' Suzanne is the best kind of friend, always ready to take your side and it was comforting to be reminded that Henry had been in hospital himself when Mum had her fall. But it had only been an overnight case, they weren't exactly about to read the last rites. If he needed nursing care when he came out it was only because Henry was such a demanding patient, every twinge of discomfort showing as a grimace of pain and forbearance.

'She is my mother,' I said, 'I should have checked that she was all right.' I thought I'd get one more round of sympathy from Suzanne but I was out of time.

'Go then,' she said, briskly. 'Go and see the old cow, tell her she ruined your life, get it all off your chest. Job done. Maybe this is your chance to take the power back. And if she really doesn't want you there – well, imagine her face when you walk in!'

I could imagine it well enough - unmitigated horror. She had told me about her pretty little house, it's garden with its apple and pear trees, the bulbs she had planted, the tiny pond where frogs probably sat on lilly pads, probably waiting to be turned into handsome princes. It seemed the sun always shone (but not too hot), it rained (but only the odd refreshing shower) and snowed only in order to turn the landscape to a fairy grotto. I remembered the extravagant descriptions she had sent Nanny of our farm and our blessed lives. I doubted that she would be eager for me to witness the reality.

'The past is over, she has her life, you've got yours. Move on, Mattie.'

But the past is never over. And your mother is your

mother no matter how you feel about her.

She hooked up her bag with one finger, balancing it on top of the folder she held clutched against her chest and swept out. Friends. You just can't rely on them.

Perhaps she was playing devil's advocate, but anyway that was the effect. Because suddenly I saw clearly that I wouldn't go, and that Mum wouldn't want me to. We'd never got on, it was better to maintain our distant relationship at – well, at a distance. The guilt lifted and I set off for modern poetry with unusual enthusiasm.

It was an unexpectedly lively session. Jason – troublesome, argumentative - wanted to know why they couldn't study song lyrics rather than Sylvia Plath and when I tried to call his bluff by saying he could and to bring something in next time (the need to source anything at all would be obstacle enough), there was a furore over which songwriter was most worthy of study. It made for an entertaining interlude if not a useful one. I often suspect that Henry's students toy with him, and I know that mine do the same to me. Though I only see it afterwards, when I see the expression of triumph on their faces as they catch each other's eye.

I caught up with Suzanne in the café at lunchtime. As I sat down she was studying her hummus sandwich doubtfully.

'What do you think this is?' She poked at a bit of wilted green. I shrugged, grateful that I always brought a packed lunch. College lunches had a knack of putting you off your food and anyway I liked to leave something out for Henry. Which made it convenient for me to have the same thing. Suzanne said I encouraged him to be dependent on me but I liked to know he had eaten and if he had to go the kitchen and make a decision about whether to have eggs or a sandwich then he would end up having neither. Whereas if a sandwich was ready and waiting then he'd eat it and we'd both be happy.

'Compromise is the secret of a happy marriage,' I'd told her. 'But you're not happy,' she'd said, and I didn't have an answer for that.

'Anyway,' she said, as she picked out bits of green from her sandwich. 'I've been thinking, and I reckon you should go to England.' My heart sank, clearly she wasn't as good a friend as I thought. 'You've got unfinished business with your mother, it's your opportunity to lay it all to rest. Before she gets laid to rest.' She clapped her hand over her mouth in mock horror, but she said what she thought, it was one of the reasons I liked her. 'And it'll be a chance for you to think about your future. A chance to get some distance from Henry.'

'There's already distance from Henry. Sometimes we're like two strangers living under one roof.'

'Strangers who still have sex though.' She stopped inspecting her sandwich and laughed out loud at what she'd said. 'Strangers who still have sex - maybe the sex is wilder than you're making out!'

I laughed too but I blushed. Changing the decor wasn't the only thing I thought about when Henry was pumping away on top of me.

It was as well we didn't have children. Henry was sad about the miscarriages of course, and sad for me because he loved me back then, but children would have been a disaster for him. Most people want to see their genes passed on, and he was no different but for him the fact of not being the centre of the household, would have been too high a price to pay. He needs constant attention. He needs calming when he gets overwrought about the progress of his work or lack of it; he needs encouraging when he has failed and praising when he has succeeded. He has depressions which come from nowhere even when things are going well, and equally arbitrary bouts of euphoria. In both extremes he needs company and a moderating influence. I've been a distraction for him and he, now I come to think about it, has been the same for me. I expect a lot of marriages are like that.

And what's true love anyway? You fall in love, you fall out again. You can't expect it to last, nothing does.

'Love isn't all beating hearts and throbbing passion,' I said.

She said, 'It is if you do it right,' and I didn't argue.

'Come for the weekend,' she said. 'We're going to the beach house. We'll get pissed and you can forget all about your damn mother and fucking Henry.' She laughed again, 'And you can take that anyway you want.' She lifted up her crisp packet and tipped it up, sucking the few remaining crumbs into her mouth.

Henry hated the beach and he wasn't keen on Suzanne's husband who liked to fish and play squash and tell lewd jokes while he prodded steaks on the barbecue. Henry definitely wouldn't go.

'Love to,' I said.

I walked in from college planning to tell Henry about the weekend at Suzanne's beach house. But before I could speak he told me there was a message on the answer-phone. It was from Joanie. I hadn't spoken to her in more than thirty years.

We are at the station, and Nanny is crying. Mum is saying, 'For goodness sake, Mother, you'll set the children off.' Auntie Joanie puts her arms round me and pushes a silver chain into my hand. It is the one she always wears but there is a charm on it, a rabbit. 'I want you to have this,' she says. 'It's to remind you of the rabbit song. Whenever you think of it, I'll be thinking of you.'

'Aren't you going to phone her back?' said Henry. The message said Mum had had a relapse and was back in hospital. Not to worry but Joanie thought she should let me know.

'What will the time be in England? Will they be in bed?' I knew it would be early morning there, I was just playing for time. 'She says not to worry, so hopefully it's not too urgent…'

'You haven't spoken to your aunt in all the years I've known you and now she's phoned,' said Henry. 'It sounds urgent to me.'

I replayed the message and took down the phone number. My heart was beating as I dialled and I didn't know if it was because I was worried to hear bad news about Mum, or about speaking to Joanie again. All the things I'd bottled up down the years. Now the subject matter was determined for us and I was glad about that.

Her voice was deeper, not a young woman's voice any more, but there was no mistaking it. 'Auntie Joanie.' I'd meant to drop the 'Auntie' but at the sound of her voice I had no choice. There was a catch in my throat I hadn't expected.

'Mattie? Is this really you?' She sounded excited,

breathless almost.

'How is Mum?'

'Not too bad, you're not to worry. I hope my message didn't frighten you. She had a little turn and they took her back into hospital... She didn't want me to call at all but...'

'But she is okay?'

'Oh yes. Nothing to worry about. Nothing specific, nothing serious. But she's not so well as she was and, well, sometimes she seems a bit confused. And you're a long way away, I don't expect she keeps you up to date. I just thought... you know, if you were planning to visit at all, you might want to do it sooner rather than later. There's the angina, and since that accident with the bus she isn't always quite her old self...'

I couldn't imagine Mum being other than she had always been. Tough and fearless, decisive, strong. I wondered what the new self would be like. Maybe we'd get on better...

'And you, Mattie? How are you?'

We talked then, stilted and a little awkward. She told me that Mum said I had a lovely house and loved my job. Did I love my job? I *did* my job, that was nearer the truth. But Mum would talk it up, of course she would, she didn't know any other way.

'Yes, I like it well enough. And how is Des?'

She said Des was well, was watching morning television that very minute. I remembered him when they were courting, how I was in awe of him, he was so tall, and his voice was so deep. And I was jealous of him too, when we sat in the tea shop before we went away, knowing we were leaving and he would still be there with her. Tears were pricking my eyes and I thought this is ridiculous! How can I still be upset after all these years? But she had turned me into an eight year old again and despite myself I remembered the photograph of the blue bridesmaid's dress.

Somehow I finished the phone call and Henry took the phone from me and replaced it in its receiver.

'Is it bad news?' he said, his face a mask of concern. But the bad news was from a long time ago, it had nothing to do with now.

'It's just relief,' I lied. 'Mum's not too bad. But I'm going to visit. I should have gone before.'

'Yes, yes, of course, you must.'

'And we're nearly at the end of term.'

'That's good,' he said, 'You should be back in time to come to the annual conference with me.'

Ah Henry, I thought, still getting your priorities right. He turned towards the CD player, and now he paused with the CD half out of its case. 'Do you want me to come with you?' He was standing very still, I could see the tension in his shoulders.

'No, you need to finish your research. I'll be fine by myself.'

He relaxed then and put the CD on, as relieved as I was.

After dinner he settled down with a book and I started my marking but the phrases swam in front of my eyes. Joanie's voice had been a key to unlock memories I didn't even know I had. I told Henry I had a headache and went to bed early. But I couldn't sleep. It was as though the floodgates had opened.

I remember it. I remember it all.

Chapter 12

Mattie

I remember it. I remember it all.

I asked Daddy once what it was like when he arrived in Australia, all by himself. He got off at Fremantle, which was a bare wharf with a few big sheds and some railway lines. Our ship had docked there and I remembered seeing it and feeling sorry for the people who were disembarking there. But that was because I thought our port was going to be in a big town like London with shops and everything and wherever we lived, that's what it would be like.

I told Daddy thinking he'd laugh, but he said everyone thought that. Daddy said he never thought he would settle down in Australia but now he had and I would too in time. He said he hadn't wanted to come at first but Mummy had been dead set and she had been right as she always was. He said there was lots of opportunity out here and it wouldn't be long before we'd have a farm of our own and then it would be a dream come true.

I said, 'But Daddy, weren't you sad to leave everyone

at home?' He looked so surprised, as though it wasn't something he had ever thought about, though I thought you would be thinking about it all the time.

He had a pack of cards in his hand and he shuffled them, then made them fly from one hand to the other. Then he turned them over so they were face up and did the same the other way. He flipped them over, cut them, made them fan out. He hardly ever did card tricks when he worked at the mine but once we moved away from Mrs Donnelly's he didn't go out so much after work and he'd started again.

'Why are you asking that?' Daddy said. 'Don't you like it here?'

'Everyone at school has nannies and grandads, and aunts and uncles. They visit them or they go to stay. We don't have anyone.'

He laughed. 'We'll visit everyone in England one day, or they'll come here. Think how much fun that will be.' He held the pack out to me. 'Pick a card.'

I took a card. Four of diamonds.

'Don't tell me what it is. Now memorise it.'

I slid it back. It was Daddy's favourite trick. We knew the form, but we always behaved as though it was the first time we'd seen it.

'We took a risk, but it's been worth taking, hasn't it? We wanted a better start for you and Bobby and we'll own our own farm in a few years. Couldn't have done that back in England.'

He reshuffled the pack, cut it, put the bottom one on the top and cut it again, then a second time. Then he held it up and there was my card. Four of diamonds.

Daddy is working at a mill. This is the second mill he's been at. I hope he won't change jobs again. But he is at home more than when he worked at the mine, and not so dirty, so that's all better. I like my school here more than the other two schools but it is in the town and that's six miles away. Our nearest neighbour is two miles down the road so there is no one to play with, only Bobby.

At night when Bobby and I had gone to bed, you could hear Mummy and Daddy whispering to each other, arguing. I didn't like to hear them. In lots of ways Daddy was my friend more than hers because Mummy would still get in a temper if you ate the last cake or if something got broken, but Daddy would catch my eye and if it was something I'd done he'd wink and say, 'Rose – it's my fault – I thought that cake was going to waste. I'll bake some more tomorrow.' And that would make Mummy laugh because Daddy wouldn't have known where the flour was kept or even that cakes had flour in them. Or he'd say, 'I meant to tell you about that cup that got broken – it flew right out of my hand.' And she'd purse her lips and get on with what she was doing. Then Daddy would come over and whisper to me that I wasn't to do it again, whatever it was, and that he was covering for me just this once. But he always did. It was like our little secret.

It was always Daddy who helped me with my homework. He had left school at fourteen, but he knew about a lot of things and he'd read whatever he could get hold of in the army. He didn't know much history and what he did know wasn't much help, but he knew loads about geography, and lots of odd facts about famous people. He was good at maths too, and even if he hadn't done something before he could often work things out from the text book.

He was in favour of me going to college when I was older. I wanted to be a teacher, an English teacher because that was my best subject. Mummy thought it was a waste of effort when there were so many other things to get on with. 'What's the point of a college education?' she'd say. 'That's the beauty of Australia, they judge you on what you can do, not on a bit of paper.'

Whenever she said that Daddy would raise his eyebrows at me and wink.

One day Mummy got a letter from Grandma Marshall to say someone she knew had a son who was in Australia looking for work and she had let him have our address. His name was Edward Handy, and it turned out this was Uncle Eddie. Mummy flew into a rage and said Grandma Marshall had no right sending all and sundry to our house, but Daddy said that was no way to carry on and his mum probably thought she was doing us a favour sending us another Pom for company. Daddy said we probably wouldn't hear from him anyway, but we did and Daddy invited him to come. Bobby and I were very excited.

Uncle Eddie was even better at card tricks than Daddy, and he liked to play about and tease Mummy. Sometimes she would lay the table and then he would hide the pepper pot, and pretend he hadn't seen it when she asked. She would get madder and madder because she thought she had put it down somewhere, and we would all sit there trying our hardest not to laugh. Then she would turn her back for an instant and he would put it back. She would say, 'You'll be the death of me'. She pretended not to like his larking about but she did really. She said he had a glad eye for the ladies, but his eyes both looked the same to me.

In Australia Mummy was different, Daddy was different, even the air you breathed was different, and the land was so flat and everywhere so hot. You could see for miles and miles, but there was nothing to see just the heat rising off the land. I felt like Alice down the rabbit hole, falling and falling, and all you could do was feel the air rushing past and wait to hit the bottom, and the air was hot, so hot you could hardly breathe.

Daddy got a job in a sugar mill. Mummy said it would be much better than the mill he was at now but it was miles away. We couldn't go with him straight away because he had to find a house for us to rent. Mummy told him, 'You better make a better job of it than this one!' This house has holes in the floor but still it is better than when we lived in the tenement and all the families had to share the sink and the toilet.

Some people bought wood for their stoves but Mummy said why pay for it when you can get it for free, so most days we went out collecting sticks and dead wood. Daddy had made a little trolley from an old tea chest and we piled the wood up on that.

There was no postman to bring letters, you had to walk to the post office to get the mail but we were used to that now. One day there was a packet for us. It was much smaller than the parcel of comics Nanny usually sent but it was still exciting to get something in the post. Mummy wouldn't let us open it until we got home but it said on the outside that it was from Auntie Joanie so then I was even more excited. It was about the same size as the paper patterns Auntie Joanie used for dressmaking. I was sure it must be the pattern for my bridesmaid dress. Perhaps she wanted Mummy to make it for me. Mummy would have to get a sewing machine, that would be the only problem, or maybe she could sew it by hand which Auntie Joanie always did for the hems and buttons. Or maybe it was just some pictures of the dress she was having made, and when we went home for the wedding it would be all ready for me. When I thought about us going home I was so happy I wanted to hug someone. I thought Mummy and Daddy must have enough money for the fare by now.

When we got back home I ran to get the scissors to cut the packet open, and Bobby climbed up on a chair to watch. Mummy opened it carefully. When she peeled back the paper there was a fat envelope inside and a small box. It was almost definitely a dress pattern in the envelope or perhaps it was some material that the dress was going to be made of, and the box was for a head band or ribbon for the sash. She'd always said I'd have a sash. Mummy opened the small box first.

Bobby said, 'It's cake! Why is she sending us cake?'

Mummy lifted the cake out from the box. One thick slice cut into four fingers. There was white icing on the top and marzipan. I hadn't had marzipan before and didn't know what it was called until Mummy said. I didn't care what it was called. I was too busy waiting for her to open the second parcel.

Bobby said, 'Can we eat it now?"

'No, it's special, we'll have it for pudding.' Mummy wrapped it up again and picked up the thick brown envelope. As she opened it she said, 'Mattie, I forgot to tell you about the wedding.' I clapped my hands with excitement – so she knew Auntie Joanie was sending us the dress pattern. I leaned in to see better as she opened the packet. I couldn't wait to see what the dress would be like. I was expecting the see-through paper that patterns were made of but instead Mummy took out a pile of photographs. She said, 'Doesn't she look a picture!'

She handed it to me and for a moment I didn't know what I was looking at. It was a bride in a white dress and she looked like Auntie Joanie, but obviously it couldn't be Auntie Joanie because she hadn't got married yet. Then I wondered if they had dress rehearsals for weddings the same as for school plays, and she was showing us how she would look on the day.

Mummy said, 'Auntie Joanie was really sorry but I said you're a big girl now, you'd understand.'

Mummy said, 'I meant to tell you before but I've been so busy.'

Mummy said, 'Always so much to think about. I forgot all about it.'

I looked up but she looked away and I knew she hadn't forgotten at all. I looked at the photograph and I felt sick. How could she have got married without me there? With no one to carry her train?

Mummy put her arms round me. 'Come on, lovey, don't cry.' Mummy never called me lovey. That was an Auntie Joanie word. It made me cry more. Mummy gave me a squeeze. 'We should be happy for Auntie Joanie, not crying all over this lovely cake. You'll melt the icing!'

And then Mummy picked up another photograph. She picked it up slowly and I knew even before I saw the picture. It was the bridesmaid. Mummy turned it over and read what was on the back. Her name was Theresa, she was a niece of Uncle Des's. Auntie Joanie wrote that her dress was pale blue. She didn't mention the Alice band with the flowers or the sash or the satin shoes but you could see them in the picture.

I knew now why Auntie Joanie had never answered my letters

Mummy said not to take any notice, it couldn't be helped. 'You can't expect the poor girl not to get married just because you're not there! Anyway, it was only registry, I don't suppose you missed much.'

Mummy put the cake in a tin to have later and Bobby lost interest then and ran outside. I stood looking at the photographs and when Mummy turned to put the tin on the shelf I knocked them to the floor.

The people who loved me had forgotten about me already. I wasn't special any more, Auntie Joanie had called me 'her special' but all she'd sent me was a piece of cake the same as she'd sent everyone else.

'Do be careful,' Mummy said, kneeling down to pick them up. 'Look this one's got dirt on it now.'

It was the one of the bridesmaid and I was glad.

'Don't upset yourself, we'll meet loads of people over here who'll want a bridesmaid, you'll get your chance.'

Mummy was stacking the photographs up, and I felt so sick looking at them, I didn't want to ever look at them again. I didn't want them in our house, I wanted to forget all about them, all about everything we had before we came here.

'You took me away from everyone I loved,' I said to Mummy. 'And everyone who loved me. And now they've forgotten me.'

She looked so surprised. 'What about Dad and me? What do you think – that you could have stayed? Get on with you. Come here -' and she opened her arms wide. 'Don't cry, lovey. Come and have a cuddle.'

And I did, I let her cuddle me. But it was a quick hug really, that's all it was. She wanted to get on with the dinner. 'It'll all be fine, you'll see,' she said. But it wouldn't be fine, nothing would be fine ever again. And I hated Mummy then. I hated all of them for forgetting me. I knew then we were never going home, not now, not ever I ran into my room and threw my silver chain with the rabbit charm under my bed, right to the back where I wouldn't see it ever again.

Chapter 13

Rose

Joanie says Mattie is flying over. Don't know why Joanie's been poking her nose in. I'm fine. Not like I'm dying or anything. Joanie thinks I've gone a bit gaga since I fell off that bus but I only had a bit of percussion, nothing to make a fuss about. Not percussion. The thing where you go unconscious. Anyway, I don't want Mattie wasting all that money on the fare, I said ring and tell her I'm fine, but Joanie said she's already booked her flight. Maybe it's going to be a surprise and she's bringing Richie. He'd come if he could, that I do know.

Mattie

The stewardess brings me a coffee and a sachet of pretzels. The man next to me doesn't want his and offers them to me. Henry doesn't like salty snacks and I'm always watching my weight so I never buy them. Eating a whole packet feels very wicked. So I eat both packets. It feels like an act of rebellion against Henry, which is ridiculous but it does anyway. Odd how your life can become restricted without you even realising it.

But a few pretzels isn't enough to take my mind off things. How will I feel if she doesn't get better? Or what if she does but she can't manage at home by herself? I can't see her going into a home. Will she want to come back to Oz with me? There's room, we could make one of the bedrooms into a lounge for her. That's the beauty of a bungalow, so adaptable. We should have stayed in our previous house, then there wouldn't have been room... No, I'm joking! If you're listening, God, that was a joke! But maybe she'll be fine. She's bounced back before.

Mum went to England to see Nanny and never came home again and now that she's in decline I've come running just like she did. And probably with the same guilt and regrets. Strange how history repeats itself.

The man on the other side of me wakes with a jolt, almost knocking my drink from my hand. He raises his head slowly and looks around. When he meets my gaze he seems surprised to find me here. His eyes are red rimmed, sticky with sleep.

'Sorry,' he says, 'I must have dozed off.' He introduces himself and offers his hand. It is moist with sweat. When he turns away to speak to the steward I wipe my palms on my jeans.

Such a long flight. And yet not a long flight at all compared with the sea voyage coming out here; scarcely believable in fact. Weeks and weeks. It seemed it would never end. Henry and I were talking about it while I was packing and he said 'That journey was life changing and this one will be merely clothes-changing'. That made me laugh, particularly coming from Henry who wouldn't change his clothes at all if I didn't put them out for him.

Henry drove me to the airport but I didn't let him come in with me. I have a horror of goodbyes, so as soon as he had lifted my case out of the boot I hurried in to the terminal. It was only as I walked towards check in that I realised I hadn't even hugged him.

I've brought books but the biography Henry recommended with such enthusiasm is heavy-going, and besides I had forgotten there would be a film to watch. We never go to the movies, Henry says what's the point when you can see them on TV eventually but we rarely do that either because he says there's so little that's worth watching. I've watched one with a car chase in it. Henry would baulk at a car chase though this one displayed an artistry and imagination that Henry would have appreciated in a different context – if, say, it had been exhibited as a video installation in a gallery in Sydney, and described in the catalogue as a comment on society's love-hate relationship with commercialism and consumerism at the dawn of the twenty first century. Or something. Poor Henry.

The man in the seat next to mine is asleep again by the time I need to get out. I speak to him and nudge him with my elbow but he just snuffles into his chest and his head drops lower. His hair is receding but there's a longer lock by the side which has stuck to his face. He's dribbling. Say what you like about Henry, he'd never do that.

They turn the lights down in the cabin and suggest we try to sleep. I draw the blanket round my shoulders and snuggle down into it, trying to relax while retaining just enough tension so that I don't slide into either of the men next to me. Henry asked if I was going to travel business class but I balked when I saw the difference in price. Time now to regret that petty meanness but I am my mother's daughter. The memory of being poor stays with you, even though it's just a memory. I close my eyes.

It is 1961. I am fifteen and we are living on the farm. There is more money than there used to be but even so Mum says I should be out at work, a great strapping girl like me. Dad says not to take any notice. My best friend at school is Lindsay Saunders. The most popular girl in the class is Becky Devlin and she is having a party. She has invited the whole class and that includes us. Becky has an older brother and there will be boys there. We are beside ourselves with excitement.

I plan to wear a shift dress that I will make myself. It will have a slash neck and be loose fitting so it won't need a zip. Zips are tricky. I will wear my hair in a pony tail.

'You needn't think you're going,' Mum said when I made my announcement.

'Mum! Everyone's going!'

'Everyone but you then.'

I said that wasn't fair and she said life wasn't fair. 'You can't expect Dad to run you back and forth all the time.'

'I'll ask him and see what he says.'

'Oh he'll do whatever you ask him, he's soft as butter where you're concerned, But that doesn't mean it's fair to ask him. You know how hard he works. Don't you think Dad and I would like to go to parties sometimes?'

I didn't think they would like to go to parties, not sometimes, not ever. Or anyway, not Mum. Mum didn't like getting too friendly with people, she said other people were too keen to poke their noses into other people's business. Dad would probably like parties - he used to play piano in a hotel - sometimes when we met people in town they would say how good he was and when would he come and do it again. But Mum had put a stop to that.

When I told Lindsay I couldn't go her dad said he could take me. When she heard that, Mum said she wasn't about to be beholden to anyone, they'd only come back expecting you to do the same for them some other time and then you'd be obligated and you'd never hear the end of it. And she said if I thought I could blackmail her into letting me go, I had another think coming. Even though I hadn't done anything, only told Lindsay I wasn't going. She said Dad would take me there and back. And that's where I met my first boyfriend.

Brian wasn't in our class but he'd come with Becky's boyfriend. He wasn't bad looking but he had glasses that made his eyes look small, and spots on his neck. He had combed his hair into a quiff for the dance and when they played Elvis Presley he struck a pose, and I realised that's who he was trying to look like. He didn't, but I liked him anyway. He asked me to dance but he wasn't very good and his knees kept knocking against mine. Afterwards we didn't know what to say to each other and he went back to sit with his friends and I went back to mine. Lindsay said, 'I'm not being funny, but what did he ask *you* to dance for?' I had thought the same thing but she didn't have to say it. After we danced a second time he wanted me to go outside but Becky had told Lindsay that he had wandering hands. It seemed to me that if they were wandering somewhere you didn't want you could always move them to somewhere you did so when he asked again I said all right.

On the way home Dad said, 'Did you have a good time?'

I told him about the food, which was good - sausages and things on sticks – and that I had danced with a boy who seemed nice.

He said he was sure to be a nice boy, because I was a sensible girl. 'But you can't blame your mother for worrying. We were young once, though you might not think it. We know what young lads can be like.'

'Stupid and spotty?' I said, and he laughed.

On Monday at school Lindsay said, 'Did Brian kiss you?' I said maybe he hadn't done it right because it was supposed to be magical according to the magazines I'd read (and make you feel like marshmallow according to Becky who had been going with boys for ages and knew everything), but it wasn't magical and I didn't feel like marshmallow. What I didn't tell her was that even though it wasn't magical or make me feel like marshmallow, it did make me feel hot in my stomach and maybe now I understood why Mum didn't want me mixing with boys.

After Becky's party Lindsay asked me to go for the weekend because her mum and dad liked me and thought I was a good influence. Lindsay's mother was a teacher which was what I wanted to be. She liked talking to me about teaching and she told me stories of funny things that had happened. They had lots of books at their house, a whole bookcase of them. When I got married that's what I was going to have. In the meantime she said I was free to borrow whatever I wanted.

One night they went out leaving us to look after

Lindsay's little brother. Lindsay wasn't usually allowed to have people round while they were out but her mum said she knew I was sensible. I blushed because we'd asked our boyfriends to come over.

After they'd gone, Lindsay sent Alvin out in the yard to play on his bike so that when Brian and Andy arrived we could listen to records but Alvin kept coming back in wanting us to play with him. On the last time it was just as Lindsay and Andy were having a kiss and he said, 'I know what you're doing, I know what you're doing,' even though they weren't doing anything .

Lindsay told him to go back outside but he wouldn't. He came in and plonked himself down next to Andy. You could see there was going to be no getting rid of him. I was mad because it was the first time I'd ever been alone with a boy with no adults around.

'Let's get some orange squash for everyone,' Lindsay said, looking at me. I was about to say I didn't want any but then I saw she was giving me 'the look' such as she'd give me at school when she wanted me to leave whoever we were with and go into the toilets to hear some gossip she'd just picked up. Becky or even Lindsay's mum would roll their eyes when they saw that look and say, 'What's she up to now?' But Brian was talking to Alvin and Andy wasn't as bright as either Becky or Lindsay's mum and didn't notice anything.

In the kitchen she shut the door and looked around as though she thought her mum or dad might be hiding behind a cupboard.

'Let's take it in turns to play Old Maid or something with Alvin,' she said.

'Lindsay, if I wanted to do that I'd have stayed at

home with Bobby.'

She rolled her eyes as though I wasn't even as bright as Andy.

'You and Brian play, and Andy and me can be in the bedroom. Then we'll swap.'

I considered. 'Won't Alvin wonder what you're doing in the bedroom?'

'I'll say he's helping me with my homework. I'm always getting stuck, he's got no reason not to believe that.'

As for me, she assured me he wouldn't even ask. She said her mum and dad were always saying what a nice girl I was, so whatever I did he'd think must be okay.

We took the orange squash back in. Andy looked surprised when she asked him to help with her homework but she gave him the look and that shut him up even though you could tell he had no idea what it meant.

They were in the bedroom a long time, so long that I had to go and knock because otherwise her parents were going to be home before we got our turn. I tapped on the door and there was some moving and shuffling about, before she opened it. She looked irritated to see me and I wondered then if she'd really meant for us to have a turn at all. She said she'd be just a few minutes, and soon she came back, straightening her hair and pulling down her skirt which had got very creased.

When we got into Lindsay's bedroom I sat down on the edge of the bed and Brian put his arm round me. Then he put his hand on the outside of my bra, and then on the inside. And then suddenly there was Lindsay banging on the door hissing that we'd been ages and it was their turn again.

After that Lindsay's mum and dad often used to go out and leave us babysitting Alvin. Fortunately none of the adults realised. Mum used to say you couldn't trust most boys as far as you could throw them. And Dad would say, 'well you trusted me,' and she'd laugh and say that's how she knew.

The man in the window seat gently prods me awake, wanting to get past. He breaks into my dream, sending me down a different avenue.

Suzanne says my mother is jealous of me. That's what she came out with when I went to the beach house for the weekend. We were sitting on the patio under the awning while Neil turned steaks on the barbie.

'Why would my mother be jealous?' I said 'She always did whatever she wanted.' I'm not sure I've ever done anything I wanted. Dad always did whatever she wanted too. And he adored her. Henry doesn't adore me, he's just married to me, not the same thing. And Mum wasn't jealous of me marrying Henry, she can't bear Henry. She doesn't think sitting at a desk writing a book counts as work. She used to scoff when he said he was going into his study to work. "Work?' she'd say, 'Reading a book - call that work?' As for his lecturing – 'Well, anyone can talk, can't they. It's not like he's teaching children, not like he's teaching anyone to read or add up or do the accounts. Students – adults – should be out at work as well, what's the matter with them?' According to Mum, the only point of education was to fit you for a job, and a better one than you could get without an education.

Suzanne says I've been ground down. She says it's been easier for me to go along with whatever my mother says. But did I have a choice? She had all the power when I was young, and by the time I wasn't... well, maybe I did get ground down. What's that they say – if you keep doing what you're doing, you'll keep getting what you're getting. So I stopped doing what I was doing. Stopped answering back, stopped fighting her. I could see Dad could never win, so how could I?

But one thing I did disagree with was when Suzanne said Henry manipulates me. I might not be stronger than Mum but I'm a damn sight stronger than him, for God's sake. Henry and I don't argue often but when we do I'm the one with the smart retort and quick comeback. It mystifies Henry, I see it in his face, that while he's searching his brain the size of a planet for the bon mot I've shot back with my limited selection from the shorter English and nailed it.

'I'm not talking about that,' Suzanne said, leaning forward, focused and intense so that her wine tipped in her glass and almost spilled. 'He doesn't have to say anything. He has a way of letting you know and you fall into line'. I poured myself another glass and told her she was talking rubbish. Henry is about as threatening as a hamster. Maybe less so, a hamster can bite. He never tells me what to do, never even suggests what I should do. It's all the other way round: me laying his clothes out. Deciding what he will have for his lunch.

'And I might be wrong,' she went on as Neil brought our steaks over, 'but you used to ask us over and now you don't.' I reached for the pepper, not looking at her. 'You invite me, but you don't invite us both any more. You used to.' I picked up my cutlery, still not looking at her. Now she was putting me on the spot.

'Henry doesn't like socialising, it's not personal, you know that.'

'He likes socialising when it's his own friends, doesn't he? You're always moaning about cooking for them.'

I protested that I wasn't always moaning, but that was just to shift the focus. I remembered the last two occasions Neil and Suzanne had come over. Henry had got up from the table as soon as we'd eaten and gone inside claiming an urgent deadline. I knew he didn't have a deadline. When Francine came with Steve it was pressure of work that had him taking his coffee into the study. After a bit you stop inviting your friends, it's easier that way. But Henry had never said he didn't like them, didn't want them to come, he'd never objected in anyway at all.

I wasn't about to let Suzanne know that despite being married for about a hundred years I'd never noticed that my strings were being pulled. What else hadn't I noticed? Was it really me who wanted to move to this house, which I don't actually like, or was it him? This one was much more convenient for the university. It unsettled me and I argued back and forth with Suzanne, more than I should have. Well, we'd both had a bit to drink by then. But she'd put my back up and the weekend ended on a sour note.

The man in the window seat comes back, interrupting my thoughts again. But Suzanne's words about Henry manipulating me are foremost in my brain now. Henry has never made any remarks about my weight. Wouldn't dream of it. And I've appreciated that. But if he'd been here on this flight and seen me accept that second bag of pretzels, his eyebrow would have risen. Just slightly. Imperceptibly. Almost. And I wouldn't have taken them.

The man in the window seat has a paunch, it collapses over the waistband of his trousers. Brian would probably have a paunch by now, and with his hair receding where that quiff had been. He was proud of that quiff, and I was proud to have a boyfriend with a quiff, acne or no acne.

I was not in love, but I was in love with the idea of being in love. Of having a boyfriend. I was adolescent, nubile, though that wasn't a word I'd have known. I was maturing. My bras were too tight, my cups runneth over. I saw in the mirror each day how my body was changing. I knew I was changing with it.

I had made a new skirt, cutting up an old flared one. It came to my knees, but it seemed short after the calf length skirts we all wore. It was a rush to finish it but I got it ready by the time they were to come. I was checking how I looked in the mirror in my bedroom when Mum walked in. She stopped short.

'What are you wearing?' she said, and the colour rose up her face as fast as if it was filling with boiling water.

I thought it was because I'd cut up the skirt. 'I couldn't have worn it any more,' I said, 'the zip was broken.' I didn't mention that no one was wearing flared skirts in that style any more though that was the main reason. 'Anyway, you must have seen me making it.'

'Well, you're not wearing it.'

'It's the new fashion.'

'Not around here it isn't, my lady.'

She was right, no one was wearing them yet, but I'd seen them in Lindsay's magazine I was going to be setting the trend. When the girls at school saw it they would be so envious

'Do you want everyone thinking you're a slut? Now

take it off.'

'They'll be here in a minute!'

'Then you'd better be quick.'

I turned away, because you couldn't win against Mum when she'd made her mind up. I got the shift dress out that I had worn for Becky's party. Mum said, 'I thought you were wearing that on Christmas Day.'

'But it's the only thing I've got.'

She opened the wardrobe and took out the blouse and the skirt I wore if we went into town but lately I was growing and the blouse pulled tight across the chest. I put it on and Mum gave an exaggerated sigh as she tried to pull the sides of the blouse closer together.

"I don't know what Dorothy will say,' she said, as though it was my fault I didn't have things to wear. And that reminds me – Dan's a nice boy but I don't want you in the bedroom. I want you in the living room and with the door open so I can see you.'

I felt the colour rush into my face, even though she knew nothing about Brian and my evenings at Lindsay's house. But I bounced back with a quick retort.

'Just because you couldn't be trusted - ' I said, and I was just referring to what Dad had said, it could have been a joke really. But she grabbed me by the arm and for a moment I thought she was going to hit me.

'What did you say?'

'Mum – I only meant – .' She stepped back, still glaring and I remembered then, something from years ago, on the ship coming over. Mum and Uncle Eddie, on the deck, behind one of the lifeboats. On the farm, Mum and Uncle Eddie in the kitchen giggling. I didn't know why it had popped into my head. But at that moment we heard the truck outside.

Dorothy, Sophie and Dan were going to stay with us for a few days. Dan had changed, he had grown up since we last saw them. His hair, which he used to have in a crew cut, was longer and had turned out to be curly. It was the colour of honey. He eyes were dark grey though sometimes they looked green. Somehow he made me feel shy.

Their life was very different from ours. They lived near a town and it had a cinema and Sophie was up with all the latest films. She said she had a boyfriend. 'Haven't *you* got one?' she asked. 'All my friends have, I thought everyone had.' I couldn't tell her about Brian, you have to be careful who you share your secrets with. She told me all about the places she went in town, and about one of her friends who was rich and gave her clothes she had finished with. Dorothy was running her own business and it was doing very well, so they had more to spend than we did. Mum wouldn't have let me buy the things that Sophie had. If I wanted something I had to make it. That's why I'd made the skirt. The skirt I'd planned to wear for Dan.

After lunch Dan wanted to have a look round the farm and see how the animals were doing. Bobby said he'd go, and I said I'd go as well. Mum pulled a face. 'Well, that's a turn up for the books,' she said.

Sophie said, 'You needn't think I'm coming,' and I said, 'Thank goodness for small mercies.' It was supposed to be a joke but it was too near the truth and she saw that. She gave me such a look. Dan said, 'Come on, Soph, we're all going.' But she flounced off to my room and slammed the door. Dan shrugged. 'You better say you're sorry,' he said. 'You don't want to get on the wrong side of her.'

But she was already on the wrong side of me with her superior ways, so I thought we were even.

We were a long time wandering around the farm because Dan was interested in everything, but he particularly liked the pigs and after he'd helped Bobby feed them he said he'd stay and watch them for a while. I said I'd stay with Dan even though I couldn't see the attraction. They were only pigs. 'What about the chickens, I thought you were helping,' Bobby said to me.

'I'm being a good host,' I said. 'I'll feed them tomorrow, and then you can be the host.' From Bobby's expression anyone would think I'd never fed them before.

'I'll feed the chickens if you want,' Dan said. 'I just want a few minutes here first.'

Bobby hesitated, but it was less boring to feed the chickens than hang around looking at the pigs, so he went off.

'Funny old things, aren't they?' I said, just for something to say.

'Look at how happy they are,' he said

'They can be very sweet.' I said, for no reason, sounding really stupid. I wondered now if it was such a good idea to have come out here with him. Now we were by ourselves, I felt self conscious and awkward, in my blouse that was too tight so I had to hunch over to stop it gaping.

Dan leaned over the pen, oblivious to the smell. 'They're like a little family,' he said, 'when you see the piglets with the sow, all feeding away, snuggling in together.'

It was ages since Alice had any piglets, I didn't know

what had made him think of that. But then he went on,
'There were pigs at the place they took us to. We all liked
feeding them, it was a chance to get outside by yourself.'

I didn't know what to say to that. 'Was it very
horrible?' I said, knowing it was stupid even as I spoke.
He held on to the side of the pen and stretched his back
out.

'I'm going to have a wander around,' he said. 'I'll see
you back at the house later, we can play Monopoly.' We
didn't have any games like that, and they brought theirs
with them when they visited.

I watched him go, hands in his pockets, head down.
'I could come with you if you want,' I called. I couldn't
tell if he had heard me or not.

In bed that night I asked Sophie what it was like in
the children's home but she said her Mum said it was
better to just forget about it.

The day before they were to go home Dad was to drive us
all into town as a special treat. But on that morning over
breakfast Dan said he didn't think he'd bother. He said he
wanted to make the most of being on the farm, and he
wanted a bit of time to himself to spend with the animals.
I hadn't expected this at all. I wanted to go into town, we
rarely went, but on the other hand, town would be there
long after Dan had gone home. I said there were a few
things I wanted to get on with myself.

Mum said, 'What things? You can't get into town
fast enough usually.'

I said, 'Things, that's all. And I don't fancy going in
today.'

'Come on,' said Sophie, cajoling. 'I want you to show

me all the best shops.' That decided it because I didn't want to hear any more about how wonderful things were where they lived.

'It's your fault,' she said, turning to Dan. 'She's only not coming because you're not, and now you've spoiled everything.'

Dan shrugged, resigned. 'It's no big deal. I'll come then.'

I was just about to say that after all I'd go too when Dorothy said, 'Don't badger him, Sophie. If he'd like to spend time with the animals, let him.'

After the others had gone, Mum said we might as well make ourselves useful and wash up the breakfast things. I cast an apologetic look at Dan but he was already on his feet. 'Your mum cooked it,' he reasoned, 'it's not fair that she should wash up as well.'

'Danny my love, if only Bobby was here to hear that,' Mum said laughing.

Afterwards I walked with Dan around the farm, and hung around while he sat on the fence musing, looking at the cows, or leaned into the pen where Alice was dozing. Later on I took him into the barn and we climbed the ladder into the loft.

'You should come and stay at our house,' he said as we sat down, our legs hanging over the ledge. 'Sophie would love showing off to you.'

'Do you think she shows off?'

'Don't you think she does?'

We laughed, conspiratorially. 'What's her boyfriend like?' I asked.

He laughed again, disbelieving. 'Did she tell you she's got a boyfriend?' Then he shrugged. 'Maybe she has.'

He paused. I was aware a question was coming. 'Have you got a boyfriend?'

I hesitated. I didn't want him to know about Brian, but I didn't want to give the impression I was a complete novice.

'No – well, not really.' I paused, hesitating. 'Have you got a girlfriend?'

He leaned over to peer over the edge, then drew back, began scratching at a bit of straw that was stuck to the floor. Then he turned his head on one side to look at me. 'If you came to stay you could be my girlfriend.'

He must have seen me blush. Something fluttered in my stomach so violently that I sat up, thinking I was lying on something. I folded my knees under me, pretending I had just been changing position. He asked me if I often sat up here, because he liked the feeling of being above the world, away from everyone else. He moved to lie on his stomach, peering over the ledge. The hair at the nape of his neck curled, like the tail of a little animal, pointing down his back. I wanted to see his face, so I moved to lie next to him.

'You've such tiny hands,' he said. He measured his against mine, the heel of his hand brushing my wrist. He talked about his favourite subject, music, as he traced a pattern across the back of my hand. But I wasn't really listening. Our fingers became entwined and now that was what I thought about: the roughness of his skin, the pale pink of his fingernails, the dirt under the one he had scratched at the ground with.

'Do you want to be my girlfriend?' he said, and when I looked up I realised how close to him I was, how close our eyes, our faces. I knew he had asked me a question but it didn't feel like I needed to answer. He leant forward and his eyes closed as his lips brushed my mouth. His lips were unexpectedly soft and warm. So this is what it was like.... Nothing that I had felt with Brian had prepared me for this.

He drew back, uncertainly. 'Do you mind?' I shook my head, amazed that he needed to ask. Didn't he know that I had been waiting for this since I first opened the pages of Romeo? This was what I had dreamt about. He brushed his finger across my cheek, sweeping my hair behind my ear. Then he pushed me on to my back so that he was leaning over me.

'I'm glad we didn't go into town,' I said, suddenly embarrassed by the silence, and then more embarrassed at my admission.

'So am I,' he said. Heat rushed up my body, from my thighs and up into my chest. He had wanted to be alone with me! So this wasn't an accident! Now he undid the top button of my blouse. He traced his lips over my collarbone, so gently, barely touching me. At the brush of his fingertip against my nipple I trembled. I was hardly aware that my hand had found the belt of his shorts until I realised I was struggling with the buckle.

Suddenly I heard Mum calling. I opened my eyes and met his, wide with fear and astonishment as mine must have been. We leapt up rearranging our clothes and he was halfway down the ladder before she appeared in the doorway.

'I've been looking for you all over, I'm getting lunch ready.' She looked from Dan to me and her eyes narrowed with a hint of suspicion. I was still fumbling with the buttons on my blouse. 'What were you up to up there?'

Dan brushed his hands down his shorts and rubbed at his legs to shift the dust. 'I've never seen up there before, it's amazing isn't it, the farm so big and yet you manage it all.' He saw her looking at me and added, 'Mattie thinks something bit her neck, but I can't see anything.'

She strode back to the house with Dan by her side, and they talked of farm work, and what there was to be done and how long the various jobs took. I followed behind and as we crossed the yard Dan turned and winked at me.

The following day they were to leave. I had gone into my bedroom for a last look round to check Sophie hadn't left anything. As I turned towards the door, I realised Dan was behind me. We stood looking at each other awkwardly. Then he held his arms out and I seemed to fall into them in a single movement. He pulled me so tightly into him I could hardly breathe. 'Mattie, Mattie,' he whispered against my hair.

I turned my face up and he leant down towards me.

'Dan, are you ready?' It was Dorothy, calling from the yard.

He heaved a sigh as he pulled back but I clung on wanting it to last for just a moment longer. Then he stepped back, holding me by the shoulders at arm's length. 'Come and stay with us,' he said. 'I'll get them to fix it up.'

I nodded, smiling. Then he was gone. I watched for a moment, seeing his long strides, the flow of the muscles across his back as he crossed the hallway. I was swept up by what had happened between us, I could hardly breathe, hardly move. Suddenly I came to and went hurrying out, but he was already in the car and Dorothy was backing out. Sophie blew me a kiss out of the window. I waved until they were out of sight.

When they had gone I ran up to my room and got out my notebook, the one Mum didn't know about. It was an awakening. Does that sound melodramatic? It was nothing like I had thought. I was ashamed I could feel such things. I was excited that I could. It was like nothing I'd ever known, or expected, like stepping out of time and into a new dimension, where you didn't have to worry about school or home or whether you were too fat or not pretty enough. I ripped out the pages where I had recorded some nonsense about Brian (who I called Elvis just in case Mum did know about the notebook) and wrote, 'Hello Me,' because I was meeting this new person for the first time, this Mattie who Dan had breathed into being. Inside me was a place I hadn't known about. I liked that place and more than that, I liked that person. She was wild and unafraid, and under Dan's fingers she rose up to fill the horizon. And there was nothing Mum could do to stop her.

I wrote: 'He is my waking breath and my sleeping sigh.' (Because even in my mystery notebook, I wouldn't risk naming him.)

It was agreed we could stay for the week and Dad drove us over. Sophie was all right at first but she didn't like it when I wanted to go for a walk with Dan by myself or even when we sat by the brook dangling our feet in the water. 'You needn't think I'm playing with Bobby,' she'd say, even though Bobby was happy to play on Dan's bike or to help Dorothy in her shop and didn't need playing with. Dan said it was nothing, she was jealous because they were seeds of the empire and they'd had to look out for each other.

'Seeds of the Empire?' I'd never heard of that. I rather thought I'd have liked to be one. He said I definitely wouldn't but then he clammed up and wouldn't say any more.

But the next day when we were sitting on Auntie Dot's back step sucking on home-made ice lollies I tried again. She didn't have any lolly sticks and we had to lick them as they melted in the aluminum molds. I'd often heard Dorothy and Mum and Dad whispering, shutting up when I came into the room.

'It's what they called us,' he said at last. 'Seeds of the Empire: the children who were sent out from the British children's homes. They told us we were going on holiday.' A sliver of ice lolly slid out of the mold and he scooped it up off his leg. It left a sticky trace that glistened on his tanned skin.

'It was a lie and we knew that the minute we stepped off that gang plank when we arrived.' He was staring at a heap of stones that were stacked a few yards away, He picked up a pebble from the ground and hurled it at the pile. 'As we came down, we could hear children screaming. We didn't know why then, but it was because they were separating the boys from the girls. The brothers from sisters... '

I didn't know what to say and I was embarrassed that I had asked. We finished our lollies and I took the molds indoors to be washed.

On our last night Auntie Dot said we could all sleep out on the veranda, but Sophie got in a sulk because she didn't want to be on the end and she went back into the house.

So then there were just the three of us. When Bobby was asleep, Dan crawled under the covers with me.

I cried when we said goodbye and he promised he'd write to me. Every day I waited for his letter but when one came it wasn't from Dan.

Chapter 14

Rose

I can't seem to stay awake. I start to come round then I drift off again. I can hear voices sometimes, Joanie and Marian, and once I thought I heard Richie but perhaps I was dreaming. It might all be a dream. Maybe I'm only dreaming I'm in hospital.

'I think she's waking up.' That's Joanie. I'm trying to speak but she can't hear me. I want to say: Pipe down, woman, I'm talking to you!

'She's a better colour than yesterday.' Why are they whispering? Joanie said she's phoned someone and they're on their way. I listen out to hear if Richie joins in, but it's just the two of them. Or maybe it's Richie that's coming.

'Is it Richie?' I ask.

'I'll be going,' Joanie says, 'Des will be wanting his dinner.'

'Is it Richie?' I'm shouting now.

'Does she seem restless to you?' Marian says. 'I hope she's not in pain.'

Joanie says she will speak to the nurse.

Someone lifts my arm and something cool is rubbed

on it. Then there's a faint scratch. I sleep.

Mattie

Mum wanted to take me on holiday to England and my first thought was: I'll be away from Dan for a month. Which was a stupid thing to think because I hadn't seen him for over a month already and he hadn't written either, and I'd written to him twice. So I said I didn't want to go which was also stupid because we'd never had a holiday before, of course I wanted to go. But Dan... how could I leave Dan? Supposing he was arranging for me to stay again and it would turn out to be the very dates we'd be away?

I got in from school and there was a parcel on the draining board and Mum picked it up and handed it to me. No one but Nanny ever sent parcels but I knew at once from the writing, even before Mum spoke, that it was from Dorothy and I tore it open so fast that Mum called out, 'Steady on, you don't want to spoil what's inside.' It was a checked blouse, she had made for me. Sophie had one the same and I'd admired it when we last saw them. 'Try it on. You can take it on holiday!' Mum said, but I threw it to one side, searching for a letter. There was bound to be a letter. Of course there was a note from Dorothy saying she hoped I'd like it. But surely there would be something from Dan? Then I saw it, folded inside the parcel and stuck down with sticky tape. I headed for my room to read it, my heart pounding, only remembering the blouse when Mum called me back and thrust it into my arms.

The note was from Sophie. She told me she had a new friend at school, and about a boy who liked her, and about a new book she had just got. And that Dan had a girlfriend. The girl had long blonde hair and even though she was stuck up and everyone at school hated her, Dan thought she was the bees' knees.

When Lindsay got the school bus I told her I was going to England in the school holidays. She was impressed and she shouted to Becky that I was going abroad. Becky said her auntie in England was always asking her to go but she didn't want to. She said her mum said the only thing England had that we didn't was rain and cold and we could mostly do without that.

I told my boss at the garage where I worked at weekends. He'd given me a rise already and I'd only been there three months. He said the customers liked me and I knew they did, always wanting a laugh and a joke. Sometimes they said things that were quite rude and if Dave heard he'd tick them off. 'That's a bit near the knuckle,' he'd say, 'Or watch your mouth, mate, she's still at school, you know.'

Sometimes instead of working in the garage, Dave's wife would get me to look after their children which I liked because I was going to be a teacher so it would be good practice. They had three children: Freddie, Catherine and Sally. Freddie was five and Catherine was three. Sally was still a baby. Linda, Dave's wife wanted a job of her own, she said it was lonely stuck in the house all day. Dave would say, 'Then work in the garage like you're supposed to,' and she'd say, 'You don't keep a dog and bark yourself.' She started cutting people's hair, the only hairdresser's salon was in town, so you could either have your hair cut in her kitchen or she'd go to your home. When she was working Saturdays Dave got someone else

217

to cover the garage for me and I looked after the children. I did some evenings too.

When Mum heard I was babysitting she said she hoped I wouldn't end up as a skivvy, and they better not think I was going to do all the cleaning. I told Mum I just had to play with the children. It seemed like an easy job to me. There was only a bit of washing up and cleaning and I didn't mind that, it was only what I was used to at home. I helped Freddie with his reading and soon he and Catherine could both say their two times table which I did with them like a song. Dave gave me a bit extra, he was so impressed.

Dave said it'd be really good if I could find someone to cover for me while I was in England. I was glad he made it sound temporary but I wasn't sure who I'd ask to fill in. I didn't want anyone winning the children over or chatting to Joey too much. Joey was the son of the caretaker at school, and he did odd jobs. With his fair hair slicked back and his tight jeans he looked just like James Dean. When he walked by whistling, or climbed up the ladder to fetch a sneaker or something off the school roof that one of the boys had thrown up there, we'd all stop what we were doing and nudge each other, especially if he had his shirt off. And now I knew him to speak to because he used to bring his dad's truck to the garage to fill up at weekends, and if Dave wasn't working the pumps I had to help and to take the money. At first I was so shy I could hardly answer when he spoke to me. Everyone thought he was gorgeous and they were so jealous that he knew my name and said hello when I walked past. I liked being the only one Joey called by name.

I thought perhaps when the time came I'd ask

Lindsay to cover my job while I was away. She had got some acne lately, so I didn't think he'd fancy her.

Joey had an open topped truck and once when he passed me on the road coming home from school, he picked me up. We got talking and it turned out he came from near Darwin not far from where we used to live. We even knew some of the same people. He'd moved down here with his dad when his parents split up. He gave me a lift a few times and then I got involved with a drama production at school, or said I did, so I could hang around for him until he finished. I had to meet him down the road so none of the staff saw. He wasn't allowed to date anyone from school though that had never stopped him.

Joey was fun. He was nothing like Dan and that was in his favour. I didn't want to be reminded of Dan. If Dan could find someone else then so could I. Joey was older than Dan, and by a few years, and he played guitar and could sing like Elvis. He hadn't had much of an education – he lived with his dad and he'd left school at fourteen which lots of kids did, so he wasn't the intellectual type I fantasised about, but he was the type the other girls fantasised about – and I'd got him. He might not know about books but he knew all the other stuff, like about film stars and rock and roll, and a lot of other stuff which you could tell by the way he leant against his truck with a cigarette in his hand. He was sexy and confident and when I was with him I thought I was a bit like that myself. I thought of it as my 'Hello me' from my notebook coming out to play. I didn't care if Dan didn't want me, I'd found someone even better.

He kept the back of the truck lined with old sacks so

it wasn't too bad for lying down on. It was mostly too hot to be in the cab. He'd park somewhere quiet and we'd be alone there for hours – well, an hour anyway. I couldn't be out too long. Sometimes I told Mum I was babysitting for Dave and he'd drop me home afterwards. Dave often did that so she didn't even question it.

My periods were always irregular so I didn't think about it for a month or so. And several girls in my class had started to put on weight, suddenly getting coy in the showers and keeping their backs turned. I reckoned we couldn't all be pregnant and I didn't get morning sickness which was the only other symptom I knew about. I would have liked to check how you could tell but I didn't know who to ask. If I'd asked Lindsay she would have wanted to know why I was asking. I wasn't a good enough liar to pretend it was just a casual enquiry. And I reasoned it wasn't as easy to get pregnant as people said and it was probably exaggerated just so you wouldn't try it. Auntie Joanie was married ages before she had any children, and Auntie Marian didn't have any at all.

I wished I could speak to Dan. But I didn't want him to know, he had already moved on, forgotten all about me. If he didn't want me, then I didn't want him either. Joey was seeing Wendy by then, and when I passed him in the school grounds he acted like he didn't know me. I used to try to get a desk by the window so I could watch him. It was hard to see him and know I wasn't his girlfriend any more. In magazines it said if you wanted a boy to be interested you should play hard to get so I thought if it seemed like I wasn't too bothered, he'd come back again. That's why I hadn't written to Dan, but that hadn't worked either.

Joey used to take his shirt off when they were laying bricks for the new school building. Mrs. Sykes made us pull the blinds down so we couldn't see him.

Then one morning I woke up and realised I knew and that I had known all along. That was the only morning of the entire nine months that I was sick.

When I got in from school Mum was sitting at the kitchen table. It was a rare thing to see Mum sitting down during the day, she was always busy. I cut myself a slice of bread - I was always starving when I came home – and then I got a drink of water but mainly it was to avoid looking at her. I kept up a commentary on what I'd done at school that day, which was also unusual, we didn't often talk except about what chores needed doing, but I couldn't bear the feel of her eyes on me.

She didn't answer me at all. Then finally she said, 'Is there something you want to tell me?' Her voice had a strange, tight sound, as though her throat had gone very small. I said I didn't think so.

She said, 'Who is he?

I laughed and said, 'Who?' It was as though if I ignored it, we could all stay as we were. Even if it were only for another day, even just a few hours. Because once we all acknowledged it, then life would change and I was scared. I didn't know what would happen next.

I shrugged as though I didn't know what she was talking about and went to put the bread on the grill. She caught my arm as I passed her and gave me such a slap across the face. She had never hit me before. I moved away to try to get to the stairs. I wanted to make

221

everything be normal.

'Who is he? Who is he?' she yelled, and she snatched up a tea towel and whacked me with it. I could feel her spittle on my chin and her hand was digging into my wrist. I turned away and as I did so I realised I was taller than her. I hadn't noticed that before; she was so huge in presence and personality, she ruled the house so it seemed impossible, but there it was. I could see the top of her head; she had to raise her chin to meet my eyes. It seemed then that after all I had some power. Boss me as she might, my body had the power to disobey her. She would never make me do as she wished again, not unless I wanted to do it.

I walked to my room and I felt stronger than I had ever felt before.

Of course, that was complete nonsense. From then on my mother would have power over me in a way I could never have dreamed of.

I stayed in my room and Dad came up later and asked who the father was, but I wouldn't say. When I opened my bedroom door, I could hear Dad downstairs weeping.

Rose

There's a big desk down the end where they all congregate for changeover. They think I can't hear what they're saying but I can, ears like a hawk I've got. No, not a hawk, hawks don't have ears...what's the thing with ears... rabbits have ears, no that's not it. Mattie was the one with rabbits, always going on bunny rabbit this, bunny rabbit that. What are they going on about Mattie and rabbits for? Now they're starting on Richie, I knew they'd be getting on to him next. It's that Irish one with the big laugh, thinks she knows everything. She's been reading my notes, thinks she knows all about Richie. But she doesn't. No one knows, no one needs to know. Len said I was wrong, but I wasn't.

Tell you what it is, he's phoned. That's why they're talking about him, he's phoned and he's on his way. I told them he'd come.

Fast asleep, and she wakes me up. What's the matter with them? Fast asleep I was.

'Rose? Do you want something for the pain, darlin'?'

I haven't got pain, just tell me when he's coming!

'She's very restless tonight. See how she is later.'

Mattie

I wheeled my case through, past all the signs for 'Mr Lawford', 'Mr Angus Prentice', and 'Miss Smelly' (surely a mis-hearing of 'Miss Melly'? I hoped so for her sake) but I couldn't see Joanie. She had said, 'Everyone says I'm the image of your mother so you're bound to recognise me,' but there was no one who looked like Mum here. I came all the way through the cordon and onto the concourse and paused to look around. Soon I was the only person left apart from an Indian woman in a sari with three children. Suddenly someone spoke behind me.

'Mattie?' I turned. The woman was small and slim. She had the family nose but Joanie used to have thick black hair falling in waves down her back. This woman's hair, though still black (as was Mum's – hardly a speck of grey in it) was short and fine and wispy, like a baby's. Either the person who told her she looked like Mum was given to exaggeration, or Mum had changed out of all recognition in the last five years.

I said, 'Joanie?' although what I really thought was that this was some other relative come in her place.

She nodded, and her eyes were filling, and her mouth was struggling to hold the smile. Now she reminded me not of Mum but of Nanny though Nanny would have been far younger than this when last I saw her. Joanie was old. I felt foolish and unkind for all the childhood resentments I'd saved up against her. It was more than twenty years since I had sent her the miserly piece of wedding cake but I blushed for it.

I said, 'How's Mum?' She nodded indicating that she was satisfactory, but her eyes were still brimming and I didn't know whether that was out of emotion at seeing me or sadness at Mum's condition. I hesitated, wondering whether to embrace Joanie and in the hesitation the moment passed. I stepped back and she turned to a grey-haired man hovering behind her. He was tall and upright, smiling but uncertain. 'Des, look lively. Come and give Mattie a hand with these bags.' She sounded exactly like Mum did when she used to boss Dad and as she turned back to me there was Mum in her smile.

As we walked to the car she told me how Mum was and they took me straight to the hospital.

Her face was a waxy yellow and her lips had lost their colour. She was always a big woman, not fat but ruddy-cheeked and healthy. Her hand, resting on the hospital sheet, was a bony claw.

I turned to a woman who sat by the bed leafing through a magazine. Her hair was cut into a neat grey bob and she wore a peach blouse with a dark skirt and court shoes.

224

'Mattie?' she said, rising to greet me. 'You must be exhausted, come and sit down.' She pulled up a chair for me. This must be my aunt Marian. She was between Joanie and Mum in age but I'd hardly known her, she moved away before I was born. 'She's asleep now but she was awake earlier. She's been very poorly but she's picking up. It's sure to make a difference now you're here.'

I didn't answer. 'Speak to her, she's sure to respond to your voice.'

Clearly Mum hadn't given them much idea of our relationship. 'Mum? Mum, can you hear me?' I leant over her, checking she was breathing, and I could see her chest moving up and down the merest fraction. She opened her eyes, then closed them again. I didn't know if she recognised me or not.

Marian's detached four-bedroomed house was on the other side of town from where Mum and Joanie lived. I had barely noticed the landscape on the drive from the airport, but now I was struck by the narrowness of the roads and that the sun was shining.

'I thought it would be colder,' I said, already regretting that I hadn't brought more of my lightweight summer clothes. I thought I'd need to buy cosy long sleeved sweaters here, maybe even a coat.

'It's warm for autumn,' said Marian, stopping at a junction so suddenly I almost hit my head on the windscreen. 'It's not always like this. Though it's certainly warmer than when you were a child. No central heating, do you remember? Everyone had chilblains. When I was a child they used to sew you into your winter clothes.'

I remembered chilblains. Fat red lumps on your toes,

that itched so badly Auntie Joanie would cut my fingernails to stop me tearing at them. She used to rub them with an ointment that looked like earwax.

We passed a park, lush and green, but so familiar, it was almost like being in Brisbane. Some of the trees were even the same. I should have expected that, it's not as if we didn't see English TV programmes. But seeing it for real was different. And so different from the little I remembered. No bomb sites, no rain.

'I don't suppose you remember much about where you used to live – certainly it was nothing like this,' Marian said, a hint of pride in her voice. 'This is very much the up-market end. We might not own the land your family had in Australia but we've done all right for ourselves.'

I'd always known mum was in competition with her sisters but I hadn't thought that maybe they were also in competition with her. Or maybe it was mum's boastful letters that had done that. Or perhaps it was just Marian, she did have a hint of the snob about her. But if she wanted me to be impressed, I would act impressed. It was kind of her to put me up, and acting impressed was a small price to pay. Besides, maybe I would be impressed.

The house was modern and squeezed into a cul de sac of others of similar styles. As we pulled in to the drive Marian remarked that hers was the largest of the six houses. She opened the front door with a flourish. The wide hall was immaculate, with carefully placed china ornaments and objet d'art on the radiator shelf.

'It's kind of you to let me stay,' I said, as I followed her upstairs. 'And at such short notice.' I was glad I wasn't to go to Mum's house. She wouldn't have liked me poking about in her things and anyway I didn't want to be there alone. Better to be somewhere with other people.

'My pleasure and I'm lucky to get you – if Joanie's grandchildren hadn't been staying she'd have insisted you went there, but her house is much smaller than this, you'll have more room here. But I'd have had to give in because she was far closer to you all than I was.'

'Well, that was all a long time ago.'

She paused on the landing and smiled. 'To you, maybe. Time moves differently as you get older.'

'I am getting older,' I said. 'I'm nearly as old as Nanny must have been when we left.' We were both silent for a moment, reflecting. Nanny had seemed so old. But she must only have been in her fifties, that's all.

She led the way into my room. Immaculate magnolia paintwork; duvet of snowy white with a broderie anglais edging. 'Women seemed older in those days. My mother – Nanny - always seemed old to me, but that's how it was. They had hard lives and it tired them out earlier.'

'Mum has had a hard life,' I said.

'I suppose she has. She never complained though, it was what she wanted. I don't think Nanny ever had what she wanted.' She laughed suddenly. 'Perhaps that's why she complained all the time.'

'Beautiful room.'

'I'm glad to have someone use it, to be honest. My sister-in-law comes sometimes but that's all. It's nice to have some company in the house.'

'It's a big house just for you.'

'I keep thinking of down-sizing, but I like the garden and the neighbours are good. Being on your own you need that. And I'm a long way from needing warden assisted and all that.' She paused, embarrassed perhaps

227

because it was likely that this was exactly what Mum would need. She straightened a curtain. 'Poor old Rose. She's been very happy in that little house.'

I unzipped my case while I considered the implications. I'd steeled myself for the worst to happen, but in my heart I thought this was all a false alarm and she'd make a full recovery. She'd soon be back in her house, waving goodbye as I left for the airport.

'You look exhausted,' said Marian. 'Why don't you have a lie down and I'll bring you a cup of tea?'

But there was too much to think about, I couldn't have rested. I said I'd change and be straight down. After she had gone I took out the picture of Richie and put it on the bedside cabinet.

I picked up my phone to call Henry but it wasn't his number that I dialled, and when I heard the voice I knew it wasn't an accident.

Chapter 15

Rose

It's so noisy in here, they let visitors in any old time of day. Mattie has already gone but Joanie and Marian haven't taken the hint. Joanie keeps saying, 'We'll just give it another minute, see if she stirs.'

I was drifting off again, all warm and peaceful and then I heard Marian say, 'Mattie's got a picture of Richie. I took her in a cup of tea and I saw it on her bedside table.'

Suddenly I was wide awake but I kept my eyes closed.

'What does he look like now?' asked Joanie

'It's not recent, it's when he was in his teens. Don't you think it's a bit odd?'

'No, I've got photos all over the place. The grandchildren, Sian's wedding pictures. There's even one of you from when we had that day out.'

'No, I mean, that she hasn't got any others. None of Bobby, or his children. Not even one of her husband.'

'Not surprised from what Rose has said about him.'

And then they were getting their coats on. I listened as hard as I could in case there was any more but when I peeped out they were already half way down the ward, and laughing now, Richie forgotten about.

I felt a pang for Mattie. I knew that photograph, I had the same one. It was taken at Richie's birthday party, before Len fell ill, before all the unpleasantness. Richie was happy then. We all were.

Richie was the darlingest little baby. He had a mass of hair when he was born, black as night. He lost it in a fortnight and it grew back blonde and that's how it stayed. He had tough little limbs even as a newborn, and the grip of ten men. He held my finger tight as tight and I thought it's all right, Little'un, I won't ever let you go, not ever.

His first cot was just a drawer but that wasn't unusual back then and I didn't see the sense in buying something fancy even though Mum had sent some money and that's what Mattie said we should get, as though he was some little doll to be played with. She used to carry him round the farm in her arms, pointing out the chickens and the pigs, singing him little songs.

They were my happiest years, on the farm with Richie running around in his rompers. I've still got his first pair of shoes, though I've never been one to be sentimental. Once Richie was born, the fact was if nothing else had gone right with us emigrating, then just having him would have made it worthwhile. Whenever I picked him up a little shiver of love went through me. I can get it back just remembering.

Sometimes I'd be rushing down for the milking or getting the eggs, or just getting a meal ready for when Len would be in – and I'd catch sight of Richie playing with the toy farm that Len made and I'd stop and think, this is what it's all been for. We're all here, and we're doing well, and we've got everything we wanted.

When he was fourteen months I couldn't wait any longer to show him off, and we finally went home, back to England. It was the ideal time, not only was there Richie for them to admire, but we were buying the farm after years of renting. Len came as well. Not Mattie, she was at work by then, and we needed Bobby to help out on the farm. Eddie was there but he couldn't manage on his own.

I did feel bad not taking the kids along. It seemed mean to be spending all that money on the fare and not include them. But how could we?   We couldn't take Bobby and leave Mattie behind. And we couldn't take Mattie, because who knows what she'd come out with? Len said who cares what your mother thinks, let them come. But I couldn't, I'd look a proper Charlie if Mattie started opening her mouth. But I did feel bad about it.

Richie was as good as gold on the plane. I'd given him a little drop of brandy – just a touch on his tongue – to make him sleep, and each time he seemed like he might get a bit fractious I gave him another little taste. Worked like a dream.

But he was wide awake and squirming out of my arms as I carried him down the basement steps to my mother's. The handrail was rusty and if my hands hadn't been as tough as old boots I don't think I could have held on, the stairs were that steep. I don't know how Mum and Dad managed, especially if it was icy.   As I got to the bottom the door opened and Richie gave a sudden lurch. I almost fell down the last step, and Richie flew straight into Mum's arms.

'My, but you're a big boy,' she said. She held him out

to look at him but he was fighting to get down and she stood him on the bottom step laughing. 'You were just like that!' she said, wistful. 'Always wanting to get down and run about.' He pushed past her legs and toddled up the hallway to meet Dad who was on his way from the scullery. Dad leant down and scooped him up and this time Richie let himself be held. He always preferred men. He pulled on Dad's moustache. 'Giddy,' he said. It was an all purpose word that could mean anything from dog to ice-cream, but Dad thought he was saying 'Grandaddy' and was enchanted. He carried him up the garden and I knew he'd be taking him to see the chickens, forgetting that Richie was at least as familiar with chickens as he was.

After they'd gone my mother looked at me. Then she put her arms out and hugged me, without a sound. I hugged her back awkwardly. We'd never been affectionate.

'He's a poppet and no mistake,' she said.

'Len, she's talking about you,' I said, teasing. Len put the cases in the hall and followed her into the living room. 'Where's my girl?' he said. His hug for my mother was everything mine hadn't been. Mum wept. 'Oh but I've missed you,' she said.

Len sat down at the square oak table that filled the centre of the room. It was still protected by an old velveteen table cover in maroon and navy blue, same as ever. The colours were different but otherwise it was identical to what she'd used since I was a child. I'd always thought they were ugly and age hadn't improved them. The table underneath, I knew, would still be pristine, and destined to stay that way. My mother didn't plan to have anyone damage it or even set eyes on it in her lifetime.

I sat in the old armchair by the fireside and looked

around to see what had changed. The house seemed to have shrunk, though otherwise it was the same as when we'd lived there, only older and more drab. There was no carpet on the stairs. I'd forgotten that. When she first moved in she wouldn't have any put down because she wasn't staying.

'Are you still planning to move?' I said.

'Can't stay here,' Mum said. 'With all this damp.' It was like I'd never been gone.

There were black and white photos of Mattie and Bobby on the heavy Victorian sideboard, of a day out they'd had with Mum and Joanie shortly before we left. And there was one in colour of Joanie's girls, and one of Michael's son. Outside in the garden, the sun was bright and harsh, made your eyes ache to look at it, but not bright enough to light up the scullery, or this room, which was joined to the scullery by permanently open French doors.

Mum busied about at the sink and then came back with mugs of tea on a tray. The mugs had thick lips and heavy handles, but for all that, two of them were chipped and one had a crack down its length. She was always heavy handed washing up. I watched her as she set the mugs down. She was going grey, and her once thick hair seemed, like baby hair. She was fatter round the middle, but her arms and wrists were like sticks. She had bunions, great fat things that pushed out through the hole she had cut in her slippers. A pair of maroon shoes sat by the hearth, so misshapen they looked as though her bunions were still in them.

'So how's my Mattie and Bobby?' Her eyes were shining and I could see how Len and me being here was bringing the children closer. It was Mattie and Bobby she really wanted to see. Bobby didn't have any memories of England, and only a hazy recollection of his grandparents, so it made sense for him to stay and help Eddie on the farm. I felt mean though, when I looked at Mum, seeing her face all hope-filled remembering. But what's done is done.

We got out our photos and she had a few tears when she saw Mattie and Bobby, and stroked them gently, as though she was touching their cheeks. 'Shame they couldn't have come too,' she said. 'I bet Bobby would have loved it. He could have gone over the park with Dad.'

'Mum, he's a teenager!' I said. 'The only place he might want to go with Dad is to the pub.'

After we'd drunk some of Mum's horrible tea – she added sugar whether you wanted it or not – she said, 'I've got something to show you. Wait till you see this!' She beckoned me through to the scullery. At first glance it looked the same, with the old brown shallow sink and the wooden draining board, but then I noticed that where there used to be a cupboard, there was a spin dryer. Michael had bought that for her, and he'd promised her a washing machine if she wanted one, but she wasn't sure about that because she'd have to lose another cupboard. 'And I don't see the point of it really – what's a bit of washing?' I had to watch while she took the lid off and then showed me how the dryer worked. I'd been planning to tell her that I was getting a washing machine – well, I'd been thinking about it anyway – and looking forward to how impressed she'd be but now that was spoiled. She told me Michael and Joanie said they could share the cost of putting in central heating but I pointed out that radiators take up a lot of room and you can burn yourself on them if you're not careful. I didn't like the idea of Joanie and Michael lording it over me. As I pointed out, all the pipes would have to run along the floor and the walls, she wouldn't want that. Mum said she hadn't thought about that and she'd tell them she wasn't interested.

'He's a sturdy little boy,' she said, looking out of the scullery window to where Richie was crouching down picking something out of the dirt. 'Who does he take after, would you say?'

'Mum, he's adopted!' I said, quick as winking. 'He doesn't take after any of us.'

'They say they grow to look like their adopted family, don't they?' She looked from me to Len. Len looked away and picked up Dad's newspaper from the table.

'That's dogs and their owners, isn't it?' I said. Mum said she thought it was both and I agreed just so she would shut up about it.

Later, while we ate bacon and eggs and Richie had a nap on the sofa, she mouthed, 'Do you know who his real parents were?' I wasn't sure if she was sounding me out, looking for me to slip up, so I just went over what I'd said in my letters.

She shook her head sadly. 'Poor little lad. He's bound to want to know who his real parents are when he grows up, isn't he?'

Len gave me such a look but I ignored it. Then he got up and went outside for a smoke.

There was a heat wave that month and the humidity in my mother's house was stifling. The air was as still as if a storm was threatening. On our second day we went round

235

to Joanie and Des's new house – a town house terrace - they were doing it up themselves. Des was a bus driver, and Joanie had never worked full time but still they'd managed it. It didn't seem right to me; Joanie and Marian had got everything just by sitting on their backsides doing nothing. Mum said Joanie worked hard. She was a waitress! How hard could that be? Let her try milking seven days a week and see how she got on. Len said you can't think like that but I thought it anyway.

Marian and Reg arrived and they wanted to hear all about the kids and see where we lived or they said they did, but what they really wanted was to tell us about what they'd been doing and how much better they had done by comparison with us. Reg had been studying for his accountancy exams when we left, and now he had his own practice and they lived in a detached house backing on to a little stream. I told her all about the house we were planning to build – how we'd been renting the farm but the owner had decided to sell. So we were going to knock down the old house, which was a bit ramshackle and build a bungalow.

Mum said, 'A bungalow!' I knew she'd be impressed with that. A bungalow had always been the height of affluence to her.

From the minute we'd emigrated, I'd tried to fit in, tried to think of myself as Australian, but it always felt like just that, like I was trying. But now it was obvious that's what we were. I said to Len, 'Instead of whingeing Poms, we sound like whingeing Aussies – full of how much better everything is there than here.'

And Len said, 'But it is better!'

Len? Are you here, Len? They say the dead come to greet you when your time's up. I can hear a whispering now and then but I don't think that's Len. Why would he whisper? He had a loud voice, hearty. If he was here he'd be saying, 'Now then Rosie, chin up, it might never happen.' But it has, Len. It happened a long time ago.

After Dad died Mum told me she sensed his presence in the house. I said, 'Where?' She said, not exactly *in* the house, more by the outside privy. I said, 'He'll be still waiting for his turn then.' He always complained we took too long. But by this time she had an indoor one, I don't know why he'd still be standing out there in the cold.

I can't say I ever sensed Len around after he died. It was a relief to tell you the truth, after seeing him so ill. If I did ever sense him close I'd have a few words to say to him, I can tell you. 'What did you do it for?' I'd say. 'Were you born stupid, or did someone teach you?'

I think he's keeping out of my way. He knows when I get to the other side he's going to get a proper earful.

They finally discharged me. About time too. I told them, the only way you're going to keep me in hospital is to tie my kangaroo down, sport. They didn't get the joke. No sense of humour. And not that they'd have taken any notice of what I wanted anyway. But they had some emergencies come in and they needed the beds. I'm probably the only person in the entire country who is grateful there's a bed shortage.

Mattie is staying with me for a few days, just till I get back on my feet, as she puts it. Not that there's anything wrong with my feet, not that the chiropodist can't sort out. But the doctor wouldn't have let me come home without someone in the house so lucky for me that she could come. She has lost a bit of weight since I last saw her but it suits her. I always say you look younger with a bit of fat on your face. Fills the wrinkles out. But she hasn't got any wrinkles. She gets that from me. I had a lovely complexion before I got ill, my face was smooth as a baby's bottom. A pretty old baby admittedly.

But I've lost a lot of weight with all this hospital malarkey. When I lift my arm up the skin flaps around like an empty carrier bag blowing in the wind. And I've got jowls now. My mother had jowls.

We had scrambled eggs for lunch. Not as good as eggs from your own hens but she'd done her best.

'I thought Henry might have come over with you,' I said, shaking some salt on the eggs. She was never any good with seasoning. As I said it I wondered if she'd think I was having a dig at him. I wasn't but we have to tip toe round each other a bit. It always feels like we might be on the verge of falling out.

'He's got a lot on at the moment,' she said.

'Just thought he might have liked to come. Busy with his work is he?' Now it definitely sounded like I was having a dig. She looked up and she was waiting for me to say he wouldn't know hard work if it came up and bit him, just because that's what I used to say. But he was her husband and it wasn't for me to criticise, not when she had put herself out to be here. And whatever I thought about the beardy waste of space, he was her choice and you could bet your life she'd rather be there with him than here cooking scrambled egg for a miserable old cow like me. So I stuffed some toast in and kept quiet.

After lunch Mattie told me that Joanie and Marian were coming to tea. Apparently she thought it would be a treat for me. I ask you, what sort of treat is it to have your sisters call round? One or other of them was round every day in that hospital – a treat would be not having them call round.

She means well, I know, thinks a bit of company will take me out of myself, but I don't want taking out of myself, I'm perfectly happy as I am, thanks all the same. Anyway, I said, that's not the point is it? She said, Well, what is the point and I told her, The point is I had it all marked out to watch Columbo this afternoon and now I'll miss it. She said it's not like you haven't got a video, I'll record it, you can watch it later. But I don't want to watch it later, I'll be watching Corrie then. Columbo only works if you watch it in the afternoon, otherwise you notice what a load of old rubbish it is.

So anyway there's a knock at the door and Joanie rolls in, loaded up with cake tins and goodness knows what, anyone would think we were starving and she's wasting her time because Mattie's on a diet and sultanas give me wind. In no time Marian is tucking into the cake. I don't know how she keeps her figure (any more than I know how she walks in those shoes).

'How is Henry managing without you?' Marian asks Mattie when we're having our tea. 'You must be so proud, being married to a doctor.'

I have to avoid looking at Joanie because she knows my opinion: well, I ask you, calls himself a doctor but what sort of doctor is it that can't write you a prescription? Mattie always tells me, 'He's a doctor of philosophy' like I wouldn't know the difference. She thinks just because I didn't go to college I'm stupid. Always got his nose in a book pretending he was working. How can you call reading a book working? They never had any children. I'd told Joanie, I don't reckon he knew where to put it. Len thought he was all right, but that was Len all over, seeing the best in everyone. Look at Dirty Dinah!

So Joanie is telling us about something Des did when he tried to work the washing machine and we're having a laugh and I'm just thinking this isn't so bad, and what do you know, they start on about Richie, wanting to know where he is, and what he's up to and everything. I should have known he'd be next on the agenda. I look at Mattie and I know she's going to open her mouth, so I try to catch her eye, but she's cut herself some cake, diet or no diet, and then she starts on about how long it is since she heard from him! What choice do I have? I chuck the cup in the air and there's tea all down me, all down my nice clean skirt, and over the chair, spots on the carpet and everything. Fortunately the skirt is polyester, and the dralon's had worse on it so I just had to cross my fingers it would sponge off.

They rush about getting kitchen towel and checking I've not scalded myself with the tea and by the time they've mopped everything they've forgotten about Richie. But why she can't keep her mouth shut I do not know. She knows I don't want her talking about him. What's done is done, no sense upsetting the applecart now.

But the truth is, I don't understand why he doesn't get in touch. Whatever we did, we thought it was for the best. He knew we loved him. Maybe he'll come for the millennium. I think he will, I've got a good feeling about it. Millenniums don't come round very often, you'd want to be with your family. I've told Mattie, it's my dying wish to see him again. She said, Mum, you don't get to have a dying wish until you're dying.

Why doesn't he get in touch?

Len and Bobby took Richie fishing as soon as he was old enough. Len said they never caught anything if Richie was along because he was so excited he'd be running up and down shouting. On the way home sometimes Len would buy a fish and Richie would come running in with it, dripping blood and guts across the floor, and pretend he'd caught it himself. I always made out I was impressed and amazed, and he loved that. I'd cook it for our tea and while he ate he'd be saying how delicious it was, exchanging looks with Len and Bobby and laughing, thinking I didn't know.

He was so kind when Len was ill. He was a teenager by then. A young boy shouldn't have to see his father like that. He'd take him out in his wheelchair down to the shops, or out for a drive. Richie isn't big built, but there was nothing of Len by then, and he'd heft Len up and settle him in the front seat. Sometimes I'd go but mostly it was the two of them. Richie would say, 'I'll take him out, it'll give you a break, Mum' but that wasn't the reason. He liked to be alone with his Dad, talking over whatever it was they used to talk about. Once Len started going downhill he relied on Richie for everything, well, we both did.

It's history repeating itself, Mattie rushing over to see me, thinking I'm going to pop off. She doesn't say so but I know that's why she came. Same as I came rushing over when my mum was ill. I don't suppose Mattie wants to see me, any more than I wanted to see my mum but it's good that she's come. It looks bad if you only turn up for the funeral. I've got no time for those people who come creeping round when you're dead who wouldn't give you the skin off their rice pudding when you were alive. Buying flowers you're never going to see. Get them something now, while they can enjoy it, that's what I say. And not flowers either, waste of money they are.

So like Mattie, I came back to England when Mum was at death's door and would you believe it, she started picking up on the instant I arrived and was back in her own house within a fortnight. Len said I'd cured her, I said No, she's got better just to spite me! I bet that's what Mattie's thinking!

My mum was so much better and I had a few weeks left on my return ticket, so I booked a coach trip to the Lake District. Might as well make the most of the time, never been that far north before. I made my mind up while I was away that I wanted to talk to Mum, about what she'd done all those years before. To have it out once for all. And then have done with it.

But while I was away she had a downturn. I walked in and there was her dinner still on the table from days before, and food going off in the fridge. When she saw me she thought I was her mother; the next day I was her sister and then she thought she was a girl again and Dad was still alive. Two days later, I was getting her a bit of lunch when I heard her neighbour shouting. I ran out and the rain was throwing it down and there was Mum lying on the basement steps. She must have wanted to go out and slipped and toppled backwards, there was blood in her hair and on the step. While I sat with her, holding an umbrella over our heads and waiting for the ambulance to come, she came round and started to speak. She said, 'Rosie, Rosie, you know I meant it for the best,' and I held her hand and I said, 'It's all right, Mum...'

She didn't really say that; she never regained consciousness. That's life for you.

Chapter 16

Mattie

At the traffic lights Marian leaned over to look in the mirror and dabbed at her lipstick with her little finger. Her silver hair swung as she moved. I'd moved back in with her – Mum said she wanted to see how she managed by herself which was a surprisingly diplomatic way for her to tell me to push off - and I reckoned I could go home in a few days. In the meantime I might as well enjoy the trip. We were on our way to the theatre. The play was 'The Dolls House' which Marian described as 'one of those plays with a lot of talking in them.' I was excited to be going to a real English theatre. 'Typical Victorian architecture, very ornate. A bit too fussy really. Very old fashioned.' Marian said it as though that was a bad thing

'It's not easy being married a long time, I know,' Marian was saying. She had got on to the subject of her late husband Reg and how in many ways life had taken a more interesting turn since he had died. Marian now found herself free to develop a whole new social life whereas when Reg was alive he only wanted to sit at home and study his coin collection and have her in attendance while he did it.

'That's really not fair, is it,' I said. 'In a marriage, you should both be able to follow your interests.'

'Well, of course in an ideal world,' she answered. 'But marriage is all about compromise, isn't it. One of you has to give in.'

It was just the sort of thing I always said myself. But hearing it coming back at me, I realised I no longer believed it. Why shouldn't you both get what you wanted? Wasn't that fair?

She paused at traffic lights and I gazed out at the narrow terraced houses. Yellowing net curtains fluttered at the window of one, its peeling paintwork in contrast to the pristine brick cladding which fronted the houses to either side. Litter was blowing in the street, and a school boy grabbed his classmate by the shoulders and tried to push him in to the road. Marian hooted and braked, and the car stalled.

'But you and Henry seem to have made a go of it.'

'Oh yes, we muddle along,' I said.

'That's as much as any of us can do,' she said, starting the engine up again. 'Once you've made your life with someone you might as well stick to it. I can't imagine having the energy to start over again with someone else, can you? All that upheaval!'

I laughed along with her though there was nothing funny about the efforts Henry and I had made to rejuvenate our flagging sex life. At one time Suzanne had started cutting out relevant features for me from her magazines and I read them to Henry as he sat perusing some worthy tome in bed at night. He raised his eyes heavenward at the one about pretending you were strangers meeting at a hotel, just as he did at the one about eating food off each other or that I should meet him at the door wrapped in clingfilm.   It was a relief that he felt like that; I couldn't see that eating stuffed olives from Henry's navel with the line of grizzled grey hair over his belly or having my breasts flattened by see-through plastic would do the trick.

But we followed advice that involved romantic weekends in expensive hotels, candlelit dinners and holidays by the sea. We enjoyed the locations even if we rarely enjoyed each other. As I gazed into his eyes through a haze of candle smoke, I would hear myself discussing what work needed doing on the house – Henry was no handyman and there was a never ending list – mending the fence, cutting the hedges, redecorating the utility room. As we walked briskly by the sea, passing couples who wandered more leisurely hand in hand, he would describe his latest research project, his hopes for his next book, the shortcomings of the latest batch of students.

'If you ate ice cream for thirty years you'd get bored with it,' Suzanne liked to say. 'There's more chance of me having an orgasm driving over a bumpy road than with Neil.' But sex isn't only about orgasm. Neil and Suzanne were friends, they did things together, had fun. They teased each other, laughed at the same things. They cared about each other.

Suzanne counselled against comparing sexual fantasies with Henry but she was too late. Henry's sexual fantasy was a dull affair, more concerned with it being carried out in a forbidden place like the library reading room than with the detail of what was done there. There must surely have been more to it than he was willing to reveal   - perhaps the reading room was peopled with blonde nymphets reading out glowing reviews of his latest work.

Suzanne said, 'Why don't you say you fantasise about him dressing up like a French maid? At least you could get the cleaning done.'

'What are you laughing about?' asked Marian, bringing me back to the present.

'Men,' I said, not wanting to go into details.

'Oh I know,' she said. 'But you have to feel sorry for them, they can't help it.'

I agreed, and I did feel sorry for Henry. And I felt most sorry for him every time I thought of Dan.

Six months ago: I was visiting Dorothy. She was on holiday at Noosa, so I drove up for the day, it's less than a couple of hours from home. I used to come here with Henry when we were first married. The national park is right on the ocean, we used to walk for hours, that's how he got interested in bird-watching. And the beaches are spectacular, though Henry was never much of a one for swimming. He would sit with a book while I took a dip.

It was a few years since I'd seen Dot. Her face was a patchwork of lines, crisscrossing her cheeks. The sun hadn't been kind to her.

I had no idea that Dan was staying with her until he walked in carrying a bottle of wine and baguettes for our lunch. Dorothy laughed to see my astonishment. 'Didn't you realise he was here?' She gave him a squeeze. 'He drove me. He's a good boy to his old mum!'

Dan grinned and placed the wine on the table. 'Sophie is coming too,' Dorothy added. 'Both my Seeds of the Empire together again.'

Dan turned to me in that same old languid way, and held his arms out to me. 'Come here,' he said, and we hugged.

Dorothy had run out of milk so after lunch I walked down to the shops with him. The pavement was bustling with holiday-makers and it felt strange, not just to be with him, but to be with him where there were other people. We had only ever met on our farm, or at his mother's quiet bungalow but I was glad of the other people and the boutiques, the swimwear shops. It made it easier to make conversation.

'Do you want a coffee?' he said and even though I didn't I said I did. We sat at a pavement cafe, our chairs positioned facing outwards, ostensibly watching the bronzed and the beautiful pass by. He sat with his long legs stretched out, his arms folded across his chest, looking into the distance more than at me. I wondered if that was because the sun had been unkind to me as it had to Dorothy. Certainly I didn't have the skin of a sixteen year old any more and definitely not the figure, whereas he was still toned, and the few lines around his eyes and his mouth were enhancing rather than the opposite. The cappuccino machine frothed and hummed as we talked of our respective family members, what we had done in the ensuing years. And then we should have gone back. Dorothy would be waiting; maybe Sophie would have arrived. But he made no move to go and neither did I.

Maybe it was talking of Dad's illness, of Richie's sudden disappearance that made it feel like a day for sharing confidences.

He turned to look at me. 'Are you happy? Has life been good to you?'

It was so unexpected I couldn't think what to say. 'Yes, I think so. Yes, definitely. I've been lucky.'

'Me too. Bitch I was married to left me, that was a stroke of luck!' He must have noticed my shocked expression because he put his hand on my arm. 'Just kidding! She wasn't really a bitch, or not all the time. But she did leave me and that saved me the trouble of leaving her. But I wish I could get those years back. Do you ever feel like that?'

I'd never thought of it like that, but it gave me a sense of unease, not only that there were years I'd wasted but maybe there were years I was going to go on wasting.

'Five years thrown away in that marriage, and another four being a Seed of the Empire. That's a lot of years.' He picked up a sachet of sugar and shook it against the table. 'Did I ever tell you about that?'

In the years since I'd first heard him mention the term I'd read about the children shipped over here from British children's homes. Of the establishments run by nuns who strapped you if they found you sucking your thumb in the night; how everyone had to sleep facing the same way, on the right hand side so their hearts were closer to God; of boys who had to build a two storey building, lifting heavy stones up scaffolding, boys with no shoes, unprotected from the poisonous building materials. Boys whose records were misplaced or who were given the wrong ones, children who would never be able to trace their origins however hard they tried because their records no longer existed.

He signalled for another coffee, raising a questioning

eyebrow at me but I shook my head. I wanted to go. Dorothy would be waiting. Why spoil it with ugly memories.

'They told us we were going on holiday,' he said. 'They said they were giving us a new start. And their version of that was to separate everyone up. Brothers, sisters, all separated. When the boat docked and we started disembarking the screaming was what you heard first.'

'Dan – ' I put my hand out tentatively to his. The mood of the afternoon had changed, I wanted to stop now. I was sorry for whatever I'd said that had unearthed this outpouring. And it was beginning to rain. We were sheltered by the awning but beachgoers were running to their cars, holding towels over their heads.

'We were lucky though,' he went on, 'somehow Sophie and I ended up at the same place. We didn't see much of each other but at least we knew we weren't alone.'

Dan paused while the waiter set his coffee down. 'We were known by a number not a name,' he said. 'I was eighty-seven. Why would people do that to kids? If you wet the bed, they put the blanket over your head and made you walk around like that until it dried. They told us no one wanted us and our mothers were dead and that's why we'd been sent away. I knew that wasn't true. On the other hand you'd think: well, why did she send us here? You think your mother can do anything. You don't think you can be sent away and she knows nothing about it.'

He was silent, stirring his coffee. I had the sense he was barely aware I was still here. I said, 'Do you think we should be on our way? Dorothy will be wondering where we are.'

He stood up, the muscles in his jaw tense. I glanced around and realised the café was virtually empty. It had been buzzing earlier, but I'd hardly noticed people leaving.

'You can't blame the Aussies,' he said. 'They thought they were giving homeless kids a new beginning. It's the people who shipped us off without a second thought who are to blame. People say to me, why didn't you ever go back to Britain? But how could we? That's where the bastards all lived.'

I thought perhaps some of the people running the homes might share some of the blame for their cruelty. But he was telling his story, not asking for a balanced discussion. We stood looking out at the rain that was now a heavy downpour, measuring the distance if we made a dash for it.

He nodded across the road. 'Once we cross over we're mostly sheltered until we get to the hotel entrance.' He took my hand, ready to cross. 'Sorry for all that,' he said. 'Haven't talked about it since I was a kid. Somehow you brought it all back.'

Vehicles were trundling past in a steady stream from the car park but a gap was coming up. 'Okay, now!' he said and we both ran.

Rose

My neighbour called the doctor in today all because when she came round with my Daily Express I hadn't got my slippers on. As if that's any reason to call the doctor. I said it's only a bit of swollen ankles, it's not as if my leg's dropped off. She said she thought I'd had a turn. I said, is that the medical term for not being able to get your slippers on? She didn't laugh. No sense of humour.

Mattie had arrived by the time the doctor came. I was sorry now I'd sent her back to stay with Marian, but we're not comfortable together, no point pretending we are.

The doctor said, 'And how are you coping generally?' I thought: better than you from the look of you. His eyes were all bloodshot and his cuffs were frayed. Either he's on the bottle or his wife's left him. Course I didn't say anything. He wouldn't know a joke if you poked him in the eye with one which from the look of him someone might have done. I told him there was some bicarb in the cupboard and he could bathe them if he wanted. (I didn't really, you can't afford to offend these medical people, they'll have you back in hospital before you know what's hit you.)

I said I was managing very well. And, I said, you needn't think you're getting me into one of those homes. I've seen some of those granny stackers, all the chairs round in a circle like some great Indian pow wow. The television on all day with the sound turned down, smelling of wee and cabbage. Mrs Hazel from down the road went in one and when I called in she was in a queue with five other old souls, all in wheelchairs. I said what's going on? And the matron or whatever she calls herself came hurrying over saying, don't mind them, they're just waiting for toileting.

If I ever go incontinent, I'm going to get those paddy knickers, like a baby's nappy. I might get some anyway, save getting up for the lav in the middle of Corrie.

When Richie phoned I told him if I'm ever so gaga I have to sit in a queue for toileting, just hit me over the head and have done with it. Well, that's what I'll say when he does phone anyway.

'No one is talking about a home,' the doctor said. 'I'll ask the district nurse to call in,' he said. 'Have you got meals on wheels?'

Well I hadn't and the day I need them you can take me out and shoot me, but he meant well so I tried to look interested. Apparently there's two sorts of meals on wheels now, they can bring them to you all ready to eat, or they can bring you frozen dinners like you buy in Iceland, or in Waitrose if you've got a pension the size of the Bank of England. I asked what sort of thing they were and he said there'd be shepherd's pie, or fish and chips or Irish stew. And a pudding. Very reasonably priced, he said, and I thought I bet they're not as reasonable as scrambled egg and a banana off the market. He said they were all very nice. I said, have you tried them then? Course, he hadn't but he said a lot of his patients had and loved them. I said, 'Would these be the same patients who love the Homes you think so much of, and who are so gaga they get put in a queue for toileting?' He said he'd write me a prescription and that I should make sure I got some gentle exercise.

'You need to keep moving about, that's the best thing for swollen ankles.'

I pointed out that keeping them up would be the best thing surely, otherwise everything just drains down into them. That's gravity. But they weren't listening. He said once Mattie had gone back to Oz I might need some help and he could arrange for someone to help me into bed at night. And to be there when I got up in the morning. I thought: Eddie would jump at the chance! But I didn't say anything.

'It's probably a good idea,' Mattie said. 'When I came

yesterday, you'd only just had your breakfast and that was almost midday.'

'I'd had a lie in. I don't know what you think I have to get up for. I'm entitled to it, I've worked all my life.'

Mattie sighed. Dr Red-eye sighed. I sighed, just to be sociable. He adopted an 'I'm the doctor, I know best' face. 'You have to keep your strength up, so you can't go missing meals. If someone helped you get going in the mornings, life would be easier for you.'

I remembered the times I'd be getting up early on the farm, feeling half dead if I'd been working late the night before. Sliding out of bed, moving around the room with my eyes half shut, falling asleep in the middle of milking. Shame I didn't have people around to make life easier for me then, when I really needed it.

'We can get you a little safe for keeping a spare front door key in,' he said. 'They fix it on the wall outside. I'll get you a leaflet.' He had leaflets for everything, that one. 'Then when the carers come they can let themselves in. There's a special code, only the carers' organisation would have it. It saves you getting up to answer the door.'

'I thought I was supposed to keep moving about?'

He said he'd get me a leaflet anyway and off he went. I still can't get my slippers on though. You have to laugh, don't you?

Mattie

Joanie knows about Richie. She hasn't said as much but I see it in her face, a look of expectancy when his name comes up. She is waiting for me to say something, to confirm what she already knows.

Dad knew that Joanie would work it out for herself.

He and Mum quarrelled about it, when it was first discussed: Mum's Great Plan. She was so determined, so adamant that everyone would believe what they were told. I can see them now, in the newly painted kitchen, Mum, arms akimbo, with those yellow gingham curtains behind her, those curtains she was so proud of.

Dad said, 'Just tell them the truth. It'll be a shock at first but they'll get used to the idea and that will be the end of it.'

She said they would never get used to it. That it was something they would hold over me forever, and not just me, but her too.

Dad said, 'But your family are thousands of miles away – even if they did, what would it matter?'

She said it mattered to her. And all the time the argument was going on around me I was dreading the moment one of them would say: 'We'll put it up for adoption. That will solve everything.' Because then who would know there had ever been a baby? We rarely saw our neighbours, and certainly none of the family in England would ever find out. I stood still while the battle raged around me, afraid that if I spoke or moved they would think of it for themselves.

But adoption was never mentioned. Not then, not ever.

Mum devised a story about a cousin whom I was to stay with during the last months of her pregnancy to help look after her children. Then we were to say – when I reappeared with a baby – that the cousin had died and the father couldn't cope with the new baby so Mum and Dad had agreed to adopt it. This story was just for people who knew us here. Family in England knew we didn't have a cousin, so they'd be told that the baby was the child of the people I used to work for, and the mum was very ill or maybe she had died.

Dad said it was wicked to tell a story like that and anyway the whole thing was ridiculous. He said he didn't agree with lying whatever the reason.

'This isn't lying,' Mum said. 'It's self protection.'

'Protection from who?'

The colour rose up Mum's neck like a pitcher filling with water. 'You run the farm and I run the home, and this is what we're doing so you can bloody well stop arguing about it.' Dad was astonished, she never spoke to him like that. 'And you, milady, can get out of my sight, you're the cause of all this. Get up to your room.' I was already half way out of the door but she shouted after me, 'And don't come down until you're ready to say who the father is.'

So that was it, everything was to be kept secret. Which, it seemed to me, was ridiculous. The girls at school would see me getting bigger, and I liked the idea of that. I would tell Lindsay – you have to tell someone – and even though I'd tell her it was a secret and not to tell anyone it was Joey's baby, she'd spread the word. And I'd like them knowing; it would set me apart, make me important. Before Joey I had been a nobody, but now I would be unique. And they would be envious. Joey! A few of them had claimed to have gone all the way but Lindsay and I thought they just said that for effect – now they'd be the ones taking me on one side to find out what sex was like. I would be Someone. I would fascinate and intrigue. And Joey would have to get back with me. At least for a while.

But when I came down to breakfast the next day Mum said, 'I don't know where you think you're going.'

Dad was pulling on his boots but he stopped and looked up, as mystified as I was. 'She's going to school, where should she be going?'

'We're going into town, I'll find a doctor. We need to get her looked at.'

'I need to get to school,' I objected.

'You can't go to school with a baby in tow, you might as well leave now' Mum said.

'But what about my exams?'

'You should have thought of that before you got on your back.'

'Rose!' Dad was as horrified as I was but perhaps not by the same thing. How could I leave school? What about college? I might have to miss some schooling when the time came, but I could catch up again.

'You can go to Dorothy – stay there till you have it. You don't show enough for anyone else to have noticed yet.' She looked up suddenly. 'Have you told anyone?'

I shook my head. 'No, no one.' Until a few days ago I'd thought it would all go away. I'd thought it wasn't happening and I was imagining things. I was Mattie Marshall, fifteen, top in my year, I was going to college.

'Good. I'll call in at the school, and say you're leaving. I'll say you're ill at the moment and as soon as you're better you're starting a job.'

'You can't just leave school.'

'Of course you can and you've got a job to go to. I'll say you're moving away and starting work as a nursery nurse. The woman just had a baby and she needed someone straight away. They won't be bothered anyway as

257

long as they've got something to write in their records.'

I thought of Mrs Sykes, my English teacher, who would be so disappointed and mystified and my eyes filled with tears. She was always so encouraging. But people dropped out of school all the time to help on their farms or in their family businesses. And what about Lindsay? She'd be so hurt that I'd left without saying goodbye. I thought about writing to her, but what would I say? And then she'd forget me, my only friend, and she'd forget me. The way Auntie Joanie and Nanny had forgotten me. She would speculate and wonder but then I'd just be someone she used to know. Ultimately no one would find it remarkable. I was nobody, I'd always be nobody. The waters would close over me like someone who's drowned.

'And you can stop with the waterworks,' Mum said. 'You needn't think that's impressing anyone.

It was a long three months, working on the farm, waiting to be deemed big enough to be sent off to Dorothy's. In fact I did write to Lindsay, but only to say what Mum had said. That I'd already left to work as a nursery nurse, for someone Mum knew who lived miles away and who needed help urgently and it'd be a good job for me. I had to say that, she said, or else Lindsay's mum would be driving her round here wanting to know what was going on.

So as planned, when I started to show I went to stay with Auntie Dot. Mum thought it was for the best – get me away from prying eyes, she said. But that was for her benefit not mine – I was excited about my baby, I could feel him kicking, I liked to look in the mirror and see my belly growing. I couldn't wait to hold him and dress him up and show him off to people. I didn't tell anyone who the father was. I had no power in any of this, but I had that.

Dad drove me there and we sat in silence for most of the four hour journey. There was so much to say but nothing that could be spoken of. He didn't agree with sending me away but this was another argument he had no chance of winning.

Auntie Dot heard us drive up and came hurrying out. Sophie was with her but she hung back as though I might be contagious. Her expression was both horrified and admiring. I was an accident she couldn't look away from. I was the person who gets run over, the one about whom you say, 'It could never happen to me.'

Dorothy clasped me in a bear hug, then pushed me back to look at me. 'My poor darling,' she said. I thought she would shout at me, would feel something of the disgrace Mum did. But she brushed my tears away and moved quickly to stop me picking up a bag even though it was a small one, containing only a flask of water and some fruit that we had brought for the journey. 'No lifting,' she said. 'I'll take that.'

I watched, wondering, as she walked into the house with Dad beside her. A few days before Mum had had me help her move the refrigerator out to clean behind it.

'I thought your stomach would be bigger,' Sophie said, as we walked indoors.

'I thought yours would too,' I said, not knowing what else to say. But she laughed, and everything was all right between us. 'I've got some magazines to swap with you,' she said, 'wait till you see what I've got. You did remember to bring yours?'

In the turmoil I'd forgotten all about them, but Bobby had heaved a pile out from under my bed. 'Don't forget these,' he'd said, gruffly, not looking at me. They were crammed in my suitcase. He was nowhere to be seen when I left. He didn't like any sort of scene. Dad said he'd seen him biking up the track as fast as he could go.

'Has Dan still got that girlfriend?' I asked, sounding as casual as I could manage.

'Girlfriend? Dan hasn't got – ' she broke off and colour spread into her face.

I knew then. How could I have been so stupid? Hadn't Dan warned me not to provoke her?

We walked in silence, and then she said, 'Look, I didn't mean anything. I was kidding! You left me out of everything last time. I was getting my own back.'

That still didn't explain why Dan had never written. 'And what did you say to Dan?'

She shrugged. 'I was mad with both of you. I told him you'd written to say you had a boyfriend.' Suddenly she stopped and gave a little yelp. 'And you obviously did!' She nudged me, trying to make a joke of it all, wanting us to be friends again. For a moment I was going to sulk, make her feel bad, but what was the point. Everything had moved on.

As we crossed the yard, Dan was kneeling down by their truck tightening up the wheel. He glanced up at me without getting up.

I had Richie at home. Not our home, obviously, I mean Dorothy's. It was five a.m. on an August morning and by the time the midwife arrived I was holding him in my arms. I'd heard that first babies can mean a long labour, but he was four weeks early and came quickly or that's what they said. It didn't seem quick to me. But once it's behind you, no pain seems as bad as you thought it to be at the time. Auntie Dot was there with me, holding my hand.

He cried straight away and I held him in a blanket until the midwife came to cut the cord. He had a mop of black hair which he lost entirely, and when it grew back it was blonde and stayed that way. I looked at him hard in those early weeks to see who he looked like, but mostly he was himself and unlike anyone else at all, though he did have a passing resemblance to every other baby I'd ever seen a picture of. But it was only passing because in all other respects I knew he was superior to every baby ever born.

Dorothy had made a cot for him in a drawer padded with a folded blanket, and it rested on top of the chest by my bed. We wrapped him in a fine woollen shawl in pale cream that she had knitted. He was so tiny, and so new. It seemed scarcely believable that yesterday he hadn't existed, yet today here he was fully formed, his own person. I know now I was only thinking what every mother thinks, but it was still a miracle however many people thought those things before me.

Dorothy showed me how to breast feed, warning me that it takes a while to get the hang of it, but he sought my nipple instinctively, gripping with those tiny fingers, his hands coming round my breast. His eyes were squeezed tight closed. When, shifting position I inadvertently disengaged him, his mouth sought the air desperately, sucking and searching until he could latch on again. Seeing him in that moment was the single most moving event of my life. I had been frightened of what I might feel when he was born, frightened of how he would look, who he would look like, that I might even hate him for the disruption and distress he had brought with him. But already he was the most important person in the world and I loved him more than anyone, even Dad. Where he had come from, who he had come from, was immaterial. I felt serene and fulfilled. If I never did anything else of worth in my life, still I had done this one thing, brought this new life into the world and I would love him as much he deserved for as long as we both lived.

When the midwife had gone and I was sitting up in bed, washed and freshened, Dorothy brought me a cup of tea and sat by my bed.

'He's perfect,' she said, leaning into his makeshift cot to look at him.

'Do you think Mum will think so?'

'Everyone will think so. And he's going to be a real good looker when he grows up.'

'Can you tell that already?' She laughed. 'You're good looking yourself, so how can it be otherwise?' She caught my eye then, and got up to rearrange his shawl, and I guessed she thought she had been indiscreet. It hung in the air, the need to say something about the father – yes he was good looking, no he wasn't good looking. He was tall or short, fat or thin. I picked up my tea and sipped. 'I'm thinking of calling him Richard,' I said. 'Richie, for short.'

She tucked the baby in, stood looking in at him. 'Is that after anyone in particular?' she asked, still not looking at me.

'I like the name,' I said.

'It's a lovely name,' she said. 'He looks a Richie.'

'You've chosen a name already?' said Sophie, entering. 'I thought you weren't sure. I thought you were going to go for William or Robert.'

'He looks a Richie,' I said, because now that Dorothy had said that, it seemed that it was always destined to be so.

'Well,' said Dorothy. 'That was quick. Sophie, go and tell Dan he can come in now.'

'Tell him yourself,' Sophie replied.

He appeared immediately, he must have been waiting just outside the door. He stood hesitantly on the threshold, brushing his hair from his forehead. His thick fair hair flopped straight back again. He licked his lips uneasily. 'Come and look,' Dorothy said, 'He won't bite you.' She laughed. 'He hasn't got any teeth yet.'

Dan smiled uncertainly and came forward. I wondered if the baby's hair would be as thick as Dan's, but of course it was dark then, it wouldn't grow fair until later. He peered into the drawer. 'He's very small.'

'That's what they're like. If they were any bigger you couldn't get them out.' She laughed, but Dan blushed to the roots of his hair and I did the same. 'But he's big considering he's a few weeks early.'

'Are you all right?' he asked. 'I heard... I mean...' I realised he must have heard me crying out. Probably the whole state had heard me.

'I'm fine now it's all over,' I said.

He stood there awkwardly, looking as though he wished he were anywhere else but couldn't think of a reason for excusing himself. 'When will you be up and about again?' he asked suddenly, as though he was a drowning man and had suddenly seen a lifebelt.

'She'll need a few days' rest,' Dorothy said. 'It's hard work, she hasn't just been lying here you know.'

Sophie said, 'Mum, you're being very embarrassing. Why don't you get the dinner and I'll sit and look at the baby.'

Dorothy laughed, and got up. 'Not lost for cheek is she – I haven't exactly been sitting about with my feet up!' But she said it good naturedly, and moved back for Sophie to take a seat. Dan grasped the opportunity the diversion created to get out. I watched him go, remembering.

Later, as I sat in bed nursing Richie, Sophie leaned over to see his face more closely. Suddenly she looked up at me.

'Does he look like the father?' she whispered. She had read my mind and it was eerie to hear my own thought spoken aloud.

'I already told you,' I said. 'He hasn't got a father.'

Friends of Dorothy's came to visit, bringing home-made biscuits or fruit for me, and for Richie a rattle or a ball made of wool or dress fabric. They cradled him if he was awake, and cooed over him if he was asleep. They made a great fuss of me. Sometimes I would be aware of lowered voices in the kitchen, but I don't know what Dorothy was saying to them. Perhaps she said I was a widowed cousin come to stay, but I don't think so.

'Your mum will be different when she sees him,' Dorothy said.

'Different?'

'She won't be so hard on you. It was a shock for her, you know. To her you're still a little girl. It takes a mother a while to get over something like that.'

But for all Mum's ill temper and insistence on sending me away, she hadn't been hard on me. She had let me keep my baby. Our relationship would be different now. We might never have the close relationship that Dorothy had with Sophie, maybe I would never be her favourite child, but she had come through for me when it mattered.

'Do you think she'll still want me to go home?' If I stayed here Mum wouldn't have to worry about people finding out I had a baby and I could go back to my studies. I could go to classes at night while Dorothy or Sophie minded Richie, or get a tutor who might come out to the house. Living in a town made things so much easier. And Dan was here, he could help out too.

Dorothy said gently, 'I think your Mum's mind is made up. But it will all work out, these things always do in the end.'

There was a tap at the door then, and Dorothy's next door neighbour pushed it open and glanced round. 'Now where's the new mother then?'

She handed me a gift wrapped in tissue and leaned into the cot. Richie stirred and she picked him up.

'I'll bet your mummy is proud of you,' she said to him. She looked across at me. 'And this little man is going to be proud of his mummy too, aren't you?'

It was the last time anyone would call me that. I often thought of it afterwards, though not as often as I think of it now.

Rose

I opened my eyes and there was a terrible smell. I was on the carpet, and I was cold, so cold and I couldn't move my legs. They were numb and stiff. And I must've been lying on my arm, because that was numb and stiff too. I could hear the television but I had my back to it. The clock on the mantelpiece said 9.20. It was light outside so it must be morning. So why was the television on? I never put it on before the afternoon.

My head hurt and I felt sick. And thirsty. If I could pull myself up on the stool maybe I could stand up... but I couldn't move and even if I did I wouldn't be able to lift my arm up that high.

Everything hurt. And I was so cold. And wet. Why was I wet? And what was that smell?

Then I realised what the smell was. Bloody hell.

'Why didn't you ring me?' Joanie asked when she'd cleaned me up and I was sitting on the sofa with a blanket round me. I was still cold, felt I'd never get warm again even after the hot shower.

'I couldn't reach the phone,' I said. Was she stupid? Didn't she think I'd have rung if I could?

'But it's here on the table, just where you'd fallen,' she said, mystified. And I remembered then. After I fell I'd picked it up but I couldn't remember her number. Me, who had never needed to write a number down, and I couldn't even remember to work the redial.

I must have been on the floor all night. They called in as they were passing on the off-chance I wanted a bit of shopping, otherwise I could've been there forever.

There was no need for the doctor once I'd been helped up off the floor but Joanie called him anyway. It was a different doctor this time. He said he'd like to admit me for a few days. 'Keep an eye on those wounds.' He said they could be dangerous in someone my age.

'Not as dangerous as being in hospital,' I said. 'All those diseases. Send me back there and you might as well write out a death certificate and have done with it.' I gave him my special look that can make a grown man wither.

'I don't suppose it's as bad as all that,' he said with an attempt at cheeriness. He looked to Joanie for help, but she didn't answer.

'And I haven't had a stroke, if that's what you're thinking!' I said. 'I tripped over my slipper, could happen to anyone.'

Joanie walked him to the front door and I heard him say, 'I think we should admit her to see what's going on. And you might want to start considering how she's going to manage in the future. There are some very good care homes around, it might be worth thinking about.'

'I heard that!' I shouted. Damn cheek.

With the doctor gone, Des came back into the living room to do what he could with the stains on the carpet. He dabbed some washing up liquid on a cloth and gave it a scrub. It wouldn't show, or not too much. I'd always favoured patterned carpets, so that was lucky.

Chapter 17

Rose

I said you are not getting me back in that hospital, and that's final.

Chapter 18

Rose

I'll be glad when visiting is over. At least in your own home if someone comes knocking that you don't want to see you can pretend you didn't hear. Just sit there with the TV turned up and ignore them banging on the window, trying to see through the net curtains. But in hospital there's no getting away from them. Those double doors swing open and your heart sinks. And it's bad enough with your own visitors, but her in the bed next to me has got three daughters and they've all got kids under five, so there's a constant coming and going, constant screech of kids crying and chasing each other round the beds. Yesterday one of them wheeled her buggy in and parked it right by my bed, so I couldn't get out even if I wanted to. I said to the nurse, 'It's supposed to be two visitors only' and she said, 'Ah but Rosie, you wouldn't be denying Constance the joy of her grandchildren, now wouldja?' And then she said, 'And you haven't got visitors, have you darling', so she could have your whatdyamacallit – allocation.' I'd liked to have given the lot of them my whatdyamacallit – piece of my mind. But you have to watch your step in here. Upset the nurses and who knows what medication you'll find yourself on.

It's just like I've never been away, except no Enid or Mary. They say it's an exacerbation of this thing I've got, long name, never heard of it but it's not terminal, and they want me in for a few days for observation. What is there to observe, I'd like to know. I sleep, I wake up. That's it. It's not like there's much for them to observe.

I'm on a different ward this time. The last ward was divided up with partitions so you had half a dozen little wards of six beds, which was nice really, you could get a bit of community spirit going. But now I'm on Cataract ward, and we're all set out in twos with a little partition and I can't get out of bed so I can't see anyone else. Mattie says it's not called Cataract, it's Catterick. No sense of humour, that one.

I'm glad I've given up walking, because I've no idea how far it might be to the loo. Now I ring my buzzer and they wheel a commode along. Good for resting the legs, not so good for the bum. It's not easy, going with just a screen round you. You don't want to do anything that might make a smell, but there's not much you can do on a commode that doesn't, is there? I've constipated myself holding on so as not to go in the middle of dinner, or tea time, or when visitors are in (and visitors are always in. Maybe I *should* have the commode when they're in. It might put Constance's grandchildren off coming). And if you leave it till night time then you can be pressing that buzzer for ages before anyone notices you.

Mattie also says it's probably not advisable for me to go back home. I said, 'How can they stop me? I'm not a prisoner. I'll go where I damn well please.'

'And how are you going to manage that?' she says, 'Unless someone brings you a wheelchair. And if they did, then what are you going to do? You couldn't get in a car, could you? And let's just say you did – when you got home, how will you get up the stairs?'

'I'll crawl if I have to. They can't keep me here against my will. I haven't done anything wrong except to get old.'

She hands me a tissue. She says, 'Come on, Mum, don't get maudlin.'

But I have, I've done a lot of things wrong. I look at Mattie sitting there, came all this way to see me, and I don't mean just over from Marian's. And I think, why did I do it? It was a mean thing and I knew it was. I thought it was for the best – but best for who? Why did I ever think it was a good idea? She was never a bad kid and it could happen to anyone. Oh Richie, Richie, please come back. If he'd only come back.

The nurse is pulling the screens round. 'There, there Rosie, it's just the medication, people often feel a bit weepy. Depression is a side effect.'

I almost laugh at that – you're in an ex-workhouse surrounded by the dead and the good-as-dead, screaming kids, grieving relatives and the only thing to look forward to is being dead yourself – and she thinks you're depressed because of the medication. But at least that stops me bawling. And the nurse is hushing the three year old twins and telling Constance they'll have to limit her visitors if she can't keep them quiet so it's not all bad.

I suddenly realise Mattie has been patting my hand. She draws it away awkwardly as I calm down. We don't do much touching, her and me, it makes us uncomfortable.

'Don't know what came over me,' I say. 'But I doubt it's PMT – haven't seen a period in a hundred years.'

She laughs and the nurse says, 'That's better Rosie, that's more like it.'

'We'll keep trying to contact Richie,' Mattie is saying. 'If he knew you were ill I'm sure he'd come. He'd certainly call.'

I turn away. The screens are blue with lavender squares on them, some sort of abstract design. On the last ward they were also blue but they were flowers. And straight away I make my mind up. I've been dwindling away, to tell you the truth. Feeling sorry for myself, feeling there's nothing ahead, nothing to look forward to. But of course there is. I'm not that old. Seventies is nothing for these days. Or eighties, whatever it is. I read of someone, in her nineties, goes paragliding. If she can do that I'm sure I can get out of bed. Maybe not right now but I could work on it. They've said I'll be getting a physio, so it shouldn't be that hard. And Richie won't want to find some old biddy sitting up in bed grizzling into her bed jacket. Sitting on a commode making the room smell.

I don't want to be a bed blocker, I've heard them say that about Gracie opposite. She can't go home and they can't find a care home that'll take her. Well I'm not that bad, nowhere near. Homes would be crying out to have me, I reckon. Cheer them all up a bit, bring a bit of life in.

And I can't go back home. I keep saying I want to, but I don't. It was horrible, stuck on that floor all night, couldn't get up, couldn't find the phone. I was so scared. You suddenly find your body won't let you do what you want it to, it's frightening. They say it was just one night, but I reckon it was longer than that. Felt like a week. And

I was so cold, never been so cold, because the heating switches off at ten. I remember I wet my pants, and for a moment, it was lovely, that warmth, so hot down my legs. And then straight afterwards it went clammy and cold, and my legs went like jelly. Then in the night it was worse, I couldn't help it, couldn't hold it any longer. The smell was terrible, all in my lovely living room. There was a blanket on the back of the chair that I used to pull over me if I had a nap, but I forgot all about it. Never even noticed it. And the phone. Picked it up and I couldn't think what you had to do, which numbers you pressed. Couldn't remember at all. I banged on the wall with my stick but my arms were so weak it hardly made a sound. Anyway him next door has his music on so loud he'd just think I was complaining again.

It's quiet when all the visitors go and dinner is over and they turn the lights down. Not quiet like when you're at home, but the noises are softer. The nurses do their best to keep the noise down. I'm sorry I complained about Constance's grandchildren. I like kiddies around, truth to tell. Richie was a poppet at that age.

Mattie had been working at the garage at weekends and after school but she swore it wasn't Dave's and I thought it better not be – wouldn't wish a start like that on a poor innocent baby – those close-together eyes and a nose so big it entered a room half an hour before he did. But who else could it be? She didn't have a boyfriend, I knew that for a fact. First off I thought it was Eddie, God forgive me. Well, she was growing up and I'd seen him noticing her, and you know what men are. And who else was there? Drove me mad not knowing.

Course I could never get her to say. She always was a secretive one, scribbling in that notebook and in code so as I couldn't read it – as she thought. Or maybe she didn't think it. Just a load of old nonsense anyway but she never wrote anything about a boy, just some pop star she was sweet on. She must have thought if she ignored it, it would go away.

Stupid, I know. But it's the sort of thing you do think when you're young and not had much experience.

I don't think a day went by that I didn't remind her what a fool she'd been and how she'd ruined everything for everyone. And part of me was thinking if it was her fault then it was also my fault.

But then Richie was born and I forgot everything. The minute I held him I knew he was a gift from heaven, and I wanted him for my own.

Come on, Richie, where are you?

FOUR

'Oh bring back my bonnie to me'

Chapter 19

Mattie

I rang again. Joanie and I looked at each other. We could hear a commotion behind the door and voices, and then with a rattling of locks the door was opened. The woman was about my age, with an eager expression and orange hair. Her heavy tortoiseshell glasses were probably a fashion statement in their day, but that wasn't recently. Still, we weren't here to pronounce on the sartorial elegance of the staff.

'Sorry to keep you waiting,' she said, pleasantly. 'One of our residents had a little accident and we were giving her a bit of help.' Behind her a younger woman in an overall was leading an elderly woman towards a lift. The elderly woman seemed not to want to go.

'Do come in. I'm Maureen, the manager here. And you're - ?' I confirmed that I had phoned this morning and that she was expecting me. She stepped back for us to enter, then took the few steps down the hall to where the elderly woman was holding on to the side the lift entrance and refusing to budge.

'Una can be very determined,' Maureen said to us, somewhat cryptically. To Una she called, 'Now go back to your room like a good girl and Anita will bring you a nice cup of tea.'

Una didn't look as though she wanted to be a good girl and Maureen went to her and gently but firmly prised her fingertips from the doorframe. Una set up a wailing complaint as the lift door closed behind her. Maureen turned to us with a smile as though nothing had happened.

'Let me show you round. We're having some extension work done.' Maureen showed us into the residents' lounge. On the wall hung two large prints of landscapes which would have added a note of serenity but for the violently patterned wallpaper, a swirling abstract of lilac and lime green. 'We'll be decorating in here next,' she said, 'but you can't do everything at once. I'd like to change some of the décor – it gives you a headache doesn't it?'

Joanie suggested that something plain would be more restful and Maureen agreed. 'Though the advantage of pattern is that it hides the marks. We had one resident who'd throw his tea up the wall if he got in a temper. So then this paper was a godsend. But if we had waterproof we'd be all right with plain, I suppose.'

She led us down a narrow corridor, the walls of chipboard to waist height, the upper sections being entirely of glass, to give an uninterrupted view into each room presumably. The partitions seemed rickety and out of keeping with the high ceilings and solidity of this big old house. It had been modernised with 'modern' meaning tacky and temporary. I made a further mental note not to be so judgemental and that the décor was about the practical and not the aesthetic.

'Now this is the only room I've got available at the moment. Not the best view in the world.' The window faced on to the blank wall of the house next door. 'But it is a single. You said you wanted a single, didn't you?' I nodded. I couldn't imagine what Mum would think of sharing with a stranger but apparently sharing was the norm not only in this care home but the three others I had phoned. 'It's very comfortable –' She indicated the single bed, the high backed easy chair with it's worn arms, the scratched teak coffee table and heavy oak wardrobe – 'and on this floor we have the shower – so that would be very convenient for her.'

'What do you mean – the shower?' Joanie asked.

The woman looked nonplussed. 'You know – shower. A spray of water – '

'I know what a shower is,' said Joanie with exaggerated patience. 'But you're not suggesting it's the only one on the floor?'

'No, not the only one on the floor.' Joanie's exaggerated patience was matched beat for beat. 'The only one in the residence. The other floors have baths in their bathrooms. With a hoist obviously for those who can't get in unaided, which is a lot of the residents to be frank, or they wouldn't be here. But we've just had this shower put in. There's a seat there too. And room for an assistant if they need help with washing. This used to be quite a big room for a single, so they took a bit off to add a shower to the bathroom next door. It's worked quite well, I think.'

The installation had made the bedroom an awkward L-shape, the short part too narrow to be of much use. Maureen put the light on. It was only three in the afternoon, and the sun was shining outside, which you could tell from the ray that bounced off the wall of the house next door. I thought of Mum's bright bedroom, and her cheerful living room. I looked at Joanie.

Maureen said, 'Will she be self funding?'

'What's that?' Joanie asked.

'You know – will she be paying her own fees or will the local authority be paying? I have to ask because the local authority don't actually pay enough to cover for this single room. Their payment would only be enough for a shared room, but we don't have any available at the moment. So either she would have to pay all of it, or if she didn't have quite enough you'd have to top up the difference.'

'She hasn't got any money to speak of,' Joanie said. 'So how much is it?' Maureen repeated what I'd already been told. Joanie had thought it was a mistake when I told her

'Well, I can't see how anyone could afford all that,' Joanie said. 'You can rent a flat in Mayfair for less than that.'

'Ah but not with full time nursing care,' said Maureen presenting the well-rehearsed information with a flourish. 'It's the twenty-four hour care you're paying for. Staff are very expensive. Agency staff even more so. And we have had to refurbish to meet new guidelines, which all takes money.' She adopted a thoughtful expression. I had the impression that the thoughtful expression had also been done many times before. 'Has she got her own house? If she sells it she'll be all right. That's how most people pay their fees, unless they've got a large amount of capital put by. There's a lot of red tape attached but that's mostly what happens.'

I thought of Dad's pride, when we had the farm that he was building up, something which we would inherit. Well, that never happened, but his consolation was that we should all be left provided for. It was what he had worked for. As for Mum, she'd always been careful about how much she paid for things, always had an eye to value for money. She would never agree that swapping her little house for this dingy dwelling with its rickety partitions and unrestricted view of a brick wall was a good investment.

'What happens when the money runs out?' I said. Based on current fees, if Mum sold her house she would be out of funds within ten years. Ten years in this pokey room. It felt like a prison sentence, but with no time off for good behaviour.

Maureen smiled the smile of one who is issuing news which will bring instant relief. 'The local authority take over of course. We don't throw them out on the street! But of course that could mean moving to a double room.'

'A double room?' asked Joanie, hopefully, as though running out of money might end up being a good thing in the circumstances.

'A double room but with two people in it,' I explained.

'Some people prefer it,' Maureen said airily, without elaborating on who these people fortunate to be ending their days sharing with a total stranger might be. She led the way back downstairs. 'It's hard when people have to lose their own homes. There's no denying it. But if they can't look after themselves, what choice is there?'

Joanie nodded. 'When my time comes they can take me out and shoot me.'

'Shoot you?' said Maureen huffily. 'These days you can't even keep someone comfortable without they do an investigation.' I realised that in her terminology, keeping someone comfortable might mean more than plumping their pillows up.

We had come back down from the bedrooms and now we were standing awkwardly in the hallway. Apart from the low murmur of the television, playing for its sole occupant in the lounge, all was quiet.

We stood there looking at each other. She knew what we thought of her establishment and that we, and our aged relative were too good for it. But she also knew that, when it came down to it, we might be grateful to get it.

'Bring your mother for a look around,' she said, falling back on her training and overcoming the hostility that our demeanour had surely provoked. 'She might like to meet some of the other residents. Lionel is a bright spark, she'd be sure to like him. But don't leave it too long.' I thought she meant because Lionel might find himself being made comfortable any minute, but she went on, 'Because a single room like this will get snapped up very quickly.'

'Not by me it won't,' I whispered to Joanie as she closed the door behind us.

Rose

Mattie said, 'You'll like it, it's a nice big room,' like I was a child, not someone with her own three bedroomed house and paved patio. 'And what do you want with three bedrooms anyway, now you can't manage the stairs?'

I can manage. Just because I don't run up them like a two year old any more, and she isn't much faster with that great back side on her.

'Just come and look at it,' she said. 'You'll have your own bathroom.'

'I've got my own bathroom,' I said. 'Two of them, thank you very much.'

Mattie pursed her lips. She was going to end up with those nasty little lines on them like I've got if she wasn't careful.

'Rosie, Rosie, cheer up, this isn't like you,' says Sister when she comes on duty. Big woman, loud laugh. 'You'll like it there, it's a lovely place. Or are you sad to leave us?'

She thinks she's joking, but she's right, I don't want to leave. I've had a lot of changes in my life and I don't want any more. I'm too old to be frightened but I am. Well, apprehensive. I'm being taken charge of, they want to take me over. Think they know best. But I am in charge. It's still my life. Might be a bit of a rubbish life, but it's mine.

'The manager is a lovely man,' she says. 'You're lucky to get in there.' She is the one doing the reference for me, confirming I'm not nuts in the head or incontinent. Actually I am a bit but they're so desperate to free up the beds here they'll say anything to get you out.

'It's a lovely place, you'll enjoy it,' she says.

'You go then,' I say. But she's already off up the ward singing away and doesn't hear me.

Chapter 20

Rose

I told them, I am not going into a home and that's final.

Chapter 21

Rose

So here I am at DunMoanin'. ('It's called Meadowfields!'
Marian said. No sense of humour, that one. And I don't
know why it's called Meadowfields either, we're right next
to a dual carriageway.)

Most of the staff are black. Or do I mean coloured. I
forget which it is you mustn't say. Anyway, most of the
white faces are the residents, that I do know. Except for
Mrs One Leg in the wheelchair, and I don't know what she
is. Her face is sort of grey, like a cup of tea that's been
standing for a long time and got a skin on the top. Do
black folks have nursing homes of their own where white
staff wipe their bums and feed them mashed potato? I
hope so, it's only fair. Or maybe they don't get old and
dwindle away, maybe they're tripping the light fantastic
right up till the moment they drop down dead. That's
what I'd like, something quick. All this waiting around for
Godot drives you mad, not that I know who he is. Marian
keeps saying it and then she laughs so it must be some
kind of joke.

I've got quite a nice little room. Mattie says it's tons better than all the other places they looked at. Purpose built, very modern, not one of these conversion jobbies. I've got my own bathroom and a shower with a seat in it, and they keep it all very clean. If there's ever the faintest whiff of anything they're out there squirting the air freshener until it smells like a tart's boudoir.

This morning a very nice little girl came in and gave me a wash, Polish I think, not much English but she smiled a lot and so gentle. She was wearing a green uniform. Green uniforms mean they don't know much, not to be confused with blue uniforms which also mean they don't know much, only they've got a qualification to prove it.

Timbo has a blue uniform, he's from South Africa. He's lovely and actually he does know much, he knows very much. Sharp as a sharp thing he is. And actually Timbo isn't his name, it's Tembi, but I heard it wrong the first time and now I only remember what it should be after I've said it. He doesn't mind, he thinks it's my pet name for him and I suppose it is in a way. He's only a boy, not more than early thirties. It's no life is it, running round after old people, but he says he doesn't mind, he says he likes old people. He says he got into nursing after his grandfather was ill and now when he looks after any of us he thinks of him. I said was it my moustache reminded him, but he didn't get the joke. He said, 'But Rosie, you don't have a moustache!' Which made me think maybe I do have one... He likes helping people, not like that girl with the dyed hair, she'll give you a poke when she's passing if you're not careful. I woke up crying the other night when Timbo was on and he sat and held my hand for ever such a long time until his buzzer went off. He said should he call Mattie, but what could be better than having a young man by my side, and even if it's not the one I long for most, still he reminds me, and that's a comfort in itself.

He did his best to cheer me up. When I said to him, sitting here with a young man is just what the doctor ordered – and how many more chances will I get? He said a young thing like me had lots more ahead of me and all the men would be after me. We laughed. When Joanie comes we tease him over which of us he's going to run off with. Joanie said he could have us both if he wanted a threesome. What a thought. All that wrinkly flesh slapping about, can you imagine. Poor boy, it's a good job he's got a strong stomach.

The woman in the room opposite has her TV on loud enough to wake the dead (which might come in handy in here). Anyway I asked Bessie (green uniform) to get her to turn it down, but the next day it was just as loud again. She must be bedridden, you never see her in the dining room, and her bed has sides on it, padded like a soft cushion. I asked Bessie what was wrong with her but she said she didn't know. I think she did, just didn't want to say, probably some confidentiality thing. Though what is there to be secretive about in here, I'd like to know? They gave me a booklet of their aims when I arrived, all about preserving the dignity of the elderly. Once you've spent half an hour on the toilet calling for someone to come and get you off it, dignity is something you stop worrying about. They have a quota on incontinence pads. Apparently you're not allowed to wet your knickers more than six times a day, after that you have to sit in it. It's a government regulation.

After Mattie went I got Bessie to wheel me down to the lounge. Blind Arthur and Mrs One Leg were on the chairs at the side and Mrs Give-us-a-kiss was in front of the telly, same as usual. She's Scottish and she only says two things. Sometimes she says, 'I'm going home Sunday,' but today it was the other one. She drives Blind Arthur mad. She shouted out that she wanted a cup of tea, and he pipes up, 'you've had your tea' and she says, 'Have I?' And he says, 'Yes.' And she says, 'Well, give us a kiss then.' So he says, will you shut up, and she says, All right. Give us a kiss. The first time I heard them I thought it was like a double act. Now I think it's like a comedy duo where you know all the punch lines, and they weren't that funny to start with.

Eddie came in yesterday. He's stopped talking out of one side of his mouth now. So either he's got better from his stroke, or he's given up trying to look like Robert Mitchum. No one knows who Robert Mitchum is anyway these days. Not sure I do. Was he the one played whatshisname in that film? No, it wasn't him, it was that other one…

Eddie says he can bring me any fruit I want because he passes the market so it's no trouble. I'd prefer it if it *was* trouble, I don't want him calling in all the time, not in here, catching me stuck on the lavvy calling out and no one taking any notice. I never thought he'd turn out to be the healthy one. I thought it'd be me visiting him in somewhere like this. But now I'm his leisure pursuit. I'm the way he passes a Tuesday afternoon, his equivalent of bingo and the sing-along they lay on here every day between two thirty and four.

That's when we do 'activities.' They hold it in the downstairs lounge which is bigger than the one on my floor, there's a piano and everything. They wheel everyone in, everyone who can't walk that is, the rest shuffle in on their zimmers, then we all sit round in a circle. On a Thursday it's music – some old chap comes in and plays for half an hour. He says, 'Now who'd like a request?' and whatever you ask for he can't do. Unless you ask for 'Tea for Two' or 'Chopsticks' and then you're laughing.

Yesterday it was aerobics. You sit in your chair and see if you can lift your arm up and if you can't then you lift up your wrist or your finger or whatever. If you can't even do that Tracey comes round and lifts it up for you. She says, 'Come on Glad, you can do it,' even though Glad is half asleep with her tongue hanging out. Then you have to make your ankles do circles and after that we play a game where they give you a plastic quoit and you have to chuck it over the plastic pole which she brings round to each of us and puts it so close you'd have to be dead not to be able to. And there were still some who couldn't do it. Suited me though. I won that. There's nothing wrong with my arms and as for circling my ankles – I could do the Cancan up till a month ago. Len said I could have been a Tiller Girl in my day. Course no one knows who they were any more.

Today it's bingo. They have these plastic wipe-clean bingo cards and Tracey shouts the numbers out. The helpers have to give some of them a hand because half of them can't hear and the other half can't see and that's not counting the ones who think 'eyes down' means it's time for a nap. Still, it breaks the day up. I won some talc from the Co-op, and there's always a packet of Maltesers and everyone watches to see who gets it because that's the prize everyone wants. I gave my talc to Mattie as a thank you, because she does her best, I shouldn't go on about her. She was that thrilled you'd have thought it was a bar of gold. Filled right up, she did.

Mattie told me she knows Eddie visits like it's some big secret.

The one with the dyed hair came and gave me my shower today. You only get it once a week if you can't do it yourself. I'm down for a Saturday morning, which means I'm nice and fresh for the weekend. Though seeing as every day is the same in here, it doesn't make any difference which day it is. She's not very patient, that one, and she gave my head a yank when I didn't put it back far enough when she was washing my hair. Timbo would be more gentle, but you wouldn't want a young lad doing your bits and pieces. I mean, for myself I'm not bothered one way or the other but it wouldn't be very nice for him. I don't suppose it's very nice for her either, come to think of it.

The food isn't bad, and a lot better than hospital. They have a menu and there's supposed to be a choice but everyone gets the same so I don't know who does the choosing. My guess is it's the chef. Chooses what he fancies cooking. He wears a proper chef's hat and apron, I reckon he bought it at a fancy dress shop. I told Gwen, who sits next to me at dinner, I think he was trained at the same cookery establishment school dinner ladies go to. Only he's not that good! But I was only kidding. He's all right. He likes me because I have a joke with him. He always says he'll be round later to take me out to the pictures, and I say make sure Timbo doesn't see you, don't want him getting jealous. Gwen just sits there. Sometimes she's with it and sometimes not. She told me she had two sons the first time I met her, but the next time she said she didn't have any.

I don't have Dr Red-Eye any more. Apparently I'm outside his territory so I've been allocated the doctor that comes in for anyone whose doctor has dumped them, like mine has. Dr Harris or Dr. Horrid as I call him. I bet he still doesn't know if I'm a man or a woman. Not because of my moustache either, ha ha. He stands looking out the window, probably checking none of us is trying to do a getaway in his car. He keeps his distance. Maybe he thinks being gaga is catching (and maybe it is, because I think I'm going a bit funny myself and I was fine when I came in). He said was I allergic to anything, but he asked Amma, the nurse, not me, and then he said I was to have something three times a day, and she wrote it down. I said, 'Thank you, doctor,' very pointed, but he didn't answer. Amma patted my hand and said she would be back with some medicine in a bit and I'd soon be feeling better. I like Amma. I've a mind to write and complain about the doctor but I keep forgetting to ask Mattie to bring notepaper in. Anyway what's the point – they'll see the address and think I'm half daft anyway, or I wouldn't be here.

Mattie

'Why don't you have your yoghurt?' I said. Mum is supposed to have one each day to counteract the effects of the drugs she's on. 'Strawberry, your favourite.'

'Just because it's my favourite, doesn't mean I want it

every time. There's such a thing as variety, you know.'

I made as though to put it back in my bag at which she held her hand out. We went through a similar charade most days. I didn't mind. It was a way of injecting a change of pace, however slight.

'I don't know why you have to bring it. They're supposed to give me all my food here.' She took a spoonful and a strawberry rolled off the spoon on to her lap. She put it in her mouth and rubbed at the mark with her finger. 'Look at that strawberry,' she said, scathing, picking out another one. 'When you think of what we used to produce – we'd have been embarrassed if this was the best we could do. And our milk…' She gazed into the distance, remembering. 'The cream on it, and the colour…' She sighed. 'Our water had more goodness in it than this.' She laughed suddenly. 'Remember the time Richie made himself sick? He couldn't have been more than six or seven. I had some milk in a basin in the fridge and a basin of cream was next to it. He dipped his cup in the cream by accident, a great mug full. Never seen anyone look so green.'

'That wasn't an accident,' I said. 'He wanted the cream and pretended he got confused. He was perfectly able to tell the difference.'

Mum looked surprised. 'Do you think so? No… he always told the truth with me.'

'You didn't see him that morning you let him stay off school.'

'He'd been bilious all night. I couldn't possibly have sent him, poor little mite.'

'He came running in to me singing, 'I'm staying off school, I'm staying off school,' and then he did a forward roll and a somersault.'

'You're remembering wrong... he didn't feel well enough to be left, I had to take him with me when I tended the animals.'

'And what did he most like in all the world?'

She smiled, suddenly recognising his cunning. 'Little scamp.'

Mum came with Dad to pick me up. I heard the truck pull up outside and had Richie in my arms already to show him off. I could hear them out in the yard, laughing, Mum and Dorothy. Then the door opened and she came hurrying over. 'Now let's have a look at him.'

She took him from me, I don't think she even noticed me.

'There, now, look at you!' She rocked him, holding him tight against her chest, then brought his face close to hers. I felt a sense of unease, maybe the fear that she might have a cold or some kind of infection she could pass on to him.

'He hardly wakes in the night,' I ventured.

'That's my poppet,' she murmured to him. 'Who's a good boy then?'

Dad was peering over her shoulder, trying to see past her head. 'Let's have a look, let the dog see the rabbit.'

She shifted slightly, but it was to block Dad's view, not make it clearer. 'Don't crowd him. There'll be plenty of time for you later.'

Dad stepped back, raising his eyebrows at me. Then he came over and drew me up to hug me. 'How's the apple of my pie?'

I cried then, big fat tears that came out of nowhere.

'Well, I didn't expect that!' he said, laughing. 'Aren't you pleased to see your old dad?'

I nodded, the tears still flowing. It was the relief of being someone's child again, instead of someone's mother. If I'd realised how permanent that was going to be, I'd have cried even more.

Over dinner Dorothy said, 'Mattie could stay on another month or so, you know. She's no trouble and we all love little Richie.'

She was carving the chicken as she spoke. She didn't look up but I was watching her face, saw a slight twitch around her mouth. I thought, 'She doesn't want me to go,' and my heart leapt up.

'I'm sure Sophie will be wanting her room back,' Mum said, helping herself to a potato.

'No,' Sophie said. 'I like the company. And I love the baby, it'd be lovely if they could stay.'

I glanced towards Dan. He was handing round vegetables and didn't seem to be listening.

'It'd be no trouble,' Dorothy said. She gave me a plate and there was a smile in her eyes.

'We've got everything ready for him at home,' Mum said. 'Len's made a proper cot for when he's bigger, and I've got some clothes all ready for him. And Bobby is so excited, it wouldn't be right to disappoint him.'

'Mum is going to paint the little room next to ours for him,' said Dad. 'It's not many babies who get to have their own room.'

It was at the other end of the landing from my room. 'Will I be able to hear him from there?' I asked, alarmed. 'Supposing he wakes up crying in the night?'

'He'll sleep in with you, same as here, to start with,'

Mum said. 'Once you've stopped the night feeds he can go in there. We've got it all planned, you don't have to worry.'

Dorothy caught my eye again. She said, 'Rose, she's been such a good mother, you would hardly have believed it. She's a natural. If he cries she has only to look at him and he hushes up.'

'Not like Sophie then,' Dan said. 'If she looks at him he starts howling.' Dad laughed, but Dorothy said, 'Dan! Rose will think you mean it.'

Then dinner was over and as we finished clearing up, Mum said we would be on our way. 'Now did you think about what I said?' Dorothy said, wiping her hands on a tea towel. 'She can stay until it's convenient for you on the farm. No trouble at all.'

'It's convenient now,' Mum said.

I was wiping the table over in the dining area, trying to pretend I wasn't listening.

I heard Dorothy say, 'Don't be too hard on her. It could happen to any of us.'

Mum put down the dish she was drying. 'Hard on her? I'm going to make it easier than anyone could possibly imagine. She'll hardly know she had a baby.'

The three of them stood at the gate to watch us pull out, Dorothy with one arm round Sophie and the other dabbing at her eyes. Dan turned and went back into the house as soon as Dad started the engine but I waved to Dorothy and Sophie until they were spots on the horizon.

We didn't talk much on the journey home. Mum cooed over Richie each time he stirred, and we took it in turns to hold him. She had brought a big straw basket to carry him but it was easier to nurse him than balance it on our knees.

When we got home she showed me the preparations she had made – his cot in a drawer, just as the one at Dorothy's - and after she had changed his nappy she dressed him in a little outfit she had made. Cotton rompers, much too big for him, his skinny legs poking out like two bendy sticks. 'Doesn't he look grand?' she said, holding him up. His feet looked purple despite the heat and I longed to get the bootees Dorothy had knitted back on.

I held my arms out, 'Come to mummy,' I said.

Mum froze in the act of handing him to me. 'Now that's enough of that.' She ignored my outstretched arms and held him against her shoulder, swaying gently. 'You remember what we agreed.'

There had been no agreement. She had said what she had said but it was ridiculous to think it would ever happen. She was overwrought, as we all were. She had said things she didn't mean.

'I'm his mum,' she said. 'He'll grow up calling you Mattie. We'll tell him he was adopted, and you're his sister. That's all he needs to know. All anyone needs to – '

'But – '

'No buts, my lady. Start as we mean to go on. Otherwise there'll be all sorts of confusion. If this is what we want everyone to believe, then this is what we must believe ourselves.'

'He's my baby,' I said. She was putting him into a little cardigan. That was my job.

'Not any more. I'm sorry, but it's how it has to be.'

I was crying now, not like before, cuddling Dad. This was different, pain that came from deep inside, far down inside, where Richie had nestled for nine months while he grew, I felt my insides writhing and churning.

'Come on now.' She set him into his makeshift cot and pulled the sheet over him, tucking him in tightly. 'You'll thank me in the end. You'll be free, you can do whatever you want with your life. But he'll be here for you to see and make a fuss of, just as though he was really your own.'

I opened my mouth to say he was my own, but she wasn't looking at me at all, her gaze was focused on Richie. 'He'll have everything,' she said. 'We'll see he wants for nothing, me and your dad.' She knelt down by the side of him. 'Who's his mummy's cherub then?' she said.

Dad made a baby swing for Richie when was a bit older. It hung from the door frame in the kitchen, so when Mum was preparing a meal he could sit there and watch her. She put him in it as soon as he could sit up, padding him all around with cushions. I didn't often see him in it, he was in bed when I got in from work, and in his cot when I left in the mornings, and if I had charge of him at weekends, I would push him out in his pram. But whenever I came in at night I'd see the indentation in the cushions from where he had sat, and as he got bigger sometimes there was a dribble of rusk on the wooden bars of the baby swing, or dripped on to the floor beneath. On the day we moved from the farm, I looked at the rings in the door frame which had supported the swing and which Dad had never removed, and thought of how things had been.

I missed the first time he rolled over, stood up, said 'Dadda'. 'Mumma' came much later when he could already ask for a drink or 'banky', his bit of chewed up old baby blanket that he couldn't sleep without. Mum said there was nothing special about the first time a baby did a thing, seeing as they would do it plenty of times afterwards. But still, she'd talk about it when it happened. 'Look, it's his first tooth!' 'He took his first step today. He was so pleased with himself, you should have seen him!'

He was good with his hands from young, dexterous with building bricks and molding plasticine. Dad bought him a toy farm which he adored, all the more because the real thing was just outside. From the plasticine he made wonky animals with large misshapen heads. There was an elephant and a tiger, barely distinguishable from the cow and the dog. We still thought this showed signs of artistic gifts and creativity. As soon as he could walk he would run to meet me when I came home, holding out his newest creation. Occasionally he was allowed to help mum with the baking and would bring me biscuits, an unappetising shade of grey, his having picked up the dough repeatedly to inspect it, maybe dropped it on the floor. But you had to eat it, he'd watch to see you did. He liked toy cars, playing for hours with the ones that had belonged to Bobby. Bobby was very good with him, nursing him when he was tiny and I was at work and Mum was busy with her farm chores. He took turns to sit with him all night when he was three and ill with flu. Dad made him a carpentry set with a little wooden hammer and fat pegs to be hammered into a tiny work bench. When Dad was doing bits of woodwork Richie would take his set out to him and play nearby. Afterwards Dad would bring him back to the house carrying him on his shoulders while Richie swayed to right and left, striking out at imaginary villains with his toy hammer.

For me, there was always a bond between us and I thought that even though we couldn't speak of it, there would be for him too. But one day, he was four, it was not long after his birthday, and I checked him because he was poking our dog with a stick. She was so placid, she wouldn't turn on him, but she was weary in the heat and kept moving away, and each time she found a new patch of shade he followed and prodded her again.

'Richie! I told you, no!' I said, because it wasn't the first time. He did it once again and now I took the stick from his hand.

He had a temper, young as he was. 'You can't tell me what to do,' he screamed. 'You're not my mum!' And he ran out into the yard yelling for Mum. When she came in I heard him telling her I had hit him with the stick. Mum brought him back into the kitchen and said to him, 'Now you tell Mattie what you just told me.'

He pursed his lips together tight and refused to answer, and Mum told him not to go telling lies about people because you would always get found out. She sent him outside but he glared at me from behind her back and pulled a face. I pulled a face back and he ran off. It was a trifling little incident but I knew then he didn't feel for me as I did for him, and never would.

'Little tinker,' Mum said.

I always planned to tell him one day that he was mine. But I was frightened. Suppose they sent me away and I couldn't see him? And when do you tell something like that? When he lay in his cot, laughing and reaching out for my fingers? When he sat on my lap while I turned the pages of the picture book and made animal noises for him to mimic? When he was curious, pointing and asking endless questions about the world – yes, that wouldn't have been too soon. But he would have told mum and dad and then they'd have sent me away. By the time he was old enough to understand that this was a confidence he must keep, he was too old to tell it to.

And anyway by then I was getting married. We moved to Brisbane and then I only saw him for the odd weekend. Richie was seven and Henry said it was time to make a break. Time to accept the inevitable and let go.

Henry said that Mum was right. That it was in Richie's best interests for them to bring him up, and mine too. He had the benefit of two parents, security both emotional and financial, and with no doubts about either his future or his past. He said I should be grateful that Mum had made it possible for me to live an independent life, unencumbered by the burden of an illegitimate child, with the stigma that implied as well as the weight of responsibility. I said: How can I put it behind me, he's my baby? Henry said: You're being sentimental.

Henry said: 'And if you had told him, what would you say when he asked who his father was?' I'd told Henry it was Joey, the good-looking golden-headed assistant caretaker at school who had plucked me out of obscurity (I didn't tell Henry that he'd dumped me right back in it again). I'd told Henry that Mum and Dad had taken a particular dislike to Joey and that's why I wouldn't tell them. Henry isn't a curious person, he was happy with that. I think that Henry saw me as a fallen woman and himself as both my patron and rescuer, and that's love of a kind, and over time it developed into something more enduring. Perhaps not enduring enough in the end. It has lasted us thirty years, but thirty years is not the same as forever.

I still have one of Richie's plasticine animals, the elephant, though it's unrecognisable since a leg and its trunk broke off, and it was fairly unrecognisable even when it had them. It's in my suitcase, in the little satin pocket.

We sat in silence while Mum ate, the only sound the applause from a game show that another resident was watching in the bedroom opposite. 'Shall I shut your door?' I suggested.

'No, they don't like it if they can't see what you're up to.'

'I suppose it's so they can check that no one has fallen out of bed.'

'It's so they can check if you've got any biscuits for them to go at.'

I switched on the television in the hope there might be a news item or current affairs programme that might give us something to talk about. Mum's horizons were shrinking to the walls of the nursing home, peppered with petty resentments and aggravations. We watched the end of a programme about how to do up your house and make a profit. She was scathing about the suggestions of the pundit ('the only way they'll make a profit is if one of them falls off the ladder and they get some insurance'). After that they trailed a programme about the Sydney Opera House. Mum was never one for the arts, but Sydney was Sydney. I turned to her but she had fallen back on the pillows with her mouth open. Her glasses were askew on her nose and I took them off and placed them on her bedside cabinet.

I wondered how long it would be before she woke up. I'd be flying home soon but I needed to talk to her first. I couldn't keep putting it off.

Chapter 22

Rose

I still miss Len. He'd have livened the place up a bit, given us a turn on the old Joanna, and he had a good voice too. They wouldn't be sitting here asleep with their mouths open with him around.

Poor old Len, I did my best for him but I wasn't cut out for nursing. The farm was what I liked, managing everything, keeping everyone going. I couldn't keep him going though, not in the end. It was the compulsory purchase did for him, no matter what they put on the death certificate. He'd never had a day's illness before that.

We'd been away for a few weeks, Len and I. A little holiday up country, the first we'd had in years, but the farm was in safe hands with Bobby in charge and Richie to help. When we got back a letter was waiting. Bobby didn't say anything till we'd opened it but I realised afterwards that he knew. The two adjoining farms were affected too and he'd already heard the news from them. They were putting a road through.

Our farm. Len always called me the love of his life,

but I wasn't, the farm was. And mine too, if you didn't count little Richie.

It took three years for it all to go through, what with the appeals and so forth. I don't think I had a good night's sleep for the whole of it. Lying there listening to the sounds of the night, the silence that wasn't silent at all really, but you hardly noticed unless you made yourself listen. As familiar to me as the sound of Len's breathing. Not that he slept either. I tried to keep my eyes shut but if I got up I'd see he was lying there with his eyes open staring at the ceiling. I used to wonder what Bobby would do, the farm was all he knew. And it was supposed to be Richie's heritage too. That's what we'd said, our two boys will take over the farm one day, when we can't manage any longer. The house was beautiful, we built it ourselves, everything we'd ever dreamt of. I had such plans. They'd all be married and at weekends I'd have everyone over for barbies, and the grandchildren would come and stay, or else they'd arrive early and help me set the food out. I saw it all. I can see it now.

A year into the appeal I walked out into the yard and he was holding on to the fence, doubled over, coughing green slime on to the ground.

'It's the new feed. It catches in my throat,' he said, when he had caught his breath.

'We should stop using it then,'

He wiped his mouth on his sleeve. 'Stop nagging, woman and fetch me a smoke.'

I had some in my pocket and we both sat down by the fence. 'You ought to give up, it can't help that cough.'

'The fags are the only thing make it feel better.'

'Ah, so you admit there's something up?'

'Only one thing up with me, sweetie.' He raised an eyebrow and cast me a wicked sideways glance. I tossed my head back and laughed. Same old Len.

It must have been six months later when he finally went to the doctor. They did blood tests then they sent him for an X-ray. They still weren't sure so they sent him for another one. The day before the biopsy they wanted a urine sample and we had to drop it in at the urology unit.

I knocked on the door and a harassed voice called to come in.

'Urine sample,' I said, needlessly because that's all they did in that room. The table was covered in little bottles. Mostly the same hospital issue that we had, but some were in whatever bottle people had got at home. One looked like it had had held Lucozade or something. The person had filled almost half of it. It put me off fizzy drinks for a while I can tell you.

'Put it on the table,' she said.

I looked at the array, and looked at Len's specimen. The doctor had scrawled the name on the label on the side, but it was virtually illegible. One or two other bottles had equally indistinct labels. I said. 'The way the doctor wrote it, it's not very clear.'

'That's fine,' she called, not turning round. 'The doctor will send me the form, I'll sort it out.'

It's not like me to be intimidated, nor Len. I could win prizes for sorting out what's what. But I looked at Len and he shrugged, and we left it there on the table. I blush to remember it but I think inside we knew, that whatever the urine sample did or didn't show, it was never going to make much difference.

They gave him six months to a year, but he lived

another three. Bloody minded, that's what it was. He was damned if he was going to let them put a time limit on his life. But he was so ill a lot of the time, it wasn't what you could call living.

We had to stop having relations once he became ill. He couldn't manage it with the medication and he was tired all the time. I made an effort for a while, but it embarrassed Len, he thought it was the man's place to do everything. Then towards the end, his bits and pieces seemed to wither away. It was the opposite of what happens to a little boy – as a boy it all drops down, and for Len it all went back in.

Well, I suppose that's where it went, anyway it all disappeared. He was left with a little bud, like a cocktail sausage. It made things very difficult for him in hospital when he couldn't get up in the night for the toilet. The nurses would leave him a water bottle, but he couldn't get it in it, his penis was so shrunk it wouldn't reach. I felt sad for him, men are proud of what they've got and there was nothing wrong with Len's in its day. When he was discharged and back home I tried to help – he'd stand by the side of the bed holding on with one hand to balance, and the other holding the bottle, and I'd hold his penis in place for him. It's strange, feeling someone weeing. Not something you want to think about too often. And you had to hold it down, or it'd flip up and spray the walls, the bed, everywhere. That's not something you let happen a second time, I can tell you.

With me looking after Len, it was just the two boys running the farm, though we kept up a pretence that Len was doing his bit, just as we pretended he was only ill temporarily and he'd soon pickup again. Richie had worked alongside Len since he was a tot and he took over all the heavy work that Len had always done. Even when he was at school, he'd stay up all night if a cow was calving. Now he gave up any kind of life and he was up at the crack. Sometimes he'd come in at night almost too tired to eat. Never complained though, and I think he liked the responsibility. Sometimes he'd send Len in for a lie down and take over whatever it was Len had been trying to do.

'What d'you think I'm here for?' Richie would say, 'You don't keep a dog and bark yourself,' which was one of Len's old sayings.

It was hard seeing the farm being broken up. You can't get sentimental about animals on a farm, no sense in getting attached to them, but I don't mind telling you I cried parting with them. It wasn't like you were sending them off to market or for slaughter because it was time and it was what you'd decided. This was arbitrary. Their lives were over because it was time for the road to come through, and that's all there was to it. And our lives were just the same.

We bought a bungalow. Nothing like the one we'd built ourselves but it was nice enough and all on the level so Len could get about. Len didn't need the wheelchair until right at the end. Before that he could just about get down the garden and around the house. He liked it out there, pottering around seeing what veg I'd put in, and watching the few chickens we'd kept. Well, we wanted something to remind us, and you can hardly have cows in a garden. Richie was working at the garage then, in town. It was supposed to be temporary in the beginning, but he was good with mechanical things and they were training him up. If things had worked out differently he'd probably have had his own place in the end.

We used to sit on the veranda of an evening just like before but we weren't kings of all we surveyed any more. We knew life was winding down for us, the best of it all behind us. One day he was nestled in the big chair surrounded with pillows and suddenly he heaved himself up on his elbow – and that was a big movement for him then – he was on oxygen, tube in his nose and everything. And he said, 'Rose – what was it all for? Did we do the right thing? Leaving England?'

I looked him straight in the eye and I said we'd done it for the children and we'd done our best, no one could have done more, and of course it was the right thing. We'd had a good life and they'd all done well for themselves, Mattie and Bobby couldn't have done better wherever we'd been, and Richie would be the same.

He fell back exhausted with his eyes closed and I held his hand. I don't know if he believed me. Why would he, I didn't believe it myself. Bobby was out of work for ages. He only knew farming and he could only get casual work what with the nearest farms having been bought up, the same as us. And he wouldn't leave us the way things were. Even after he got married they stayed at the bungalow, they didn't move out until they got the pharmacy to manage and that was just before Tamsin was born.

That compulsory purchase order did for us. I didn't feel the same about anything after that and I know Len didn't either. Bobby said we could get another farm but they didn't pay us what it was worth. But then they could never have paid what it was worth to us.

Mattie

On the bus back from the nursing home I thought again about trying to contact Richie. He ought to come, no one knew how long she might have. And if we got together again, we could draw a line under things. He must know we love him. He surely knows whatever we did was because we thought it was for the best.

Maybe if I contacted the friends whose addresses we still had, and explained that Mum was ill, then they might go the extra distance and try to get a message to him. Bobby was coming over himself next week but maybe he could make some calls before he came. He didn't have much time for Richie, but in the circumstances... Bobby had always said it was our fault for spoiling Richie so that the first time something happened that didn't suit him he couldn't cope with it. He said we'd brought it on ourselves.

We'd had such a row after the reading of the will. We all went back to the bungalow after the solicitor's but we were so angry, each in our different way, that we couldn't help each other. I was mad with Mum, and Bobby was furious with all of us.

'What did you expect?' Bobby said. We had come out on to the patio at the back of the bungalow. Mum was in the front room sitting on the sofa going through the photograph album, looking at pictures of Dad and weeping.

'There was always going to be trouble in the end. You can't keep this sort of thing secret forever.' Bobby was so easy going, it was a rare thing to see him angry and

I hardly recognised him.

'It wasn't my idea to keep it secret at all.'

'Then why didn't you tell him?' he said.

'Why didn't *you?*'

'It wasn't my secret to tell. I said right at the outset I wanted nothing to do with it.'

Bobby's wife Donna was hovering in the background. I noticed she had had her hair coloured and wondered why I was even thinking about such a thing right now. 'Keep your voices down,' she said. 'You don't want Mum to hear you.'

'I don't care if she hears me or not,' I said. 'There are too many things we're not allowed to speak about in this family, it's about time we did some straight talking.'

'And you think now is a good time to start?'

It was distressing to hear Bobby so enraged. He sat down on one of Mum's wooden patio chairs. It creaked as he leant back on it. He was developing a paunch, and his face was ruddy. I hoped he didn't have high blood pressure. Uncle Michael died of a heart attack.

Donna sat down next to me. 'It's a shame Henry isn't here, he's always so calm, isn't he?'

But Henry had left for a short lecture tour the day before. The will should have been straightforward and there didn't seem any need for him to be there. She was right, Henry would have been a calming influence, but that was primarily because he didn't take much interest in family issues. Now I thought about it, I was surprised that Donna had come. Except that she and Bobby rarely did anything without each other. Perhaps she thought he would be upset and would need her support. Well, she was right on that count

'Somebody should check on Rose,' Donna said. I took that as my cue and went back inside.

Rose

It's all single beds in here and that doesn't seem right when you've spent your whole life in a double.

When we were growing up we were all in the same room, Marian, Joanie and me, and the single bed was mine and they shared the double because I was oldest. But Marian was such a whiner and a fidget and she used to carry on so that often she'd have my bed and I'd go in with Joanie. Anyway, the point is, a single bed is hard to get used to when you're used to a double. You can't stretch out and you turn over and you're almost falling out. You get very hot too, because they put plastic mattress covers on in case of accidents. I said to Bessie, the only accident I'm likely to have is if a car comes in and runs me over. She looked at me like I was barmy. No sense of humour.

There's no air either, the windows are fixed so they only open a fraction. Timbo says it's for safety so you can't fall out. I say it's to stop you throwing yourself out. Timbo says, 'Rosie, Rosie, Rosie, what will you come up with next?'

I didn't have a visitor today so after lunch I went into the lounge. I'm back on the zimmer again now, I can get around quite well. The lounge is a bright sunny room, done out very nice and curtains with those fancy tie-backs. A bit twee for my taste but very nice. There's a bookshelf with paperbacks and a whole stack of jigsaws and board games. I've never seen anyone use any of them. Mrs One

Leg has a newspaper sometimes if her daughter brings one
in, but mostly we don't bother. Mattie brings me in the
TV listings but I don't look at it any more. Sitting in my
room doing nothing, it's as quick to flick round the
channels as look it up in a magazine. I read the horoscope
sometimes just for a laugh. But as I said to Joanie, 'It
doesn't matter what star sign you are, they never predict
you're going to spend the week sitting in a chair watching
telly and waiting for the next meal to show up.'

I thought Gwen might be in the lounge but she
wasn't. Timbo said she wasn't feeling well today. Mrs One
Leg was there but she looked right through me, and when
I said 'Good afternoon' to Blind Arthur, he said, 'What's
so good about it? Who is that anyway?' I thought to
myself, he's got out of the wrong side of the bed. Shame
he isn't in one of them with the sides on.

The racing was on the telly but no one seemed to be
watching it. Mrs One Leg and the nice woman, forget her
name, was dozing but the minute I turned over for
Countdown, Mrs One Leg jerked up – 'Who's changing
the channel? I was watching that, I've got five pounds on
the favourite.' She lives in the past that one, who is there
in here to put a bet on for her?

I sat down by the window where you can see the
traffic going by. A bus passed and I thought I saw Richie
on it, upstairs at the front. But that was daft. Why would
Richie be going by on a bus and it was years since he'd
worn a school uniform.

I'm glad Mattie didn't come today. Yesterday she started
asking about the will again. Course, she's trying to blame
me, same as always. I said Len did as he liked, always had

and it was nothing to do with me. Which is true. As if I'd have let it all come out that way. So I told her I was feeling tired because she knew the consultant said I needed plenty of rest, but that turned out to be the wrong thing because instead of going home she started fussing around, have I got this, have I got that, am I sure I'm happy here. I said, 'I'm stuck in this room, surrounded by a load of other people who are half daft – and that's just the staff – and I can't even wipe my own backside without help – what do you think?' So then she starts crying.

'Oh come on,' I said, 'look on the bright side. If I was back home, you'd be the one wiping my backside.' She had to laugh at that. And as I said to her, anyone who's travelled halfway round the world with two kids in tow can surely manage to survive an en suite and all meals laid on.

I had a little rest then and I must have dozed off because when I opened my eyes she'd gone and Timbo was bringing my tea in.

Mattie

I took Mum out to the park this afternoon. She's been a lot better these last few days. She wanted to walk so it took a while, but she needs the exercise, and it isn't as though we were in a hurry. She was being quite amenable, telling me all about the nurses when she was in the hospital. I think she'd forgotten I used to visit her there. Sometimes she's as sharp as a razor and other times, she sounds like her brain is clogged up with cotton wool.

The gardeners were digging over the flowerbeds, clearing the remains of the summer blooms and replanting for winter and we paused to watch them. Mum pointed

out the various plants and their names and I pretended I
didn't know. She's seen our garden often enough but she's
got the idea that it's all Henry's doing; because I didn't like
farm life she thinks I don't like gardening, but they're not
at all the same thing. But she doesn't listen. She gets an
idea in her head and it's there for good.

There were three gardeners, one mid thirties, about
the age Richie will be now, a younger one and an older one
who was sinewy and tough and reminded me of Dad. He
was balding though; towards the end Dad was grey and his
hair became fine and wispy. You could see his scalp
through it. We had to take care brushing his hair because
his scalp bled so easily. The young one was eager: digging
a hole, picking up a pot and tapping it against his leg,
setting the plant in the soil, all in the time it took the older
one to wipe the sweat from his brow. He did a lot of
leaning on his shovel and watching; he wasn't like Dad in
that. When the young one made a comment about it, the
older one said he was supervising. The one who was like
Richie worked fast, but with care, planting with precision.
I knew Mum must be thinking of Richie too. Each time
he bent over she said to me, 'I hope he's watching his
back.'

It was pleasant in the sun, unusually warm for the
time of year, Mum said, and the sweat was running off the
younger two. The younger one took his shirt off, pulling it
off over his head. His back was white and his arms were
brown, he looked like he was still wearing his white tee
shirt. You don't see skin as white as that at home. Mum
said why didn't I give them a biscuit. I couldn't see that
was the thing at all, in this late summer heat, and I made a
remark about Alice Through the Looking Glass, but she

didn't make the connection. Mum was never much of a reader. She'd finished the bottle of water I'd brought, so biscuits were all we had. 'They might be hungry,' she said, 'it won't hurt to offer.' I knew why she wanted me to ask. The middle one had reminded her of Richie too; she was thinking that he might be working somewhere, hot and hungry, and glad of something to eat, even a biscuit with the chocolate running off it.

The older man didn't want one, but the other two took two each. The one who reminded of us Richie came over to where Mum was sitting and started chatting; he said if she had any cold beers in her bag, he'd have one of them too.

She said, 'if I'd known the park was going to be full of good looking men like you, I'd have brought a crateful.'

They had quite a joke together. Mum's a coquette, even now with her ankles hanging over her shoes, and the toe part cut out for her bunion. He said were we sisters, and Mum said it'd be the ugly sisters then, and so it went on. I just smiled, I never know what to say in these situations.

On the way home we passed the paddling pool. Two children were splashing and a woman in a flared skirt was sitting on the edge with a toddler on her lap. The edge of her skirt was lapping in the water. The toddler was just in a tee shirt and his nappy and was struggling to get into the pool.

Mum said, in a raised voice for the woman's benefit, 'The edge of that concrete is very sharp, you want to be careful.' The woman ignored her, or didn't hear, anyway she held the child out over the water, skimming his feet along the surface. Mum said, 'They can catch all sorts.

You never know what's in that water – dogs wee in it.'

'You didn't used to be so fussy,' I said to Mum. Richie could barely walk when she had him helping us fork the dung on to the barrow. Mum laughed and said farm muck was clean muck, not like the mess people make.

On the way home, I asked her again about Dad's will, but she said who knows why men do anything.

Chapter 23

Richie

They made me look like an idiot. Everyone in the entire family knowing but me, lying to me all those years. All my life. And the way Mum used to go on about Mattie, and I listened to her, so I thought the same. Lazy, shiftless, good-for-nothing, she said. Well what does that make me? And why didn't she tell me herself, why did she go along with it? Maybe when I was little she felt she didn't have a choice, but when I was grown up?

Did they really think it'd never come out? My guess is they didn't think it through, or maybe they didn't know it'd work out that way. See what happened, Dad died and we all went to the reading of the will at the solicitor's office in town. So anyway, the house and quite a lot of money went to Mum, and then there was another amount to be shared between each of us children, Mattie and Bobby and me. That was one reason I wanted to go, because people where I worked told me I'd get less, being adopted but Dad had always said I was the same as if I'd been theirs, and I was relieved that he'd kept his word, even though I knew he would. But where money's concerned people don't always behave like you think. Then there was another amount of money and that was to be divided equally for the grandchildren, that was Tamsin, Sandy and Warren. And then the solicitor looked up, and he said, 'And Richie'.

I said no, I'm not a grandchild, I'm one of the children, you included me already, with Mattie and Bobby. And the solicitor looked at Mum, and then he looked down at the will and he didn't answer. He looked embarrassed and I thought it was because he'd made a mistake.

Everyone got up then and thanked the solicitor and all that stuff, and I sat there wondering what's going on and why is no one saying anything? Bobby and Mattie shuffled out and they never even looked at me. Then Mum kind of grabbed my arm and pulled me out because I wanted a word with that solicitor but she said she could explain. And I still didn't get it. My first thought was, maybe Dad loved me so much, more than the others, so he named me in the will twice, but that must be upsetting for Mattie and Bobby so that's why they were acting funny. But I knew that didn't make any sense. I was such an idiot!

Mum told me in the car on the way home. I said, 'But you're my Mum,' because you can't just rearrange everything in your head all in a second. It took me a good long while to take it in, and she's driving, trying to look at my face without looking like she's looking. So then I said, 'So who's my real father?' and my heart was pumping. I felt so sick waiting for an answer I wished I hadn't asked at all. I was thinking of all the people we knew who it might be – and I thought Please don't let it be Henry. If she'd said it was Henry I'd have cut my fucking throat. But you know what she said? She said Mattie never told them who the father was. I didn't believe that, they just didn't want me to know, like they didn't want me to know anything about anything. Except for Dad. Because he had fixed it for me to find out, and even though it wasn't the best way to find out, at least now I'd know and not live the rest of my life like a fucking idiot never knowing who I was. Plus he'd fixed it for me to have more money than any of the others. So Dad was okay in my book. And probably he woulda told me sooner but Mum wouldn't let him, and Mattie. Fucking bitches the pair of them. I hated Mum – Rose! - so much at that moment. I kept thinking, but Mattie is my sister, she always made such a fuss of me, she was always so lovely, even though Mum always said bad things about her I'd always felt they weren't really true. Now I thought they were true, and she was worse than Mum had ever suggested, because why, when she was taking me for ice-cream when I was a kid, or pushing me on the swing, didn't she just lean over and whisper it? What was so hard about that?

I hated her and I hated Mum and it was a toss up right then who I hated most. Mum always told me I'd been chosen but that was lies – I hadn't been chosen, I'd been dumped on them. I'd been an embarrassment they'd tried to cover up, like a bad smell and everyone pretends it's the dog. How'd you think it feels to find out your whole life has been an embarrassment to everyone? I felt like the car was filled with red, like a thick hot red blanket that had got dragged over your face and wouldn't let you breathe. Mum went very hard faced and silent which was her way when she was upset, but who cared if she was upset? I was glad. I hoped she'd be upset the whole rest of her fucking life. I hoped they both would.

I'd never thought much about who my real parents were. Wasn't bothered. But I had an idea, maybe my dad was a racing driver, and my mum could've been one of those leggy models you see them with, and they hadn't been able to keep me because they both had high-flying careers and a kid wouldn't fit in. I had it all worked out. And now whaddya know – my mum is a lying scheming bitch with a fat arse and my Dad is probably some jerk who – Christ, I can't even think about it. Anyway fact is I never did investigate my real parents because Mum and Dad always said it was better not to know and that if my parents had decided to give me away it would have been for a reason and digging it all up again might only stir up trouble. And I believed them! Well they've stirred up trouble now.

Chapter 24

Mattie

We usually tried to stagger our visits so that we didn't both arrive at once, but when I got there Amma was changing Mum's dressings, so I went into the lounge to wait for her to finish. I had just picked up a magazine dated 'September' without specifying which year (but from its dog eared condition it didn't seem to be this one), when Joanie walked in. She was wearing a new red jacket; she did a twirl for me to admire it, and added a few dance steps when I didn't immediately notice the shoes. I nodded towards Blind Arthur who was asleep, and she pulled a face and put her bag down with care so as not to wake him.

'Charity shop,' she whispered, sitting down and taking one shoe off for me to inspect the designer name in the insole. Joanie wasn't usually label-conscious but she loved a bargain. 'I was going to tell Marian to pop in there, they had some that might fit her. But then I thought, if she knows I shop there, she won't think they're good enough for her.' Mum always said that Marian thought she was a cut above her sisters and we both laughed.

'Have you been waiting long?'

I shrugged. Time seemed to stop in this establishment. 'Long enough to read the problem page and the horoscope. According to this I'm going to fall in love and will have to consider my options, but I don't know if that was last year or the year before.'

Joanie delved in her bag and drew out a box of liquorice allsorts. 'I brought her these but we might as well open them. She won't miss a few. 'She's probably not supposed to eat them anyway.' She passed me the box and I picked out a pink coconut one. We sat in silence for a few moments, while the bulges in our cheeks reduced.

'Funny isn't it, ' she said, as we watched a car pull into the car park below. A young man hopped out and lifted a folding wheelchair from the boot. 'Years ago I gave up expecting to see you again. And now here you are, and we've had all these months together.'

I nodded, sucking on the liquorice at the centre of the sweet, unsure what to say.

'I always wondered how you would turn out.'

She spoke as though the process was finished, though it seemed to me I was changing all the time. I said, 'I used to wonder myself. Somehow I didn't expect it to be like this. I imagined I'd always be twenty-five with a figure like an hour glass. Now it's more like a beer glass.' That was a joke of Mum's, I wondered why I was repeating it.

Joanie pulled a face. 'Don't know why you say that. You've got a lovely figure.'

'But only from the front. Mum always said I took after Nanny – she calls it the Marshall bum. She says it's like carting your own sofa around.'

'If you ask me, your mother is jealous.'

She offered me the box of sweets again and I took another one. We sat in silence for a few minutes. Then she said, 'Poor old Nanny. It was so hard for her when you went away.'

'It was hard for everyone.'

'You were her pride and joy. Bobby too, but you especially. He was happy playing by himself but you liked to be with us, reading us a story you'd written, or a poem. Or asking things. You were so inquisitive it used to drive us mad sometimes.'

I checked my watch. I must have been here almost half an hour. I peered towards the door to see if the carer was coming yet. I didn't really want to discuss all this.

'We used to think it must be terrible for you,' she went on, oblivious. 'In some ways you hardly knew your mum, well, not compared to how you knew us. I'd take you to school and Nanny would pick you up and give you your tea. Or I would if I wasn't working. It seemed to me you only saw Rose at bedtime.'

I got up and walked to the door. 'If she doesn't finish soon, I'll need to be going.' I was flying home the next day and I had a few things still to do. Joanie and I had passed the time since I arrived in the country without dwelling too much on this aspect of family history, and I didn't want to start now. I'd forgiven and forgotten whatever petty resentments I'd been harbouring all those years and there was no sense in digging them up now. Joanie was a good person, and whatever she had done, she would have thought it was for the best. I was old enough to understand how that can be misunderstood.

'You were always drawing and writing,' she went on. 'I bet I've still got some of your drawings up in our loft.

323

And I know for definite there's a Christmas card you made the year you left. Two donkeys looking at the manger. I said to Nanny, 'She can even draw a donkey!" She smiled fondly, remembering. I remembered too. The picture was on stiff white card and I'd coloured the ground yellow to be straw. Mum wasn't sentimental in that way. When we had packed up her things when she moved back to England, there was nothing from Bobby's or my childhood, though we found Richie's first pair of leather shoes. I remembered him wearing them.

'That's one of the first things that struck me,' Joanie went on, 'We knew it would be hard for you, going there, and when we didn't hear I said to Des, that's how hard it is. She can't even bear to write about it.'

I nodded again, wondering what I'd put in those letters if not what it was like out there. It seemed to me that was all I would have done: moan on and on about how I hated it.

'What did I write about then?' I asked.

Joanie looked surprised. ' I'm not complaining, don't think that. We all sympathised with how you must have felt. Rose didn't say much of course, but we could tell something wasn't right. I used to say her letters are full of what she isn't saying. But that was her all over. We guessed there was some problem with Len, but then we'd known that before she went. But they obviously made a go of it in the end.'

'I wrote whenever Mum wrote,' I reminded her. They weren't short letters either. I tried not to feel irritated that she could remember some old Christmas card but not my outpourings.

'It was a long time ago,' she said gently. 'We all

remember things differently, I suppose. Your Mum used to send those aerogram things – you know, just one sheet and you fold them over and stick them down. She used to write right up to the edges and all down the sides too – she was never one to waste anything. We should have realised there wouldn't be room for you to write on there as well.'

'Mine were on ordinary paper,' I explained patiently. 'She used to seal them inside.' But even as I spoke, I understood, and I felt the heat rise up my body.

How could I not have realised? It was later, when I was older and had in any case ceased to write to them at all, that Mum started using air envelopes and pads of paper, each sheet no thicker than tissue. But when we first arrived it was always aerograms – a single sheet that you folded over and sealed along the gummed edges. If you added an enclosure you would have had to pay extra postage and then you might as well have sent an ordinary letter. And Mum would never have done something that would incur some added cost. So what had she done with my letters?

Joanie leant back to look at me. 'Are you all right? Shall I open a window?'

'I wrote to you,' I insisted. 'Every week.'

'There were the letters you wrote from the ship, which Rose must have posted when you docked. After that you probably just never got round to it. Or perhaps you started letters but didn't finish them, that's easily done. But you got ours, that's the main thing. You knew you hadn't been forgotten about!' She said it with a little laugh, an attempt to lighten the mood that had descended.

It was getting dark outside and Tembi came and switched the lights on. 'She shouldn't be too much longer,' he called. His voice woke Blind Arthur and Tembi went over to him and settled the rug over his knees.

'Mum always read your letters out,' I said. 'It was a ritual we had, something to look forward to after dinner.'

'Even the ones we sent you? They were only bits of nonsense but they were supposed to be personal. We wanted you to have something of your own.' She laughed. 'That's why we didn't use aerograms ourselves.'

Amma came to the door, pulling a plastic disposable apron from her waist. 'All done,' she said amiably, 'you can go in now.'

Joanie thanked her and stood up but I didn't move. I thought I was going to cry. But not me, it was Mattie, eight, who wanted to cry. I could see her there, in that hot stuffy room with its grimy walls, and she was hunched over crying; crying because she'd never be a bridesmaid or anyone's special, crying because she'd been taken away from everyone she loved, and now everyone she loved had forgotten her. While outside Mum hung washing and Dad rocked back and forth on the one good kitchen chair shuffling his playing cards.

'We better go in, if you're in a hurry,' said Joanie. '

I stood up, though my legs were trembling. I felt nauseous but I had to say it now, or there might never be another chance. 'Joanie,' I said, 'there's something I have to tell you. About Richie.'

Chapter 25

Rose

They marched in and you should have seen them. There's Joanie done up like a dog's dinner in a jacket so red she looked like a walking blood transfusion, and Mattie all black round the eyes where her make up has run. And thick as thieves, the pair of them. I didn't like the look of that.

'What have you two been up to? No good from the looks of you,' I said trying to make a joke of it.

'You may well ask,' Mattie says, as if I was actually interested. I was only asking to be polite.

I don't think they stayed above ten minutes, don't know why they even bothered coming. Joanie left me some liquorice allsorts but they were open and she'd already gobbled half of them. Damn cheek.

Mattie

Joanie had made a chicken pie. The pastry was light and fell in crisp flakes from my fork. The underside of the crust was moist with gravy. I closed my eyes.

'Your pie tastes the same as Nanny's,' I said.

Joanie laughed, 'I think not! Nanny's pastry was like a wad of cardboard. She always made it too thick, and it never cooked through properly. Your grandad used to say he'd rather chew the draining board.'

And yet the taste was so distinct, the gravy so rich… but Joanie went on, 'It's my pies you're thinking of. By the time you were old enough to remember, I did most of the baking. Where I worked it was only a short bus ride away so I'd be home in time to cook the dinner. I always preferred to do it if I could.'

I remembered then, Joanie coming in from the scullery, holding the pie dish, saying, 'Ow, ow, it's burning me,' because she was holding it in a folded tea towel and it wasn't thick enough. Grandad was at the table, holding his cutlery in his fists, and Nanny said, 'Hold your cutlery properly, Fred, I don't want the kids picking up your bad manners.'

Des cleared the plates, telling me to stay put when I offered to help, and Joanie poured tea. When I tasted mine, I was back in Nanny's living room, sitting on her lap while she held the cup for me to sip from.

'There must be lots of things you want to know,' I said. On the drive back from the nursing home I had told her that Richie was my son, but not the details.

'Only tell me what you want to,' she said, topping up our cups. 'It's nobody's business but yours.'

'Don't let Mum hear you say that,' I said.

In the next room Des had switched on an American cops show. Sirens wailed and shots rang out. One of the voices sounded like Bruce Willis.

'I've never told anyone who Richie's father is,' I said.

Joanie stopped in the act of closing the door to

muffle the shoot-out. 'And maybe you shouldn't tell me either,' she said. 'If you've kept it to yourself for so long, you must have had a good reason.'

'I haven't even told Henry,' I said. 'Or Dan.'

'Who is Dan?' she asked, closing the door.

It was time to bring him into the open along with everything else. 'Dan is the man I should have married,' I said.

If things had gone differently, Dan might have been the father. He could have been, if we had made love that day when he crawled under my covers on the veranda. Sometimes I pretended that we had. That Dan rolled me over with a passion and we grappled there on the rough wood amidst the scuttling insects, that he was tender and loving, enflaming me with his warm breath and soft caresses. And Richie had his good looks. He could have been Dan's. So sometimes I pretended to myself that he was, because Joey had hurt me, and I didn't like thinking about it being him. But even if I didn't think about it, I knew it was him, of course: Joey, who could get any girl he wanted, Joey who had more hands than an Indian god (when I first saw a picture of one it was Joey I thought of); Joey, who wouldn't take no for an answer (but then who would have answered 'no' when they were with Joey?). Joey wasn't the ideal candidate to be your baby's father, but he was good looking, the girls all liked him. He had treated me badly, but that was how he treated all the girls, he didn't go out of his way to be any different with me. Later I would tell Henry it was Joey. I told myself it was Joey.

But I don't think it was Joey.

We were the third week into our relationship, Joey and me. That was a long time for Joey, I was doing well and the knowledge made me special. And I needed that boost to my ego after I heard via Sophie that Dan had someone else. When I was with Joey I forgot about Dan and how losing him felt like a part of me had been cut out. But if I was to keep Joey there were certain things I would have to do. I understood that, but it was worth it, and after the first time I thought we were in love. Certainly I was. I didn't know then that having sex with a man can make you fall in love with him, whereas for a man having sex can make him fall out of it.

On this afternoon a group of us drove into the outback. Joey and I rode in his truck, his friends were in two old cars. Late on in the afternoon, Joey drove us off to be by ourselves. We were in the back of the truck, we'd been there a while kissing and doing what you do, and then just as Joey was lying there having a smoke, we heard a noise. Joey kneeled up and suddenly a voice said, 'You know we can see you?'

It was Todd, Joey's friend, who had come out in one of the other cars. He was standing by the truck staring in. I was not fond of Todd. He was what Mum would have called 'full of himself.' He was jealous of Joey, though Joey couldn't see it, and he didn't like him spending time with me, even though Joey would always have been spending time with some girl, that's what he was like. Todd jerked his head towards where the others were sitting on a patch of ground that rose up. They were some distance away but I remembered that Todd had some binoculars. Joey had told me they had had fun one afternoon at Todd's house spying on people out of his window.

Todd said, 'Whaddya think?' He spoke out of the side of his mouth in a lazy drawl, the words running into each other. Joey spoke in a similar way, and Todd spoke that way to copy him. Joey didn't answer at first, just looked back at him. Then he looked at me. I didn't say anything because I was so shocked seeing him there, and I was trying to cover myself over with the sacks. But feeling Todd's eyes on me was a powerful thing, even though I didn't like him. Or maybe not liking him made me brazen. Now he would see that Joey and I had this special bond between us that Todd didn't have with him, and certainly didn't with any girl because no one fancied Todd. As I moved to rearrange one of the sacks, my shirt fell open. I had good breasts for my age, and why shouldn't he see what kind of a girl Joey had got for himself? I looked at Joey but I didn't want to seem like a prissy schoolgirl so I shrugged in a casual 'okay with me' kind of way that was also meant to be non committal because I wasn't exactly sure what Todd was asking.

Then suddenly Todd was getting into the truck and saying something to Joey. Joey laughed. I started doing my shirt up again, thinking after all we'd finished but Todd said, No, don't do that.

I looked at Joey but he was watching Todd unbutton his jeans. I knew now what they meant and what was going to happen. I started to get up but Todd pushed me back, not hard but I lost my balance. I looked at Joey for help but he was just standing there and his face was getting the heavy look he got when we were doing it.

Todd said, 'I'm not gonna hurt you. I'll just put it in a little way and if you don't like it I'll take it out again.'

They both laughed at that and Joey said, 'Oh she likes it.' His voice sounded thick.

I couldn't look at Todd. In that moment all the confidence Joey gave me melted away and I knew this was a terrible, terrible thing, and would be the end of everything. I should have said no, or fought harder, I might have got away even though Joey was holding my shoulders down. But it was already all over for me; I thought I was special to Joey but now I could see what I was and all the fight went out of me.

Todd's breath smelled of cheese and cigarettes. It hurt with Todd but that wasn't why I was crying. I'd let something happen that shouldn't have happened and now everyone would think I was wicked or else stupid and I didn't know which was worse.

Joey drove me home afterwards and I cried all the way. As we approached the farm he said, 'You better do something about the way you look unless you want your mother finding out.'

When I got in she was in the barn. I went straight up to my room and when she came in later I was already in bed. I told her I had a sore throat and must be coming down with something and she said sleep was the best cure and I had done the right thing.

I told myself it was Joey's baby, even though he used a condom and Todd hadn't, because part of me had loved Joey. But I could never tell anyone else. Not when I couldn't be sure who the father was – and when the choice was between someone with bad breath who spied on people with binoculars or Dirty Dinah's son.

Yes, Joey was Dirty Dinah's son. Joey Donnelly.

Small world isn't it?

Joanie took my hand when I had finished. 'If only we'd known,' she said.

'If only it hadn't happened,' I said, with an attempt at a smile. Except that then I wouldn't have had Richie and Richie was my phoenix risen from the ashes. Before he flew away. Now all I had was more ashes.

Our tea had gone cold, and Joanie called Des to ask if he'd make some more. 'Still sitting here jawing?' he said good-naturedly when he brought the tray in.

When he had gone out again, discreetly closing the door behind him, I said, 'You can tell Des. In fact, I'd like you to. I think it's time everyone knew everything.' Because, as I said, 'What good has it done everyone to try to hide it all?'

She gave me a look I didn't understand. 'Not your mother for one thing,' she said.

Rose

I just happened to glance down in the car park and I caught the top of his head. I'd know it anywhere. I stood up so I could see better but he'd already gone into reception.

I said, 'Arthur – you won't believe it. My son's come to see me. All the way from Australia.'

He said, 'You haven't got a son.'

I said, 'What are you talking about? I've got two.'

He said, 'Oh no you haven't. Who are you anyway?'

And they say the blind have a well developed sense of hearing. You need a well developed sense of humour in here. I said, 'Give us a kiss then,' just to confuse him. He didn't answer but Mrs Give-us-a-kiss looked up – 'Did I say that?' she says. Daft as a brush the lot of them. Us. The lot of us.

I hurried back into my room, because I didn't want Richie seeing me in this cardigan, it had porridge down the front, and when I saw someone sitting in my chair for a moment I thought he'd beaten me to it. But it was Mattie, sitting there with a face like a wet week in Widdletown.

'Look lively,' I said. 'You'll never guess who I've just seen.'

She didn't answer, just sat there. 'I'll give you a clue,' I said. 'He's got fair hair and he's a member of our family.' Still nothing. 'We haven't seen him for fifteen years.'

She said, 'Mum, every day you think you've seen him.'

'Well, you'll see for yourself in bit,' I said. 'Now help me look for my blue cardigan.'

She just sat there. Then she said, 'I've come to say goodbye. Have you forgotten I'm flying out today? But you won't be on your own, because Bobby is arriving next week.'

'Bobby is?' That was something to look forward to then. I'd definitely need a clean cardigan on then, he might be bringing that wife of his along.

I had forgotten Mattie was going, but anyway I couldn't worry about that now. Not that I was worried. She could do what she wanted, always had. Though why she was in such a hurry to get back to that useless lump of a husband of hers I couldn't think. Never done a day's work in his life, all that sitting about reading and writing.

'Don't get maudlin on me,' I said. 'Best to leave with a smile on your face.'

'You lied to me,' she said.

I opened the drawer but my cardigan wasn't in there. 'I did not,' I said. 'Anyway, lied about what?'

'Why didn't you send Nanny my letters?'

I almost laughed at that. It had only taken her forty odd years to find out. And I thought she'd have rumbled me the first time she didn't get a reply. All the time she was growing up I was waiting for it, but nothing. Now this.

'It was for the best,' I said.

'How could it be for the best? Making me think they didn't care about me? Making them think I didn't care about them? Joanie said it broke Nanny's heart.' Her lip was trembling. But that was years ago. Why stir it all up now?

'Clean break,' I said. 'Didn't want you clinging to the past, always thinking we were going back. Better to put it behind you and move on.' I'd read that in a magazine in the lounge just this morning. Seemed like good advice. It's what I did think anyway.

Mattie got up and walked to the wardrobe. 'You might as well change anyway, that cardigan has got porridge on it.' She checked through the hangers. 'I can't see it in here.'

I remembered now. Mrs One-Leg had had one on just like it yesterday. Bet your bottom dollar that was mine. They make you sew name tags in everything in here but then they don't read them. The one who brings the laundry round, I don't think she can read anyway, not the Queen's English, she can't talk it anyway. I said to her, 'What language do they speak where you were born?' She said, 'English, I was born in Glasgow.'

'It wasn't about me at all, was it?' Mattie went on. 'You couldn't bear them knowing back here what it was really like. You were spinning your yarns, painting some bright picture of how wonderful it all was. You cared more about not losing face than about who got hurt.'

I could tell she'd been going over all this in her head. Probably been up all night planning what she'd say and for the briefest moment, my mother's face flashed into my mind, right out of nowhere. Looking at me, smiling. I hadn't thought of her for years, not like that. There she was, playing with Bobby on the lino, building a stack of the wooden bricks her neighbour had given him. She was good with the kids, my mum, you had to give her that, much better than me. Having them for me while I was at work, feeding them. She'd give them breakfast as well if I was late in a morning. You know, I'm not sure I really appreciated it. When you're young you don't, not really. She was my mother, it was what she did. What she was supposed to do. And anyway she owed me.

'Have you any idea what it felt like, collecting the post and always hoping, feeling sick every time there was nothing? Never ever getting an answer to my letters?'

Suddenly I realised Mattie was going on again. But she wasn't getting away with that. While we were airing our complaints, I had a few of my own.

'Don't come to me talking about lies. Who was it would never say who Richie's father was?'

She looked me straight in the eye. 'All right, I'll tell you. It was Dan. So now you know,' she said.

'Dan?'

'Of course it was Dan. Think of the hair, who else would it be. Who else did I know?'

I looked at her while I weighed it up. It made sense. I'd always had my money on Dan, well, hoped it was Dan, to tell you the truth though I'd never thought the dates tied up. But she'd answered just a bit too quickly. She was hiding something. You don't keep shtum about something for years on end and then come out with the truth just like that.

But before I could say anything she went on, 'That isn't what I wanted to ask you about though - '

'Oh really? There's a few things I want to ask - '

'I've been talking to Joanie.'

I saw it coming then, like when I'd gone tumbling off that bus, and I knew I was falling but I couldn't stop myself. I sat down on the bed.

'You've lectured me on my morals my whole life,' she said, 'but you're not so lilly white yourself are you?'

It must have been leaning over the drawer too far that had upset me. The blood was rushing to my head. I told her: You know I'm ill and my heart's not good. I said you should take more care, you should be ashamed of yourself coming in here talking to me like this, upsetting me when I'm poorly.

I shut my eyes and she rang for Timbo because I could feel a pain in my chest and I wanted my angina spray which was in the pocket of the other cardigan, the one I couldn't find it seemed to me, though I knew that couldn't be right because I had it this morning.

But even with my eyes shut, I could see her there. Blue winceyette pyjamas with daisies on, Joanie had made them for her for on the ship. We were by the lifeboats and I looked up from his kiss and there she was, eyes black and sparkling, hair so dark you could hardly tell it from the sky.

I'd turned my face away and when I peeked again, she'd gone. Kids weren't allowed up on deck at night. If she'd said anything, I'd have had her. But once I was back with Len, it was always there in the back of my mind, that she might let something slip. Even if she didn't know what she'd seen, Len would have known.

But it was too late to hurt me with all that, no point going on about it now. Only it turned out she wasn't talking about me and Eddie at all. Not the way I'd thought anyway.

She stayed until after the doctor had gone. He told me to rest and not get too excited, but I was all right again now, especially now I had my cardigan. Timbo had got it back off Mrs One Leg.

I said to Mattie, you'll be cutting it fine to get to the airport, but she said there was plenty of time. I'd have preferred her to go, but she thought she was doing me a favour staying with me. We were pretending that nothing had happened, that we hadn't said the things we'd said. I only had half an hour or so to get through and then she'd be gone for good.

'I wonder what's happened to Richie,' I said, filling in the silence. Well, you can't just lie there saying nothing. 'I'm sure it was him I saw. Go and see if he's talking to the manager. It must be hours since he parked up.' Anything to be rid of her for a bit.

'Mum, Richie isn't here, you know that. We don't even know if he's had our messages. He'll come in the end, I expect so anyway, but don't get your hopes up just yet. We all have to be patient.'

Patient? Who's been more patient than me the last

fifteen years? But he would be on his way, I knew it. And the millennium was coming, they're already planning the decorations they're going to put up here. He'd be bound to come for a special thing like that. I'm not likely to see another one! And you get a sixth sense where your children are concerned. Not where Mattie is concerned obviously, but the boys.

I said, 'Isn't it time you were going? You know what the traffic can be like.' I'd heard all I needed to know, more to be honest. I'd taken it on the chin for now, but once I got to thinking about it I was going to want to keep that angina spray to hand, that's for sure.

But she moved to the armchair and settled back in it, like she had all the time in the world. Then she said, 'Why didn't you tell me what happened to you?'

'Help me off with this cardigan, would you?' I said. She didn't move at first, then she got a frown on her face, but all the same she came round the bed and pulled the sleeve for me so I could get my arm out. It's this arthritis in the fingers, stops you getting a grip.

'Mum,' she said. 'I know. Joanie's told me.'

'She knows everything, that one, what do you need to come bothering me for then? And I suppose you've been telling her about Richie then. Right little mothers' meeting that must have been, sorry I missed it.'

'She had guessed about Richie. I'm talking about you. She said you had a baby.'

It was a bolt out of the blue but I didn't miss a beat.

'Yes,' I said, 'and her name was Mattie, then I had another and we called him Bobby.' She stood there, looking at me. 'Joanie's going gaga, she should be in here with us,' I said. 'She's getting everything muddled in her head. Nanny went the same way in the end.'

She picked my good cardigan up from the chair where Timbo had put it and helped me on with it. 'Shall we have a cup of tea?' I said. 'I didn't fancy it before but I wouldn't mind now.'

She got that long suffering look on her face and went next door. They have a little kitchen area off the dining room where visitors can make their own drinks. They have everything there: tea, coffee, squash. Not as good as at home but not too bad.

I felt a shiver run down me even with my cardigan on. I could see him now, little mite, wrapped up in the shawl I'd made. I should never have listened to my mother, I knew it as soon as I saw him. But it was too late then, we'd put everything in motion. Mum said it was for the best. No one would know, and life would go on just as before. Len would come back from the war and marry me like we'd planned, and be none the wiser. 'What's the point of upsetting Len?' she said.

Mrs Meredith's son thought he had seen Len killed. It was a week before we heard he was all right, and by then I'd drowned my sorrows with a boy from two streets away who was home on leave. I'd been at school with him and he'd always had a soft spot for me. Poor old Eddie. I took advantage of him really. I needed someone and he was there. It was only the one night. I was foolish and more than that, I was unlucky. So to keep quiet seemed no more than common sense the way Mum set it out and by the time Len was home for good, it was history. I never told Eddie. I loved Len and we were going to live happy ever after.

But when I held the little mite, before they took him

away, I knew I'd never love anyone the way I loved that baby. I begged Mum to let me keep him – but she wouldn't hear of it, and I was too frightened to take it on alone. It wasn't like it is now. You'd be an outcast, and how could I have supported us? She said it was for the best but it wasn't best for me. I told her I'd never forgive her if she made me give him up. She couldn't say I didn't warn her.

Mum sent me down to a home for unmarried mothers in Brighton. You weren't supposed to know where the kiddies went, but I saw the couple come in. There was only me gave birth that week, so I knew why they'd come. I knew her. Not to speak to, but she used to catch the same bus as me when I started work and I knew where she got off. Funny really, I was sent miles out of everyone's way, and here was this woman who virtually lived on our doorstep. Afterwards I used to go round there and wait outside the house to see if they came out. They'd got him a proper pram, I was glad about that.

Then one day I saw a new family was living there. I knocked at a neighbour and she told me they'd emigrated on some scheme. I'd thought the pain couldn't get any worse. But knowing he'd gone far away, where I could never find him, I hated my mother more than ever.

It was only later that I heard of the Ten Pound Pom scheme and I knew right away this was the answer. Maybe it would take me nearer my baby. And it'd pay my mother out like she deserved.

I stood there at the factory notice board, and already it was coming to me: the image of my mother on the station platform, waving bye bye to her pride and joy, the two apples of her eye. That was fitting thanks for what she'd done to me. She'd taken the apple of my eye from me and why shouldn't I take hers from her?

Mattie came back in carrying a tray. She brought biscuits too. I wondered where she'd found them. The staff usually eat them before we can get any. Or was that in the hospital?

'Are you going to tell me?' she said.

'Going to tell you what?' I said.

And then suddenly she was going. She stood up, brushed the crumbs from her skirt and pulled her jacket on. Watching her, I wondered why I made remarks about her weight. She wasn't fat at all. 'You've lost a bit of weight, haven't you?' I said. Her little face lit up. Poor old Mattie. It wasn't her fault she hadn't been born a boy. Or that she'd seen me and Eddie on the deck that night.

'I've dropped two dress sizes in the last year,' she said. 'I wondered when you'd notice.'

'You know how it is,' I said. 'You get an idea in your head and you stick with it, whether it's true or not.'

'I'm sure Richie will be in touch soon. We've sent your address and all our phone numbers to everyone we can think of,' she said. 'And if we still don't hear, we'll just keep looking.'

'I'll keep my tidy cardigan on anyway,' I said. He could turn up any time, he might not want to tell them he was coming.

She took longer to go than I'd have liked – I can't bear long drawn out goodbyes. I got off the bed and went to the window to watch her walk across the car park. I had to lean on the windowsill, and it was a bit uncomfortable. I was getting that pain again. When she got to the end of the path she turned and waved. Poor old Mattie. She always said I'd taken her away from everyone she loved and who loved her, and I had. I hadn't planned for it but it was true and I was sorry. She hesitated for a moment, then she was gone. I stood there a long time.

Mattie

I am dispossessed, I belong nowhere. This place with its cold winds and grey skies is not the home I remember. I have one memory of rain and that is of it beating against the scullery window while lightning crashes and Joanie hugs me on the sofa. I am afraid and she is saying why don't we do some drawing, you can use the coloured crayons.

I must go home. Home to my house and my own kitchen where the sun shines in the windows and lights up the hall if you leave the door open... no, because Henry is in the kitchen, he has just come in from his study, he is wanting to know why coffee isn't ready yet; he is, gloomy so the writing hasn't gone well and if I ask the gloominess will turn to silence and the silence will turn to depression which will somehow be my fault and forgiveness will only be achieved days later without my ever knowing when or why. No, I must go home but not to that home. Where is home? To my bedroom with the cream walls and cool sheets, delicate with their embroidery edging and the pale satin appliqué? But Henry is here too, and I must not put the TV on because he will want to read in bed, and his light will still be on when I wake at three and he will be asleep with the book in his hand and his mouth half open...

I can smell coffee, the air is filled with it, and the sound of a cappuccino machine. There is a buzz of conversation, voices raised because the cappuccino machine is loud, and the sound bounces off the wall so that sometimes we have to stop speaking entirely until it stops… I am looking around, the tables are full, we have always found a seat before but maybe not today, but where is he, he's late…and then I see him. He sits waiting because he has arrived already, and his coffee will be cooling, that's how long he has been here, but he is unconcerned at my lateness, only delighted that I am here now. Dan rises to meet me. He kisses my cheek in a way that to the casual observer will imply the platonic, while I savour the tenderness that lies behind it. But today I take his face in my hands and kiss him properly, deeply, not caring who sees. The cappuccino machine disappears, the conversation dies, we drift away to our own secret place. I have come home.

Rose

I was just thinking I'd get back into bed when a car pulled up. A man got out and went round to the back seat. He lifted out the biggest bouquet I'd seen since Dorothy's wedding – her husband likes a lot of show. I watched him as he walked in. It was the same man I'd seen this morning, the one who looked just like Richie. But how would I know what Richie looked like now anyway? Mattie was right. I did think all men with fair hair looked like him. I was going as barmy in here as the rest of them.

I lay down on the bed then and I thought: So this is how my mother felt. This is how it feels when you know you'll never see them again. My poor old Mum…. I could have brought the kids back with me for a visit, where would the harm have been? We could have afforded it, it was what Len always wanted. And that ache I've felt all these years not seeing Richie... What would it be like to have that last forever, to die without ever seeing them again? But maybe that's what will happen to me. Maybe my mum had the last laugh after all.

Thinking about it was bringing on that pain in my chest. I lay down on the bed and pulled the cover over my legs. If it didn't ease off I'd ring the buzzer. I couldn't remember where I'd put my angina spray.

I hadn't been asleep for more than a minute when there was a tap on the door. It was Timbo, his voice all a-quiver with excitement, like he'd just won the lottery or was going to tell me I had.

'Rosie, Rosie,' he said. 'You've got a very special visitor.'

ACKNOWLEDGEMENTS

Revenge of the Ten Pound Poms is a work of fiction. However I am grateful to *The Ten Pound Fare by Betka Zamoyska* for a vivid picture of life for British people who emigrated to Australia in the 1950s, and also to *The Ten Pound Immigrants by Reg Appleyard.*

I'd also like to thank my husband John for his patience, help and support in preparing this book for publication. Writing it was the easy part.

ABOUT THE AUTHOR

Lynn Peters was born in South London and read English at Cardiff University. Her writing career started with poems on sex and relationships for Cosmopolitan and these were soon appearing all over the world. The poem 'Why Dorothy Wordsworth is not as famous as her brother' has appeared in numerous anthologies and continues to be broadcast and used in study materials for schools and universities as far afield as Finland and Japan.

Lynn's poems brought her to the attention of publisher Simon & Schuster, for whom she wrote three novels: Immaculate Misconceptions, Premature Infatuation and Reading Between the Lies (currently being adapted as a musical). She also became a features writer for magazines in the UK and USA (including for the American magazine Redbook for which she was a contributing editor) and simultaneously began writing for TV and radio including the multi-racial sketch show The Real McCoy (BBC2) and The Little Big Woman Radio Show which she co-wrote with actor Llewella Gideon (BBC Radio 4).

A collection of Lynn's poems, 'Why Dorothy Wordsworth is not as famous as her brother' is now available.

Lynn lives in South London and Brighton.

www.lynnpeters.co.uk   email: lynn@lynnpeters.co.uk

Why Dorothy Wordsworth is not as famous as her brother and other poems **by Lynn Peters**

Why Dorothy Wordsworth is not as famous as her brother
'I wandered lonely as a...
They're in the top drawer, William,
Under your socks -
I wandered lonely as a -
No not that drawer, the top one.
I wandered by myself -
Well wear the ones you can find.
No, don't get overwrought my dear,
I'm coming.

'I wandered lonely as a -
Lonely as a cloud when -
Soft-boiled egg, yes my dear,
As usual, three minutes -
As a cloud which floats -
Look, I said I'll cook it,
Just hold on will you -
All right, I'm coming.

'One day I was out for a walk
When I saw this flock -
It can't be too hard, it had three minutes.
Well put some butter in it -
This host of golden daffodils
As I was out for a stroll one -

'Oh you fancy a stroll, do you?
Yes all right, William, I'm coming.
It's on the peg. Under your hat.
I'll bring my pad, shall I, in case
You want to jot something down?'

Printed in Great Britain
by Amazon

59799060R00213